The An

ANN FOWERAKER

All characters in this publication are entirely fictitious and any resemblance to real persons, living or dead is purely coincidental – except for Sir Tim Smit, who has kindly given me his permission to be himself in this novel. Other than Eden (where I have taken liberties with the layout of service buildings and where the fictional procedure and personnel structures are all my own) no organisations are real or represent real organisations in Cornwall or elsewhere.

First published 2013
by Pendown Publishing
Cornwall, United Kingdom
PendownPublishing.co.uk

To my little bruv love & best wishes

Ann

To friends and family - for your patience

– this one was a long time growing

***

The Angel Bug

'These memoirs may be the only evidence left of what really happened, where it came from and how it spread.'

When Gabbi Johnston, a quiet, fifty-something botanist at Eden, was shown the unusual red leaves on the Moringa tree, she had no idea what was wrong. What she did know was that the legendary Dr Luke Adamson was arriving soon - and that he would insist on investigating it.

This is the unassuming start to a maelstrom of discovery and change - with Gabbi swept up in it. What starts out as an accident turns into something illicit, clandestine and unethical – but is it really, as Adamson claims, for the good of all mankind?

***

'The Angel Bug', Ann Foweraker's fourth novel, is set mainly at the Eden Project in Cornwall, UK. This is a contemporary novel combining science fact and fiction, told by the people at the heart of the discovery.

The Angel Bug

The Angel Bug 1

Gabbi - October 18th

Thirty years should change a man, I thought, but looking at the handsome face on the huge poster it didn't look like it had done much to Luke Adamson's features except, perhaps, make him look more rugged, a man to be taken seriously.

I hadn't mentioned knowing him when it was first mooted that he might be able to fit the Eden Project into his UK trip; publicising his book and film, rumoured to have made him a millionaire already. *'Jungala'* was a box-office phenomenon, though it started out as a serious film on 'Man's relationship with plants and the importance of preserving biodiversity'.

It shouldn't have made it as a blockbuster movie, however, something happened in the filming; the 'baddies', a real threatening force, turned up and turned Luke into an Indiana Jones character. Added to that, in the three years it took to film, two major breakthroughs in treating terminal illnesses in man had been developed from extracts of plants hitherto only known and used by natives of the rainforests. With his superb on-screen presence, deep knowledge of his subject, film-star good looks and some excellent cutting, the serious ethno-botanical study became a mainstream 'true-life' film complete with soundtrack and an eco-song reminiscent of 'Born Free'.

You see I knew all this, I'd read about it in the papers; his name, as always, drawing my eye and, despite my conscious thoughts, my interest, I'd even gone up to Plymouth to see the first screening. So why hadn't I said anything to Mikaela when she was bubbling on about 'how wonderful it would be', and 'what a coup it would be', and 'wasn't he the most sexy scientist out there'? Well, I knew myself too well, I knew if I'd said anything that I'd have blushed, and then there would have been that kind teasing that they went in for in the Eden family, and I didn't think I could cope with that, and they would have no idea that it would be difficult for me.

The Eden family, that's how I felt about them all, a great bunch of people that easily became friends as they seemed to have, at their core, the same values. To me they had been a true life-line, welcoming me in and giving me both a focus in life and the gentle external framework I had needed to grow into a stronger person when my main support had been so suddenly cut away.

Well I'd had a month to get used to seeing his photo everywhere, even in my local Co-op, and now his visit was only a couple of days away. I wasn't really worried, I told myself, even at university he'd been one of the 'celebrities' and I was definitely 'one of the others'. He probably wouldn't recognise or remember me, so it wouldn't be anything to be fussed about, I told myself - again.

'Gabbi!' Mikaela called, waving me over as soon as I reached the open-plan office floor of the Foundation building. When I got close enough, Mikaela swung her chair round to face the others too, 'Hey, listen – Luke Adamson's emailed me. "So looking forward to seeing the eighth wonder of the world! I have heard so many good things about the Eden Project – and as it is the last date on my tour I intend to take a break and see a bit of Cornwall while I'm there. Recommendations welcome." Wow, what do you think? What would a guy like that want to see?'
'He's American – anything older than 200 years should do the trick,' cut in Andy from the plant pathology desk.
'Cynic!' Naomi muttered, her eye to a microscope.
'He's used to old buildings,' I murmured, seeing him standing under the arch of King's College, then, as Mikaela turned a puzzled face to me, I added quickly, 'PhD at Cambridge.'
'So he did!' Mikaela turned back to Andy, 'So, maestro?'
'So, it had better be King Arthur then, Tintagel, um, some of the prehistoric stuff, Men-a-Tol,' Andy offered, pushing himself

back from his desk, 'Coffee anyone?' Heads were shaken, one hand up, Andy shambled off to fetch one for himself and one for Naomi.

'You know I keep thinking this is his first UK visit, when it's just his first visit to this part of the UK!' Mikaela beamed brightly, 'I'm sure we can find some really Cornish places to recommend to him, might even be able to escort him round a bit,' she added with a twinkle in her eye.

I smiled at Mikaela's enthusiasm and thought he'd probably be quite happy to be escorted by Mikaela. Twenty-eight, pretty, long-legged, blonde and shapely, Mikaela was the antithesis of the dowdy scientist, very much the sort of girl Luke used to go for, I thought, and the type who went for him back then. I didn't suppose he'd changed in that respect either.

By mid-afternoon, truth be told, I was feeling a little drowsy as another restless night caught up with me and I was finding the rows of figures in front of me swimming. Somehow, while Eden was between senior botanists, I had ended up with the role, partly through an odd deference to me as the senior by age and, I believed, an acknowledgement of my organisational skills. I shook myself and, deciding on a restorative cup of tea, pushed my chair away from the desk. As I did so my phone rang, sliding the chair forward again I answered with a voice much brighter than I felt.

'Hello, Gabbi Johnston.'

'Gabbi! Josh here, I'm in H03. There's something not right with the Moringa – I think you had better come and take a look.'

From the designation, H03, I pictured the slight, pale boy, Josh, standing by the Orang dan Kebun, the Malaysian house and garden area in the humid-tropics biome.

'All right, Josh, I'll be right down,' I said already standing as I replaced the phone. A quick whiz down to the pit was probably the best antidote to the lethargy I was feeling anyway.

Picking up my mobile I headed out of the Foundation building, turned sharply and collected my bike. As a health and lifestyle statement and as a method of keeping fit I kept a bike at Eden for getting around. Easy on the trip down into the pit, as the site of the biomes was appropriately known to the employees of Eden, but a darn sight harder on the muscles on the way back up to the administration buildings on the rim.

I felt that sense of wonder and exhilaration that I always did as my pedal strokes brought me in sight of the Eden that everyone recognises from books, TV and adverts, the soap-bubble constructions piled against the sides of the once raw granite china-clay pit, then, as I neared, the panoply of the temperate zone, the largest, the 'outdoor biome'. All of it looking both small and vast at the same time.

After walking briskly through the jungle conditions of the humid biome I was perspiring slightly by the time I reached H03 and there was Josh standing beside the Malaysian house, keeping out of the way of the visitors who were wandering, gawping upwards, stopping and bending to read notices, children dashing back and forth to drag parents on to the 'thing' they'd found, or trailing behind, tired and hot.

'Hi!' Josh said when I stood beside him. 'You have to get to the higher side to see it.'

We walked with the crowd round the edge of the garden, but where the rest flowed onwards we stopped and stepped to the far side of the path.

Josh raised his hand and pointed to the top most leaves of the Moringa oleifera.

'There!' he said, 'Earlier, when it was clouded over, I could see quite clearly that the top-most leaves are going red.'

The sky beyond the ETFE bubble biome structure was bright now, I shaded my eyes but I still couldn't see the leaf colour properly; the higher delicate fronds were just dark silhouettes.

A family came and stood between us and the tree. The mother read from the guide in clear tones. ' "Moringa oleifera, also know as the Horseradish or Miracle tree, has edible leaves, beans, flowers and roots." I wonder if it's the roots that give it the Horseradish name. "Beside it stands the Neem tree known throughout the East as the world's most useful tree, providing medicine, fuel and food." Well that sounds impressive for one plant. '

The family stood a moment or two looking the two slim trees up and down, the younger boy pointing out the bean-like seed pods. They moved on, the mother reading the next section as they walked.

'I'm going higher,' I said. 'I can't see well enough from here.' Josh nodded assent and followed me as I turned and took a near vertical route up through the planting to get as high as possible.

Now I could see. Josh was right; there were a significant number of leaves turning red, as if for an early autumn. Yet these trees shouldn't have an autumn, shouldn't be changing colour.

'What's the watering like?' I asked

'Fine, checked that, no problems now or recorded.'

'Hmm, okay, well we will need leaf samples anyway – so dehydration can be ruled out while we look for other baddies,' I smiled. 'Could you arrange that for me Josh?'

'Sure, only one for you, or one to each?' he said, meaning, a sample for the plant pathologist and one for the entomologist too.

'Better make it one to each, thanks,' I said frowning, 'Better make them bio-safe and labelled urgent. Okay?'

'Okay, no probs!'

No probs! Indeed! Big Probs!! I thought as I sweated the bike back up the slope. Perhaps I should have had a sample sent to Mikaela too. It might be easier than actually telling her that there was a problem with the Moringa. Of all the trees in all the biomes, why did it have to be that one? A paraphrased Bogart said in my head, if no other plant, Luke would certainly zero in on his pet, the tree that made his name in ethnobotany! Back at my desk I bashed Moringa oleifera into the Forestry-Compendium website to check out if it had any history of turning red, and what the cause might be.

Andy and Naomi were heralded by their voices, obviously in heated discussion, followed by their persons as they came up the central staircase into the light and airy office space.

'But it could be Thrips Palmi,' Andy was saying.

'What, with the quarantine measures all in place? Besides it isn't as if it came from some dodgy place.'

'Well, Kew has been known to have its own problems with diseases and vectors.'

'Do we have a new problem?' I cut in.

'W04, some die-back *co-incidentally* right beside the new introductions.'

'Which were quarantined for three months as usual!' Naomi retorted.

'Anyhow, we'll know soon, samples coming over pronto.'

'Well we're going to be busy then, I've asked for you to see some from the Moringa as soon as they come in. It's a bit tricky, it's the last tree we want to have a problem with just now,'

'Why? Any time is bad for any of them isn't it?' Naomi said, shrugging.

'Ah, but Luke Adamson's coming and he's sure to make a bee-line for it.'

'Why's that?' Andy said as he sat down.

I looked at Andy and Naomi, both of them looked puzzled, and young all of a sudden. I smiled, 'Well back when you two were in nursery school, Luke made his name with the first comprehensive ethnobotanical study of the Moringa.'

'Oh dear!' Andy pulled a mournful face, waggling his head in a mocking way.

'Oh dear, indeed,' I almost laughed, Andy, at least didn't seem in awe of the superstar.

The three of us busied ourselves in the portacabin laboratory at Watering Lane, Eden's nursery a few miles west of the main site, each wearing the standard kit, lab coat, latex gloves, and, when we were cutting, goggles.

'So,' I said firmly, looking up from my microscope, 'it's definitely not a dehydration problem, these cells are as turgid as we could wish for.'

'And so far I have found no signs of microbacterial infection,' added Andy. 'So I'm going to culture some sections, especially of the red cells.'

'You just do that!' Naomi said to his back as he went into the second half of the lab.

'Nothing?' I asked, looking across to her. There was an atmosphere between them that I couldn't quite put my finger on, though it might have just been the cross accusations over the source of the plant infections.

'Nothing, certainly on this sample, I'm off to take a good look at that tree and the area, put down a few sticky pads to see what insect vectors I catch.'

'Okay. I have to admit I'd rather we found something concrete before Adamson turns up.'

Naomi turned and gave me a quizzical look as she hung up her lab coat. 'I don't know why *you're* worrying, Gabbi, that new senior botanist will be here tomorrow and she can talk herself out of any hang-ups Dr Adamson has about our trees.'

Naomi just about slammed the door behind her, leaving me wondering what had ruffled her feathers. There was something in the way that she had said 'senior botanist' that suggested that the new boss was a problem, but, as I had not been in on the day of the appointment I'd not met Dr. Ananias. I had heard that she had made an impact on all of them in different ways, some by her looks, some by her 'air' and some by her obvious intelligence, however, perhaps not all opinions were favourable. I recalled that Naomi had been unusually reticent at the time.

I turned the leaf over again; the under side was a definite red, not unlike many plants that have a red underside to reflect light back through to the chlorophyll-bearing leaf tissues. I began to wonder whether the Moringa had the ability to adopt this red pigment in reduced-light circumstances. After all the ETFE bubbles of the domes did not allow a hundred percent light through them, then add to that, the fact that many of the largest of the trees in the tropical biome had grown so fast, faster than had been expected, that they had already needed pruning to prevent them reaching the skin of the dome, and so they were cutting out even more light.

'Hey, Andy,' I called. 'I'm going over to reception to see if I can chase up anything on Moringa and low light levels.'

'Okay, catch you up later.'

I cleared and washed up, then hung up my lab gear and left the laboratory. I glanced up at the vast range of glasshouses that had brought on the bulk of the trees and plants needed to create Eden, and now continued that work, with the sideline of producing plants for sale in the shop. Reception was a building that looked, appropriately, like an overgrown garden shed. Inside, it had the appearance of belonging to a set of artistic hippies; six-foot butterflies hung lazily on fine threads from the ceiling, a foam rubber and papier-mâché tree wound itself around a central pillar, and collection boxes for all kinds of recyclable stuff were everywhere. The reception desk itself was little more than a bare board and unmanned as usual, yet above it hung the ubiquitous picture of Luke.

'Hiya, Jim,' I called as I circled round to a spare computer.

'All right?'

'Will be if we can sort out this blessed Moringa before he comes.' I nodded to the picture.

'Yeah, I heard you had a problem. Anything I can help with?'

Jim was one of those truly green-fingered horticulturalists that make you believe in such things; anything he touched grew.

'Not unless you can tell me why these Moringa leaves should turn red with no obvious reason. I'm just looking up the likelihood of a change to utilise reflected light, though there was nothing in the Forestry guide'

'No watering problems?'

'Nope.'

'Hmm, light sounds like a possibility then, and that guide's not infallible. I'll leave you to it,' he added as he left the building.

Half an hour later Andy broke through the trance that I'd sunk into as I flicked from article to article dealing with plants that utilised the red underside of their leaves. There were no cases where Moringa had exhibited this pattern of adaptation and the only plants where the colour changed, as opposed to always being red, had a well documented histology that demonstrated that they were always ready and willing to change as soon as the light levels decreed it.

'Ready to go back?' he asked.

'Yep, might as well, not getting anything useful here. Of course I might be on to a new research paper,' I grinned. 'The adaptation of Moringa to life under ETFE.'

Andy grinned back; he knew how little I wanted to do any such thing, even though progress in the scientific world was made just that way. I'd said often enough that I was so glad I didn't have to jump through those hoops as I had no ambition now to be a botanical high-flyer. After all I'd seen at first-hand what it meant. James had been at the top of his field for decades and it had driven him to despair at times, especially when out 'scrounging' for research funds, yet it still amazed me when he threw it all in and retired at fifty, many of his colleagues were just getting into their stride at that age.

We were no further on when I left for home. I drove my mini quite sedately, there being no need to hurry home, and the twists and turns of the high-banked hedges and the road between them meant that being ready and able to stop within a few yards of spying another vehicle was a distinct advantage. My mind wasn't on my driving however; it was still on the problem of the Moringa.

Within fifteen minutes I pulled into my own drive. The sight of the house, low-browed over heavy granite with the sea glinting in the distance, as always, gave me first that surge of joy, now followed by a tang of sorrow. Sometimes, like today, I thought about selling, but I truly doubted I'd find another that gave me that delight on seeing it and there would always be the sorrow of James' absence wherever I lived. The house had been my choice anyway, that sort of thing not being of interest to James, he'd just asked that the place should have a good sized garden. The garden was now a bit of a problem to manage. It was getting on for an acre and James had only just about got his vegetable garden going and an enormous herbaceous border planted when he collapsed with a massive heart attack whilst digging.

While I unlocked the door and went straight through to the kitchen, automatically putting the kettle on and flicking the answerphone off, I allowed myself to think about James. So often I had to stop myself thinking about him when I was alone, as the pain seemed to overwhelm me too easily when I had nothing else to think about. At work I could allow myself to think of him, knowing that I would be shaken out of my reverie by something going on, someone talking to me.

I'd been with James for over thirty years, he'd just started his PhD in Botanical Science and I was a second year student in the same subject when we met. I was working in the labs he used for his studies, and we got talking. He wasn't the tall, dark and dashing type, more the tall, intellectual and serious type, but above all he was a really good person; kind, helpful, generous with his time, honest and dedicated. As I got to know him I found that I not only admired him but missed his presence when he was not working in the labs.

It took him a couple of months to ask me out. I recalled with a small smile his later confession that he'd been trying to make himself ask me out for all of one of those months at least, terrified that this 'exotic creature', as he called me, would laugh at him. Little did he know at the time that I was as shy as they come, and had it not been for the fact that we could talk in a detached, professionally scientific way to each other I probably wouldn't have spoken to him at all.

People said we made an interesting couple, he at over six foot, alabaster skin, blue eyes, auburn hair, and me, a foot shorter, with a mass of unruly ebony hair, slightly olive skin that tanned easily and dark almond-shaped eyes.

I poured my tea and wandered into the open-plan dining area; as I did so I caught sight of myself in the mirror and stepped closer. That ebony hair was now tempered with what would be a sprinkling of grey if I didn't disguise it with a chestnut dye, giving my hair instant highlights, and was far more controlled and controllable than it used to be by being well cut and twisted back into a knot held fast by one of my collection of unusual clips. The skin still looked good all things considered, but there was no hiding the lines round the eyes, so called laughter lines. If only.

With a blush I suddenly realised I was looking at myself and wondering what Luke would see.

The Angel Bug 2

Luke October 18th - 19th

The Great Hall was packed, the front rows were loaded with the elite of the university but, as far as I could see, the rest of the audience were the well-heeled environmentally-conscious middle-classes that I'd grown used to over the month of the tour in Europe.

I was prepared, hell, I knew my script off pat so that I spoke without notes. The lecture was carefully tuned to keep the audience awake, smiling, nodding at the wisdom pieces, anxious where they needed to be and enthusing just at the point where the talk finished and the book signings began. I'd worked out what I wanted to say and then, ignoring the publisher's suggestion to 'just be yourself', I'd turned to the guy who'd worked the script for the narration on the film, a guy who could work magic with words. It was well worth it. Every time I spoke the audience was spellbound.

The Dean was at the lectern, giving me the 'big build up', Cambridge-style, almost off-handedly, reminding the assembly that 'our speaker this evening' was also a product of their own hallowed halls. It made me think for a moment on the difference between countries. Back home at Harvard I'd had a much better introduction, and I'd not even attended that university. The Dean, turned hand outstretched - my cue - and with a smile I stepped out onto the stage. The Dean waited near the lectern, so I had to cross most of the stage to get to him. He shook my hand, faced the audience and, with a turn of his hand towards the lectern, left the stage.

So there I was at the lectern but with no notes to put down on it. I still stood there, just to start off, I told myself. I gripped both sides of the lectern like a drowning man clutching a plank; I couldn't let go of the damned thing. My fingers felt slippery and I was suddenly aware that my heart was beating faster than normal. This was ridiculous - I'd given this talk so many times and to so many illustrious groups. I mentally shook myself, smiled at the audience and began.

'Good evening,' I coughed and then continued, 'this evening I want to take you on a journey, a journey that will lead you to stand beside me in a fight to save one of the worlds most valuable resources…..'

I found myself rushing my words, and I kept returning to the damned lectern as if it really did hold a set of notes. A part of my mind, not occupied with delivering the speech, realised what was wrong; every other time I'd felt totally relaxed, the audience with me - this lot were not playing the game. In the first few rows there were many with pursed lips and raised eyebrows. For the first time the carefully planned script sounded too much like entertainment and not enough about the real issues and the concrete science behind it.

'….. so this is where we come to, could it possibly be true, as the indigenous peoples believe, that the mother forest has everything to cure all man's ills? That it is part of God's care, if you will, to provide our redemption from all the ailments man is heir to? Our journey has demonstrated how we live only by the grace of plant life. Could it be that we may live even healthier, even longer, without pain or disability, if we can only understand the gifts that are provided? And here's the bottom line. To understand such things, then we need to be able to find and test them. This takes time, time that is running out as six percent of the rainforest is destroyed every year, meaning that your cure for cancer, your cure for Alzheimer's, your cure for infertility, your cure for arthritis, may be lost forever. Thank you.'

The applause started and grew; I gave a small bow and turned to leave the stage. There, hurrying onto the stage was the Dean, florid faced with hand outstretched. What the hell?

'Wonderful, wonderful,' the Dean pumped my hand and turned out towards the audience, the clapping dying quickly. Only then did he drop my hand. It was all I could do not to wipe the clamminess off onto his suit jacket.

'I'm sure we were all fascinated by Dr Adamson's talk, and I'm sure that some of you will have questions,'

I felt a flush of annoyance, it was explicit in the contract that there would be no question time, but I was trapped, and looking round I could see at least half a dozen of the audience indicated questions by a discretely half-raised hand. I smiled grimly and walked back to the lectern, the beaming Dean in tow.

I scraped up a decent answer for the first and second questions, and headed off the third as I could see I was going to screw it up if I tried to answer properly, the figures were just not there at my fingertips. Their questions were pointed and deeply scientific, in every posh-brit syllable I felt an underlying criticism of the popular appeal of the book and the film and it was unnerving. It had been a long time since I'd been dealing with the nuts and bolts of the work that they were asking about. The past four years had been spent either in the jungle, doing bits for the film, editing or writing the book.

The fourth question was not much better and I knew my answer did not carry the required scientific rigour. Ridiculously, I began to feel out of my depth, as if, out there, were my former professors scrutinising me and my work. Indeed, from the number of white and balding heads I could see they probably *were* sitting out there.

More hands were raised. At that point, feeling sick, I leant over towards the Dean and said just that. The Dean, all hesitant and bluff at the same time, waved both his hands at the same time as if to ward of a host of mosquitoes, and then patting the air, apologised that 'Dr Adamson will not be able to answer any more questions this evening as he is feeling under-the-weather'. He added that he was 'sure that Dr Adamson would be glad to discuss matters of interest tomorrow as he was staying for another day'. He turned to me, beaming and nodding, at which I found myself nodding back.

Next morning, I lay awake listening to the breathing of the young woman lying beside me. I'd not had such a disturbed night since I left the jungle. Was it just being back here at Cambridge or was it the debacle last night? Well it was a new day and as far as I was concerned I was not going to be available to discuss anything.

My departure from the hall had meant fewer book sales than were usual, according to Kayleigh, so it had hit my Rainforest Foundation, and for that I was annoyed with just about everybody who'd had anything to do with the set-up for the lecture. I was lying there blaming them all for how it went wrong, and that included the pretty airhead, Kayleigh, lying beside me.

I slid from bed finding the floor cool beneath my feet, and padded through to the bathroom. On my way back I grabbed a towel and wrapped it round my waist. A quick glance told me that Kayleigh was still asleep as I turned to stand at the un-curtained window, drinking in the ancient city as it came sleepily awake in a misty morning. After a few moments my perceptions shifted, the window replaced by a movie screen as memories came flooding through. God! They had been electrifying times. I felt my blood stir as I thought of those years.

I saw my first immature awareness of the place, soon subsumed into an overpowering urge to beat it and everyone else at their own game. This place was supposed to be the best in the world; then I would be the best in it, no matter how I achieved it. I felt a smile touch my lips as I thought of the non-academic goals I'd set myself. Every one of them achieved, well very nearly, even if I'd had an advantage over the competition in both looks and provenance.

Rowing had been a first love from my early days on the New Hampshire lakes and later at Johns Hopkins, but at Cambridge the competitive edge took me over. There weren't many other scientists on the crews and I worked really hard to dispel the 'weak scientist' prejudice that some of the crew members had. It meant being harder and meaner than they were. Harder meant I'd trained twice as much, meaner meant that at the crucial team-choosing time I'd zeroed in on a guy who'd been hassling me from day one. If he wasn't calling me a 'Yank' then it was the science thing or because my hair was long and blond. So when he'd called out 'Hey Blondie, did you forget your handbag?' I'd walked over, punched him out and then turned away. He'd come up fighting mad and launched himself at my back, whereupon I'd grabbed his arm and folded forward tipping him over my back to land flat on the floor at my feet, only I didn't let go of the arm, feeling something give as his body cracked down. Others had caught up with us by then; I shook my hand free of his and stepped back. He clambered up but the rest of the team held him back, and plenty said he'd asked for it. The fractured wrist put him out of the running, and me firmly into a place on the winning team for that most prestigious of races - the Oxford and Cambridge boat race.

I had worked all hours on the first piece of 'competitive' work and still found time to sweet-talk and bed the girlfriend of my main rival. That was the way I found out about the progress he was making, and how I came to the conclusion I'd have to upset the other guy's experiments somehow, as they were proving too successful. In the end it was nothing to get into the other lab at the end of the day and turn off a switch. It could have been anybody that turned off the wrong switch, easily done, and weeks of preparation and incubation were wrecked in a single night of cold. It was all I needed to get the edge to complete and write up my work successfully by the deadline, whereas my competitor struggled to get to the end of his experiments. I took the girlfriend too, for a time, not for long, just about the length of time it took her to find out about the others.

For intelligent women they weren't that good at working out my game, and boy were they intelligent! Just chatting to them was an intellectual sparring match in itself, and remembering that sent a shiver through me. That Kayleigh had to go, a PA from the publishing house, supposedly organising my tour, she was attractive in just the way I liked, and fell readily into bed, but talking to her was like conversing with a TV guide. If it wasn't on the TV, then she didn't know anything about it. She seemed to live in a reality show and knew all about the goings on in the soaps almost before they did, but intellectual conversation, even about books or publishing, seemed completely beyond her.

'Hey!' I shouted close to her ear. 'Are you going to get that useless head of yours off the pillow or what?'
'What?'
'Yeah, right, listen up, I'm not intending to hang around here to be quizzed. I want transport out booked, pronto, I'm out of here by ten at the latest.'
'Oh right,' she glanced at her watch. 'I'll just grab a shower.'
'No! I want that transport arranged first – then you can do what you like because I'm going to do this last tour date on my own.'
'But Luke,' she started her voice almost a whine. 'I'm coming too, aren't I?'
'Don't you ever listen? No, I'm going alone. You were great. I was glad to know you, but this is it, goodbye. Got it?'
Kayleigh pulled the sheet up over her breasts, her eyes wide, shaking her head slightly. 'Just like that? You cold bastard, just like that?'
I shrugged and started to pick out clothes to dress in, then realised she hadn't moved. 'Phone! Now!' Kayleigh jumped and,

still clutching the sheet to herself, wriggled across the bed to the phone.

'Okay, Luke - er Dr Adamson? I've booked you a taxi, but where will you want to go, like, your flight to Newquay isn't until tomorrow, and you were supposed to be a guest of the University until then.'

'Screw that, can't you get me down there today?'

'Well, I don't know – I'll see, it might not be easy, being a small airport, and I don't know how many flights there …'

I cut in 'Find out then! And if it's an okay then get the hotel booking moved up a day too.'

'Sure, fine, right away.'

I was pacing the room, wondering if even going to this last venue was worth it and why on earth had I allowed myself to get worked up over nothing. It was this place. I'd had come out top in everything; academic, sport and personal ambitions were all met, yet I'd never felt accepted, and I realised that still bugged me.

The Angel Bug 3

Gabbi 19th October

One of those beautiful frosty mornings that make winter worthwhile greeted me as I drew back the curtains. The sun glinted off the sea and on myriads of hoarfrosted points in the garden, for a change I felt refreshed and ready to face the day. It was my usual half-day so, as I was going into help at the St Piran's Society in the afternoon, I dressed for comfort rather than style. After a quick breakfast I set off for Eden aiming to get there early to make sure everything was tidy in preparation for the arrival of our new senior botanist.

The sun had not yet worked its way into the pit and the domes were in shadow but light suffused the top floor of the Foundation building as I climbed the central stairs, assuming that I was first in, as usual. Suddenly I realised there was someone there already, sensed or heard a movement, I didn't know which. I gripped the handrail at the top of the stair and tried to identify the direction the sound came from, swinging all round to take a three-sixty degree sweep of the place. A woman suddenly threw open the door of the coffee lounge, I jumped, even though I'd guessed there was someone about.
'At last!' the woman snapped, 'does no-one work at this place?'
'Sorry?' I began.
'Sorry? It's gone eight and not a soul about, not even on the desk.'
'Well, that might be because Karen doesn't start until half eight,' I said quietly, while telling myself I ought to check that this formidable woman in the tightly tailored black suit with red blouse and shoes was really the new senior botanist. I took the final step to the top of the stairs and held out my hand, 'Allow me to introduce myself, Gabbi Johnston, botanist.'
The woman did not immediately offer her hand to be shaken, she held her note book to her and gave me an all encompassing

look, making me feel about twelve years old and wearing the wrong fashion, again, then suddenly there was smile from the carefully painted lips, the hand and a firm emphatic grip.

'Dr Sapphira Ananias, *senior* botanist, I don't believe I met you when I was appointed, *Gabbi*. Tim Smit tells me it's all first name terms here,' she raised her perfectly arched eyebrows.

'Yes, to names, and no we didn't meet, it was one of my half-days, that day,' Again I felt wrong footed. 'I came in early to make sure everything you would need was on your desk ready.' Sapphira just tilted her head in query.

'As, as,' I felt my confidence leaking away, 'as I have been sort-of covering the job whilst the appointment was made.'

'Sort-of? Well, I suppose they couldn't get anyone really suitable for such a short time, even for a post as crucial as this.'

I was lost for words, said nothing, but wondered if Sapphira had given Naomi some of this treatment. It would have done nothing to endear her to anyone, yet Andy and Tim spoke highly of her. I became aware of an expectant silence.

'Have you found your desk?' I said and started to lead the way to the desk in the centre of all the others, slightly larger, to take the extra sets of files and books, but otherwise not dissimilar to those surrounding it. 'Here,' I smiled at the area I'd made tidy, clear and clean as it never was when used by its previous owner.

'No.'

'No?'

'No, this will never do —how can I be expected to work professionally in the middle of this entire melee,' she waved her hand to indicate the desks of the rest of the team.

'It's how it's always been done here at Eden, so I understand.'

'So, maybe it's time for a change,' she let her gaze sweep round the large open space.

This was a space designed not to have separate offices, to be light and generous not boxed in and tight, a place where work was shared by everyone in the 'family'. However, I said nothing, I knew that this was not something I could affect but already I sensed that there would be consternation amongst the tight-knit

24

group of scientists used to interacting merely by looking up and speaking.

'Well, er, would you like a coffee, or something before the others arrive?'

'And what time do they deign to arrive?'

'Their day starts at nine, unless they've had an emergency call of course.'

'Nine. Oh very well, black coffee.'

Counting under my breath I went to get a coffee for her and a herbal tea for myself. I reached for a refreshing and relaxing peppermint tea as I waited for the kettle to boil. Emergency, I thought, well, was the Moringa an emergency? Should I tell this woman about it now – or leave it? Feeling cowardly I decided to find out the results from the cultures and the sticky pads before saying anything.

'Coffee!' I said brightly as I offered her the mug of Eden's-own coffee. Sapphira looked at the mug, but didn't reach for it. Only then did I realise I'd used the mug brightly splashed with the words 'A Mug for a Muggle!' against a blue moon, but that the second half of 'muggle' would be lost against the curve of the cup. I turned it slightly, smiled and said, 'Harry Potter fan, it's our plant pathologist's really, we tend to bring in our own distinctive mugs, you know.'

With a sour look Sapphira took the cup, sniffed it suspiciously then set it down.

The sound of the door opening and closing downstairs broke the moment's unease.

'Morning Gabbi!' called Karen from the desk below.

'There's Karen now,' I smiled, glad that she was in well before her start time. I whisked over to nearer the top of the stairs and called down, 'Hi! Be down in a tick to sign in, just checking our new senior botanist has everything she needs.'

Sapphira was now standing near the centre of the floor, looking first one way then the other, I walked towards her and she marched away to the nearest end, where she stood glancing from the first elegantly arched polished wood roof truss to the end wall. 'You run along and get signed in, I will be perfectly alright once I can see the alterations I will require,' she said in dismissal.

It didn't take much to see that the area being studied would cut off a beautifully large office if Sapphira ever got the go-ahead, though I couldn't see Tim wearing it, as a separate office seemed to go against his philosophy. Run along, indeed! I thought as I descended to greet Karen.

'Oh! I didn't know *she* was here already,' Karen hissed.

'You don't like her?' I whispered back.

'Well, it's only from the one time I suppose,' Karen backtracked a little, 'but she made me feel like I didn't exist, and if I did then I was about as useful as, as a maggot.'

'Mmm, she does seem to be a bit aloof, but then again I heard good reports too, and she is highly qualified and experienced.'

'You know your trouble Gabbi?'

'What?

'You are just too damn kind and always trying to find the best in people,' Karen broke out into a grin. 'Perhaps she was just putting it on for the interview and really she's just a great big sweetie.'

I couldn't help laughing; Karen really *was* a sweetie and would always help anyone who needed it and certainly didn't deserve to be put down.

I was just signing my scrawl on the new page when Andy rolled up.

'And a very good morning to both you lovely ladies!' he boomed as he dumped his battered briefcase on the desk and swung the book round to sign in. 'All ready for Dr Ananias?'

'Hardly, she beat *me* in,' I whispered.

'Andy!' a pleased voice sang out. Andy swung round, Sapphira was descending the stairs as if making an entrance at a ball, slowly, a gentle sway of her tailored hips as she stepped. 'I just knew you were a stickler for time,' she came across holding out her hand to shake his. 'Early! Not, surely, to be here to greet me when I arrived?'

Andy's eyes sparkled, he took her hand and for one awful second I thought he was going to kiss it rather than shake it.

'Well, I did rather hope to have been here, but you know…' his voice trailed, he let go of her hand.

She smiled, glanced at me, 'Gabbi has been showing me the office area, though I want your opinion on a little idea that I have, come,' and she turned and led Andy upstairs, he following obediently. I turned and looked at Karen, who merely raised her eyebrows so high that they disappeared under her light fringe.

More to get out of the office than for any other reason I took myself off down to the domes and into HO3. I pushed fast through the paths to the Orang-dan-Kebun. I was hoping that by being early the sunlight would come in at an angle to illuminate the topmost branches, but would not blind the observer below. I climbed higher through the plantings until I gained the best view. There was no mistaking the redness now, more than the few original leaves were coloured, in fact I estimated that at least thirty percent of the tree's leaves were now showing red undersides, yet there was no leaf fall, and from my vantage point they seemed to be turgid, not showing any signs of flaccidity through droop. I sighed, well the Moringa really wasn't my problem anymore; perhaps I'd better just get it over with and inform Sapphira. Even as I thought this, I knew I didn't like the idea; I wanted to know what was wrong with the tree for my own satisfaction. I was just leaving the biomes when I caught sight of Naomi striding along, head down; she turned abruptly to come in my direction.

'Naomi?'

Naomi's head shot up, her face, which for a second or two showed a scowl, cleared in an instant to a wide smile, 'Oh, Gabbi! Glad I met you!'

'You okay?'

'Humph. Well, I don't know – I was when I arrived this morning but two minutes in the office and I don't know. Have you met her yet?'

'The senior botanist? Sapphira? Yes, earlier.'

'Sapphira?' Naomi's voice was filled with unusual venom. 'Dr Ananias, to me – apparently. And she had the cheek to tell me to get her a cup of coffee while she chatted with Andy, oh, and while I was there, was there anything Andy wanted. Like I am some waitress or something, and you'd be more polite to a waitress!'

'Oh dear, perhaps she thought you were getting something for yourself...' I began.

'Oh no she didn't – I had just said to Andy that I was off to check the sticky pads on the Moringa, nothing to do with coffee.'

'Did you get it?'

Naomi looked up in the air, then suddenly down. 'Yes,' she sighed. 'That's why I am now in such a foul mood! Never mind – want to come and check the pads?'

'Okay, just been there as it happens,' I said as we retraced my steps. 'The red-leaf has progressed down the tree, about thirty percent now, I'd say.'

'Shit! And you are sure that Adamson will want to look at it?'

'No, not sure, of course not – just knowing his interest I thought it likely, though it's a long time ago now.'

'Well, if it provides a problem for Dr stuck-up Ananias, I'm bloody glad!'

Naomi and I returned to the Foundation building together, 'for protection' as Naomi put it. We came out onto the first floor to see Jim and Andy manhandling the large desk out from its usual position down the room towards the end. The reference shelves that stood at that end were shoved together on one side with no room between them. A quick glance round showed me that Sapphira was not about. I was on the pair of them in an instant. 'What are you doing? Did she tell you to do that?'

'Down,' Andy puffed, then stretched his back.

'No, we just thought we'd surprise her, she's had this little idea you see, to have her area just a bit away so if she needs to work on anything serious or see someone confidentially, then she's not going to cause us any problems in moving or working extra quietly.'

'And she was saying, oh, well I will have to see if I can arrange for caretakers or someone, and we just thought, didn't we, well, she's popped out for elevenses, we'd do it and surprise her,' Jim finished.

I looked at our head horticulturalist, usually so level-headed. 'Really? And you didn't wonder why this has never been done before by our other senior botanists?' I shook my head. 'Anyway, unusual to see you over here before lunch Jim?'

'Yeah, well,' Jim said picking up his end of the fully loaded desk. 'Just came to welcome the new senior botanist, didn't I?'

'Well, don't put your backs out, you shouldn't be doing it that way anyhow, you should have emptied it first,' I said turning away to look at Naomi.

'Oh my! What a piece of work!' muttered Naomi and took herself and the sticky pads off to her desk and microscope, now marooned on one edge of a gaping space.

'Hey everyone! Oh good grief! What's happened here?' Mikaela made her usual exuberant entrance then stopped short when she saw the new arrangements. Jim and Andy were just relocating the last of the filing cabinets and only the chair remained to indicate where the senior botanist's desk had been. Up at the end, the reference book shelves were still crowded together.

'What do you think?' Andy called, cheerily. 'And we haven't done our backs in,' he added sticking his tongue out at me. I merely shook my head at him with a wry smile on my face, it was like trying to chastise a Labrador puppy.

'Well, I think it's really unfriendly to put her desk down there, wouldn't she prefer to be with us, all together?' Mikaela asked.

'Mikaela – it was her idea, to give us space, only she thought she'd have to wait – months – to get it done,' Andy said.

'Oh, right.' Mikaela said thoughtfully, as she sat at her desk and wiggled the mouse to bring her computer to life.

I stood a moment looking at the desks that were left, I couldn't help feeling that the ragged hole in the conformation represented more than just a move of furniture, it was a disturbing sensation with a tingle of premonition to it. I shook myself. 'We ought to rearrange our desks as well, make it more – well, bring us back together.'

'Yeah, well, that'd be good,' Andy started. 'We'll think about it then move them all at once, eh?'

'Oh stewpots!' Mikaela gasped. 'Another email from Luke Adamson! He's changed his arrangements and is arriving today on the one-thirty flight to Newquay! He presumes that arrangements will be made to meet him. He will now be alone as he has dispensed with the services of his publisher's PA.'

'Well, there's plenty of time to get up to Newquay,' Andy said.

'It's not that – it's what to do with him? I'd prepared the itinerary for tomorrow, meet the staff, tour of Eden, familiarisation with the lecture facilities, dinner and the lecture – what do I do with him today?'

'Don't worry, he'll probably want to rest up anyway, won't be bothered about what to do today,' I suggested, looking at Mikaela's troubled face.

'Not your problem, give it to *Sapphira*!' muttered Naomi, 'And there's no indication of pest predation on the Moringa either, so she can have that one too!'

I looked over to Naomi, I had never known her to be so negative, and of course her comment made the Moringa question rise to the surface again.

'Andy? Anything from your tests?'

'Not checked yet, I'm going over in half an hour – want to come and see?'

'Will do, I checked the tree this morning – I reckon we're up to thirty percent leaf colour change now, and still no sign of leaf fall or droop.'

'You're joking – that's a hell of a spread in a day, less than a day!'

I just shook my head, I had no answers.

'Forget half an hour, you ready to go now?'

I gave a tight lipped smile, nodded and collected my bag.

'You know it wouldn't be too good for Sapphira to have this problem right now, just when she's started at Eden. It'd be good to sort it out if we could,' Andy was saying as he unlocked his car.

'Not good for Eden at anytime,' I replied, wondering about the impact that Sapphira had made on Andy, usually a bit of a cynic and unfazed by authority or fame, he seemed to be reacting out of character over Sapphira.

Andy hummed a rock tune over and over as he drove, only stopping as we pulled into the site. We waved at the staff in the reception building and headed straight to the labs. Once inside we put on coats and gloves, then Andy lifted the cultures out of the cabinet, took them over to the microscopes and removed the lids. The tune started up again.

'Any joy?' I asked as the humming became quieter and quieter.

'Not a thing! All looks well, healthy, except they are the wrong colour! It doesn't make sense.'

'Well, perhaps it *is* some reaction to the lower light levels in the dome.' This idea had been growing on me; there were examples in the histology of other plants, try as we might the light levels under ETFE were lower than normal levels, and perhaps the evidence that this occurred in the wild just hadn't been recorded or if it had, hadn't yet been found by my researches.

Andy looked up at me, a long thoughtful look.

'Yep, we could say that. We could say that we were proposing to research reactions under ETFE. You think Adamson would buy that? It'd let Sapphira off.'

'How would I know?' I realised I was sounding sharper than I meant to be, but somehow didn't feel able to change it. We cleared up in silence, Andy putting the cultures back in to continue development in case they revealed anything later.

Back at the Foundation building we found the upper floor deserted. Mikaela had set off for Newquay and Naomi was nowhere to be seen. I found myself looking towards the relocated desk. It was obvious at once that Sapphira had been back in the interim, for standing on the desk was a photo frame. I really didn't want to, but somehow I found I'd wandered to the desk. Overcome with curiosity I peered round the end to look at the picture, expecting a photograph of family, perhaps husband or children, but the person in the frame wore a sort of ecclesiastical garb in an electric blue which served to enhance his tan, his clear blue eyes and white-blond hair, the photo showed him with his hands held in uplifted praise. The face was vaguely familiar, though I couldn't put a name to him.

'The Reverend Elliot Ashe,' Sapphira's voice rang clear across the room from where she stood at the top of the stairs. I jumped, for the second time that day, blushed, as I felt caught out, and stepped away from the desk.

'A wonderful and inspirational man,' Sapphira continued gliding towards me. 'I met him in California, travelled with his ministry for a while when he visited Texas - inspirational.'

'Oh, yes – I thought I recognised him, just couldn't place the name,' I muttered as I remembered seeing an advert for his upcoming mission to the UK.

Sapphira gave a tight smile as she reached me and continued in a low voice, 'If you'd ever heard him preach you'd know his name. You help at St. Piran's Society in your time off, so I guess you are a believer?'

'Umm, well I do help out there,' I felt unnerved, how did she know about St Piran's already? What did she think I believed in? If anything I believed in some benign goodness, I believed in, if not always being able to do good then at least in doing no harm. 'I suppose I believe in 'loving your neighbour as yourself',' I said paraphrasing Christ's second injunction.

Sapphira smiled, 'It's a start, Gabbi, but there is so much more that He wants to give us, you know.'

'Oh, yes, umm, well, sorry to have intruded,' I shrugged, still embarrassed at giving in to my curiosity.

'Nothing to worry about, it was a blessing to open your mind to what He wants you to know,' Sapphira said as she gracefully sat down at her desk, giving the photo a glance as she did so.

I returned to my desk, Andy looked up from where he'd settled himself in while I'd been snooping. 'What was that about?'

'Hmm. Well Sapphira was telling me about the Reverend Elliot Ashe? Heard of him?'

'The footballer?'

'No,' I laughed. 'The *Reverend* Elliot Ashe? Evangelical minister of the air, TV, net, whatever?'

'No, you know me, nothing against your beliefs, but none of it interests me.'

'No, well, it's of interest to Sapphira, apparently.'

'Really? I'm surprised she seems so switched on scientifically, I wouldn't have thought it her kind of thing. No basis in verifiable fact.'

'Well there's more things in heaven and earth,' I smiled, 'and now I'm off as it's lunch time. See you tomorrow.'

'Gabbi,' Andy beckoned me to him, and whispered, 'have you told Sapphira about the Moringa?'

'No, but perhaps I ought before I go,' I said feeling as if someone had just pulled out my plug. We looked at each other for a moment.

'No, it's okay, I'll tell her,' Andy said. 'You get off to your down-and-outs,' he smiled.

'Homeless.'

'Homeless, whatever, hey, perhaps she'll want to convert me to believing in the Rev Ashe, I might enjoy that.'

I shook my head at him in mock reproof but thanked him with true relief for opting to be the one to tell the news about the Moringa to that unsettling woman.

The Angel Bug 4

Luke 19th October

Damn crappy little airports and the crappy little planes that fly to them. I could feel myself getting angry as I waited for my luggage to turn up. The flight had been appalling. I'd been crammed in a miniature plane, dumped at this miniscule airport reception area and now there was no sign of the Eden person supposed to meet me, at least I'd seen no card flashed with my name on it.

Suddenly the bags appeared; I reached for them and snatched them up. Okay, now where's the meet and greet? I stepped towards the doors, looking all round for someone who might look like they were waiting for me. I tossed the larger suitcase down near the desk and leant over to the receptionist.

'Can you page someone for me? Someone from The Eden Project is supposed to be meeting me.'

'Of course sir, your name please?'

'My name? Dr Luke Adamson.'

'Thank you sir,' the receptionist turned slightly away from me and picked up a small microphone. 'Would the person due to meet Mr Luke Adamson please come to the reception desk. Thank you,' she smiled and continued with her work. So I started looking round, there were very few people left in reception and no one was heading in a purposeful manner my way.

Right, I've had it with this shit, I thought, I'd just decided to call a taxi and get to the hotel, then tear Eden off a strip when I got to them, when I saw this stunning blonde run into reception, her eyes were wide and her cheeks flushed, she hesitated a moment and then continued quickly over in my direction, sweeping back her hair and straightening her clothes as she approached.

She held out her hand, a broad smile in place, 'Dr Adamson, I am just so dreadfully sorry I wasn't here to meet you when you landed. I got caught up in a terrible traffic jam, an accident I'm afraid, I'm really sorry.'

I knew I was still feeling angry, but I could see a lovely little opportunity to make this woman feel grateful to me and so, as usual, I took it. 'It's not a problem, are you okay, has it upset you, seeing the accident?' I said as I shook her hand and rested my other hand on her upper arm, solicitously.

'Oh! Thank you for understanding, it wasn't nice, they were cutting someone out of the wreckage. So, um, I'm Mikaela Archer.'

'And you're from Eden, right?'

'Right, and I have my car just outside,' she turned and I picked up my bags ready to follow. 'You know I was so nervous about meeting you, and then to be late like that, I, well, thanks,' she said over her shoulder.

'Obviously not your fault,' I said smoothly. 'This yours?' I'd seen these cars around of course, a cross between a corrugated iron shed and an old-fashioned VW beetle, but I didn't look forward to the ride it might give.

'Yeah, she's called Binky, don't ask it's a long silly story!' Mikaela said patting the hood as she rounded the vehicle to unlock the door. 'Best just stick your bags on the back seat, the boot's a bit full at the moment.'

'Binky! Boot.' I muttered, hefting my suitcase into the narrow back seat, carefully stashing my hand luggage in the foot well. They must have sent a ditsy receptionist or something to collect me, I thought, as I gently lowered myself into the front seat as if it might break.

'Okay?' Mikaela, pushed the car into gear and set off. Once we were out of the airport area and on our way across country, heading towards Eden I guessed, she continued, 'Now, I presume you'll want to go straight to your hotel, I'm afraid that the reception and stuff's all set up for tomorrow, perhaps you'd like to rest this evening?'

'Well, that's a mite unfriendly, abandoning me on my first evening. You could at least offer to stay for dinner with me, if you have no other pressing business that is.'

Mikaela glanced round as if to see if I was joking, but I pulled a serious face, and thought, well she's already messed up by being late and I'd been so nice about that, so to stay for dinner was the least she could do, wasn't it? It was as if I could read her mind. She'd make some excuse to whomever need to know, I saw that click and then she turned her face to me, all hesitant smile.

'Well, that's very kind of you. So, are you happy to go straight to your hotel, and then I'll return later to keep you company at dinner, say seven thirty?'

I glanced at my watch, two thirty. What the hell was I going to do for five hours kicking around some shitty little hotel? The car gave a better ride than I'd expected, it wouldn't hurt to go further. 'I don't think so, no, I think you can wait for me to freshen up and then you can bring me back to this Eden place so I can give it the once over.'

'Oh! You do?' There was a pause while I imagined some other clogs clicking into place, 'Okay, I'm sure that'll be alright.' She was leaning forward, peering through the windshield, 'The hotel entrance is along here somewhere, ah, there it is,' she said and accelerated towards a pillared gap in a long wall. Inside we turned a sharp right to reveal a magnificent redbrick Victorian building of at least six floors, with lush green lawns to the front of it and, as we as reached it, I saw it had spectacular views out to sea. Things were looking up, at least the hotel looked classy from the outside.

'I'll just wait in reception,' Mikaela said after I'd signed in.

'Hell, no! You come on up, it's a suite, it's not as if you'll have to sit on my bed, and I won't eat you,' I knew I was laying on the American geniality, but it worked more often than not, these English girls seemed to like it.

Mikaela blushed, 'Well, alright, if you're sure.'

'Sure, I'm sure,' I said, course I'm sure, I thought, congratulating myself on my progress already.

Once in the room I took the suitcase through to the bedroom, placed it on the stand and unzipped it. I removed my jackets and flung them on the bed.

'So what do you do at Eden?' I called softly from the bedroom.

'Pardon?' Mikaela appeared in the doorway.

'I asked what you did?'

'Well, you know. I mean, I'm the ethnobotanist there and you know how that's one of the main focuses of Eden - the relationship between man and plants.'

Whoa there, I straightened, looked at Mikaela again, the ethnobotanist. This called for a slightly different game.

'Shoot, I'm sorry,' I stepped over to her at the door, held out my hand to shake, 'I didn't realise, I thought they'd sent a publicity person to meet me, pleased to meet you!' Mikaela shook my hand, blushing again as she realised she'd never introduced herself properly in the first place, still holding her hand I leaned forward and kissed her on her cheek. 'You know you blush so damned prettily you would make a man find some way just to make it happen,' I said softly beside her ear. At which she blushed again, but did not draw away. I stepped out of the personal zone, and as I thought it would, it made Mikaela lean ever-so-slightly towards me, which told me that she was ripe.

I turned away, back to my unpacking, 'I'll get this stuff hung up,' I said indicating the clothes laid on the bed, 'then a quick shower and you can show me your Eden.'

'If you like, I'll hang that up, while you shower'

'Well that real nice of you Mikaela. Not your job of course, but really nice of you, if you don't mind?'

'No, that's fine,' Mikaela came into the bedroom, glanced around to see where the wardrobe was and opened it ready to fill. I disappeared into the bathroom.

Ten minutes later I returned with a pure white towel wrapped around my waist, my scarred torso showing tanned and toned above it. 'Thanks,' I called, as Mikaela had returned to the sitting room.

'No problem,' she called back and I saw her glance in my direction just as I appeared in the doorway. I held the door as if I was about to close it, but stood there looking at her for a very long moment, long enough for her to see that this was one hell of a fit looking guy, regardless of age.

Half an hour later and we were just pulling into the entrance to Eden.

'Here we are!' Mikaela sighed

'We are? I see nothing!'

'Promise you,' Mikaela had a smile in her voice, 'We are at Eden, I called ahead and those who are here will meet us at the visitors centre, so you get the same experience that all our visitors do.'

'Okay, lead on!' I said, feeling much better and more relaxed, a pleasant evening lay ahead of me, very pleasant if Mikaela came across....

I realised later that Mikaela had parked deliberately so that the view of the domes was obscured then and while she led me down the path towards the visitors centre. As we rounded the last bend the centre itself now blocked any view.

'All the plantings and art works on the outside are part of the temperate biome,' she explained.

'Sure, but where's the bubble structures?'

'Here's the visitors centre now,' Mikaela said. There were three people walking up towards us and as they reached us she stopped and turned to me, 'and here are some of the team, may I introduce the senior botanist, Dr Sapphira Ananias, Andy Peters, plant pathologist, Naomi Jamison, entomologist.   .

'Delighted,' I said. 'Great to be here,' pumping hands and smiling my very best at the women in the group. Very nice too, in quite different ways; the senior botanist, dark and sophisticated and the entomologist, graceful, black and beautiful.

'Please, come through here,' Sapphira said leading the way through the visitors centre to the stunning panoramic view of the bowl that was The Eden Project, the bubble structures making an impressive backdrop to the plantings and buildings in front.

I was actually impressed, though I'd thought I might not be. There was a strange other-worldly quality to it, yet very English for all that.

'You must be exhausted after your journey, would you like a cup of coffee first? It's made from our own coffee beans,' Sapphira offered. I accepted and we sat overlooking the view making small talk about my tour, the film, my current projects.

'Tomorrow we'd planned a full tour, before the public come in, but is there anything you'd like to see now as a taster?' Sapphira offered. The Andy guy sent her a sharp glance, but she didn't seem to notice it.

'Well, let's see now, I'd certainly be interested in looking round your humid biome.'

'Of course,' Sapphira said. 'I'll escort you round and Mikaela can meet you at the end to return you to your hotel. We'll meet up with the whole team tomorrow.'

We all stood, handshakes were shared, but as I followed Sapphira out, a glance back showed me the other three, heads together and looking towards us; which made me wonder what was going on.

'And this is the Orang dan Kebun, where we've recreated a Malaysian home with its traditional garden and surrounding plants.'

'Complete with Neem and Moringa I see,' I said casually, following the line of the trunks upwards. What was that? I looked round, there didn't seem to be any artificial lighting that could be shining onto the Moringa, what was it?

'Yes, traditionally extremely useful trees, and over here … '

'Is there something wrong with the Moringa?'

'Pardon, no, over here, you can see…'

'No, pardon me,' I said stepping back and shielding my eyes. 'The leaves are going red – it has a problem.'

'Oh that, no, it's just a reaction to low light levels caused by growing it under ETFE.'

'And your evidence for that?'

'Well, we are still in the process of researching the phenomenon, it's not unknown amongst jungle plants you know.'

'I know, the anthocyanin layer, and I also know Moringa extremely well, what have you done so far?'

'If you must know I only took up my post today, and have only just been told we had a problem. My team are looking into it and I am quite sure we will manage to sort it out as soon as I can focus on it.'

'Sure,' I said backing off, this was one hell of a good looking woman, almost as full of herself as I am, I didn't want to blow my chances, after all, I wasn't about to ration myself. We worked our way round the humid biome and back out into the cool fresh air of an autumn afternoon. Sapphira called up Mikaela to be ready to meet us.

I said my thank you and farewell, leaning in to kiss Sapphira's cheek as I did so. I winked at Mikaela and followed her out to the car.

'Well what did you think?' she asked as we reached it.

'Really impressive,' I said and was rewarded with a dazzling smile. Easy.

'Fine, so bye for now, and I'll see you at seven,' I said.

'Oh, seven, okay.'

'In the bar for an aperitif before our meal?'

'Well, I really can't, I'll have to drive you see and…'

'Nonsense, take a cab, my treat.'

'No, really, I'm happy to drive.'

'I insist! After all you are doing me the honour of coming all the way here to keep me company.'

'Well, okay, thanks, I'll do that.'

'That's better.'

I went to the window and pushed the curtains right back, I can't stand closed curtains, not since I can remember, then stood looking out at the wonderful view; something about the English countryside is able to make even the simplest bits look terrific. The pocket book size of everything makes the small differences stand out and be noticed. What the hell, I thought, I might as well take a breather and enjoy this place a bit more, so I grabbed a jacket and left my room.

Outside the hotel I walked round to the front overlooking the sea, beyond a raised grass bank I could see a path, which, when I made my way to it turned out to wind its way around the cliff edges in both directions. Seeing the edge of a cove with golden sands and pinnacles of rock I decided to head towards it. The path was well walked, though narrow, and for the most part kept as close to the edge as I wanted to be, in fact at places I wondered how long the path would survive come bad weather. I rounded a small headland only to find that the path now took a detour inland, yet I was sure I could see it return to the cliff-edge just the other side of this wild area marked only with a battered 'private' notice. I looked around, not a soul in sight, the land looked so unkempt, it wasn't as if I'd damage any crop or whatever, so I pushed down the barbed wire and stepped over. The going was rocky underfoot, and I made sure to watch for any sudden drops, just in case the area was really barred because it was unsafe, but there was nothing to worry about, just waist high bracken and gorse. The other side of the patch, however, was guarded by a mass of bramble bushes reaching both ways, I found a bit of stick and beat them down and high-stepped through them. I made it to the barbed wire line with barely a scratch and a just small snagged thread in my jacket.

Now the cove was close, invitingly spread out in front of me. The path continued across the top, but a winding set of steps and pathway obviously led down. Feeling really alive and surprisingly happy I set off down the path, gaining speed as I descended. Suddenly the shale slipped sideways beneath my leather soles and carried my legs out from under me, over the cliff edge. Unable to stop I grabbed for the vegetation beside the path to stop my fall, the pain of the gorse spikes almost making me let go, but holding on to prevent worse. I dragged my legs back over the edge and sat up, gasping for breath and laughing at the same time, I thought of what the press would make of it – the intrepid Dr Adamson, beaten by a Cornish cliff path! I sat on the path, pulling dead gorse spikes from my fingers, then turned and stood up carefully. The drop from this point was still a good thirty feet onto jagged rocks, I gave an involuntary shudder and, glancing at my hands, decided to go back and get cleaned up before Mikaela returned.

The shower was good and hot, though not as powerful as I liked, British plumbing never really made it on that score. My hands stung like fury and to add to the damage to my shins I found a graze down the back of my leg I'd not know about. As I towelled myself dry I thought about the evening and how to play it. Now I knew Mikaela wasn't just some airhead, I may need to play a longer game, but that would only make it more fun. I grinned at my image in the mirror. Oh boy, didn't I just love English girls!

At seven I wandered down to the bar, and so was there, all gentlemanly, when Mikaela came in looking wildly round, her face broke into a smile of relief as she spotted me.
'You are looking lovely,' I said, stepping in to kiss her cheek, stepping back to admire her. And she was, she'd put on a classy looking dress, and with her hair pinned up she looked special. The blush came easily to her cheeks and she allowed me to buy her a Kir-Royal before she'd even thought.

'So, what got you interested in ethnobotany?' I asked as we waited for our desserts to arrive.
'You!' Mikaela said, her eyes shining and her cheeks aflame with almost a bottle of wine she'd downed since the Kir. I'd made

sure we'd had two bottles, when she opted for the white, I'd gone for a red and topped up her glass whenever it slid below half.

I dipped my head and looking back at her raised an eyebrow, 'How's that?'

'Long before, long before the film and everything I had read an article you wrote about the inter-relationship of man and plants. It just got to me, you know, straight to that part that makes ultimate sense to me. We weren't put on this earth to exploit it, land, plants, animals, any of it, we were here to work *with it* in harmony,' she gave a small laugh. 'Listen to me! You know all this, you wrote the book.'

'Ah! Not me personally then? What a disappointment,' I leant in close, teasing her with my eyes.

'Well, not then, I mean I had no idea who you were.'

Good girl, falling.

The desserts came and the conversation drifted to the quality of the locally sourced fresh fruits and clotted cream.

'How about we take a coffee and liqueur up in the suite?'

'I really shouldn't,' Mikaela said. 'We've got an early start,' she giggled, 'some bigwig film star coming to look us over before we open,' her eyes twinkling at me.

'He won't mind if you're a bit hung-over, promise,' I said leaning in and giving the slightest flick of my head in an upwards motion.

'Okay, just one, then I must get back.'

Good girl. I indicated to a waiter and asked for two Irish coffees to be sent to my suite.

We were barely inside the room when the knock came on the door and a waiter brought in a tray with the Irish coffees, placed them on the table and left closing the door gently behind him.

I settled myself on the sofa and stretched myself out, pushing off my shoes, 'You don't mind?' I said looking up at Mikaela where she stood, wavering, between the window and the end of the sofa.

'What, oh no, not at all,'

'Come and sit down then,' I patted the sofa beside me just once. 'The coffee'll be too hot yet.' Touching the fabric with my palm made the prickly sensation return to my hand, I turned it palm up to look.

'Oh. What happened to your hand?' Mikaela said, dropping herself beside me to look. My palm was reddened with numerous pin-pricks of deeper red.

I grinned, 'I'll only tell if you promise me, absolutely promise, never to tell a soul.'

Mikaela looked up at me, her face very close to mine.

'I promise,' she said, wide eyed.

I leant forward, searched her eyes a moment, found no resistance, leant on in and kissed her. She kissed me back, then drew away with a small gasp.

'To seal your promise,' I said with a light wink, and a smile that disarmed the moment. 'I was bushwhacked by a cliff path, nearly had me over the edge, just grabbing a tough old gorse bush stopped me plunging into the sea!'

'No!'

'Oh, yes I'm afraid. That's why you can't tell! Really, so reckless, leather soles on a downward path!' She was smiling now. 'So,' I said, taking her hands, 'you really must not break that promise.'

'I won't.'

'Good. I'll hold you to it,' I said and drew her closer. 'You really are something,' I whispered, kissing her again before she could speak. This time she didn't pull back, this time I felt her soften, I released one of my hands and let it slide up to the nape of her neck, and down to massage her spine, down again to her thigh, sliding gently towards the top. Then, carefully working my way down again, kissing her, being kissed, this was working well. The hand massaging her back again, drawing her closer, I could feel her body move to the rhythm, down, sliding up under her dress, to the smooth flesh of her side. I was really hard now, finding myself drawn on by old familiar urges.

Mikaela pulled back. 'No.'

'Come on, you want this,' I whispered and drew her back towards me pressing my hand against her naked back. 'You're so beautiful, you know, a real peach, just beautiful.'

'No, I …'

'Oh but you are, how could a man resist, eh?' resuming the massaging, the light kisses falling on her shoulder, neck, lips and again harder until she responded. 'Better,' I breathed. 'Come on,' I leant her back a little, paused, to look in her eyes, damn. Her eyes were wide and she was shaking her head slightly, but enough. 'No,' she said, pulling herself up a little. 'No, not, not, no.'

'Mikaela?'

She shook her head, 'Sorry, I should never …'

'Hey, Mikaela sweetie, I like you, I like you a lot, and we're getting on so well, don't worry, no problem.'

'I really have to go now,' Mikaela pulled herself back from me and stood, I could see she was unsteady.

'Okay, we'll call that cab and then you'll go,' I called reception for them to call a taxi, then went over to where Mikaela stood, holding onto the back of the sofa. I came up behind her and ran my hands down her bare shoulders. She didn't move or complain so I repeated the movement, gently, caressing, then leant in and kissed the nape of her neck.

'Please, don't,' she murmured.

'Fine, no harm done, fine with me,' even I could hear the sting of disappointment in my voice.

The phone rang. Reception, the taxi was waiting. Cursing myself for pushing my luck too far, too soon, I escorted a flustered Mikaela down to the taxi. 'See you tomorrow, Mikaela,' I said, 'see you tomorrow.'

The Angel Bug 5

Gabbi 20th October

'You have all let me down, have you any idea of how embarrassed I was for you, and for Eden, at the moment when Luke Adamson told me that we have a real problem with the Moringa oleifera? And then questioned my knowledge when I offered him the answers *you* gave me – at the last moment, may I add – so that I had no chance to verify your wild hypothesis,' Sapphira had started with her voice low and calm. I thought Andy and Jim were both looking appalled, Naomi looked straight at Sapphira and Mikaela had her head hung, eyes hidden beneath a curtain of hair, as they had been since she'd arrived. I hardly knew where to look, as Sapphira continued with her voice growing raw and jagged, I felt so guilty for letting Andy be the one to pass on the Moringa problem.

'So unprofessional! So incompetent! When they asked me, begged me, to take over here at Eden I was told I had a top team of dedicated personnel, now I find I have dross that can't be bothered to look after the plants, can't be bothered to do their research, can't be bothered to inform the senior botanist about the most important failing in the place before an important visitor, not just any visitor but one who actually knows what he's looking at, comes along and points out that incompetence!'

The men looked at the floor, no one else moved.

'Don't you think you are being a little unfair,' I began.

'Don't *you* presume to tell me anything! After all, what do you know? This mess is all your doing anyway – you were supposedly in charge.'

'The problem had only just been spotted and we were working on it on all fronts, I did point out that he'd want to see it.'

'You did, did you? Not to me you didn't. Why not? Did you want to show me up, put me in a bad light?' A strange look came over her face. 'Did you want this job by any chance? Do you have a grievance that I have it?'

'No! I didn't even apply.'

'Just as well, under-qualified and out of date at that. So whose stupid idea was it to suggest to me that it might be due to growing under ETFE?'

'It's a possibility,' Andy cut in before I could say anything. 'It's just that we've not had time to find out what it is at all, just time to discount some of the easier things to rule out.'

'I see! So you'll be the best person to explain all that to Luke Adamson when he arrives full of criticisms and spouts off to the press. And talking of him arriving, Miss Archer, where is he? I had expected you to collect him today.'

'Sorry, I couldn't, um, I couldn't drive today, car problems, so I've sent a taxi for him.'

'Time?'

'Sorry, time, any time now, really.'

'Incompetence!' Sapphira muttered and turned away from them to look up the path. 'Get up there,' she said over her shoulder. 'Make sure he feels welcome, perhaps we can pull something back from this.'

Mikaela looked up, looked around as if to check that it was she who was being spoken to, then, wincing in the bright sunlight, she walked slowly up the path towards the parking area. I watched her for a moment then began to follow, feeling she needed some support today.

'And where do you think you are going?' Sapphira snapped. 'You, here, and the rest of you. This is what we are going to do – we are going to get him involved in the search for the problem with the Moringa. That way we can use the spin that we have brought in 'the expert'. Whatever turns up then we are covered and he is in it with us, so cannot reproach us.'

'He's only here for a day, what could he do?' Andy started.

'How long doesn't matter – as long as he's in on it.'

'Besides, he could be here for longer – remember he wants to look around Cornwall,' I offered, though saying it made me feel like a collaborator.

'Ideal! Now we only have to get him involved.'

'He's coming,' Jim said, nodding in the direction of the path.

'Welcome back, Dr Adamson,' Sapphira called as they approached.

'Pleasure to be here again, Dr. Ananias,' Luke beamed.

'Please, Sapphira, we all use first names round here.'

'It's Luke, then, Sapphira, what's the plan?'

'First an apology, Tim had hoped to be here to meet you now, but he's not got back from London on time, rail hold-up somewhere. Right now, come and meet some of the Plants team you missed yesterday then we'll give you the deluxe tour before a lunch with Tim and some of our other teams.'

'Lead on.'

Sapphira turned towards the others, 'Andy, and Naomi you met yesterday,' she indicated the pair who dutifully smiled and nodded a greeting. 'May I introduce our chief Horticulturalist, responsible for the growing of the plants at our Watering Lane Nursery.'

Jim leant forward, hand outstretched, 'Jim Borlase,' he said, and was given the big American handshake. I was watching Luke, I hadn't been able to take my eyes off him from the moment he appeared. The years really had been good to him, he looked as good in life as on the posters, and despite myself there was something happening to my pulse rate.

And this is another of our botanists and she is the one who is supposed to be looking into the Moringa difficulty,' Sapphira added.

'Gabbi Johnston,' I said, smiling at him and holding out my hand, inwardly smarting from the jibe that Sapphira had aimed at me.

'Pleased to meet you, all,' he said shaking my hand briefly and encompassing us all in his glance. 'And if you want any help with the Moringa I will be delighted to take a look,' he added, looking back at me as he did so. I felt my heart thump as I noticed a faint look of puzzlement flit across his face.

'That would be wonderful, an honour, thank you,' Sapphira cut in quickly, drawing him aside. 'Perhaps after your lecture, I understand you are staying with us for a few days.'

'Well, yes, I had thought about seeing something of the countryside while I'm down here,' he said, turning his head back towards me, a glance that, seeing it coming, I managed to avoid.

As I followed along in the 'grand tour' I wondered at my own reactions, wanting and not wanting him to recognise me, certainly not wanting to actually tell him. Sapphira started well on the main principles behind Eden and its plantings, stuff she must have mugged up on prior to her interviews and appointment, I supposed, but was clever enough to hand over to the rest of the team, one by one, as her specific knowledge became sketchy. I was almost in a daydream, sub-consciously giving the plants we passed the once-over for health and well-being, and on another level working out what more we could have done in the case of the Moringa since we found the problem. I had tuned out the explanations from my surroundings, my mind on another agenda entirely, when I heard my name, and from the tenor it sounded as if this was at least the second time Sapphira had said it.

'Sorry?'

'I had just said that you were the first to notice the problem and so it was your call.'

'Well, sort of,' I guessed that though we were nowhere near the Moringa that the conversation must have reverted to the problem. 'You have to understand that this is a problem that only came to light forty-eight hours ago, if that, and we have taken samples, cultivated cells, set traps for insect vectors and monitored the progression in that time. Unfortunately we have not been able to identify the actual cause of the problem at the moment, but of course any indicators we need to look at or procedures to be followed that you might suggest would be very welcome.'

'Sure,' Luke said looking at me his head slightly tilted as if listening for some distant sound. 'Okay, perhaps we can have a look at it together, after this lunch thing?'

I glanced at Sapphira as she'd previously suggested that he start tomorrow; Sapphira's raised eyebrows didn't give me any answers.

'Well, whenever you like, but won't you want to rest before your performance?' I could have bitten off the words, they sounded so trite. He grinned, and gave his head a shake.

'Last in a mighty-long tour of lectures, I think I know my script now. No this afternoon suits me.'

'Fine, I'll come to meet you after the lunch finishes.'

'And I'll look forward to it,' Luke said, his eyes slightly narrowing, though holding his smile, as he looked at me.

As soon as I could decently leave the group I rushed back up to the Foundation building and logged on to search the internet again for clues to the problems with the Moringa, 'Anything,' I murmured to myself, 'any new idea to pursue this afternoon.' There was nothing in the recorded studies to give me a clue of where to go next. Perhaps Luke would be similarly stumped, I thought, and wondered why I was feeling so concerned about what he'd think of my scientific credentials, what did it matter what he thought?

Three o'clock saw me pacing up and down in the Link, the section above the restaurant area that joins the Humid Tropics Biome to the Warm Temperate Biome, trying not to get in the way of the visitors and keeping an eye on the lunch party below in the restaurant. I could see that both Luke and Tim were as animated as each other as they talked over their coffee, the other lunch companions seeming not to get much of a look in. Ah, movement at last, a few people were making 'I must leave signals' and shaking hands with Tim and Luke and going on their way, Tim listened to something Luke was saying, then looked up, scanning the Link walkway. His gaze found me and he raised a hand. I raised mine in return and started to walk down to meet them.

'Well, I'll hand you over to the tender care of our Gabbi, I am sure she will look after you as she seems to look after everyone in the team. I look forward to your lecture tonight.' Tim said before shaking Luke's hand warmly once more and leaving us.

'Okay now we're alone you can put me out of my misery. I do know you, don't I?' Luke said, lightly touching my arm.

I felt the blush zooming up my face. 'Well, it was a long time ago, and I'm amazed you remember me at all but yes, we have met, at Cambridge, Gabriella Angellenzi then, I married James Johnston.'

'J J!' he said suddenly, 'the lucky dog, how is he?'

I took a breath, 'Passed on,' I said. 'Two years ago.'

'Oh, gee, I'm sorry to hear that.'

'Thanks. Well I won't say I've got over it, because it wouldn't be true, but I have come to accept it now.'

'What was it? Sudden?' his voice low and full of what sounded like genuine concern.

'Oh yes, sudden and instantly fatal, massive heart attack, no warnings.'

'Jesus! Whew, shakes a man up a bit I can say – being the same age and all,' he shook his head as if trying to rid himself of the thought.

I swallowed. Somehow this was harder than I'd expected. He looked up at me again. 'And you, how have you managed?'

'Day to day to start with, but then they're a great lot here, helped me though it, and Emma came back over from Australia for a few months.'

'Emma?'

'Oh sorry, Emma, our daughter – she's living in Australia doing a PhD in Anthropology in Sydney.'

We'd started walking as we talked, into the Humid biome, moving towards the Orang dan Kebun, and in its garden, the Moringa.

'So how did you end up down here?'

'Here, because James took an early retirement and wanted to move down here to Cornwall,' I heard Luke give a sudden exhalation of breath, almost a 'huh?' so moved straight on to an explanation. 'He was fed up with the constant begging for money for research, the doing the rounds and making the bids taking more time than the research grants gave time for the work. He, we, decided that quality of life was missing, so we tried for it here, and it was working, until – it happened.' I knew that my eyes were beginning to fill, but could do little to stop them, it seemed to have been so long since I'd talked about James to anyone new, I looked away, scanning the tree tops for the hexagonal structure beyond. I felt his hand on my arm and turned, his hand slid down to my hand, took hold of my fingers in his, so caring and gentle, I had to look at him.

'I really am, really am sorry Gabriella, I didn't mean to bring it all back. Come here.' He drew me to him and I leant into him, wondering at the feel of a man's arms around me, letting my tears flow into the fabric of his shirt. After a moment I drew a deep breath and brushing my eyes with my fingers stepped back.

'Oh dear! Sorry. Now, we have a job to do – I think.'

'Gabriella?'

'Everyone calls me Gabbi now.'

'Not me. I always thought it a magnificent name that just suited you all out. Gabriella, would you be my guide in the time I have down here, before I go back to the US?'

'Of course, as long as I can be spared here, and that means we've got to get this Moringa sorted,' I waved my hand at the offending tree, its uppermost branches blazing with their reddened leaves.

'Okay, deal. So you've looked at the leaves, insect vectors, watering. What else?'

'Taken cultures from the affected leaves, which, by the way seem to be healthy in every way apart from the red colour, and I'd better admit to this, as Sapphira has her sights on me over it, it was my suggestion that the red might be a reaction to the lower light levels under ETFE, just a hypothesis, considering the range of jungle plants that exhibit this in the lower light levels below the canopy.'

'I can see the reasoning, but 'a hypothesis' is not how the lady put it, and I have to say I haven't found any such reaction in Moringa in the wild – but then they aren't usually in lower light conditions either.'

'And that's where we are, any ideas?'

'Yeah, have you looked at the root structure?'

'No, what would we be looking for?'

'Disease, fungal attack maybe?'

'But then the tree would show some kind of weakness or failure, leaves actually dying rather than just changing colour.'

'No leaf fall or deterioration at all?'

'None caused by the leaf colour change.'

'Okay, so, you've covered most bases, I'd still like a look at the roots.'

'Okay, how about tomorrow morning before the public gets in?'

'Hell no, I want to get right in there now and take a look, waiting would just be wasting time.'

I looked at him for a moment, there was no doubt that he meant it, and Sapphira really wanted him on board so that he was tied in. 'Okay, I'll just call up one of the horticultural assistants and some equipment and we'll go for it.' I stepped to one side of the path and called through to Josh, asking him to bring some tape to cordon off the area along with tools for digging, a brush, sample bags, a knife and a saw. Glancing at Luke I added that gloves and a small tarpaulin for kneeling on would be useful and that we'd be in the area somewhere near, waiting. Josh sounded really keen and said at the end. 'Wow, Luke Adamson, working at Eden!'

We were looking at the slate grey West African Totems, carved for Eden by a renowned West African sculptor out of old timbers from the Falmouth docks, timbers that had started their life as West African trees, when Josh appeared on the scene, his wheelbarrow loaded with gear. It took only minutes for us to reach him, by which time he'd strung some tape around the corner of the Orang dan Kebun garden and hung a sign on it advising people to keep away for their own safety.

Luke grabbed the shovel, lifted it out, 'Strange looking shovel?'
'Cornish, traditional, can get you something different if you like,' Josh said.
'No, no need, won't be using one,' he lifted out a trowel. 'This'll do,' he knelt by the trunk.
'There's a tarpaulin, stop you getting dirty,'
Luke laughed, 'Oh, don't worry about me, Gabriella.'
Josh looked from Luke to me and back. I took the tarpaulin out and laid it next to Luke, kneeling on it. 'We're not all as gung-ho as you, you know.'
He laughed again. 'Yeah, its coming back, you always were a little mother weren't you?'

I could feel Josh's eyes on me, knew he was wondering what was going on here, and would soon air his views over coffee to the rest of them. I looked up at him.
'You didn't know that we were at Cambridge at the same time, did you?' Josh blushed and shook his head. 'Different years, didn't expect Luke to remember me at all, but there you go.'

Luke had dug and scraped the soil away from one of the roots and was working his way along it, clearing the soil, stopping to brush away loose dirt from the finer roots.
'Hey, hey. What's this?'
I leaned over to look and there, seemingly attached to some of the roots, were dark reddish nodules about the size of small peanuts.
'Are they attached?'
Luke brushed again, lifted a fine trellis of roots and sure enough the nodules were hanging like tiny sparse potatoes.
'We'll have some of these for a start,' he said, 'these are not usual on Moringa – I can tell you that for free.'

It took another quarter of an hour to check that there was nothing else extraordinary about the root structure, and to have collected quite a crowd who watched this 'film star', actually doing 'work' at Eden, complete with the background sound of cameras and mobile phone videos whirring. The disturbed roots were carefully re-laid and the soil replaced. With the samples in a collecting bag we left Josh to tidy up and ensure the area had extra watering to counteract any desiccation caused. Luke had the biggest grin on his face as we took the quick exit out of the biomes and hurried to get back up to the Foundation building.

I dashed into the building to get my car keys and tell someone that we were off to Watering Lane, to the labs, with some samples, but as no one from the team was about, I left a message with Karen at the desk, in case anyone asked.

We climbed into my Mini and were swiftly on our way to the other site.

'So, tell me about Sapphira.' Luke said suddenly.

'I can't.'

'What, confidentiality?'

'No, I really don't know anything about her, she's only been here a couple of days, as in, this is her second day in charge. So, I'm not even being good or coy, I really don't know anything about her.'

'Okay, I'll believe you. What about Mikaela? You know I took her for some personnel go-fer when she met me at the airport?'

'Mikaela is a great girl, good brain if a little taken up with the more flashy aspects of ethnobotany, but that suits here as getting the message across to everyone is a major part of the Eden thing,' I thought about Luke's reputation of old, and added, 'She's got a long-term boyfriend, Jono, seems the right sort.'

'Okay, and your entomologist, I forget her name.'

'Naomi, first class brain and dedicated. What's this, twenty questions on the people here?'

'Nothing, just curious.'

I shook my head and smiled as I turned the car in a tight right hand turn and into Watering Lane. I waved at Jim as I pulled up and took Luke over to sign in at reception.

As I led him towards the row of portacabins, Luke was staring round him, distracted.

'Where are your labs then?'

'In here.'

'What? You have to be joking. These are your lab facilities?'

'Yep, well, they do for what we need, and if we need more we have links with some big university labs, you know scanning electron microscopes, the works,' I said, hooking a lab coat down for Luke and shrugging into one myself. I pulled new gloves out of the box and put them on the table, and goggles beside them.

'Okay then, I'd like tray, a block, distilled water, some slides. Do you have a microtome?' I nodded 'Need to use that then.' I slipped on gloves and collected the equipment together. Luke washed a root nodule down with distilled water and then turned to me and asked for a scalpel.

I fixed a blade on and handed it to him. As he sliced through the nodule it bled scarlet onto the block. For a second I thought he'd nicked his finger and it was blood, realising as I thought it that he'd not put gloves on.

'Luke, there's gloves here.'

'Don't fuss, little mother, hate the things. What do you think of this? I've never seen anything like it!'

'It's extraordinary, so bright.'

'Sure is – I must get a slide done, perhaps the structure can tell us a little more. Some fungi can have such colouration bleed.'

I watched as he quickly and deftly used the microtome to cut a thin slice of the nodule and prepared a slide.

'Set the rest of this to cut properly with the gear,' he said not even looking at me.

I picked up the sample and took it to another area of the lab and started the process to prepare it so that when it was set in paraffin wax it could be sliced ultra-thin to give the best view of the structure.

'This the best scope you got?' Luke muttered.

'Yes, here in the labs, it should do for structure.'

'Yeah, okay.'

I watched him gently move the slide.

'Hey! Come and look at this – what do you think?'

I moved in and looked down the eyepiece. The picture wasn't that clear, the cells had suffered a great deal of trauma being sliced unprepared, tearing and squashing them sideways, but the overall structure of the nodule was evident. I stood up and then bent again to look, moving the slide slightly.

'It's very reminiscent of nitrogen-fixing nodules, isn't it?'

'Hmm, my thoughts exactly. Though I can tell you for free that they don't have an association with Moringa, no way, I pursued that one into the ground years ago.'

'So, what is it?'

'The hell I know, but I do know I'm not letting up on this thing until we have an answer.'

The Angel Bug 6

Luke 20th October

I was beginning to think that lunch would never end, though Tim's a great guy the rest of them were plain dull, perhaps just English, what the hell, eventually people are shuffling to their feet, shaking hands and moving off, and although I've had this question nagging me, who was that woman? I'm usually very hot on names and faces but even having both wasn't helping. Something strange happened when I shook her hand, not electric or anything, just strange, something that needs experimenting with to check that it wasn't just a fluke.

Tim looked up towards the Link and raised his hand. She raised hers in return and started to walk down to meet us. Hell, she'd been up there looking down at us, for how long?

'Well, I'll hand you over to the tender care of our Gabbi, I am sure she will look after you as she seems to look after everyone in the team. I look forward to your lecture tonight,' Tim said, shaking my hand again and beaming at us both.

We watched him weave his way out of the restaurant and before she said anything I got in first. 'Okay, now we're alone you can put me out of my misery. I do know you, don't I?'

She blushed, oh so pretty. 'Well, it was a long time ago, and I'm amazed you remember me at all but yes, we have met, at Cambridge, Gabriella Angellenzi then, I married James Johnston.'

'J J!' I said, everything falling into place, Gabriella! And still gorgeous. 'The lucky dog, how is he?' Instantly I knew it wasn't good; there was this flash of pain across her face.

'Passed on,' she said, 'Two years ago.'

There are only platitudes to say at this stage, so I say them, what else, yet this news hits home in a way that other deaths hadn't, I mean, we were the same age, same line of business.

I asked a few questions to orientate myself with this news and we walked as she told me how come she was down here in the butt-end of England, I saw that remembering was becoming too much and it was all I could do not to wrap her up in my arms, but that would have scared the hell out of her I'm sure, so I reached out and touched her arm gently, she turned towards me and as the tears filled her dark eyes, I slipped my hand down to her fingers and drew her towards me. Just for a moment, to comfort her, experiment one, result, same as before, strange. Too soon she pulled herself together and became all business-like, and though I secured a promise for her to show me round the area after the show she was all fired up to look at the problem with the tree.

Nothing much seemed to have changed since the day before, though it was hard to tell, perhaps there was an extra intensity in the red of the uppermost leaves. There didn't appear to be any fallen red leaves in the immediate vicinity. I ran her through the tests they'd done and decided that the only place they hadn't considered was the root system, so I opted for that, least it made it look like a new contribution.

Wasn't long before she called up some lad with the gear and I started working. Real cute, she was, fussing over me, making sure I didn't get dirt on my jeans, and that brought up a memory of how she was all those years ago; looking after people, thinking ahead.

I don't think I could believe my luck when I came across these nodules on the fine root. First thought was that they might not be attached, but they were, and I knew I'd not encountered this type of structure on Moringa roots before, and I had looked since this was one area of research I'd gone into. The Moringa has an inordinate amount of nitrates in its leaves and as such is used as a green manure in some parts of the world, but how it manages to get such a build-up in its structure is a bit of a mystery, as it has no known association with nitrogen-fixing bacteria, which is the usual route for plants to get such a high intake of nitrates. My mind was in overdrive, could this be a mutation, or was there something here that I'd missed in all my studies in the wild? I had to get some of these into a lab and look at them. I did a bit more work around the roots; I didn't want to have missed anything else before we moved off.

It didn't take long to get to the other place, Watering something, but it was long enough in that tiny box of a car, I wasn't sure which frightened me more, Mikaela's dustbin or this matchbox. Gabriella 'signed me in' in some kind of garden shed then we headed for a couple of portacabins. These, my God, were the laboratory facilities; I felt like laughing, I'd had more in the middle of the jungle!

I got a nodule cleaned up and then sliced into it. It was bleeding, I mean, this red liquid oozed from the cut, so unusual, not the colour - the oozing, but Gabriella just starts fussing over gloves. Okay so nitrogen-fixing nodules usually contain leghaemoglobin and are therefore red, but I had never seen anything quite like this, and I was damned sure there was no other case of nitrogen-fixing bacteria associated with Moringa. So this *is* unusual, okay so I tell her that there're some fungi that bleed, true, but not like this, and they can have a red colour as would a nitrogen-fixing nodule, also true, but not usually as deep and bright as this. I was really pumped by now, could I be about to make a new discovery? I sure hoped so.

I got a rough un-prepped slide mounted; get Gabriella to set about prepping the rest of the nodule for high definition slices, and move to the best scope in the place. It's okay, nothing to write home about but just enough at this stage. What could I see? The structure was familiar: nitrogen-fixing bacteria make nodules with a similar structure, but I think I can detect hyphae too, suggesting a fungal association. Okay, so what are the possibilities, symbiotic relationship between fungi and bacteria and plant to provide what? Nitrogen is the obvious and given, though Moringa don't seem to need that anyway, what else?

'Hey! Come and look at this – what do you think?'

I watched her look at the sample, even the lab coat looked good on her, she moved the slide.

'It's very reminiscent of nitrogen-fixing nodules, isn't it?' she says still not looking up at me.

'Hmm, my thoughts exactly. Though I can tell you for free that they don't have an association with Moringa, no way, I pursued that one into the ground years ago.'

She looked straight at me. 'So, what is it?'

'I'm damned if I know, but I do know I'm not letting up on this thing until we have an answer!

Gabriella looked at me, then quickly at her watch, so I do too. Hell, nearly six and I still have to shower, change and be ready for a half seven start.

'I'll run you back to your hotel,' she said, not even discussing the problem, stripping off her lab coat, ditching gloves and cleaning up all at once. She hurried me out, threw me the car keys to let myself in, yelled into the hut to 'sign Dr Adamson out' and we were on the way.

'About fifteen minutes to get to your hotel, how long will you need? What about eating?'

'Half an hour will be fine, and I don't eat before a talk.'

So I'll arrange a taxi for quarter to seven, that should get you back by seven, quarter past at the very latest, is that enough time to collect yourself before you go on?' and all the time weaving through these tiny lanes.

'Sure.'

'Sure?' she said flashing me a smile.

'Sure,' I said, returning it.

So I got into my hotel room and made for the shower. The water was at least hot and it stung my hand, especially as I had to scrub at it where the red colour seemed to stain the skin. I took a mental note of this too, staining, well that would concur with fungi again, as some ancient dyes were made from fungi or their symbionts, lichens.

I got dressed for the evening, it's like getting ready for any performance I guess, I have the costume, the carefully selected range of clothes that says to my audience; adventurer, savvy, individualistic, but also an accomplished professor of ethnobotany. As I rigged myself out I wondered if that's where I went wrong with the Cambridge lot, maybe it should just have said 'professor' for them, maybe the rest of it raised their hackles before I even opened my mouth. Shit! Thinking about them was a mistake, I could feel my heart rate rising just standing there. So, I went back to thinking about the Moringa and before I knew where I was the phone rang to tell me that my taxi was waiting.

The place was packed, the audience, from what I could make of them, covering everyone from young teen to geriatrics. There were those who might be in the scientific community but there were a hell of a lot of people who looked like hippies, as if we'd dropped back thirty years, and some of them looked like they'd been that way for the last thirty years. The build-up was good and as I took the stage the last vestige of fear that it would be a 'Cambridge' repeat left me, the audience response was great.

I really used that stage, like looking down from somewhere else I could see how well I was taking the message to the people, my whole body was singing with this message tonight and I could feel the warm approval coming off them in waves. I could almost have wished for someone to offer that I answer some questions as I just knew I was flying and that the answers would be the right type.

Standing ovation; for a science lecture! My heart was racing fast, I knew, and I felt as if I was burning up, but it was a good feeling, right up there with winning everything I ever wanted to win.

Tim came on and said a few words, which resulted in another round of applause, and we were off and scooting along to a reception with invited guests and I am both ravenous and parched but on such a high it's worth it.

'Gabbi tells me that you've found something to investigate on the roots of one of our trees, the Moringa?' Tim said.

'Sure as hell have, and you know what, I'm not going to leave this place until I find out what is wrong with that tree.'

'That's good of you, but I am sure that our team could manage if you'd rather not.'

'Rather not? In fact I rather would, in fact I'd be insulted if I couldn't do it. Hey, you can use the publicity if you want.' Thinking that would buy them, because if they really wanted me out they could do it, no problem.

'Well anything, or any help you want, just ask the team, I'm sure they will be willing to assist you in any way,' he smiled.

I was really thinking on my feet now, we were coming in close to a group of people, 'Could you assign Gabriella to my team for the duration? She seems quite capable of the type of assistance I need.'

Tim smiled again. 'I'd have thought that wouldn't be a problem, just ask Sapphira if she can be spared.'

'Oh, I will. Thanks, I will,' and we were into the crowd, with pats on the back, a glass in my hand and the conversation flowing. I emptied the glass and glanced round to get a refill, which came as if by magic. A real old guy, science woven into his face, congratulated me and told me he's been trying to get that message across to the scientific community all his life and wished me luck with it. I thanked him, and at the same time I was scanning round looking for Gabriella. Suddenly I have that 'looking down on the world sense again' just as I did on stage, it's as if I can see myself standing there looking round, tops of heads, trays of food, all below me. I see her over by the door, near a buffet table. I start to move towards her, realising as I do so that I've left the old guy in mid-sentence, he'll put it down to American rudeness I guess.

'Gabriella!'

'Oh Luke, brilliant lecture! You remember Andy, our plant pathologist?' she indicated the guy towering beside her.

'Yeah, sure,' I stuck out my hand and got it shook.

'Gabbi was just telling me that you found some root nodules, any thoughts if they are of a pathological origin?'

'Not at the moment, but we'll keep you informed. I've arranged with Tim to stay on while we sort this thing out,' I said thinking that would screw him up, 'and to have Gabriella assigned to assist me.' I didn't know what I liked more, the closed look that came over the Andy guy's face or the surprise, and did I see a hint of pleasure, that flashed across Gabriella's?

'I am just so thirsty, any chance of a really tall glass of sparkling water or something?'

'I'll get it,' Gabriella said and was gone leaving me with the hulk, not that it bothered me, and before he could ask any more puerile questions I was swooped upon by some other guests, who made all the right noises and had in their hot little hands copies of the book which they hoped I'd sign. Happily I scrawled the marks that had become my signature over the tour – no author should have a long name – or write clearly enough to have to actually write it – it just takes too darn long and you get writer's cramp before you know what's going on; you can just about make out the L and the A on mine now. Gabriella appeared, her hand held the most wonderful looking long glass of clear sparkling liquid. I almost shoved aside a devotee to get at it, felt it wash a cool path down my throat. I grinned, 'Sorry, folks, I was just parched.' They made appreciative noises and thanking me again, left. The glass drained I looked back at Gabriella, 'That was good, thanks.' But even as I spoke I started to feel hot again, as if the air I was breathing was over-heated, and more, as if I were generating a heat energy from deep within my body that couldn't escape. 'Any chance of some more?' I asked, feeling that my face should be glowing like a bonfire by the temperature that I was beginning to experience.

'Yeah, okay, look, Luke, are you okay? You look a bit flushed.'

'All that adrenaline rushing round I guess, though I might grab a breath of cold air.'

'Well, hang on until I get back with more water,'

I hung on, well that's what it might have looked like, but after signing more copies of the book I felt myself rising up, I had to be a good ten foot off the ground, and rising up, almost up to the top level of the Link, I spun round, looking for her, there she was engaged by someone with a neat bald spot on the top of his sandy hair, my drink in her hand, her whole body language saying, 'let me get away you creep'.

'Ha!' I felt the laugh explode from me, and there was Gabriella handing me the glass

'What's funny?' she asked, looking more worried than before she'd left. 'I really think you could do with some air.' She turned and started away, turned to check I was following and led me out to the crisp dark of a Cornish October evening.

The cold air was good, it stroked the skin on my face and hands, I wanted to feel more of it on my skin, I stood the half-drained glass down and started to unbutton my shirt cuffs, rolling back the sleeves. I drained the last of the water, and wished there was more, that I hadn't drunk it so quickly.

'Could you, sorry, please, some more water?'

'Is that wise, you can over do water you know,' Gabriella said, peering at my face in the light that filtered out from the restaurant area.

'Last one, you have no idea how hot I am,' I said, a dirty chuckle bubbling up from somewhere.

'Okay, last one.' Nanny Gabriella said to me, in such a sharp tone it made me laugh all over again. It was no good, I just had to feel more of that beautiful soft cool air, I unbuttoned the rest of my shirt and stripped it off, stood there rotating slowly to allow the air to cool the burning surface. I could almost see the flames licking at the hairs on my arms, glowing with small pinpricks of light, each a tiny flame.

Gabriella returned. 'What! Have you completely lost it Luke?' she said, I saw she'd put a coat on when she'd collected this glass of water, stood there holding it instead of bringing it to me.

'Water,' I heard myself say and I snatched it from her hand as I swooped by, started to bring it to my lips and then, catching sight of the flicker of the flames on my arm as I did so, I doused myself with it, until there was water running in steaming rivulets down my arms, and I had lift off, flowing straight up, higher and darker, darker and higher, until all I could see were the stars, blue as ice, red as fire.

The Angel Bug 7

Gabbi 20th October

As soon as we got outside Luke started to roll his shirt sleeves up, he must have been feeling really hot as after a few minutes the cold was getting through to me and I was feeling distinctly chilled. He drained the water and asked for another, well, I know he accused me of fussing before, but I had to ask whether it was a good idea, which he, all high and mighty, found very funny. I stomped off to get another glass but took a detour to grab my coat; I wasn't intending to get frozen while hanging around outside with him.

When I got back he was stripped to the waist and turning in small circles his arms outstretched and lifted up.

'What? Luke! Have you completely lost it? Luke!'

'Water,' he said and sort of swooped it out of my hand, then, in that freezing night air he tipped it over his head and then down his arms. The glass dropped and smashed on the ground, and he kept turning.

'Luke?' worried now, I stepped in, aiming to take hold of him, to stop him, but he turned away from me, travelling and turning, faster and faster.

'LUKE!! Stop it!!' I shouted after him. 'It's not bloody funny!'

'There you are,' Andy suddenly said behind me. 'What the fuck?' But I wasn't listening as I could see Luke was losing balance, I ran towards him, trying to get there before he crashed over. Too late, he fell, made no attempt to stop his fall, just crashed flat out on his back, hands still in that strange raised position. The thud of his skull on the concrete went right through me, turning my stomach and bringing my head out in sympathy.

Andy was there almost as soon as I was.

'No, don't!' he said gruffly, just about stopping me in time before I tried to lift Luke's head. 'There might be damage, you might make it worse.'

'What?' I started, my mind suddenly full of smashed brains oozing onto bleak concrete, 'Phone!' I said, started to rise, then remembered I had my coat on, so my mobile was in my pocket. I stood and quickly punched in the numbers, soon getting through and asking for the ambulance, giving the details they needed to get here as soon as possible. By the time I'd done that Andy and Luke weren't alone, Luke had a coat over him, and Tim was encouraging the people who had come out, to go back in, as there was nothing to be done until the ambulance arrived.

Andy looked up at me from where he was kneeling. 'What do you reckon, cannabis, cocaine?'

I shook my head dumbly; I didn't want to think either. 'No idea.'

'That whirling around stuff?'

I shrugged. 'Said he was feeling really hot, looked overheated too.'

'Ecstasy?'

'What the hell would I know? I just, I just, I got him water, I even warned him about drinking too much of that!'

The ambulance came, its lights and physical presence wending its way down through the labyrinth of internal roadways to where Luke lay. He was breathing, his colour was still very high, but he hadn't opened his eyes, or moaned in pain, nothing but the steady breathing.

They were quick and efficient, a few brisk questions, then neck support, back support and up on the stretcher and into the ambulance.

'Can I come with him?' I said, it didn't feel right that he should be on his own.

'Yeah,' the paramedic said. 'You might be able to shine a light on what happened before he went over.'

'Yes, of course,' I said climbing in. 'Andy, tell, um, tell Tim I've gone in with him,' I called just before the doors closed.

'Mrs Johnston?' A young doctor stood in front of me, I wasn't asleep, more in a trance, trying to work out what could have happened.

'Yes, sorry?'

'I understand from the paramedics that you were with Mr Adamson when he fell.'

'Yes, keeled over, though he was probably dizzy.'

'Why would that be?'

'Well, he was turning round in circles, and getting faster, so, well anyone would get dizzy.'

The doctor's eyes were intent but also screwed up with puzzlement.

'Do you know why he was getting himself dizzy?'

'No, no idea, I really don't know what was going on. He said he was hot, very hot and needed to cool down, so we'd stepped outside. He asked for more water so I'd gone in to get it, when I came out he was twirling round.'

'Would you say that Mr Adamson took drugs?'

'I wouldn't know! I really don't know him that well, he's here to give a lecture and I'm sort of helping him while he's here.' I finished lamely.

He wrote something on his pad. 'So, is there someone else who would know?'

'Look, this is Dr Luke Adamson, the ethnobotanist,' I could see it meant nothing, 'Have you heard of the film 'Jungala'?'

I saw recognition dawn on his face.

'So he's here as a guest of Eden, doing his book, film, lecture tour and he's just given the most amazing lecture, nearly two hours, no notes! Was he taking drugs then? No I don't think so, did he slip himself something after? Possibly, but what difference does it make to a cracked skull?'

'Well, that's what he doesn't have, fortunately.'

'What? I heard it, such a crunch.'

'A lucky man then, no, no sign of trauma to the skull at all, but we can't rouse him at the moment and that is why we are considering the drug angle. Tell me everything that happened prior to Dr Adamson falling over.'

No trauma to the skull, I thought, how on earth could that be when he went down so unprotected and so hard? I shook myself mentally and brought myself back to tell the doctor of everything that had happened and as I did so I could sense that he was thinking of 'drug patterns'.

I was offered a cup of coffee, and then left on my own again. I kept seeing him fall, hearing that sickening crunch. What else could it be but bone on concrete? I kept looking at the time, it crept along, I picked up a magazine and began flicking through the pages, nothing caught my eye, I was aware that I wasn't really reading anything on the pages. I never did like hospitals, so much so that I went all out to be able to give birth to Emma at home. It wasn't easy, but then there were individual midwives who'd fight your corner and sign up to the cause, and I was lucky enough to find one. It was all going quite well at first, and then there was some doubt about progress and after a few more hours the midwife said that she didn't like the sound of the baby's heartbeat and that we should go in after all. 'Go in', more like rushed in, rushed to the delivery room, monitors, wires, drips, stirrups, and a forceps delivery. Everything I'd hope to avoid, but we came out with our perfect baby girl and were so happy. The next time I stepped inside a hospital was when James was rushed in, but that time there was no happy ending as in reality they knew, as did I, that it was too late, there was nothing to be done.

So I don't really like hospitals, and sitting there waiting to hear some news, wondering if there was anything I'd missed that could help them, whether Luke was into drugs, who ought to be here, ought to be told he was in hospital, I began to feel a bit disorientated and slightly panicky.

I got up and wandered about the waiting area a bit, then went back down the corridor to where a girl was working in a reception area.

'Hi' I said, getting her attention, 'I'm waiting to hear how Dr Adamson is getting on.' I saw the puzzled frown, 'he's a patient, Luke Adamson, brought it as an emergency about,' I glanced at my watch, 'two hours ago, I just have to get out and get some air, and make some calls, but, please, I will be back, I'll just be outside the front door.'

'Fine, Ms?'

'Mrs Johnston, a doctor spoke to me earlier, I really won't be long.'

She smiled her reply and I noticed she made a note on a piece of paper beside her keyboard, whether it was my name I couldn't tell, but I headed out anyway. Out, by following the exit signs, appeared to be via a maze of corridors, but I found my way, eventually passing through an enormously busy area where people sat, ate, lay on seats and generally chatted, until I whooshed out through the double set of doors.

The air was redolent with frost, the moon crisp and showing like a scimitar in the sky. I fished out my mobile and turned it on. Who to ring? I tried Mikaela, it rang, and rang, 'Hey this is Mikaela's phone, can't answer just now, do leave a message'. I didn't. I tried Andy. Phone off. I thought for a moment, the phone pressed against my cheek, so when it rang I almost dropped it. It was Mikaela.

'Sorry, Gabbi, didn't hear the phone, but got the 'missed call' text. How's Dr Adamson?'

'Well, they say he's not got any trauma to the skull, which must be a miracle, I heard the crunch, but they can't bring him round they said.'

'Oh my God!'

'Delicate question, they were asking if he'd been taking drugs.'

'What?'

'His behaviour was, well, quite odd just before he fell, you know.'

'Yeah, Andy told me, but drugs, I wouldn't know, he drank quite a bit last night, I mean, night before, you know the evening he arrived.'

'You were coordinating with his team, publishers and stuff, we need to know if there's anyone we should notify that he's in hospital, and if there is anyone who might know if he did do drugs at all, or whether it's likely.'

'Shit! Okay, I'll see what I can do, you know he fired the publishers' PA they gave him just before he came down to us, but I still have her mobile and email, I'll get back to you as soon as I can.'

'Call it in to the hospital when you find out, I have to have the phone off while I'm in there.'

'Sure, no probs, oh and Gabbi.'

'Yes?'

'Josh told us you were an old friend of his from way back, and well, I thought you'd like to know we've been praying he'll be okay, here. I mean it, Sapphira had us all praying, even Andy stood there, didn't go off on one.'

'What? Well, of course we want him better, thanks.' I said, trying to take this vignette in, unable to imagine it.

Sapphira must have made even more of an impression on Andy than I thought, the image of him even staying round for a prayer meeting was hard to grasp, and I just couldn't understand how someone would actually orchestrate a group prayer amongst a bunch of people who's reaction to religion ranged from ambivalent to downright antagonistic. I shook my head and decided to get back to the waiting area.

I had barely sat down, and certainly not warmed up, when the young doctor appeared again in front of me. Feeling wide awake from the cold I quickly stood, 'Is he awake?' I said. I know my heart was beating faster and my hopes were high, and instantly dashed with the start of the shake of his head.

'Sit down, please Mrs Johnston,'

I sat, he sat.

'Mr Adamson ..' he started.

'Doctor,' I corrected, he looked at me, 'It's Doctor Adamson.'

'Of course, sorry, *Doctor* Adamson is in a coma.'

'A coma?'

'We don't as yet know why, or how,' he finished.

A coma. What did I know about comas? My mind started to do an analytical whirl. Scientists can't help it, they find refuge in facts, and the facts that I knew were being dragged from their dusty cupboards even while I listened.

'I've contacted someone who should, eventually, be able to put us in touch with people who knew Dr Adamson well,' I said primly. 'Is there anything else I can do?'

He looked at me, 'No, I don't think so tonight. You really might as well go home, make sure we know how to contact you, thank you for your help.'

'Thank you, Doctor, thank you,' I murmured, as he turned away and I wandered back to the receptionist to give my details before phoning for a taxi.

The house felt cold as I entered, but as it was gone midnight and I felt exhausted I decided to just crawl beneath the duvet to warm up and sleep. For the first time for a long time I dragged the spare pillows down and formed a buffer against the emptiness of the double bed, bringing my back up against their soft bulk and curling the duvet tight around my shoulders. I was so tired, I had thought sleep would come quickly, but as usual it refused, instead my mind sent me pictures from the evening, and then from the afternoon. I felt again Luke's hands on my shoulders, and experienced a small shock as I acknowledged to myself how good that had felt, and spent time analysing whether this was due to the touch of another human being, a man, or that particular man. Sometime along the way I managed to slip into oblivion.

I woke with a start, my heart beating too fast; ears straining to hear what it was that had roused me, the sun streaming in through the open curtains. One quick glance and I knew I had overslept really badly and then I heard the knock come again. Grabbing my kimono I shrugged it on and tied it rapidly, dragged my fingers through my hair and clipped it up with a barrette. I stepped quietly into the lounge, from where I could get a side view of the front door without having to get close to the window. What looked like Andy's back stood side-on to my door. Quickly retracing my steps I opened the door.

'Hi,' Andy said. 'Hope you don't mind. You know, just got a bit worried when you'd not called in.'

'Andy, you dear!' I said, 'Come in, a phone call would have done you know.'

'Well, that's it you see, I tried that, it seems to cut straight into answerphone, no ring.'

'Bother! I forgot to take it off when I got home! And last night of all nights!' Sure enough it was winking away; messages, I set it to play, hoping I hadn't missed a vital call from the hospital, but all except the first had no message, and that was Andy asking if I was okay and to call back.

'Have we heard how Luke is?' I asked as it played.

'Yeah, Tim told us this morning that the hospital described him as stable, done all the scans and they showed all clear but – you knew that he'd slipped into a coma, didn't you?'

'Yeah, they told me last night, before sending me home, so, no change. They were trying to figure it out, said he'd not had any trauma to his skull, unbelievable, but his brain must have been really shaken up, I,' I caught my breath, as a wash of memory swept over me, I heard again the sound of bone on concrete.

'Gabbi, you okay?'

'A coffee?' I asked, shaking myself, 'I need one!'

'Thanks, if you are sure – I mean, there's no need now we know you're okay.'

'There's need!' I said sticking a full kettle on, 'Back in a mo – make yourself at home.'

I dashed into the bathroom, grabbed a quick wash and ran a brush through my hair, dressed and was back in the kitchen before the kettle cooled.

'I'm afraid it's instant.' I said as I poured a coffee for Andy who looked oversized in my small kitchen, perched as he was on a kitchen stool by the breakfast bar gazing at the stunning view.

'No problem,' he said, looking thoughtful. 'Gabbi?'

'Hmm?'

'They say you knew Adamson before, from university.'

'Yes, well, sort of, James and he were contemporaries and similar fields. Different social circles generally, you know how it is in uni, Luke was definitely among the athletic and social crowd as well as the scientific, James and I were strictly the scientific crowd, so some overlap, I was amazed when he recalled me, I wasn't about to remind him!'

'Okay, how do I say this? You are such a good person, Gabbi, I'd hate to see you hurt. Look I've heard this guy has a terrible reputation with women, a womanizer and a bastard with it.' He looked so pained, embarrassed and yet obviously concerned for me.

'Oh Andy! As if he'd look at me. As I recall it is girls like Mikaela and Naomi who need to look out, they are much more his style!' I couldn't help the broad smile that I felt cross my face but I didn't want Andy to think I was laughing at him. 'Besides, with Luke in a coma it's the least of our worries.'

'No, you're right. Fine, sorry. None of my business.'

'Andy! It's a very kind thought. I could almost wish it was necessary!'

He looked at me from beneath bushy eyebrows, 'I think you underrate yourself,' he said.

The Angel Bug 8

Luke 21st - 22nd October

I let go, just as the voice told me, I'd been holding on so tight my head hurt, but now it felt good, the cool air rushing through my hair, brushing my burning skin with tendrils of ice. I tried to open my eyes, but if I did manage it then all about me was so black that there was nothing to be seen, no difference between eyes closed and eyes open. I gave myself up to the sensation of the air passing me, wondering if it was me or the air that moved, unable to distinguish the sensations.

As I became lost in the feeling, air on skin, skin brushed by air, chilled and chilling, colder and colder, losing sensation as I seemed to withdraw within myself to a small core of warmth, I became aware of a change, a visual change. Somewhere there was a lightening of the horizon, as there is before the sun rises, yet this horizon was not horizontal to the plane I felt to be upright, but vertical, a split in the darkness, growing brighter as I, or it, moved forward.

The radiance grew brighter, and I seemed to be hurtling towards it, brighter, until I felt I needed to hide my eyes with my hands, yet they would not obey my commands but streamed out behind me as if I was using them as wings or balances. I closed my eyes until my lashes touched, forming a protecting lattice-work but allowing me still to see. And so I saw when the 'sun' rose, not burning bright, beyond looking at, but tawny gold with a centre of black, shining black, a vertical eye couched in a brilliant sunglow of light. And still I rushed on, my mind deciding that it must be me that was moving, as the owner of such an eye would not be rushing anywhere.

There was a change of perspective somehow – I did not stop in my headlong rush yet suddenly I was at a distance from the holder of that eye, and was aware of a great shining light, the brightest sunlight reflected off water, off snow, eye-wateringly dazzling, and this light wrapped what should be the body of the holder of the eye, and of the other eyes that circled the head, all seeing in three-sixty degrees. Yet there was a front to this glowing face and it was turned towards me.

As suddenly as I had swept forwards I stopped and dropped to my knees, though I don't think I could have stood if I wanted to. The sound of rushing wind was substituted by a low roar, more of a rumble, and in it, or in my head I heard the word 'EVERYTHING'.

'EVERYTHING' it rang around the space, or inside my head, I couldn't tell, and I was startled to find myself thinking of the dime sweets that I had stolen from the candy store when I was six and as this memory developed, into my nostrils crept the smell of dog-shit till the taste of it coated the back of my tongue and I gagged.

Then it was gone, completely gone, but replaced with the memory of cheating to beat Lilibeth, the only child brighter than me in first grade, I almost smiled before the foul stink stuffed my nose and the gagging reflex took over and I felt tiny pin-pricks of sweat start around my hairline.

I held my breath until my ribs ached, I breathed in carefully, the reek had gone, relieved I let out a full breath and drank in fresh air and suddenly with it came the next memory and a new and more vile stench, a smell dredged up from black malodorous silt layered with partly decomposed bodies of animals, which, taken on an in-breath forced my guts to heave themselves spewing bitter water in a spray around me.

It was then I realised there were so many, so very many memories like these to come that I wondered if I would survive it. 'EVERYTHING', seemed to mean to remember every little thing that I had done wrong, everything I had done to hurt or cheat or exploit my way through life. Ha! If I was right then I was going to be here for a long time!

The brightness was still there but I could no longer divine whether the glowing being was there or not, my memories came so vividly, a wraparound movie that starred myself in different younger incarnations, and with them the most fetid stenches I have ever known, filling me so that I felt they leaked from my pores, before being swept away for different and seemingly more pungent ones to replace them. It didn't take long before the merest hint of each memory was enough to make me flinch away from it mentally hoping to reduce or avoid the olfactory onslaught. My guts were empty, retching up only bitter dregs when their churning forced something out, my skin clammy and slick. And still the memories came on. Hells bells I had only reached my university years, and there I was switching off the socket and here came the stink of hydrogen sulphide.

Somewhere in a small scientific corner of my mind I noted that I was surprised that a human being, with its inferior sense of smell, could sense and differentiate so many disgustingly putrid aromas. And that same part also recognised the effectiveness of the system as the brain had not time to accustom itself to one scent, meaning that each new one hit with a renewed and equal force.

Shaking with weakness yet firm in the knowledge that I was nowhere near the end, I tried to blot the memories by screwing up my eyes and tightening my hands into fists so that my fingernails cut into the flesh. It did not work, if anything the memories, fresher as they were, came faster and more vividly, and my body twisted and urged, desperate to spew out the effect of the stench. My callous using of my publisher's assistant brought with it a pungency that brought up more bile, vile and green/black it coated my tongue, but at least I knew I was near the end. The sight of the lovely Mikaela made me shrink as I knew a new stink would swamp me and wreak more havoc on my aching frame, yet was, as far as I could recall the last I had to worry about. Not so, I had more.

When I collapsed I don't know; I only know that I felt the cold of the ground against my cheek and opened my eyes to a pinkish glow. I tried to lift myself up, the muscles in my chest and stomach screamed at me to lie still. I was parched, felt as if I had been shouting in a dry land. As I lay there I heard music and found myself thinking of the child in the Amazon whose life I had managed to save, when she fell into the river. I'd not thought, I'd merely reacted and jumped in after her. We were both lucky that the black caimans did not get to us before I managed to scramble ashore. The scent of honeysuckle filled my nostrils and I sighed, a contentment rising up through my tired limbs.

It was then I heard her voice. Calling to me; calling me by my name. Gabriella; her velvety voice calling 'Luke, can you hear me?' Then there was music, sweet, sweet music, Beach Boys and I felt soft and at ease. I think I slept.

The Angel Bug 9

Gabbi – 22nd October

I decided to get back to the lab and take some decent slides of the Moringa nodules and to get a sample packed off to the University for a scan with the electron microscope, if Sapphira would okay the extra, and said as much to Andy before he left me to return to Eden.

Karen was wide-eyed and full of questions when I signed in, she'd heard about the spinning around thing that Luke was doing and, not for the first time that day, I was asked if I thought he took drugs. I didn't blame her, or anyone, it was strange behaviour and I could easily have accepted that theory but I couldn't reconcile that with the fact that he'd lose face by 'tripping out' at such a public scientific venue, he struck me now, as he always had, as someone who needed public recognition and approbation of his achievements, so it was not something he would risk recklessly.

Sapphira was in. Now, as I came up the steps to the higher level of the Foundation building, I was right in her sights. It gave me an eerie feeling, like entering a royal audience, as if, due to being on the stairs, I began my approach on my knees. She stared at me as I rose to the top step then deliberately looked up and to the left at the clock then down to her own desk and continued writing. I walked straight up to her desk.

'Morning,' I said, she looked up at me, tipped her head a little and raised those perfect eyebrows. 'Sorry I'm, late. I was at the hospital until very late last night. I want to get the slides of the Moringa nodules sliced and believe we need to get one sent off for SEM.' I pressed on quickly. 'I think it's important to continue the work Dr Adamson had started on the Moringa.'

'Yes, good morning. I suppose at your age I can understand your need to catch up on lost sleep. Do you really think you are the best person to continue this work on the Moringa?'

'Yes. Why not?' I snapped, steaming inside, *at your age*, flaming cheek!

The bloody eyebrows again, 'Well, if you get so tired after one late night, Mrs Johnston?'

'That's nonsense, it was more than just the lateness, and besides, Luke had asked for me to be his assistant in this project.'

Her mouth pursed. 'Very well, for now.'

'And the SEM?'

'Had Dr Adamson said he wanted that?'

'Well he intimated it, spoke of the inadequacies of our level of magnification available on site.' Even if she brought out the worst in me I couldn't tell the outright lie and just say yes.

'Very well, go ahead. Not that it matters at the moment; after all he can hardly show us up from his hospital bed.'

I ignored my desk and went straight out; I knew I ought to have checked mail, email and stuff but I didn't think I could stay around Sapphira for one more minute. What was happening to me? I could usually get along with anyone, taking a forgiving attitude to anything and anybody that came my way.

The lab was open when I arrived at Watering Lane and I wasn't surprised to find Andy there. He was ostensibly monitoring the die-back he and Naomi had been arguing about when I'd dropped the Moringa news on them, but soon after I arrived he put all that stuff away and came over to see what we had on the Moringa.

I showed him the section of nodule, now fully prepped for slicing, and he stood and watched while I set the microtome in motion.

'So dark?' he commented.

'Yeah, though I would say it has darkened while in solution, which isn't unusual.' I went to fetch a cutting board, and found that I was holding one of the ones we had used the day before. It was hard to realise it was only a couple of days before, but I knew I had one of those boards because in my haste to clear up and get Luke away to the Hotel I'd obviously not cleaned it properly. The smear on the edge showed almost black, the red of the previous day having darkened like dried blood.

'Look,' I said, 'dried, the liquid from the nodule turns almost black.' I took the board over to scrub it before I used it again. 'Thank God Sapphira can't see this sloppy lab cleaning, she's not best pleased with me being in late as it is.'

I looked up as Andy was so silent, watching the microtome.

'What is it?'

'Well, either the paraffin didn't penetrate well, didn't set, or that's a very strange nodule.' I stood and looked down; the blade was gently slicing in an ever-growing pool of deep red 'blood'. The slices were dark too, and shining wet. I wondered if they would be any good at all.

'It's a strange nodule,' I said, so quietly I wasn't even sure I'd said it.

Fortunately the slices mounted well, and the structure was clearly visible in the one I tried under the lab microscope. There was little more that I could make out though, over and above the structure that was identifiable from Luke's raw cut. Each slice seemed to have bled out, leaving them a pale pink and easy to view. I hoped the scan from the electron microscope would give us something more than was visible with the standard microscope and perhaps a clue to the actual function of the nodule. I looked at the remaining nodules in the fridge. They didn't seem to have changed, no noticeable shrinkage or 'drying out', no darkening. I cleaned up carefully and stripped of my gloves and coat. Seeing the gloves, stained red with the liquid from the nodules, sent a flicker of a question through my mind, but before I could get a handle on it Andy appeared.

'Going now?' he asked

'Yes, just um,' but it was too late, the thought had escaped me, 'just cleaning up, properly,' I grinned at him.

He smiled back at me, 'See you back in the office.' he said as he lurched out of the door.

What was it? I knew enough to let such fugitive thoughts rest, they would come back to me if I didn't try to chase them, but something told me that this question was important, so like a fool all the way back to Eden I tried to work out what it was that I had thought of, and all the time the thought kept itself well hidden.

Sapphira was not at her desk, but Mikaela, Naomi and Andy were at theirs. It was good to see all of them together again, though the desks still held their old positions, the gap looking like a nasty hole in an otherwise perfect set of teeth.
'Let's rearrange the desks people,' I said as I arrived at mine, 'How would you like it to go, all looking in at each other with a centre well or all looking out, but within touching distance and easy to turn round to see a screen?'
'All out' from Mikaela, 'All facing' from Naomi, at the same time.
'A block?' suggested Andy. 'As there are only four desks now.'
'There's that too!'
'Yeah a block would be good, not too far to whiz round,' agreed Mikaela.

We set to hauling desks around, leaving the block at a friendly angle to the stairs, Mikaela and Andy had the two facing up room, towards Sapphira's desk, and Naomi and I gratefully took the positions that put us with our backs towards her. Somehow, after that I felt much better, and settled down to send off the sample and open my mail and emails. The mail was of no consequence but an email from Worldagroforestry.com had me sitting up. They had no scientific record of any leaf colour change in Moringa, nor of any nodule formation. They did have a newspaper report from the wilds of Sarawak where an elderly woman was claiming her husband had been cured of leprosy by the 'blood' of the Moringa, which contained the word 'nodule'. They attached a report from a local paper.
Miracle cure in Sarawak

We know that leprosy is now curable by the use of antibiotics and is best dealt with at the first sign, but news from Sarawak suggests that there is a natural cure out there in the jungle that we may have missed for generations as it has been kept a secret by the man who discovered it and benefited from it. Mrs Guannionmo (66) told us of her husband's miracle cure forty years ago.

'My husband had the leprosy and was living apart from us. He had it in his hands, we feared for his life. He was digging for the roots of the wild Moringa, he told me, as he tried to tear the root from the ground he squashed the bulbs on the roots and they bled onto him. He drew out the root and cleaned it to eat it; the stain was still on his skin. He told me that he slept deeply and that when he woke the leprosy had left his hand. We asked to see her husband, but she said that this was a long time ago and now he was dead she could tell his story, he wouldn't let her say before. Other local villagers confirmed that her husband had indeed suffered from leprosy and had recovered completely and become a good man in the village.

The Worldagroforestry network tells us that the root structure of the Moringa does not include 'bulbs' or 'nodules' and as such throws dispute on the origin of these 'bleeding' bulbs that Mrs Guannionmo believes to have effected the miracle cure.

I quickly forwarded the email to the others, saying what I was doing even as I pressed send, then realising that a copy had probably also gone to Sapphira's computer, unless she'd changed the email address for the senior botanist, and would just arrive without explanation as a forwarding from me.

'What do you think about this amazing email worldagfor sent me?' I asked. All heads bowed to read the email. Mikaela's head snapped up first?

'Are our nodules red?'

'More than that, they bleed a red liquid when cut.'

'Extraordinary – but still it could just be a fiction,' Naomi said slowly.

'Don't think so, if you'd seen the way that stuff oozes, you'd describe it as bleeding, trust me,' Andy said, looking straight at me. 'Says the guy 'slept deeply' could that be a coma?'

'Gloves!' I said out loud, as the thought came back to me, 'Luke didn't wear his gloves, his hand was covered in the stuff!'

'But the skin isn't that porous, the guy in the report would have had open sores,' started Andy.

'It is if it's full of holes, 'Mikaela chipped in. 'Dr Adamson's hands were scratched to blazes.'

We all looked at her

'He'd had to haul himself back onto a cliff path by grabbing hold a gorse bush – he showed me.'

We sat in silence for a few minutes, I re-read the email. Even if it were true did it help us at all, where did we go from here?

'Have you had the nodule chemically analysed? For toxins or hallucinogens?' Naomi asked.

'No, not yet, and thanks,' I stood quickly. 'if anyone needs me I'm back at Watering Lane.' I said grabbing my stuff.

'I'll give you a hand,' Naomi said suddenly, and I glanced up to see Sapphira emerging from the lower level.

'Going back to Watering Lane,' I said to her in passing. 'Interesting email, forwarded it to senior botanist,' I added, hoping that would cover everything I needed to at this stage.

'Right, Naomi, what can we test for here and what do you think we need to send off?'

'To be honest Gabbi I don't think we can do much in that line – but I do know of a good testing lab in Cornwall, and a friend of mine works there – I'm sure I could get Robbie to do the job quickly and quietly for us.'

I looked up from the fridge where I was fishing the box of nodules out. 'Quietly?'

'Yeah, Gabbi, this might be something big, or something bad, I don't know but I think discretion is a good idea, don't you?'

'Well, I suppose it couldn't hurt,' I said. The ramifications were just beginning to sink in. Could this be a cure – and if so was it for more that just leprosy, or was it a toxin? Nothing about the report suggested the man had been damaged by the substance, but how could we tell from anecdotal information, and then there was Luke - in a coma.

'Okay, can you get in touch and ask discreetly then, we'll need to know how much of a sample he'd need.'

Naomi took out a sleek mobile and flicked it open, tapped a few keys and wandered out the door, phone pressed to her ear.

I stood in the lab looking down at the remaining nodules that Luke had taken from our red-leaved Moringa, and saw again the glint in his eye when he found them and felt again his embrace. I had to get out to the hospital and see him, even in a coma it was important to have visitors, and I felt the need to be there with him as I had been unable to be with James. Naomi was taking a long time, I was beginning to worry that there was a problem when she leapt back into the lab grinning from ear to ear.

'Whoa! That'll cost me,' she said her eyes sparkling. 'Apparently I now owe him a dinner out in the restaurant of his choice, and I don't mind telling you that dinner out with Robbie is a real treat as it will be somewhere very special, and he's quite a special guy.'

'Why do I get the feeling that Robbie is more than just an acquaintance?' I grinned. Naomi laughed, and it was great to see her laugh again, she'd been looking quite down for the last few days.

Naomi set off with two nodules, just over the fifty grams that Robbie had said he'd need to run the tests that Naomi had suggested. That left three in the pot, though there were probably as least as many again that we knew of, re-buried still attached to the root structure. I put in a call to the hospital and asked if and when I could visit. They sounded so pleased that someone was coming in and even thanked me, which I thought odd as I knew that Mikaela had been on to the publishers to get the message out to Luke's family.

After about my fifth circuit of the hospital car park I pulled into a space just vacated by an ancient and smoke belching Volvo. The air still smelt of the fumes as I got the ticket and stuck it inside my car. When I located the correct area I was asked to wait for a doctor to speak to me before visiting. In a way I was glad about that, I had a few questions and a doctor seemed a good bet for knowing the answers. It wasn't long before I thought I recognised the same young doctor who had been there last night; he nodded to the nurse at the nurses station and came straight over to me.

'Good afternoon, Mrs Johnston?'
'Yes,' I said, standing to meet him. 'I am right, you are the same doctor from last night?'
He smiled, his thin face broadening and instantly warming. 'Indeed, yes, Dr Gregory, please sit down,' he said and sat beside me as I did so.
'I was in a bit of a daze last night, just wasn't quite sure,' I smiled at him. 'How is Dr Adamson now?'
'Well he has had an EMRS and MCR – neither of which showed us any cause for concern, no trauma, no swelling, no damage to the skull. He is still in a coma and is being constantly monitored for brainwaves and heart rate but there is nothing more that we can do. However, I hope there is something that *you* can do, Mrs Johnston, we have been told that you have known Dr Adamson for a long time.'
'Well, we met at university but …' I began.
'It seems,' he cut in, 'that Dr Adamson has no-one who can visit him. Apparently he has no family, except his mother who is in the US and too infirm to travel. No close friends in the UK well, except you, that is.'
'But I'm not,' I tried, but he was only pausing for breath as he swept on.

'I'm sure you have heard how important aural stimulation is when a person is in a coma. He needs to be talked to, he needs music played that he likes, or even hates, not just indifferent stuff, it all helps.'

'Yes, I've heard that. Um, does it matter that I really don't know him that well? I might have met him at University, but haven't set eyes on him for thirty years until yesterday.'

'Oh!' the doctor sat up, looking a little lost, then he must have made a decision. 'Well, Mrs Johnston, you're all he's got, you probably have more idea of what to say, and what to play than anyone else, will you do it?'

'Of course I will. They'll give me time off, I'm sure, can I see him now?'

'Great, yes, come with me,' he leapt to his feet, the strain having left his face once more, and I followed.

The Angel Bug 10

Luke 22nd – 23rd October

All of a sudden I am standing in a valley, the sides are randomly swathed in fruit bushes and olive trees, there are clearings and in these meadows are living creatures oblivious to my presence they play and run, yet unidentifiable as they go so quickly and are hidden by so many flowers and grasses. The river to my side is crystal clear and I can see that it teems with fish and hear that it resonates with the sounds of creatures nestled in the vegetation along its banks.

There is a noise, a humming, buzzing noise that brings a melody along with it, like some long forgotten dream I think I hear a tambourine and guitar and am wondering how many roads must a man walk down before he understands.

Somewhere over a horizon I know that He waits, that shining one, waiting to rise above this landscape like the sun, but he is waiting for me to see something, waiting for me to work something out.

I start to walk along the valley, the landscape appeared to remain the same, as if I was on some bucolic treadmill, walking, but getting nowhere. I stop and look about me, there is change, the hill is higher to my right, the valley bottom wider on the other side of the river. With renewed determination I start forward again, picking up speed, figuring that perhaps this is just a very long valley.

The sound of my heart pounding takes up a beat in my ears, like someone chasing me, trying to catch me, someone grunting 'greed, greed, greed,' over and over with every stomp. Somehow this thought makes me run faster, I am stumbling over rocks and scrambling my way through dry bushes and tasting sand in my mouth before I realise that I am out of the valley.

Not just out of the valley, but it must be miles away, I turn wildly in circles but I can not see it, can not see a single green blade of grass, glint of water or smudge of fruit. The hum of life has gone, silenced. Now all I hear is my heartbeat in my ears, still making me want to panic into flight.

I turn again. The light is literally breathtaking; I gasp and fall to the floor, hiding my eyes with both forearms.

Was it in my head? In my heart? Pumped round my body in my blood? The words seeped in, pulsed in, formed themselves and reverberated. 'Man is not what man should be.'

I am lying here, wherever here is, flat and cool. Comfortable. I can hear voices. I can hear Gabriella's voice. She is calling me again. I call. 'I'm here, can't you see me?' I know the words hold still in the air, I can see them standing there, hesitant, wobbling, fading. No, don't! Go, go to Gabriella. I try again, 'I am here!' but these fade faster than the first and I feel the darkness blot them out.

The heat hits me first, so suddenly I am drenched with sweat, yet I know this high humidity and recognise the smell of the rich greenness and the leaf litter at my feet. I am back in the jungle, and despite the uncomfortable breathlessness I feel a sense of home. Standing absolutely still I start to see all the life that is there for those with eyes to see, yet even I begin to gape as I see more than I have seen in a month, crawl, creep swing, scuttle and lope past my frozen frame in less than five minutes. Out of the corner of my eye I see a flash of blue; I turn to see a bird of paradise flitting off into the jungle. It perches for a moment, and I swear, looks back to see if I am following. Cautiously, not wanting to frighten it away, I move towards it, shadowing myself with the trunks of trees, drape of roots and vines. When I am but two metres from it, it moves on again, not in a rush, not as if scared off by my presence. I follow. I follow, it plays this game with me until I find myself on the edge of a huge and desolate pit. From the pit comes the stench of explosives, the boom of an engine that says 'greed, greed' and an overwhelming sense of despair.

'I know.' I hear myself say out loud. I do know, it is part of the stuff I have been working on for so long. I understand, Man's greed is destroying the natural world, and this most precious and essential part of the world is suffering more than most.

Then I heard again that word. 'EVERYTHING' and it strikes terror into my heart, I felt faint at the thought of what could follow that word, and even as I flinched I glimpsed that first act of greed, and the vomit-inducing dog-shit smell rose into my nostrils. I was shaking as the next image crept upon me, the reason for my cheating, greed, filled my head with the reek of putrid slime and my mouth with bile. Yet even as the next started I was reasoning, is this what this is all about, a sermon from on high?

A sermon, what the heck did our old preacher used to say? Oh yes, like a recorder button pressed I could hear him clearly, and blessedly the other images stalled while his video played. 'The love of money, yea, the LOVE of money, that is the root of all evil in mankind, GREED, greed, THAT leads man astray. You shall love the Lord your God with all your heart, with all your mind and with all your body, says the Lord, and if you're loving money you can't do that.'

For the first time in my life I didn't want the sermon to end, I feel my eight-year-old feet scuffing against each other beneath the chair and force them to be still, I don't want to go back to the other set of images. In that old pine scented Church I stare up at the window and think, could this be it? Could I have been chosen to receive some vision and mission? The mere thought made me bark a 'Ha ha!' out loud, sounding like derisive laughter and I felt the sharp clip round the ear that my mother saved for such outbursts.

As I opened my eyes from the automatic closing as flat of hand made contact with head and ear I know that He is back. The light was all encompassing, no place where there was not light, no shadow, no dim corner left unlit. No corners, no end to the light.

'So is that it? I said, my voice apparently coming from something very small. 'Is that it? Okay, so now I know that greed makes everything bad. I know. I get it, I… I won't do it again.'

I didn't hear a voice; I just know that this much had been heard and that He was waiting for more.

'What else can I say, I won't,' I thought of the stenches. 'I probably can't.'

It was an affirmation, a sense of affirmation. Yes, if I tried then I would get more of the same.

A part of me stepped outside this scenario, looked at me looking at nothing. It said: why the heck have you been selected for this and what sort of mad hallucinogenic trip are you on?

I tried to remember what I was doing before this started, the usual stuff that I had been doing since the start of the book-tour; travelling, giving the lecture, moving on. The only thing I could think of out of the ordinary was working on the nodules from the root of the Moringa.

Affirmation.

'What? The Moringa?' Back within myself I was speaking into the light. 'The Moringa did this?' And I see the blood red fluid seeping over my fingers, into the scratches from the gorse.

Affirmation, and an underlying sense that it was intended.

'You made the Moringa do this?' It was like playing with a Ouija board, with only yes or no answers available.

Affirmation, and a sense that I was being irreverent.

Then there was blackness again. Not just absence of that immense light but a blackness that seemed to have a tactile quality to it, thick and viscous it seemed to envelop me and threatened to stifle me. Was it just panic that made it seem difficult to breathe? I could hear voices in the blackness, music and voices. 'How many roads must a man walk down' the word 'doctor' repeated, why would Gabriella need a doctor, I tried to turn round seeking where the voices were coming from, the music getting in the way. Suddenly the music stopped with a sucking feeling in my ears. I can feel someone holding me down, someone holding my hand, Gabriella calling my name.

Then around the edges it gets fuzzy with a warm light, seeping in from all around, and it seems to be drawing me back to that place, where I both do and do not want to be.

Yet this light is not the same, no intensity, a beautiful soft light that warms as silkily as lying in the shallows of a tropical sea. And I am lying in the shallows, the transparent sparkling water lapping gently at my chest, small fish tasting the skin on my arms. There is someone else here; I can sense them just out of my vision. They are singing. It is so peaceful I could lie here forever; in my own little bit of Eden. Ah, yes, that's where I am, I remember being here after the filming was over, a tropical island, where you could really believe in Eden, not unspoilt, of course, but not so popular and tourist orientated to be ruined. It was pleasant, and the women amenable. I froze, almost as the thought crept into my consciousness so I sensed the start of a scent, and it was not hibiscus! I banished the thought, apologised for my former self, and the smell appeared to fade away without becoming unbearable. I resumed my wave-washed idyll.

Slowly a huge snake swam up to me but my body would not respond and I could not get out of the water fast enough before it opened its jaws and swallowed my hand. I scrambled crab-like back out of the water, wrenching my arm forward and back, but the snake hung on. I lifted it up and smashed it down against the sand, again and again until it loosened its grip and disappeared in a burst of light. Shaking, I sat up and looked around me, everything was different, Gabriella was here but nothing else made sense.

The Angel Bug 11

Gabbi 22nd – 23rd October

I spoke to Luke, standing there, feeling a little foolish with the doctor looking on.

'Dr Adamson, Luke, remember me, we were at the lecture last night, before, before,' I trailed off and looked at the doctor. 'Is there anything that I should avoid saying?'

'No,' he smiled wanly, 'Though keeping it up-beat might be a good idea.'

'Of course,' I turned back to Luke. 'Hey that was some lecture you gave us all last night, a standing ovation how was that?'

I could sense the doctor smiling and he raised one hand and said softly that he'd be off now. I nodded, started to turn back to Luke, then dashed after the doctor just as he closed the door,

'Can I? Can I touch him, I mean – hold his hand?'

'Sure, that would be good. I'm sure you used the bactericide when you came in – another go wouldn't hurt,'

'Absolutely,' I said turning to see where the nearest dispenser was.

Hands cooling from the effect of the lotion I returned to Luke's side. I was thinking about music, all I had with me was my mp3 player, and all that was on that was an eclectic mix of easy listening stuff from the sixties and seventies that I used as a backing track to some of the more mundane tasks I have to do. I fished it out of my bag, I guessed that some of the tracks would be relevant, though knowing Luke so little I really had no idea which.

'Hi Luke, Luke can you hear me? Luke can you hear me? I'm going to play you some music.'

I looked at the earphones and nipped back out to rub a little lotion round them, then gingerly fitted one, then the other, into Luke's ears and pressed play, the tinny sound just about escaped enough for me to identify the Beach Boys.

When I thought the track had ended I pressed off, lifted one earphone out and took Luke's hand in mine and squeezed it gently. 'Luke, hey Luke, if you can hear me squeeze my hand.' I waited, the limp heavy fingers lying motionless in my hand.

After a few minutes I decided to move Luke on to the next track, replacing the earphone, I pressed play again, I didn't need to hear the track, I was so familiar with the playlist I knew that Bob Dylan would be singing to him now.

I spent three hours, alternating tracks and chat, hand-holding, squeezing and reminiscing – dragging up memories from the university days that were all mine but might have had some resonance with Luke's, mentioning always the places, the professors that I thought he might know. Time concertinaed, sometimes going fast when I got myself caught in a reverie of good memories, sometimes dragging as I dredged my mind for what to talk about when the next track finished. At one point I felt the tears start and didn't bother to stop them or the memory that I was telling, so clear was my vision of James.

Doctor Gregory returned, looking rested, to check on the patient and suggested that I go home for a rest myself. After a long look at Luke I decided to follow his advice. I realised I was hungry; it was later than I thought and I'd had little to eat for lunch. I decided to come back tomorrow as soon as I could get away from Eden. I had no hopes of any results being back by the next day, but I still felt there was more to be done in looking into the nodules and research on any soil-borne infections that could cause hallucinations and coma. I knew that there were both beneficial and bad things down there in the soil, things like tetanus, but didn't know what else exactly or what they could do. As I headed for home I was adding the possibilities of exotic soil contaminants to my list, many of the plants could not survive without a 'starter kit' of the right type of soil from their native lands so there could be all sorts I had never encountered in there.

The next morning the rain rattled relentlessly against the windows creating a sense of doom before I had even got out of bed. I breakfasted, dragged on a waterproof coat and ran for the car. My trusty Mini sounded sluggish as I turned her round and headed for Eden. Even sheeted in rain the place still looked a marvel and I felt a little up-lifted at least until I hit the top floor. First face I saw, steely eyes looking over tiny glasses, was Sapphira's.

'Morning,' she said, and though I was early rather than late it still seemed to carry that undertone of reprimand.

'Morning,' I called back as cheerfully as I could manage.

'Do you know how Dr Adamson is this morning?'

'No?' I start towards her. 'Have you heard anything this morning?'

'No, of course not, I understood you were liaison on this matter.'

I subsided a little. 'Yes, I see, no, I haven't heard anything yet this morning but I was at the hospital talking and playing music to Dr Adamson until about nine last night,' Damn! I meant to pick up some different music. 'He was comfortable, stable, but still in the coma.'

'Ah, I see, and will you be spending time there again today?'

'As soon as I have checked all the experiments going on and initiated some other investigations I have decided might be relevant, not only to Dr Adamson but also to the problem with the Moringa, I thought I might get back there then, unless you have any tasks I need to do?' I added to draw her fire.

'No, we can manage quite well without you. Don't concern yourself about the Moringa either, I think the solution may be to excise the tree altogether.'

'It will take a while to grow another to look anything like a tree in situ and I don't think we have one in the nursery, also if the ground is contaminated it may go the same way.'

'No, you misunderstand me, I mean just take it out altogether, no replacement, the Neem tree is right beside it and creates a focal point beside the house.'

'But, the Moringa, it's so… so what Eden is all about, man and plants.'

'Well the Neem illustrates that too, in its own way.'

'I know, I know, but the Moringa…'

'It really isn't your job to decide these things you know,' Sapphira closed the folder in front of her on the desk. 'Why don't you leave the experiment checking to, uh, Naomi, and go off to the hospital now?'

'No thank you, I'd rather not.'

'Ah, you don't trust her to get it right!'

I was alarmed at the twist Sapphira had put on things so easily, 'No, it's not that at all. Naomi is already following up one aspect and I will need her to follow up some of the new ideas I have had. She's very capable. I, I just want to check before I go, I need to know how our investigations are going for my own peace of mind.'

Sapphira took in a long breath through her nose, and then snorted it out in a quick burst. I was, it seemed, dismissed.

I went over to my desk and had just got the computer fired up when the others arrived in a very welcome gaggle of noise and bonhomie.

'How's Dr Adamson?' Mikaela asked as soon as they reached me, Naomi slipped into her seat beside me and rolled her eyes, indicating Sapphira behind us. 'How's she this morning?'

'Just don't get me started,' I hissed to Naomi, then shook my head and explained to all of them how Luke had been when I left him last night.

I ran the idea of soil borne infections and bacterial toxins or hallucinogens past them as well, with differing responses, though all agreed it was definitely worth following up for the sake of Dr Adamson or the tree. I mentioned in an undertone Sapphira's idea about excising the Moringa, to be met with the same degree of dismay as I had experienced. It was good to be with these people.

The rest of the morning sped by as we set up the tests on the soil that we could manage and Naomi committed herself to yet another meal out for the sake of some more delicate and intensive tests to be made by her friend Robbie. She left with samples of the soil from round the nodules just before lunch time and I walked up through the temperate biome, the outside area of Eden, to the Cafeteria area to grab a healthy whole-food snack lunch before heading off to the hospital.

I was well on my way before I remembered I had intended to divert home to pick up some different music, cursed my failing memory and pressed my foot harder to the floor as I reached the open road

I checked in at the nursing station when I arrived and was given the all clear to visit. Hands duly done with the bactericide I entered his room. Monitors winked and made waves. Luke lay still and pale.

'Hi Luke, I'm back. Gabbi here, how are you feeling today?' I started, feeling as strange as before, not unlike being caught talking properly to your baby when you know they are too young to understand anything you say, yet you do it anyway. 'I'm sorry but I forgot to pick up some different music so you have my hick collection of sixties and seventies golden oldies again. You'll probably come out of this hating every track and not knowing why.' I burbled on for a bit then set up the earphones and put the music back on while I thought of what else I could talk about that might have meant something to Luke.

At six I left him for half an hour and retreated to the hospital cafeteria to get something to eat and a drink, I was parched from the warmth of the place and the talking. I hit on the idea of talking about the jungle, the Amazon, the film, anything and everything that I could think of that he might have encountered or been involved with out there. It was just as well that I had seen the film as soon as it had come out.

I tried to retell the story that the film *Jungala* told. Remember, I started, remember being in the Amazon and making a documentary about the way that man's greed is destroying our very hope for the future. Remember, how you came across the illegal loggers and what happened next.

When I ran dry I put the music back on for a while and collected my own thoughts, both to try to talk about something relevant and also to think about what we knew about the possible causes of his condition. So, though I held Luke's hand in mine, I wasn't putting any pressure on it or talking to him when it suddenly moved, twitched, then flexed. I flicked my glance from our hands to his face, he was moving, trying to move his head like the earphones were annoying him, I pulled them out then squeezed his hand saying 'It's alright, it's alright.' then called as loud as I could, 'Doctor! Doctor!' letting go of his hand I went to the room door, snatched it open and, darting toward the nurses station, carried right on shouting 'Doctor!' A nurse hurried round, as I added, 'He's waking up, waking up!'

She pressed a button and followed me back to the room. I went straight to Luke and took his hand again, 'It's okay Luke, there's nothing to worry about just open your eyes and come back to us.' But already he was subsiding, the head movements had stopped and the hand twitched feebly. I turned to the nurse who was holding his other wrist, taking his pulse, knowing there were tears in my eyes, 'He was moving his head, squeezing my hand.' I said, feeling like I'd raised a false alarm.
'Well, his pulse is up, so he was probably near surfacing, it's a good sign,' she said calmly and smiled in a way that defused my concerns.

A few minutes later a doctor arrived, not the one I had met before, but a harassed looking young man with sandy hair. After a few questions he read the monitors, checked Luke over and left.

I returned to Luke's side and once again took his hand.
'Luke, can you hear me? Luke, look you gave an extraordinary lecture, felt pretty good about it, felt really thirsty and then this happened, so there's nothing to worry about just open you eyes and come back to us,' I began, this time I'd decided to tell him everything I knew about since he arrived at Eden.

When I'd exhausted everything I could tell him about the last couple of days I checked the volume on the earphones and then re-inserted them into Luke's ears as gently as I could. I pressed play, sat down and took hold of his hand once more. I felt exhausted, yet didn't want to go home yet, wondering if he was going to surface again, perhaps even wake up. I sat letting my own thoughts drift in and out, ranging from James to the Moringa, to Emma on the other side of the world and back to Eden and the new senior botanist and her effect on the team. I dozed. I knew afterwards that I had rested my head down on our hands, the creases I could see on my face proved it, but it was Luke who woke me up.

The Angel Bug 12

Luke   24th October

Gradually everything came into focus, the room looked utilitarian and clinical, Gabriella, standing, was wide-eyed and seeking my eyes and saying my name.

I tried to speak but my mouth was stuck shut.

'Hang on,' she said and with a squeeze of my hand dashed to the door and called 'Nurse! He's awake. Really awake!' and came straight back to me.

'Oh Luke, thank God!'

I try to say 'what's happened?' but there's no sound.

'Don't worry, don't worry, oh alright, here's the doctor.'

A doctor loomed close and talked to me, all the while running some checks. I opened and shut my mouth and indicated with my hand that my mouth was dry.

'Okay, that's usual, I'll get the nurse to bring you some drink,' he said as if I'd spoken. Sure enough a nurse came along with a sort of drinking tube and I sipped it gratefully. She smiled at me and I nodded. I felt so much better already, like life trickling back into my veins. All the while Gabriella stood back, keeping out of the way but now I looked for her and smiled.

'Gabriella,' my voice came out papery.

She stepped forward. 'Luke, so glad you are back with us.'

'What happened?'

'Well, what do you remember?'

'Giving the lecture, the shindig after then – well not much that makes a whole lot of sense to be honest with you.'

'I guess they will be asking you all sorts of questions, but from my point of view it looked like you got rather overheated, went outside to cool down, drank a load of water then went off your head. You were just spinning round and round then you crashed over, hell of a bump to your head, or so I thought, seems there was no damage they could find.'

'Always was a bit of a bone-head,' I said, watching her worried face.

'Well, no damage, but you were in a coma, for .. well, this'll be the third day.'

'A coma! No shit,' And almost as I say it a tiny shiver of a memory slices its way in, bad thoughts and bad stenches.

'We were all so worried.'

'But they don't know what caused it?'

'No, they asked about, well, whether you'd taken anything,' she left words unsaid hanging in the air.

'Screw that!'

'And, well not one of their tests or scans could give a reason. Perhaps you just really shook your brain up.'

'Blood tests, did they show anything?'

'Not that they've said, and they were looking at blood tests for all sorts.'

'It was the Moringa,' I said simply, from somewhere I had a conviction that this was the cause, as if I somehow knew that I had been told this in some incontrovertible way.

'What? I wondered if you'd been infected when I remembered you didn't use gloves, but you sound so sure?'

'Let's just say that we will research this together but I can tell you now that I am sure that the Moringa nodules did this.'

The doctor returned, I didn't want to take my eyes off of Gabriella, hers were looking puzzled, but he stepped close and she stepped back breaking the line of sight. I needed to know that she was on my side, that she would work through this with me, together.

'Gabriella? Together, research this together?' I said ignoring the man.

'Dr Adamson,' he tried.

'Just butt-out for a minute! Gabriella?'

'Yes, of course, Luke, please - the doctor.'

I looked up at the guy, 'I'm all yours,' I said.

They said they had to keep me in for observations, yet minute by minute I was feeling much more like my old self. Gabriella had left, apparently it was the middle of the night, and she had promised to come back the next day and take me home if they would let her.

I lay there, having been told to rest, but unable and not actually willing to sleep. I knew there were memories that I wanted to retrieve, to verify, but the more I chased them the harder they seemed to pin down. I was certain of only two things. One, the Moringa nodules had somehow caused me to sink into a coma, whether a chemical alteration or a bacterial attack I had no idea but I was certain sure of the cause. Two, that I had undergone some weird kind of aversion therapy. In the time since Gabriella left and the doc had told me to rest I had tried a few little experiments. As I lay there I deliberately remembered my episode at Cambridge, where I wrecked the other guy's experiments to steal the lead. As I started in on the memory the 'aren't I the clever guy' feeling started to build in me and then it happened, I hallucinated a smell, well not really a smell, more a stench of such putrefaction as to make me gag. Veering my memory away from this one-time triumph, the smell went too. Check, one.

Second experiment I had to wait for, I didn't want there to be any memory association with this one. Sure enough after a while the nurse comes in to check I'm okay. She was not a great looker, but good enough to let my imagination have free rein. I engaged her in a few words. Her soft English accent made up for a lot and I felt the old urge creep up on me, and it happened; just as I started in on the plot I could use to lay this little lady I almost convulsed with the shock of the stink that hit me. It must have shown as she reached forward, 'Are you okay? Is there a pain?' she asked, but by then I had banished all traces of lust and the air was clear again. I smiled at her and told her nothing was wrong,

I just remembered something important that I'd forgotten all about. Check, two.

Okay, so two trials are not conclusive evidence, and there was no way to try double blind tests on this one, but I was convinced. I lay back and wondered what the hell had actually gone on, and how. As I did so I must have drifted into sleep for the next time I was aware, it was daylight outside and a different nurse was checking up on me.

I still had no idea what had actually happened to me, yet I had this feeling that I was really on to something big, something that would take me in a whole new direction. As I lay there thinking, I considered the 'aversion therapy' I had undergone, I never have had a strong stomach for certain smells, always struggled with formaldehyde for instance, a regular aroma for a scientist to have to deal with. And the other stuff, though it seemed like a weird dream, some mishmash of stuff I had endured as a child in Church with my Ma, all of which I had rejected fully from an early age. So, how come it was so vivid in my coma dream. I find myself thinking of the last bit of the Bible, yeah, that was probably it, I had internalised a section from the readings or sermons or some such. I tossed the idea of it being relevant aside and returned my thinking to the aversion therapy.

I knew I was an incorrigible womaniser, had been called it to my face more than once but hey, they can always say no. And I did get what I wanted out of life, though I don't think most other people knew what methods I had used, but it didn't bother me. I saw what I wanted and I took it, I worked hard but made sure that it worked for me every time. So to wipe that, or make it almost unbearable to even think, let alone do, was some powerful weapon for good.

For good. Was this what it was all about? Opposite of evil: good.

Even thinking was making me tired, I longed to close my eyes and drift off yet I was almost frightened to do that in case I drifted off into a another coma, and with it the vile dreams I had endured. No, I would analyse and experiment and work out what this was going to mean for me and the future.

After running a few more memory experiments and one more 'womaniser' experiment I was satisfied that I had undergone a psychological change; now my usual behaviour and thoughts towards women and methods of behaviour had, and would be, modified by a mental association that manifested itself as an unbearable stench. How this worked I had no idea, but that it was effective I could not deny.

Was this something special to me? Would this work on others in the same way? Greed? Wasn't that the problem with the whole world, not just the destruction of the Rainforest? I lay there turning over all the ills of this world in my mind. Poverty and starving people in Africa, when at their head sat fat, rich, greedy men who even stole from the aid that was sent to help the poorest in their ravaged countries, the greed and corruption that made a vicious trail right down the hierarchies of all those agencies that had access to any funds. The war-torn regions? They weren't fighting over the ownership of the barren lands, they were cornering the market in opium, cocaine or oil and the wealth that it could bring. Religious battles? That gave me pause for thought, yet as I set my mind to it I could see that although those that actually fought may have religious zeal as their only goal, those who pulled the strings and turned their minds were comfortable, more than comfortable and wielding more and more power as a result. Greed again. Were there any ills of this world that could not be traced back to greed whether for power, wealth, sex or control? Had I been given an insight and, uniquely, a potential cure all in one go?

I turned to wondering how I could test whether this effect would be reproduced in others if it were administered to them and I turned over in my mind the suitable candidates for trial. It was impossible to trial something like this on animals and methods to take a new drug to human testing were beyond endurance. The best tests would be those where the participants had no knowledge of the effect that was being sought, or even that they were part of a trial. It would be totally unethical to administer a drug to someone without their knowledge or consent, so what was I thinking? And if this was unethical why could I think about it without the trace of a bad smell? Could it be that it was because that was what was wanted of me? I began to chuckle to myself, was I developing a Messiah complex? Well, how about that? Another experiment:

Right, I decided to plan a way that this 'discovery' could make me millions. First I would isolate the active ingredients then peddle it as a behaviour therapy at extortionate fees to cover my 'research costs'. It could be given to recidivists. This idea built rapidly in my head, there would be scores of governments wanting to buy this new wonder drug that meant prisons could be emptied of all thieves, wait, more, any crime connected with greed. Even at a modest fee this would bring in…. it happened. Suddenly there was the stench. The reality of the money to be made had carried my experiment away from my control into my own ego and desire and then, only then, it had hit. I cleared my mind swiftly to be able to breathe. Somehow the stenches varied so that I could not assimilate and get used to them, and every time they made me feel wretched.

Back to the problem of finding out if it affects everyone the same way. There was more than one hitch in this. It seemed that I had gone into a coma, not something you put someone into lightly. They would need to be monitored so that when it happened, if it happened, they could get the best and appropriate medical care. A spate of persons, associated with me, falling into temporary comas might raise some questions. Though I guess it might be thought to be a contagious condition that was being passed on by as yet unknown means. Could I get away with this? How would I find out how they had been affected, dream-wise, aversion therapy-wise?

I slept, I guess I slept, for the next thing I knew was that Gabriella was beside me again, I sensed her presence and saw her through barely open lashes, her face blossoming from concern to happiness as I opened my eyes fully and stirred.

The Angel Bug 13

Gabbi 24th October

I remembered to turn my answerphone off this time but it didn't matter, for although I had been in bed less than five hours I was wide awake and raring to go before eight. I felt unusually happy and put it down to the relief that Luke was okay, that he hadn't died on me. I didn't want to analyse this too much but put a call through to the hospital before I left the house to see if they thought he might be allowed out and if so, when.

The answer was non-committal. Not until the senior consultant had made his rounds could they say whether Dr Adamson would be allowed to leave, I might like to call back after lunch. So I agreed that I would, and headed out to go to Eden instead.

The day matched my feelings, the heavy rains of the previous day had torn the last leaves from the trees and now they lay discarded in coppery swags along the roadsides, glowing where the brittle bright sunlight hit them. Eden, as usual looked stunning, newly washed and sparkling wherever the sun touched.

On the top floor changes had been made, Sapphira's desk, though it hadn't moved, now stood at the end of a 'corridor' made from the reference shelves. To me it made her look like a librarian, though I was sure that was not the effect she'd hoped for. It did, however, cut her position off from the rest of us even more, which I suppose was what she wanted. She still had the same commanding view of the gradual ascent of anyone onto the top floor. I continued up and straight forward to her desk; the space was wider where the desk sat giving her a large rectangular office space around her position.

'Morning,' I said as soon as I was near. 'If you haven't heard, Dr Adamson came out of the coma last night, should I say, this morning, about two-thirty.'

'Well, that *is* good news. Do we know any more?'

'Not as yet, I am going to call the hospital after lunch.'

'I suppose that is the end of the story then. I do hope he's not thinking of suing or anything like that, you know what some people can be like.'

'Well, I don't think so because I do know he wants to continue the research.'

'Really?' she looked pensive. 'Well, I don't know if that's a good idea do you?'

'It's not up to me, but he was very positive about it last night.'

'We'll see. We'll see,' she murmured. 'Very well, thank you.' She smiled briefly and returned her eyes to the papers on her desk. Dismissed, I turned and made my way through the reference aisles and round to my own desk.

I was so happy that Luke had survived I hadn't thought about any consequences. He was certain it was the Moringa that caused him to go into a coma, how or why I didn't know, but that raised the problem that we might be dealing with a very dangerous substance, and I had been cavalierly sending samples of it out to all and sundry with not so much as a 'handle with care' note attached. I felt myself flush hot and cold as I thought of the consequences. I breathed deeply to steady myself, reasoning that most scientists were not as careless of their own safety when dealing with an unknown substance as Luke had been. If he had used gloves and if he had not had abrasions to his skin it might never have happened. Calm once more, I turned on my computer and it was only then that I noticed the sheet of paper tucked under my keyboard. It was upside-down and as I turned it over saw it was from Naomi and was the first set of analysis results from the nodule that her friend Robbie had worked on.

After a short preamble, the list of chemicals found in the sample and their quantities followed, as I scanned down the list I could feel my eyes opening wider and wider, it was incredible.

There were a number of unusual components but four in particular caught my eye as I recognised their relevance to the condition Luke found himself in. There were two chemicals that

I would put in the hallucinogenic realm, associated with fungi, and one in the analgesic realm associated with tree bark and one that would act as a sedative-hypnotic that was originally extracted from bacteria. There were some other chemicals that I did not know enough about to assign, and as I had suspected there was haemoglobin but not, as is usual in nodules, leghaemoglobin but the type actually found in man and other animals. This was so extraordinary that it almost made me query Robbie's competence, had it not been for the fact that this whole nodule thing was getting so weird that anything seemed possible.

I dived into researching each of the components and in no time I had both learned a lot and eaten up the morning. Lunch of a mini vegetarian quiche and I was heading for my car and the hospital. I had so much to tell Luke about the possibilities of the nodules causing his condition, but I was very aware of liabilities so I was also determined to put the blame for the contamination fully in his court. Anyway, I told myself out loud, there was no harm done, sure he was in a dodgy state for a few days but there seemed to be no harm done. If anything he seemed keener on doing further research than before so I didn't think Eden had anything to worry about.

I checked in and stepped into his room. He was lying back, pale and asleep, I went over to him worried that he may have slipped back into the coma but at once registering that he was not wired up and that there had been nothing said as I'd arrived. He stirred and opened his eyes; the warm feeling that flowed through me must have been relief.

'How you feeling?'
'Fine, tired a little, but fine.'
'I've had some analysis results back from the nodules. Do you want to hear this now?'
He elbowed his way up the bed to sitting. 'Shoot.'

'Well, amongst other stuff, that I've gone through and appears to be neutral or benign, there are two hallucinogens, one analgesic and an hypnotic-sedative, all originally isolated from plant or bacterial sources.'

'No shit?'

'And haemoglobin,' I saw him smile and shook my head. 'No, I really do mean haemoglobin, not leghaemoglobin.'

He shook his head. 'Unbelievable.'

'So if you'd worn the gloves as I asked, you wouldn't have been contaminated,' I put in to make sure he understood the chain of responsibilities.

'I know. That's not a problem. What I want to know is how much of a dose did I get from that contact?'

'Pardon?'

'Well, I got some of the juice on my skin; my skin had abrasions, it's still not like I swallowed a whole nodule of the stuff. How little of these hallucinogens and sedatives does it take to cause a coma for... how long?'

'Three days.'

'Three days, I'd say that they need a hell of a lot more stuff when they induce coma for medical reasons than what anyone could absorb through their skin, even abraded, from a smear of juice.'

'Well, yes, I hadn't thought of it like that. It could be the particular combination that engineered the response.'

'Could be, or could be that what actually gets in is capable of reproduction and develops inside the system.'

I gasped. I know I looked astonished as Luke beamed at me. 'Hadn't thought of that angle then?'

No I hadn't and yet it was entirely possible, I had been treating the information as if it were merely a combination of chemicals, yet when dealing with bacteria and fungi and who knows what else then the possibility of infection and multiplication ought to be considered with some care.

'Could that mean that you are infectious?'

It was Luke's turn to look momentarily surprised then he gave a small smile.

'I really hadn't thought of that. You are good, Gabriella, you are good.'

I felt myself blushing but ploughed on, 'You need some blood tests run.'

'No!' he snapped. 'Least not here. I think this ought to be part of our research, don't you? I mean, if they run tests here I may be kept in for who knows how long and I really couldn't stand that.'

'But you'll have some done? If what you think is right, you may relapse.'

'Sure, no problem, I can set up blood tests and have them analysed myself, I don't need the hospital to do that for me, do I?'

I thought a moment; I suppose he could, if he was worth as much as rumour suggested.

'Right, now I want out of here, they going to sign me off?'

'Seems as if we need to wait for the rounds, should be within the hour they said.'

'Or even now,' Luke beamed towards someone behind me. I turned to see the registrar and his consultant and stepped back out of the way.

'Okay,' Luke said as he settled himself in my Mini. 'Let's get outta here.'

He sounded buoyant and looked pleased with himself.

'Where first?' I asked, not entirely sure what was going on in his head.

'Hotel,' he grinned. 'For a change of clothes, then Eden.'

He looked out of the window at the passing scenery for a while then turned to me.

'What do you think, Gabriella, if you could make the world a better place, less killing, less misery, less greed, would you do it?'

'Sounds like a perfect idea, who wouldn't?'

'Well, let's say you could put something in the water, just so everyone gets some, that forced people to be less greedy, so they didn't do antisocial stuff to get rich or powerful, would you do it?'

'You mean put some drug in the water that stops them feeling they want things?'

'Sort of, I guess.'

'So they'd not have a choice, whether to have it or not, whether to change their minds or not?'

'Yep, it would have to be an all or nothing thing.'

'Not, then.'

'What!'

He sounded so startled I had to look at him, taking my eyes of the road momentarily, and in those seconds a motorbike came out of nowhere behind me and roared past so close he could have brushed my door mirror.

'Why the hell not, for the good of everyone, why the hell not?' Luke persisted.

I drove for a while, concentrating.

'Well, it's a combination of violation of people's right to choose whether they should take a medication or not and it seems like it would also take away free will.'

'Okay, I can see the first part, though if everyone gets it then it's not like some have the choice to opt out and some don't, everyone gets the same treatment. But the free will stuff, come on Gabriella that's a load of bullshit and you know it.'

'No, I think it's part of what makes us human, free will and a thinking choice. Not just driven by instinct and need, free to choose how we attain what we need, through good ways or not such good ways.'

'You mean evil.'

'Well, evil sounds a little extreme, sure some people do evil, seem evil, but many just make poor choices, choose the not so good ways to get what they want.'

'But shouldn't good triumph over evil?'

'Yes, of course, but in each individual's heart.'

'Huh,' Luke puffed and turned back to looking out of the window, and I was left wondering what the hell had got into him.

'Can you wait?' Luke asked as we drew up in the hotel forecourt. 'Of course, how long do you think you'll be? I might have a wander along the sea-front if it'll be a while?'

'Less than quarter of a hour, but you go up there, I'll find you,' he said. He left the car and I watched him hurry into the hotel.

I parked, locked the car and wandered up behind the hotel to where the view of the sea rolling in was magnificent. Ice blue to match the bright white-blue sky, the sea sparkled and foamed as it washed up on the beach below and cascaded back on itself where it met the rocks further along. I was lost in its unceasing beauty of motion when I felt Luke's hand touch my shoulder and turned to him. He looked into my eyes, close. 'It's beautiful, isn't it?' he smiled softly.

I nodded, swallowed and said, 'Eden now?' breaking the spell.

We headed straight to the Foundation building and up the stairs to the office as Luke wanted to see Sapphira. That was no problem, as we ascended we could see she was at her desk, as were two men I did not recognise at first. I hesitated, Luke just carried on in, right up to her desk. The other guys got up and Sapphira must have introduced them as handshaking went on.

I turned away and went to my own desk, fired up the computer and checked emails, while at the back of my mind I tried to place the faces I'd just seen. There was an email from Naomi, and attached was a sheet of the second range of test results that she'd agreed dinner for. The soil samples yielded no surprises. Nothing that I wouldn't have expected and perhaps less than I would, considering that the soils may have had an imported element. I felt a little deflated and became aware of raised voices.

Luke suddenly appeared round the end of the bookcases and he was not looking happy.

'Gabbi, give me a ride back to the hotel,' he snapped as he swept past. I jumped up and leaving everything as it was ran after him, glancing back at the three people left standing at Sapphira's desk, and skittered down the stairs. I only caught up with him beside my car.

'What was that all about?'

'Silly bitch won't let me do the research here, and that lawyer prat is shitting himself in case I sue and the accountant in case I claim expenses or something.'

'Oh Luke.'

'Never mind, they're happy now, they think I've gone. But you are going to take me to your lab place because the one thing I need is the nodules, then we can get on with the research anyway.'

'Well, I'm not sure I can Luke, they aren't exactly mine to give to you.'

He stood there and looked at me, shaking his head slightly, his eyes looking full into mine.

'Gabriella, just one?'

Three left out of the ground, many more in the ground, at least until Sapphira excised the tree. That did it. What was the point when she was going to have the tree taken out anyway? And here was the man who knew the tree and its ecosystems better than anyone in the world wanting to research the problem himself.

'Okay,' I said and we set off for Watering Lane.

The Angel Bug 14

Luke 24th - 25th October

It only took ten minutes or so to get to the place but by then I had seen the way Gabriella was chewing her lower lip, obviously this idea was causing her great anxiety. I had also made a decision; I needed more than one nodule. The only remaining question was did I allow Gabriella to steal a nodule for me when I knew I intended to get the rest from under the tree? Was it best to be sure of having at least one? There was no smell; so that was alright then.

At Watering Lane we pulled into the side of the track just out of sight of the wooden cabin and Gabriella hauled on the handbrake. 'Stay here!' she said and got out. I watched her walk the short distance up to the cabin and turn to go in, a second or two later she crossed to the labs.

I waited, sunk down a little in the seat, for, I don't know what reason. After ten minutes or so she came out again, an envelope in her hand, and followed by the Bear. She stepped to her right, allowing him to step in beside her on my side, so that he was looking away from me and talking. She lifted the envelope and they both disappeared towards the cabin, out of my sight. A moment later she ran back down to the car and, as she snatched open the door, she hissed at me 'Get down! Hide!' I slipped the belt free and, turning, slithered into the foot well to a kneeling position, my torso and head on the seat. These cars were not made for hiding in. I felt the car make a three-point turn and we are out of there.

'Okay,' she said almost laughing.

'Okay,' I said scrambling back up into the seat and strapping the belt across me again. 'You had company at the lab?'

'Yeah, bit tricky,' she flashed me a smile. 'I just said I was sending another nodule off for analysis, it's true, though, isn't it?'

'Yep,' I said, while thinking that I will have to get the other nodules by myself.

I got Gabriella to drop me back at the hotel and after getting her number waved her goodbye. At the hotel I extended my stay and asked for them to organise the hire of a car. I also found out where the nearest town with a largish supermarket was and got given a map that would probably guide me enough when I needed it.

The rental took about half an hour to turn up and by the time the paperwork was done it was nearly five but the answer to another query told me that the supermarket was one that was open till eight, so I took off in the car reminding myself to drive on the left. This was fine where there were two lanes to drive in, I just made sure I stayed by the dotted line. It became trickier when there was no line, and almost no width for there to be a side, and I met someone coming towards me. Thank goodness the guy I met was as good at reversing as he was driving forwards! I gave him a real cheery wave of thanks and he smiled back, real nice.

At the supermarket, thankfully out-of-town so I didn't get hung-up on small busy roads, I looked for and bought a flashlight, a small cool bag, and a gift set garden trowel and fork with pink-flower decorated handles, the only type available.

Back at the hotel I called Gabriella. 'Hi,' I said after her recitation of her number, 'it's Luke.'
'Oh, hello, is everything okay?' she sounded worried.
'Yeah, sure, just wanted to know where might be a good place to go out to sample a typical Cornish pub, not a touristy one, a real pub, like say …. what was the young guy called who brought us the tools for digging up the Moringa called?'
'Josh.'
'Yeah, a place like where Josh might go?'
'Well, um I really don't know. There's the…'
'Hey, you've done enough running me around,' I cut in. 'I've hired a car now, do you have his number? Perhaps he could give me a few suggestions.'

'Oh! Okay, if that's what you want?' she sounded put out. 'Um, hang-on, I should have a mobile number for him from work.'

She disappeared from the end of the line for a while, then 'Yes, here it is,' she reeled off a string of numbers, and then repeated them again for me.

'Luke?'

'Yeah?'

'Take care.'

'Sure, sure, don't you worry about me,' I said, feeling warm at her concern.

'Josh? It's Luke Adamson.' I let it sink in a second or two and hear him suck in his breath. 'Hope you don't mind, Gabbi gave me your number, thinks you might be able to help me, I want to go to a real Cornish pub, not some touristy place, the sort of place you and your mates would go?'

'Oh Hi! Well, yeah, sure, like this evening?'

'Like now.'

'Cool, how will you get there?'

'I've a rental, no problem, just need directions. Though your company would be good too, if you're free?'

'Really? Wow, tell you what, meet me at Eden, park in the big lay-by outside, then I can direct you.'

'Sounds perfect, thanks a lot Josh. See you soon.'

'This is great Josh,' I said nursing a pint of beer he'd called 'Betty Stogs' when he ordered it for me. The pub was low-beamed but not hung about with brasses or whimsical plates, instead it had a two real-looking stuffed fox heads, a trap of some kind, photographs of the pub itself and, most probably, the local area in various shades from black and white or sepia to fading colour prints. The people seemed to be comfortable in their surroundings and the barman obviously knew many by name, including Josh.

After the first pint I offered to drop Josh home so he could have another, he said he wasn't planning on going home as he had a little spot somewhere in Eden he could sleep in when he wanted to be out on the lash but in work on time in the morning. This was more than I had hoped, my plan merely being to glean information about Eden from a slightly intoxicated youth who seemed happy to be in my company and low enough in the pecking order not to know that I was now persona-non-grata around the place.

I was buying and he was on his third pint of lager and his second double vodka, though the latter he knew nothing about, when I asked how on earth he got back into Eden at night.

'Getting into Eden isn't a problem,' he laughed, 'just finding somewhere comfortable enough to kip.'

'Surely it's all locked up and patrolled?'

'Sure, but it's easy if you know the place like I do,' he grinned. 'I often wander though the biomes at night, all alone, it's magic.'

I really couldn't believe my luck, Josh had been the only member of general staff I had been in contact with and yet he was the one who knew just what I needed to know, could this be sheer luck or something else?

'Wow,' I said, drawing out the awe. 'Now that sounds like something I really must experience.'

'Really? Really? But you've been, like everywhere.'

'This sounds real special though, Josh, you make it sound just real.'

'Shhh!!' Josh hissed as we crept down the side of the service road keeping to the deep shadow that the rim of the pit cast in the bright moonlight. I smiled to myself. His hushing was making more noise than anything else at two-thirty in the morning. I had with me the cool bag, the trowel and the flashlight.

He paused, placing his arm across my path so as to stop me. He looked both ways in an exaggerated manner. Nothing, we stepped though the silver light to the shadow of a doorway. A key let him in and we stood in darkness so complete that it felt airless. He left my side and I could hear him edge across the room. Suddenly it was flooded in light, I glanced round, concerned that light would be streaming out, but there were no windows to this room.

'Pump house,' he said softly. 'This way,' as we exited the room he turned off the light and then, by the ambient glow seeping in through skylights along the way, he led me though a corridor to a low door that opened out into the Mediterranean biome.

All was still below us; he looked round and then checked the time on his watch. He motioned me to sit down and as he did, so I copied him. Putting his head close to mine he whispered. 'Five minutes.' We sat and watched the enclosed landscape by moonlight, the air was fragrant and everything felt peaceful.

His hand on my arm almost made me jump, but it was to make sure I was still and said nothing as a figure appeared at the top of the Link on the other side and swung a beam around the biome, he wandered down into the centre and repeated the sweep from this position, only to return to the Link and disappear.

Josh beckoned me forward and we walked quietly and slowly through the biome, taking paths that were edged with the taller plants. He was right, it was eerily beautiful, a silvered stillness. He backed me against the wall while he sneaked forward for a check through the Link, then motioned for me to follow, our only concession being to hunker down so that our heads did not show above the wall of the Link should someone look up from the restaurant area below.

A waft of warm damp air and we were in the Humid Tropics biome, the earthy scent of the place filling my nostrils with nostalgia for the jungle.

'This is the place on a cold winter's night,' Josh whispered.

'Fantastic,' I answered, wondering what I was going to do now, I had intended to get information on Eden enough to break in and take the nodules myself, alone, but here I was with Josh in tow and now I had the problem of what to do with him.

We wandered pretty much at random, Josh looking unsteadily up at the canopy and weaving around. I guess the alcohol had just about reached maximum effect; I certainly couldn't have held the total of four pints and three double vodkas that he'd consumed, that well.

'Hey Josh,' I hissed, 'Josh, buddy, hey I'd like to take another look at my favourite tree, the Moringa, where can I find it buddy?'

'Ah! The Moringa, the Horseradish tree or Miracle tree, all parts of this tree can be used, roots, seeds, bark, leaves,' he quoted at me from the catalogue in his head. 'It's over here, look while you can.'

'What?'

'Ms high-and-mighty is having it taken out. Bye-bye Moringa, no new Moringa.'

'Really?' I say, amazed but interested in his tone of voice. 'That's too bad.'

'Bad, it is that alright, bad.'

'Well, I'd like to do something about that. Hey, Josh, if I can have some more of those nodules from the tree roots, you know like we found before, I think I could make her change her mind.'

He stopped me, a tug on my shoulder to make me look him in the face.

'Really?'

'Sure.'

He stared at me for a moment and then walked off, 'Follow me!' he called, far too loud. In moments we were by the Malaysian House and there was the tree, its leaves only looking dark against the moonlit dome.

I hunkered down and got working with the trowel, the soil was soft and easy to move and in no time I had in my grasp the remaining nodules from the section of root I'd exposed before. These I tucked in the cool bag. I followed another root down into the soil, working away to trace its descent into the earth. In moments I had uncovered more of the nodules, dark and firm in my hand, these too went into the cool bag. I glanced at Josh; he had collapsed on a bench a little way up from where I was, his head lolling back, his eyes open apparently watching the sky through the hexagonal frames above. I traced the third main root down and harvested more of the nodules. My hands were caked in earth but the cool bag bulged with my collection.

'Hey, Josh, better get back, buddy.'

He tipped his face forward, his eyes pretty glazed.

'Sure,' he said and got to his unsteady feet.

'Where were you going to sleep?'

'Show you,' he slurred and wove his way through the pathways to a cabin that reeked of rubber, he reached into a dark corner and pulled a rubber airbed from the display and started to blow it up.

He gave me lots of warnings about getting out unobserved, kept stopping to say he'd better come with me, but in the state he was in I thought my chances better on my own. Eventually he waved me goodbye from the doorway of the cabin and I trod my way carefully back towards the Link. This, I felt, was the dodgiest place, and rightly so, as there was no cover and more than one direction that someone could appear from. I spied out the area well first, made a crouching run to the stairs and checked down them, then keeping low, headed for the temperate zone. I reached the door into the corridor and heaving a sigh of relief closed it quietly behind me. Once in the darkened pump room again I felt safe, I gently opened the door and stepped out. The cool of the night air refreshed me and I checked carefully before leaving the security of the shadows.

It took me another ten minutes to reach the outer rim and then the outer fence of Eden, at last I got to my hire-car.

Exhausted I fell onto the hotel bed, the nodules stashed in the hotel mini-bar fridge, its former contents standing guard on the lid, all except the one nice drop of Southern Comfort I downed to settle my nerves and ease me into sleep.

Next morning dawned bright and crisp. First problem was to get hold of some good lab facilities in the area. I really expected trouble but, after a bit of ringing round, my contacts came through good and recommended me not one, but two local and independent labs that might be willing to offer me the space and equipment I was seeking at short notice.

The first was not too positive, asked my name twice and then didn't have any reaction to it and eventually said they were at full stretch themselves but could offer me a couple of hours lab space a day, with the implication that it would be difficult. The second seemed really pleased to be able to help me, Dr Luke Adamson, as the guy who came on the phone was obviously clued up about my work and at the same time they were much more laid back and friendly. Yes they would hire out one of their lab areas, with assistant if I needed, for a week initially, no problem. I requested various instruments and equipment and was told they were all available, I agreed a hire fee and got directions.

After lunch I called Gabriella, but got her answerphone, leaving a message that all was well and I was going to a lab to work today, would call her later. After I put the phone down I wondered why the hell I'd called her in the first place, it just seemed the natural thing to do, yet hadn't exactly been part of my plan.

The lab was situated behind a farm. From the outside you might have mistaken it for another one of the farm buildings, lower than the large farm hangars but clad in a similar box-metal roof. There was a small entrance hall with a 'press bell for receptionist' and it worked, a receptionist appeared. I was buzzed through and advised to use a bactericide hand wash before entering the next area. Once in I was greeted heartily by a tall middle-aged guy with a small goatee beard and his long hair snatched back in a band.

'Jules Brandon,' he said, 'great admirer of your work, heard your lecture at Eden, really pleased to have you here at my labs.'

'My pleasure.'

'What is it you need labs for incidentally? I understood you were on the book tour?'

'Finished, last lecture was the one you heard. I am doing a bit of extra research while down here, something that came to my attention and I thought I'd look into it.' We were walking through the building and through the glass doors on either side I could see clean, narrow but well equipped labs of differing types, most with youngish men and women looking busy in them.

'Really? Any chance of knowing what it is?'

I smiled at him. 'Too early to say really, know you'll understand.'

He smiled back. 'Sure, I know, fine, well, here's your space, um, if you need an assistant I should be able to round one up, though may not always be the same one. Anything else you need call reception and they'll put you through to me. Press R on the internal phone here.'

I looked round the room, long and narrow it was equipped with centrifuge, microscope, incubator, a fresh stack of agar plates, cutting equipment and coveralls, masks, gloves – the works just as I'd asked.

'It all looks fine, thanks. Do you have wi-fi internet here?'

'Sure, login to 'thefunnyfarm' it's secured to this building only and we change the code regularly. Any problems just get back to me,' he smiled and turned to go. 'Anything else you need, just ask, we keep most basic lab disposables in stock. We usually quit by six but if you need to overrun, just ask and it can be arranged.'

'Thanks,' I said, wondering how come they had spare capacity when their rivals seemed to be so busy, it looked like an efficient and well run place. I was too keen to get on to think any more about this and donned the full coverall, gloves and mask for my first 'experiment'. I removed one of the nodules and washed it off in the distilled water. Next I macerated it in a juicer, taking care not to lose any of the liquid as I transferred it to the centrifuge to extract every drop. I drew up the resultant liquid into a syringe and sealed it off.

The next nodule I prepared and set sections to grow, with any luck, on agar plates in the incubator. I put half the remainder in the lab fridge but kept the other half in my cool bag. It was way past five and, apart from a friendly 'just passing, got everything you need?' from Brandon, I had been left to my own devices. I cleared and packed my gear ready to depart and Jules Brandon reappeared; he held a key in his hand.

'Hi, here's a key for your lab,' he said. 'We don't have cleaners in here except when they are called, the only other key is mine, so treat it as your own until you quit it. Do you need to get in at any other times?'

'Thanks,' I said, rapidly thinking about other times. 'Well at the moment it seems I don't, it depends how things go though.'

He gave a nod and a smile, 'Okay here's a personal code for you, it will get you into the building without setting off the alarms, then you'll have your key for your own lab, use the same code for this alarm, which will cut off the lab alarm in this room only,' he indicated the number-pad inside the door. He must have read the look on my face. 'We specialise in independent research,' he added, 'half the labs are hired by independents, the rest are our bread-and-butter.'

I stashed the half-pack of nodules back into the cool bag and prepared to leave. Everything was tidied away so even if the lab boss came snooping there would not be anything that would tell him what my research was about, though I was fairly confident that their facilities also depended upon discretion and that it would be preserved. I locked the door and heard a rapid beeping from the alarm as it set itself. Within seconds of leaving the building my cell phone burst into rapturous applause.

'Hi, Gabriella,' I said as it told me the caller's name.

'Luke!' she sounded really pissed off. 'What the merry hell did you think you were doing?'

The Angel Bug 15

Gabbi   25th October

The first thing I heard as I got into work was some kind of argument coming from the top floor. Karen gave me an 'I don't know' gesture and said quietly, 'It's only just started.'

I headed on up to see Naomi and Mikaela, backs towards me as they stood ranged against Sapphira's desk, she was standing behind it, fingers braced on its leading edge as she leant forward, her eyes glittering as she said something in a voice too low for me to catch, and then, as I reached the top step both Mikaela and Naomi turned as one and, at speed, headed for their own desks. My glance towards Sapphira was met with a hard stare as she straightened haughtily behind her desk then quickly seated herself. I cast a 'Morning,' in her direction which she acknowledged with a tilt of her head as she picked up her phone.

'What was that all about?' I asked quietly as I sat down, both faces were set and Mikaela looked close to tears.

'She's having the Moringa taken out *today*!' Naomi said shaking her head.

'And while we are open! Can you believe that!' Mikaela added, her voice cracking a little.

'Why? I mean, why right now? What's the hurry?'

'Seems someone has been digging round the tree, the earth was found all disturbed and dug up around the roots this morning.'

'Oh! Hells bells, how? Who?' I said, with a sneaking feeling that I knew who, but not how.

'Who knows, it's just spooked the … woman,' Naomi said. 'Immediate removal, just in case.'

'What is she afraid of?'

'Luke Adamson? Seems he is really interested in the tree.'

'Of course, we knew that, he wants to do more research on the cause of the problem, no harm in that surely?'

'Not the way she sees it, seems he might be all set to ruin Eden and everything it stands for. Better the tree goes than everything goes, is how she put it.'

'Well, anyway, I'm just writing up a 'temporary' note to go over the exhibit info. I'm saying the tree is being replaced with a new one for sound biological reasons. By the time everything is cleared it might be true. Least it should save a publicity disaster.' Mikaela said typing rapidly and hitting print. She retrieved her notice, cut it down and laminated it, waved it in a gesture of goodbye and headed out.

Naomi looked at me and was silent for a moment.

'Do you think it was Dr Adamson?'

I felt the blush before I had time to think what I was going to say. She nodded.

'Did you help him?'

'No!' I blurted. 'Just guessing the same as you, I do know he was most put out when they told him he couldn't study the nodules here, and he's not a man who takes that sort of refusal lying down, never has been.' And as I said it I wondered at his insistence on talking to Josh about pubs last night. What had he really wanted of Josh?

'Who found the disturbance to the tree roots?' I asked.

'Louise, just doing the rounds this morning.'

'Okay, not Josh then?'

'No, why?'

'Oh, um only Josh was the first to notice the problem with the leaves, I know he's been really interested in how it turns out,' I dissembled, knowing I make a terrible liar, only to be rewarded with a shrewd look from Naomi. I was saved by the trilling of my mobile, pulled an 'I'll just answer this' face and glanced at the name, speak of the devil, it was Josh.

'Hi,' I said, not wanting to reveal the caller's name to Naomi.

'Hi, um, Gabbi, I think I've made a big mistake, I really don't know. Can you come down here I need to talk to someone about it?'

'Sure, down where?'

'Sorry, down here, I'm in the Link café.'

'Sure, and don't worry,' I reassured, hastily putting two and two together and making myself worried.

'Back soon. Little problem,' I said to Naomi, leaving her with questions in her eyes.

Josh was nursing a cup of coffee and looked terrible, even his clothes looked more crumpled than usual. I fetched myself a coffee and went to sit opposite him. He looked up and flashed a near-usual smile.

'You've heard about the Moringa?' he said, his head dropping again.

'That it's being taken out this morning?'

'No!' he looked up at me wild-eyed. 'Shit, it was supposed to stop that.'

'No? You didn't know, so you mean something else, oh, that the roots had been disturbed last night?'

'Yes, that, oh God, is that why it's being taken out?'

'Afraid so.'

'Bugger! Damn! Bugger! Sorry!' he said rapid fire. 'You see it was me, well sort of.'

'Josh if it was you – well then there's no reason for them to whip the Moringa out so quickly – we just explain that….' I started feeling relieved for a second before my thinking caught up with my mouth. 'But if it was you, why? And what do you mean by sort of?'

'Well, it wasn't me that dug them up, that was Dr Adamson, but it was me got him in here. He said he could stop the Moringa being taken out if he could get hold of some more of the nodules, he said that it would be too precious to be removed if he could get some research done on them.'

'Did he indeed?' I said feeling murderous. It was bad enough being cajoled into taking one nodule, but to get me to do that when he was about to do a wholesale raid…

'Now I don't know what to do, if I say it was me got him in here then I'm for the chop.'

'No, you can't do that Josh. It might be worth trying to stall the removal of the tree if you said you'd scraped around the earth though for… for.. ?'

'To see if there were any more nodules?'

'Of course, and there weren't! Come on.'

'Where?'

'To see the senior botanist and see if we can't change her mind.'

'Okay, but won't I still lose my job?'

'No, not if you explain that you were concerned that if there were any more nodules that they might be responsible for the change of leaf colour and that you thought their removal might aid the tree's recovery.' We were powering up the back road to the Foundation building in one of the little electric buggies for transporting team members and goods around.

Josh was silent for a moment. 'Okay, I think I can handle that, and I came in real early this morning 'cos it was worrying me all night.'

'Sounds good, yes, as it was found by Louise on the morning rounds.'

'Yeah, I know, she said.'

'Oh my? So she said and you didn't say you'd done it then?'

'No,' he said woodenly. We were silent; I let the speed drop to a crawl.

'You said nothing because you were worried you might get into trouble as… as you had acted on the spur of the moment through your real concern and afterwards you knew you should have asked permission and were afraid to own up.'

He looked at me hope flaring in his face, it sounded weak, but if he could be convincing he might carry it off.

'Afraid to own up, well that bit will be easy to say truthfully,' he said as we parked before the building.

We climbed the stairs, to look at Josh you would think he was climbing the scaffold, if anything he looked worse than before his coffee. Sapphira was at her desk and gave us the merest glance as we reached the top floor. We walked towards her until we were standing at supplicant's distance from the desk. She looked up, 'Yes?'

'Josh has told me something I think you might need to hear.'

She raised her eyebrows and looked at Josh.

'I, I, er, was the one who disturbed the roots round the Moringa – I spent all night worrying about it and I had come the conclusion that if there were nodules on the tree then they must be what was causing the problem, and I knew Dr Adamson had left some on the root he looked at,' he started. I held my breath, so much for there not being any to find. 'So I decided I should remove them and any others so the tree could get back to health, I figured they were the problem, and so I did it,' he concluded.

'Without permission?'

Josh's Adam's apple bobbed. 'Yes, I, I know – I was, obsessed with it, came in ever so early and started looking, I was only going to look where Dr Adamson had been, just brush away the loose earth, but then just I kept on, kept on. Only when I finished I realised what I'd done and it was too late to ask.'

'And what did you do with the nodules?'

'There weren't any.'

'Oh no? You started by telling me Dr Adamson had left some on the tree, that's what was worrying you in the first place.'

My fingers were so crossed they ached.

'Yes he did, but I didn't find any, it was like they had shrivelled up and gone.'

'So you ran to mummy and told her the story?'

Josh looked perplexed, I blushed.

'You told your story to Mrs Johnston, not to me?'

'Oh. Yes, sorry, I was … I didn't know what to do.'

'And Mrs Johnston did.'

'Well, yes, she said we had to say 'cause then the Moringa might not have to be taken out.'

Sapphira smiled, it was not a gentle smile.

'Well, I think we still do have to excise the tree, no matter what she thinks, it is my decisions that count in this place.'

It dawned on me that whatever I did was going to meet with opposition from Sapphira and I still didn't know what it was that caused such antagonism.

'I'm sorry,' Josh said diplomatically. 'I realise now I should have come to you.'

Sapphira regarded him coolly. I said nothing; nothing I said would have helped Josh, keeping silent might.

'Okay, call it just a verbal warning. It will go on your file.'

'Thank you,' he said.

Dismissed we headed back out of the building; I wanted to talk more to Josh about last night.

'I'm sorry she made that a formal warning, Josh.'

'I'm not worried, it could have been so much worse.'

'Still, what actually happened last night, I suppose it was last night and not early this morning?'

He gave a small bark of a laugh, 'Bit of both,' he said and told me about the night and his hideaway. Somehow I'd become Mother-confessor and it was okay to tell me all.

I had work to do but as soon as I left Josh I tried ringing Luke. The phone cut to answerphone, I was so angry with him I didn't feel able to leave a coherent message. I got back to my desk without having to see Sapphira again as, according to Naomi, she'd left to oversee the demise of the tree.

'And Andy?' I asked as I hadn't seen him all day.

'Probably helping her,' she said flatly.

'Naomi?'

'Yeah,' she looked up from whatever she was writing.

'Anything else wrong?'

'Nothing much, just *that* woman, *that* woman and oh, *that woman*.'

'Has something else happened since the row this morning?'

'You could say so, just after you left she called me over to let me know that she was refusing leave for me to apply for that management course I was interested in,' Naomi put on a Sapphira-like voice '*I really don't see you as capable of running your own*

132

department anywhere. So in fact, I'd say, yes something has happened, and that I am working out my letter of resignation right now.'

'No! You mustn't do that.'

'When you are undermined, made to feel as if you are incompetent, belittled in front of other members of staff…' she turned a teary face towards me. 'This used to be such a happy place Gabbi.'

'You shouldn't be resigning, she should. Look that sort of behaviour is harassment, surely.'

Naomi looked hard at me, 'I'm not playing the race card,' she said. 'That's not how I look at things and she's been very careful not to say anything like that.'

'No, I'm not talking about that, I'm talking about if she treated any of us in that way it would be harassment, or bullying, that's it, bullying. That's not allowed.'

'But even that has to be proved.'

'If you stay I am sure she'll give ammunition enough for it to be proved, you'll have us as witnesses.'

'Only half the time, mostly it's when no one else is around.'

'Then tape it all, what the hell, devices are small enough nowadays.'

Naomi looked at me again, her face registering surprise. 'Oh, Gabbi, listen to you, what a suggestion!'

'Well,' I said a little sheepishly, 'that's what they do in books and films,' and we both laughed.

'Stay.' I said. 'Fight it!' She smiled a tight smile and nodded, screwing up the piece of paper under her hand.

Catching up with the work I had to do meant I hardly had time to think for the rest of the day or else I would have had more time than I did to try calling Luke, each time I felt the fury ebb a little until I thought I would be able to leave a coherent message the next time it cut to answerphone.

I kept to the Foundation building for the rest of the day, not wanting to be anywhere near the tree as it was removed. I got home about five thirty and decided to try Luke one more time or leave my, now composed, cutting-but-clear message on his answerphone. Hearing the phone answered tripped me back into anger.

'Luke! What the merry hell did you think you were doing?'

'Hey, hey!' his voice sounded placatory. 'What's up?'

'Only you nearly got a good lad sacked, you've stolen from Eden, you got me to do the same for no good reason, you are a conniving, cunning bastard.'

'Oh Gabriella, you've got half of that wrong, honest.'

'Oh I very much doubt it.'

'Look, let me take you out for a meal this evening,' I drew in a breath to object but he raced on. 'And I'll explain everything. Just a meal, I gotta eat, you've gotta eat, and I'll tell you everything.'

I thought, 'Life, the universe and everything' as the anger subsided a little. 'Alright,' I sighed 'but it had better be good.'

'Where do you suggest then?'

'I meant your explanation,' then caught up with myself. 'The Ship at Par is usually quite good.'

'I'll collect you at seven, okay?'

'Okay,' I said, resting my phone against my chest. What on earth was I doing even talking to this man?

I looked at myself in the mirror. I had taken more care with my appearance than I liked to admit to myself, choosing an outfit that I always thought flattered my figure and in a colour that made me look healthy even in the depths of winter. It's true about some colours suiting you and some dragging you down. There was the sound of an engine and then a knock at the door. I opened it expecting Luke, but there stood Andy again.

'Andy?'

'Sorry to just call in like this,' he said, he paused, and suddenly from expecting to walk out of the door I realised I had to ask him to come in.

'Come in, what is it?'

'Naomi.'

'Oh?'

'I think she's thinking of resigning.'

'What makes you think so?'

He lifted his large hand and in it was the smoothed-out but still crumpled sheet of paper she'd been writing on.

'Oh, I know about that,' I said in as light a voice as I could. 'She's changed her mind.'

'Changed her mind? So, do you know why she wanted to leave Eden?'

I struggled at balancing confidentiality with Andy's concern but he went on.

'About a week ago I did something a bit stupid,' he said looking shamefaced. 'Made a pass, well bit more than a pass, she wasn't keen. She seemed so down, it started like, just cheering her up, a hug, but I.. I overstepped the mark. I've always liked Naomi, I just … how can I be sure she isn't thinking of leaving because of me?'

'She wasn't thinking of leaving because of you! I can tell you that for free.' What was happening to me? Had I 'confess to this woman' written on my forehead?

He looked relieved but still puzzled. 'It's nothing to do with you or your … behaviour. You should be worrying more about Liz and the boys shouldn't you?'

Now he really did look shamefaced. 'Well, that was worrying me too, if it came out as a reason for leaving, harassment? I really didn't mean…' he trailed off. 'Gabbi?'

'Yes, you're an idiot. Naomi needs our support though, she's feeling got at by Sapphira.'

I saw the surprise in his face. 'Andy, open your eyes and ears. Notice how our new senior botanist doesn't treat people equally, some she is determined to undermine and bully.'

'Naomi?'

I tilted my head. I could have added my name and Karen's to the list but let it stay as it was, let him see for himself.

It would have been better if he'd actually left by the time Luke arrived, but it didn't happen that way, Luke's car drove up just as Andy was leaving. They stood at the gate eyeing each other.

'Thanks, bye,' Andy called as he turned away from Luke and headed for the car. Luke came up the drive but I noticed how Andy stared after him before clambering in his car and speeding off.

'Out of hours meeting?' Luke asked, with a raised eyebrow.

'Only just turned up before you, just work stuff,' I said dismissing it and presenting myself ready to go out.

The pub grub was actually rather good, really homemade from a small but varied menu, offering hearty dishes to suit the October weather. While we waited to be served I'd vented my anger at his reckless behaviour and somehow he made it all seem so understandable, right, even. Didn't I realise that Sapphira was going to have the tree taken out anyway, that was the reason why Josh was so keen to help. He apologised for putting Josh's job on the line, but hey, he was okay, he hadn't lost it in the end, had he? So somehow by the time the food arrived I had simmered down, and by the end of the meal I was positively content. Luke seemed pleased too. He rested back against the chair.

'Stuffed!' he said smiling at me, his eyes catching the light.

I felt warm and a little tipsy.

'So what are you doing tomorrow?' he said.

'Ah! Tomorrow I play hooky, I go to help out at a place called St Pirans"

'Peer run?'

'Piran, P.I.R.A.N. a Cornish saint, one of the patron saints of Cornwall. St Piran's is for homeless people, I help out just one afternoon a week.'

'And what do you do there?'

'Generally talk to them, make tea, chat, try to encourage them to stay.'

'Stay? Why?'

'Because while they are there they have to stay sober, they tend to manage to stay out of trouble, they have a warm bed, dry place to sit, a place to get it back together, advice.'

'So you sit and chat to these old guys who usually roam the streets?'

'Not all old guys, not all guys even. Amazing how many youngsters there are even here in Cornwall. Kicked out of home some of them, just have no idea of how to deal with Social Services to find housing and stuff, just roam around dossing down on friends' sofas, sofa surfing they call it, until the welcome wears thin and it's a barn or outhouse and with no food and no money they turn to petty crime.'

'Sounds grim for today.'

'But it's there, like there's this old guy, well no, he isn't an old guy, he's our age, but his lifestyle makes him look old. He used to be a solicitor, wife left him, started drinking, he says, could of course have been the other way round, he is an alcoholic. Lost everything, went from large posh house to on the streets, and eventually wandered his way down to the Westcountry because he said he had happy memories of it from his childhood. If he drinks, he steals, petty stuff, but he steals to drink. So if we can keep him in St Piran's he can, with the help of counsellors, hopefully get off the stuff.'

'And is it working?'

'To be honest, not that well. He'll go along fine for a while then something happens to upset him and he's off, gone and next thing we know the police give us a call as he's given us as his place of abode.'

'Sounds real interesting, and shows a whole different side of you.'

I looked sharply at him, but his face agreed with his words. 'Well, it's certainly different from dealing with plants.'

'Can I come along, tomorrow?'

'I really don't know.'

'You know I'll behave myself, perhaps it'll help, having a guy to talk to. Bet most of the volunteers are women.'

'Well, actually…'

'There you go, whatever you say.'

'Okay,' I said, feeling doubtful that he would really want to go when the time came tomorrow.

Luke drove us back to my place. He stopped the car and got out though he stayed by the car door.

'Goodnight Gabriella,' he said, softly.

I felt he was waiting for me to invite him in, but it hadn't been a date, and it wasn't what I wanted, was it? I stood with my hand on the gate looking back at him across the roof of the car, illuminated by the gleam of a thin-sliced moon.

'See you tomorrow,' I turned and hurried towards the door, suddenly turning back to add, 'If you're coming, be here by twelve-thirty and I'll do a lunch.' He nodded his head in reply and opened the car door to get in. I faced my own door, heart thumping in my chest. Just as I changed my mind and switched round to ask him in, the ignition caught and the headlights went on, he raised one hand and drove away.

The Angel Bug 16

Luke 26th October

I drove away from Gabriella's house both satisfied and definitely not satisfied. I had this strange yearning to be close to her, yet if I so much as thought of a way to lure her to my bed the olfactory deterrent was deployed. I almost had to stop the car to get out and retch up that good food we'd eaten earlier. This was a powerful thing that had happened to me and I began to wonder if it would work on all vices. Like the guy Gabriella had been telling me about. Was that greed? Was alcoholism a form of greed, was any addiction, surely it wasn't conscious greed, it was driven by chemical changes in the brain.

Well, there was one way to find out, I thought as I wheeled the car into the hotel grounds. I could try out the nodule juice on this guy. Was that ethical, hell I thought, no, so why did I not smell anything? I started to think how it might be done, still no signs. Was this because this was what I was meant to do? Was it because there was no greed involved, no power, just a willingness to help the guy? I had no idea but, though my mind whirled, sleep came quickly once I got to bed and with it a luminous dream that seemed to answer my problems, glimmering as clear as a true memory when I woke.

Morning saw me bright and early in the lab facilities. I checked the incubator and set about prepping an extract of the nodules in such a way that I could deliver a very small quantity in differing ways; as a liquid, as a powder and as a small solid tablet. I took a syringe of the liquid and set twenty sets of five millilitres quantities to dry, without undue heat and protected from contamination. The five millilitres of liquid I wanted to encase in capsules, like fish-oil, and the making of tablets was a matter of amalgamating the liquid with talc or chalk and something like wax to make a solid I could press into a shape.

I called reception and asked about the ingredients I required and was rewarded with an affirmative on the non-active ingredients of tablets as being in stock at the lab, though it would take twenty-four hours for an order of capsule cases, minimum order 5,000, to arrive. I asked for the order to be placed and had it put on my card.

I walked out of my lab at twelve with five folded 'papers' of five millilitres worth of dried nodule-liquid and two tablets. The tablets I had made with the five millilitres of the liquid soaked into the chalk and wax base, then pressed out into makeshift moulds, round depressions left when I'd extracted some paracetamol from their bubble packet.

As I drove to Gabriella's place I relived some of the dream. Lines of desperate people, obviously down-and-outs, were lining up to taste salvation. A new life, free from obsession or addiction, a life that offered hope in a world where greed was a thing of the past. I considered what I intended to do. It sounded like the guy was a no-hoper but in a place where if he fell ill he would be cared for, taken to hospital if that was what was needed, if he slipped into a temporary coma, as I expected him to, after all, that was what had happened to me. When he awoke I would talk to him, see if he experienced anything like I did, whether this really was the magic bullet I was beginning to believe it was.

My only concern was the dosage. I believed that I had contact with a smaller amount of the 'blood' yet it was 'blood' to blood, absorbed through an open wound. This would be ingested orally, and what the effects of digestion and dilution would be, I had no idea. Digestion itself was a major hurdle for any biological agent to overcome, with extremes of chemical pH balance combined with molecule breaking capacities. Five millilitres seemed a reasonable amount to try, even though I really did not think that the dosage was that important; I was convinced the agents actually multiplied in the body, replicated like bacteria in the bloodstream, if they managed to get that far unscathed.

Gabriella looked slightly flustered when I arrived, but at least she was alone. She'd made a hearty soup and warmed some rolls to go with it. We broke bread amiably.

'You really sure you want to come today?' she said, wiping a last piece of crust round the side of her soup bowl.

'I really wouldn't miss it for the world,' I said, then took a risk. 'You know something happened to me when I was in that coma? Changed my whole outlook on life.'

Her large dark eyes looked at me closely, she gave the slightest nod, 'A near death experience often changes people,' she said.

'It was more than that,' I began but changed my mind and decided to be more sure of my ground scientifically before I made any rash statements or alerted her to the possibility that I might just try to prove it.

He seemed collapsed in on himself. If Gabriella had not told me he was of a similar age to us I would certainly have added on at least ten years. He looked gaunt and grey, his face unshaven, his hands mottled as he held a dog-eared paperback reading at the sitting-room table.

'Hello, Simon,' Gabriella said her voice rich and warming. He looked up, his face breaking into a smile that took years off him.

'Hello Gabbi,' he said and I was surprised at the refined tone.

'May I introduce to you Luke Adamson, the ethnobotanist who made the film Jungala? Luke, meet Simon Napier.'

He half stood, extending his hand, his shoulders drooping and his eyes not quite meeting mine. 'Pleased to meet you,' he said and sat again.

'Shall I fetch us some tea?' Gabriella said, and moved off. I sat.

'Fine woman,' I said looking the way she had gone.

'Certainly, kind and entertaining.'

'Yep, she is that,' I was beginning to realise how tricky 'chatting' to him was going to be, you could hardly ask 'what do you do?' or even 'what did you do? It seemed wrong, what other gambits were there when man met man, just the usual sizing-up dance of words.

'She's taken me under her wing,' I said, 'just come out of hospital, been in a short coma,' trying to explain my presence with her.

'She's that type alright, tries to take everyone under her wing. Sometimes it's only the thought of not disappointing her that keeps me off the .. stuff.' He shook his head as if the mere thought of alcohol affected him.

'If only there was an instant cure for that, eh?'

He looked at me, his eyes stained yellow, 'If only,' he sighed, 'wouldn't that be a miracle?'

Gabriella reappeared gripping two mugs in one hand and carrying in her other hand another mug with a small plate of biscuits balanced on top of it. We both reached to help and almost ended up with a catastrophe, but gained laughter instead.

Conversation started to flow when Gabriella got going, she had obviously been thinking about items from the past week's news that she thought he would like to discuss, and he did.

'Did you hear Judge Willborough's programme on 'Unintended consequences of laws'?' she said. 'No? Well the basic premise was that sometimes a law has not been thought out to its ultimate effect and has undesired and unintended consequences. Like the law to compensate victims of crime, where the wording actually allows a criminal who is hurt during his perpetration of a crime to gain compensation as he was a 'victim', that is he was hurt, while a crime was being committed, even though it was him committing the crime!'

'That is where the profession make their money,' he said, his face showing signs of true interest.

'Surely not, they wouldn't actually want the criminal to gain compensation?'

'Not necessarily, but the sorting out of the laws, the closing of loopholes takes a great deal of court time, and makes money for some.'

I sat out, having little to offer that would help the flow of conversation, but soon realised my opportunity. Our cups were drained.

'Another?' I asked indicting the cups.

'Please, two sugars,' Simon smiled. Gabriella pointed me in the direction of the kitchen and I set off, checking I knew whose mug was whose.

So it was with great ease that I stirred in the contents of one of my folded papers into Simon's mug of tea, as if the opportunity were God given.

After a while Gabriella left Simon with promises of a good long chat next week, and with 'you will be here, won't you?' as a parting remark, she took me over to introduce me to one of the men who ran the refuge. Bill was just as I imagined a do-gooder to be, warm, cheerful and homely, with his glasses perched on the end of a stubby nose and his cheeks round and cheery. However, he did know who I was and was enthusiastic about the film and about my visit.

I feigned more interest in the organisation than I felt and I suspected him of hoping for a sizable donation. Well, I thought, as I would need to follow up my experiment that may be just the route I could go down.

'I would be delighted to give you any information that you'd like about our work here, I do hope you can spare the time to visit us again,' he burbled, then looked a little more serious. 'Would you just excuse me, and Gabbi, I need to have a quiet word with her about...' he left it hanging in the air.

'Of course,' I said, and turned away as he drew Gabriella aside a moment. I could just make out a few words. 'Care.. terribly lost.. needs an anchor. Would you?' and his 'good, good.' as I am sure she answered his query with a 'yes'.

Half listening, I casually glanced towards Simon, I don't know what I was looking for, probably just glad to see he was still upright but I was suddenly overcome by a strange feeling of benevolence, I so wanted to cure and to help, there was not a trace of wanting power or exploitation in my feeling towards this man, and that was new to me.

Gabriella was by my side.

'Luke?' she said, her voice betraying that she'd already said it once.

'Oh, sorry, lost in thought.' I said and smiled down at her.

'There's someone they'd like me to talk to, a young lad, will you be okay for a bit on your own?'

'Sure,' I said, not really sure at all. She slipped away and I remained standing there.

'Oo are you then?' a voice like sandpaper addressed me coming from a shrunken guy with few teeth and sparse hair.

'Adamson, Luke,' I smiled and held out my hand as he sidled round to face me, his head held on one side like a curious bird. His face contorted as he tightened his lips and closed his eyes, but he relaxed and stuck out his hand to take mine in a brisk enough shake.

'Micky Cordy. Wot you in for?'

'In?'

'In 'ere?'

'Oh, visiting, with Mrs Johnston. Gabbi?'

'Oh? You wiv 'er, y'lucky sod!' and he leered.

'Not *with* her, I'm just visiting with her.'

'Oh,' and he shuffled off a little. 'Oh,' he said again, 'well are you coming or not? Play chess do yer?'

'I know how,' I said, having not played for years.

'Good enough to 'ave a flutter on the finish?'

'No, and I wouldn't gamble on it.'

'You'll do anyways. Come on.'

So I followed and found myself playing chess against a man who knew what he was doing on a chess board, and listening to him tell me how he used to be a bookkeeper. 'The end of everything was getting banged up for fraud, I was just borrowing to cover m' betting losses but I gets caught and jugged for fraud,' he said. 'You can't go back to bookkeeping when you got that on your back. There comes a day, when you'd even take up religion to get you a good roof over your head.' And he winked, a wink that screwed up his whole face.

Gambling, another addiction, and surely closely linked to greed, perhaps this character would have been a better first test; perhaps I could double my chances of results.

'Fancy a cup of tea or coffee?' I asked the victor.

'Sure, coffee, if you've got summat to put in it,' he winked again, again the facial contortions.

I grinned, 'With sugar then?'

'Ha!' he said, but nodded.

Okay, I said to myself, I can put something in it, and stirred in the second paper's contents and delivered the coffee to my new friend.

'Not 'aving any?' he asked.

'Afraid I'm not up to taking British coffee,' I smiled.

'Yankee nancy,' he said amiably as he blew the surface of his coffee and tried a tentative slurp. He lifted his head and looked beyond me, I turned and there was Gabriella standing a little way off talking to Bill and with her eye on me.

'Thanks for the game,' I said to my opponent and went to her side.

'Bill, I wonder, would you allow me to make a small donation to the fund, this has been a real eye-opener for me.'

'Now that's the sort of request I like to hear,' he said shaking my hand.

'I'll pop back tomorrow then to sort it out, if that's okay?'

'Absolutely, absolutely,' he beamed.

'You didn't have to do that,' Gabriella said, her eyes gleaming.

'I wanted to,' I said

She tugged on my arm and gave me a small kiss on my cheek. It felt wonderful.

The Angel Bug 17

Gabbi   27th October

I woke refreshed and feeling cosy in my bed, alone, thinking that I had made the right choice even though a tiny corner of my mind still suggested otherwise. Despite the cosiness and the obvious coolness of the day outside I got up quickly and breakfasted lightly. I arrived at Eden over half an hour early, fished the book out from behind Karen's desk and signed in, hoping to be alone for a while. I was in luck as, since that first morning, Sapphira had converted to arriving at nine along with everyone else. My plan had been to get any office work done and out of the way before nine so that I could be out and about in the pit rather than in the confines of the office for any longer than I had to be. Being away for the afternoon had highlighted the atmosphere that was beginning to pervade the Foundation building and I wanted to be away from it.

I got the computer going and checked my emails first. Quick scan, open, check and delete the mainly science-based sales pitches, new items from your usual suppliers, none of which should have been routed to me anymore, I thought, as I was no longer holding the fort for the senior botanist.

That left three; I quickly opened the first from Worldagroforestry.com hoping they had come across another reference to nodules on a Moringa or of its leaves turning red. No such luck, it was just an update telling me that there had been a paper presented last week on the green-fertilizer use of Moringa and its place in regeneration programmes in Afghanistan. Nothing new there, except in its proposed use as a government tool, for Moringa, unusual in the high nitrogen content of its leaves, has been used for centuries as a green-manure.

Deflated, I opened the second email, from a local freelance journalist. This was potentially more worrying, she obviously knew about the removal of the Moringa, but she suggested that there was more to it, that Eden was suffering from some kind of attack on its plants, even hinting that it might not be from a natural cause, that it might be deliberate, the latter just by saying, 'who knows what it could be, there are hundreds of people each day who have access to these living things'. I could see her headlines already forming in her mind.

This had to go straight to Publicity to deal with, and another copy to the senior botanist, I pressed send with an unusual feeling of 'so there' since a quieter removal of the Moringa may have caused less interest.

The last was *from* Sapphira herself. As soon as I opened it I wished I could suck back the email I had just forwarded to her. I was suspended, pending enquiries, for 'bringing Eden and the Eden trust into disrepute'. My heart was hammering; I felt so hot I knew I must be the colour of beetroot. This couldn't be right!

I heard a noise from the lower floor, glanced at the clock, just about halfpast eight, with any luck it would only be Karen. I knew I couldn't face anyone else. I turned off my computer, grabbed my coat and bag and headed downstairs. Karen's homely face broke into a smile, 'Oh, it's you Gabbi. Whatever's the matter?'

I could only shake my head; I knew that if I opened my mouth I'd howl.

I turned the book round and signed out. Karen looked at me, tried to hold me by placing her hand on my arm, 'Gabbi? What?' I shook my head and pulled away from her and out of the door. As I slammed the car into gear and drove off she was standing at the open door looking after me. I only just missed hitting Mikaela's Citroen 2CV.

I didn't go home; I felt too bereft. I drove towards the sea, to a cliff-top car park where I left the car and climbed the last few feet to the very edge, the sea a sparkle of hammered metal beneath, the sky a fierce white above. The wind blew through me, cooling and whipping away the tears that ran down my face.

What on earth could Sapphira have that she thought would stand up to scrutiny; did she know about the nodule I had passed on to Luke? I couldn't think of anything else that I had done that could result in suspension, and on top of that it had been unnecessary as he'd gone ahead and stolen the rest. It just didn't make sense despite her attitude and behaviour this accusation was something that had to stand up against investigation, not liking me wasn't enough.

I felt another wave of self-pity as I felt the loss of those good friends that had supported me over the past two years, I knew how easily even good work-friends drifted apart when work wasn't the common factor. My tears traced cold lines across my face and I brushed them away with the sleeve of my coat and turned my face away from the sea and the wind.

This was ridiculous, it couldn't be right, I'd never brought Eden into disrepute, nothing I had done or said reflected badly on Eden. Perhaps I'd misread it. I called the screen to mind, no, I hadn't misread it, there was no room for misinterpretation, I was suspended, subject to enquiries, no date by which these enquiries would be carried out, no further details. Well there was something, I would demand to know those details, and the grounds, and I would fight this. My heart beat faster as I felt my mood change from despair to defiance. There had been nothing stating that I had to get out and stay out until this 'enquiry' was over, so I would go back armed with my list and when she told me to go I would demand the answers before I left.

I pulled open the door of the car, stood there a moment, should I take representation with me? A friend? A solicitor? Shaking my head I climbed in and was soon reversing out of the car park and heading home.

Once home I fired up the computer and tapped out the questions as they came to me. Not much of a list. How had I brought Eden into disrepute? On what grounds were they suspending me? When would the enquiries take place? What rights of representation did I have? I stared at the list, there was only the nodule that was remotely possible, yet it was no more than I had sent off to various other bodies for testing and analysis. It had to be the fact that it was Luke, Sapphira was unhappy about his visit from the word go and the Moringa problem had only exacerbated matters.

My email pinged. I glanced at the box to see it was from Naomi and clicked to open it. I felt a wave of heat wash through me, as if I'd been caught in an embarrassing situation; they all knew about the suspension. Sapphira had told them and Karen had told them about my 'distress' going early this morning and was I alright as they were all worried about me. I was not answering my mobile, apparently. I took it out and looked, it was off, I'd not switched it on in my haste this morning.

What to say? Yes, I had been suspended, No, I had no real idea why, no idea what I had done to 'bring Eden into disrepute'. Yes, I was okay. Whatever that meant. I clicked send.

Now I had to go in and face that woman and get my answers. Before I left I went and washed my face and tidied my hair, I needed a boost so changed into something that I felt good wearing, then headed out to Eden, somehow my heart dragged along, and my usually pleasant route through the winding lanes felt like a tumbrel journey to the guillotine.

I put on a brave face for Karen, smiling and saying that it was okay, it just had to be a misunderstanding. She almost broke my composure as the kindliness in her face was so clear. Up the dreaded staircase and into the dragon's lair. Sapphira sat in her splendid isolation yet it didn't matter as not another soul was around.

'Sit,' she said as I drew near.
'I think there must be some misunderstanding,' I began.
'If you think that, then you are the one who has the misunderstanding, to us it is quite clear. You are suspended due to your aiding and abetting the removal of one or more nodules from Eden for whatever purpose, with no permission and without due care and respect for the principles, rights and ownership of Eden.'

'And what do you base this on?'

'The fact that there is a nodule missing from the accounted collection and that you were the only person who had access during the time in question, other than the one who reported it missing, Miss Jamesie. Of course, you are only suspended pending further enquires, unless you choose to resign to prevent any further… embarrassment?'

'No, I won't be doing that,' I said, while thinking, Naomi? Not Naomi, surely? And feeling sick and uneasy. 'I think you will find that the nodules are all in order, just some have been sent for analysis and other tests.'

She raised her eyebrows, 'Really, then at the very least your paperwork is as sloppy as your science. You are still suspended until enquires are made. Please ensure you remove any personal items, and only personal items, from your desk when you leave and do not return unless you are requested to do so.'

'Right,' I swallowed, 'when will these so called enquires be carried out? How long, when will I know?' I could feel the tension building in me, the temptation to give in and howl as I had earlier. I fought it down, I was not going to let this woman see me break.

'You'll receive a letter stating all these details, I can't possibly tell you at this stage, it has to go through our lawyers. So, you may clear your desk now, I will come with you.' She rose and I rose, and as steadily as I could I went over to my desk and removed from it a number of files and a few other odds and ends.

'What's in the files?'

'Oh, look if you must. This one is about St. Piran's, just kept it here for convenience as I usually go straight on from here, this is my collection of Eden cuttings,'

She flicked over a few pages then slammed them shut.

'Got everything?'

'I, I think so.'

'Then, goodbye, you will be hearing from us,' she turned on her spiky heels and headed back to her own desk. I gathered up my stuff and headed down the stairs and as I did so recognised Luke's voice in hushed conversation with Karen.

'Luke?' I said wondering why he was here, had he heard?

'Gabbi, what?' Luke seemed surprised at seeing me.

'Suspended, banned from Eden until investigations are complete.'

'But why on earth?'

'Seems I have aided and abetted the removal of nodules from Eden for a third party,' I searched his eyes for a clue.

'But that's ridiculous!'

'Yes? But what are *you* doing back here?'

'Taking me to lunch,' Sapphira's voice rang out from behind me, 'Are you ready Luke?'

A wave of nausea passed though me, I shook my head to clear the feeling and stepped out of Eden, perhaps for the last time.

The Angel Bug 18

Luke 27th October

The next day found me awake early anticipating the day. I had no idea what I might be walking into. Would I find the two men I had given the moringa juice to had been taken into hospital, or that there was no change at all? Could it be that I had become, overnight, a murderer? The latter thought held me in an icy grip for a moment before I reasoned that I had survived, and had not even been in danger as such, the falling over I had done being of more concern than the effect that had held me in a coma.

I am not sure what I hoped for but when I turned up at the hostel, armed with my cheque book, I had not expected everything to seem normal. But normal it seemed. I was greeted by Bill who showed me into a small and untidy office. He offered me a chair and sat cornerwise to the desk.

'And how is everyone this morning?' I asked as casually as I could as I extracted my cheque book from my pocket.

'Fine, this morning,' he smiled. 'I fear that a couple of our guests may have smuggled in some alcohol last night though, how, is another question altogether,' he paused. 'You weren't persuaded to give cash to either of the gentlemen you were talking to yesterday were you? I wouldn't blame you, they can be powerfully persuasive.'

'No! Not at all! Gabbi had warned me before I came,' I said hastily, thinking about the hospital and how they had assumed I was on drugs through my behaviour.

'Why? What happened?' I asked.

'They were completely sozzled last night, dancing jigs and singing, though quite unlikely dancing partners, don't usually have much time for each other. Then they sort of fell into a heap on a sofa and had to be carted off to bed.'

'Are they alright?'

'Fine. They're sleeping it off. Snoring fit to wake the dead.'

Would that have been the diagnosis if I'd just gone to bed and hadn't woken up on time?

'Oh. That's a shame; I mean I'd have liked to have another chat with them.'

He looked at me and must have made his mind up about something. 'Well, with Gabbi to vouch for you I see no problem with you coming along anytime you like, while you're over here,' he said and his smile changed to a broad grin as he read the amount I had written on the cheque. 'And thank you very much indeed Dr Adamson. Thank you very much indeed.'

'Well, you may see me tomorrow then,' I said. 'This place is on my way back to my hotel.'

'And you'll be most welcome, and by then we may have found out how they got hold of some drink and they'll be fit to talk to you again.'

I left St Piran's and headed towards Eden. I had woken with the idea that having the nodules was not enough, that it was important that I could have access to the actual tree that produced the nodules and though I'd only been at St Piran's half an hour or so the feeling had grown and now I had a sense of urgency about it. The only way I could see to achieve this was though Sapphira, so I wanted to talk to her again and see if I couldn't persuade her to let me work with Eden on this project.

The receptionist was quite nonplussed when I turned up at the door asking to see Sapphira but she did make me wait while she called up. I was rewarded by the lady herself sashaying down the stairs to meet me.

I could tell that I was going to have to use all my old skills to get back into this woman's good books as the look on her face was venomous.

'Dr Ananias, thank you so much for seeing me at short notice.'

She tilted her head as if she was some minor royalty deigning to notice me, 'Dr Adamson?'

'I realise we have not got off to a good start and I would like to talk with you to see what I can do to remedy this situation.'

'How we have got on is not the problem, Dr Adamson,' she said tartly, and I realised that she was frightened of me, or frightened of what I might say to the world at large.

'Well, you know that I would always have the reputation and standing of Eden high on my priorities, I am a real admirer of the concept that Tim has based this on and wouldn't do anything to damage it.'

Fast as a rattler strike she came back at me, 'Oh wouldn't you. Dr Adamson? Stealing samples from the Moringa tree, that sounds like something damaging, and what, pray, were you going to do with the samples? Prove that we have been negligent? Show up our care methods, inability to discern the problem, aided and abetted by that incompetent woman who calls herself a scientist.'

'Whoa!' I raised placatory hands. 'Obviously we have some seriously crossed wires here, I don't know anything about stolen samples, hey, can't we go,' I half glanced towards the receptionist, 'go somewhere quieter to discuss these matters you have raised?'

It was as if she had only just realised that there was someone else in the vicinity, she turned on her patent spiked heels. 'Yes,' she said over her shoulder. 'Come up.'

She swept round to her side of the desk and sat with a wave of her hand to indicate the chair on my side.

'Dr Ananias,' I started, 'I would be most grateful if you could see your way to allowing me to continue research on the Moringa here at Eden. I understand that you have had the tree removed, what happened to it?'

Sapphira smiled. 'I did not have it destroyed, if that's what you are thinking. I have had it taken to Watering Lane and re-planted there for study, pruned a bit, I understand, to fit, but nothing that the tree cannot and does not cope with in it usual environment.'

This was the best news that I could have expected,

'I'll sign anything you want to guarantee that I'll not sue nor charge for my time,' I said as I thought of the pair of suited creeps that had seen me off before. I suddenly thought of a new angle that might make the difference, 'In fact, this way any research I do will actually belong to Eden and if there was something new enough for a paper we could be co-authors on it.' I could detect a subtle change in her demeanour, that little bit of bait was obviously on the right lines.

'Belong to Eden, you say? Well that might be acceptable. Finding the time to put in to accomplish the research may be a little difficult with my full-time post here, but…'

'Oh, you wouldn't have to, I am sure that Gabbi wouldn't mind doing the work for both of you.' As soon as the words were out of my mouth I realised I'd said the wrong thing.

She drew herself up, 'I very much doubt it, and I certainly wouldn't put my reputation on work performed by that amateur, and I am surprised that you would.'

'Well, I understood she came recommended, to assist me.'

'Yes. No. Recall, Dr Adamson that I had only just taken up my post and had not had time to assess the members of staff. Things have now come to light that have changed my mind.'

It felt disloyal but I went ahead and said 'Come to that, I really don't need any assistants and I'd still put your name on it.'

'And why would you do that?'

'Because, Dr Ananias, Eden holds the only nodules I know of and the only tree that has produced them, without these then there is no research. '

Sapphira smiled. 'Alright. I'll have a contract drawn up, just as well you don't want Mrs Johnston as an assistant, she has been suspended from her duties.'

'When? Why?' the words betrayed me before I'd thought of what they revealed.

'Incompetence, bringing Eden into disrepute, it really doesn't matter. Does it matter to you, Dr Adamson?'

'No, not as such. Really I knew Mrs Johnston's husband, from a long time ago, that's all.' I wondered if Sapphira could smell the scent of excrement wafting through the room. 'Dr Ananias do you have time to talk about this research today?' I could see her hesitation, 'We could talk over lunch if that suited you better, I realise just how busy you are.'

'I am incredibly busy, but I suppose that I could work it in with a lunch break,' she turned her narrow wrist and looked at the slim rectangular chunk of glass fastened there. 'Yes, an early lunch, though I can only spare you an hour, two at the very most.'

'Thank you,' I said as graciously as I could, an obsequious duck of my head thrown in for effect. 'Where would you like to go?' fully expecting her to say The Link in Eden.

'Oh, I believe your hotel has a good reputation, that would be fine.'

'Okay, I'll give them a call, what time would suit you?' I had never asked so many minute questions about a lunch fixture but I knew that this woman needed to feel in total control of the situation before she'd open up, especially to me.

'Twelve thirty would be fine, I really do have a lot to do this afternoon and that would give me an hour to tie up a few loose ends before we leave.'

'Fine, I'll arrange that and be back here to collect you at twelve?' She inclined her head again, 'That will be suitable,' she said with a small nod and turned her face down towards her desk. I felt, as I knew I was meant to feel, dismissed. I stood and murmured, 'Until twelve then,' and left. I looked across to the group of desks where I knew the rest of the team usually worked. It was empty.

Downstairs I was met by the enquiring look from the receptionist. 'Hi? Karen, isn't it,' I said as the name Gabriella had told me filtered in. She smiled and nodded. 'Has Gabriella been in today, I'd hoped to…' She didn't let me finish, she nodded and hissed, 'Yes, and she left, terribly upset, I had no idea what it was, not then, I asked, but she just ran out of the building. I told the others and I think they're looking for her.'

'Really? Why would they go looking?'

'They said *she*,' her eyes rolled upwards, 'has suspended Gabbi, they are worried about her, she's not answering her phone.'

'Why that's terrible, whatever for?' I whispered back.

'For?'

'What did she get suspended for?'

'Bringing Eden into disrepute, and that's something Gabbi would never do. Never!'

'No, I agree, tell her that, if you do see her, tell her that I believe in her.' I could see it was the right thing to say to this little lady but it was also the absolute truth.

I stepped out of the building and phoned the hotel, there was no problem with getting an early lunch reservation. I looked at my watch, nearly an hour, I walked over to the car and turned it towards St Piran's, I had no idea what excuse I was going to use but I just needed to know how the two old hobos were doing. After driving for a couple of minutes I had a thought and I pulled into the side of the road. I took out my phone and the leaflet that Gabriella had given me about the place and dialled the number, this was much easier. Cheery Bill answered, I recognised him at once, 'Hey, Bill, it's Luke Adamson, I was just wondering how my two friends from yesterday are now, woken up yet?'

He laughed, 'No, they've not, gave them a little shake not ten minutes ago but they are deep in sleep, if they weren't snoring so badly I'd be worried.'

'Ah well, snoring, a good sign eh?' I said hoping to encourage him in his belief, I really didn't want them hauled off to hospital.

'Thanks, somehow I really took to those old guys.' I said sounding bemused and friendly as I could

'Real characters,' agreed Bill, 'No problem, ask anytime.'

'Thanks, I may do that, bye.'

I was back at the Foundation building in plenty of time for my rendezvous. Karen leapt up as I stepped into the building.

'Gabbi's back, she's okay,' she whispered beaming, then her face fell. 'She's up there now, talking to *her*.'

'Oh right, should I not go up? Or should I?' I genuinely didn't know what to do, unusual for me. If I had to back Gabriella I would, but it would ruin the plans I had for Sapphira and Eden.

'Oh I don't know, I'd have to call up anyway before you went up.' Karen said looking worried.

'Luke?' Gabriella's voice sounding puzzled, I turned and there she was descending, her arms full of folders and bits and pieces.

'Gabriella, what?' I said, flicking a glance beyond her to check that Sapphira was not following on her heels.

'Suspended, banned from Eden until investigations are complete.'

'But why on earth?'

Gabriella looked at me hard then widening her beautiful eyes said. 'Seems I have aided and abetted the removal of nodules from Eden for a third party.'

'But that's ridiculous!'

She just looked at me for a moment, 'But what are *you* doing back here?'

'Taking me to lunch.' Sapphira said as she sauntered down the stairs behind Gabbi, 'Are you ready, Luke?'

Gabriella's face froze, she gave her head a slight shake as she closed her eyes and stepped past me, then out of the building, I felt like shit, which made a change from smelling it.

'We really don't have time to stand about,' Sapphira said into my ear as she reached me while I was still gazing after Gabriella wondering what I could have said to change things.

'You're right, let's go,' I said in a cheerful way. 'Your carriage awaits.'

The Angel Bug 19

Gabbi 27th October

I flung the stuff I was carrying in the back seat and drove off in a squeal of tyres. I told myself firmly to calm down and drive carefully as I turned out on to the main road, yet my foot kept pulsing with my heartbeat driving the speed higher and higher. I missed my home turning, not concentrating, not really even thinking about the driving, just feeling the motion and putting space between his treacherous face and mine.

Seeing a sign for the Polgooth turning I suddenly thought of St Piran's and just in time swept off the main road towards the small village. If Bill was surprised to see me he didn't show it.

'Hi Gabbi, how nice, cuppa?' were his first words, friendly, kind, I felt myself dissolve.

'Oh Bill, yes please,'

'Why whatever's the matter dear?' he said shepherding me to his office instead of a chair in the lounge. I shook my head and waved my hand a bit, unable to unstick the words without crying and determined not to do that.

'I'll get the tea,' he said, disappearing. I was grateful for that; it gave me time to pull myself together.

'I thought I'd pop in to say that I can give you a lot more time at St. Piran's for a while,' I said when he came back, two steaming mugs of tea in his hands.

He looked at me and nodded, 'Most welcome, most,' he said, 'but your work?'

I gulped hard, squeezed the ache down my throat, I searched for a word to replace the insinuation-laden word 'suspended'. 'Temporarily on leave,' I gave what even I felt to be a weak smile. 'Just until something can be sorted out – new management ideas and stuff.'

Bill smiled, 'Well, it's our good fortune and very opportune to see you today, I would say, very.'

I looked at him.

'Not only got that young lad you were going to work with but also a bit of a quandary, yes.'

'Quandary?'

'Simon and, er, and Micky,' he glanced up to make eye contact, be sure I knew who we were talking about. I nodded. 'Both of them seemed to get drunk last night, dancing and joking about together.' I felt my eyebrows raise.

'Quite, quite, not usually a pair one would say.'

No, not at all, I knew Simon found Micky to be a bit 'coarse' as a character and despite their common circumstances they did not have much time for each other, with Micky considering Simon to ''av a poker up 'is arse' as he eloquently put it to me one day.

'So, and there's no telling where or how they got any drink, we never did find any evidence, but after the dancing and singing they both fell asleep on the sofas and we carted them off to their beds, where they have remained.'

'Still?'

'Still, snoring fit to raise the dead, but quite out to the world. Tried shaking them, but nothing doing, and now I'm beginning to get a bit concerned but I don't really know why, it seems odd that's all, never had a drunk sleep quite so long or so deeply. I'm thinking I ought to call the doctor to give them a check over – what do you think?'

'Oh? I really don't know, perhaps we could look in on them?'

The sound of snoring was noticeable from outside the bedroom cubicles, two tones as if even in sleep Simon endeavoured to have a softer more refined snore. I noticed that they had been placed in the recovery position so it wasn't a restricted airway that caused the noise. I squatted down and looked into Simon's face, shaking his shoulder gently, speaking his name. His eyes remained closed and the steady snore continued, but as his snore grumbled out I noticed no smell of alcohol about him, none at all, just the usual staleness of sleep.

'I can't smell any alcohol on him?'

'Hmm?'

I stood and stepped though to Micky. Here the rasping snore rattled the windowpanes, but when I squatted down to be level with his face, forcing myself to actually smell, again there was no alcohol smell, just a different stale breath.

'Nor Micky, what could they have drunk that leaves no alcohol smell?'

'Vodka perhaps?' he said but I could tell he really didn't think so – as the liquid might have little scent or flavour but the power of it carried an effect of its own.

'I reached out tentatively and lifted one of Micky's eyelids. His eye was rolled up, almost hidden in his skull – I let the lid drop quickly. I returned to Simon and tried the same, with the same result. I felt his pulse, slow and steady, tried shaking him again; watching closely, no flicker of eyelid, nothing.

'It couldn't have been drugs, could it?' I asked.

Bill looked at me his eyes widening. 'No, at least I wouldn't have thought so, not them. Others maybe, but not, not Simon for sure.' I nodded, I really didn't see Simon taking that route, 'Nor Micky really.' Again I nodded.

'I really don't think I can help you decide Bill, but they don't seem to be ill as such, perhaps give it another few hours and see?' He smiled. 'That's what I was thinking. Let them sleep it off but keep an eye on them.'

I felt he was humouring me, finding something for me to help with, that he had decided already really, but I was grateful as it took my mind off my own problems effectively.

'So, as you are here would you like to see young Kieran?'

'Yes, I'll do that, if he wants to see me, that is.'

Bill smiled. 'I'll just pop along and see how he's doing.'

Bill reappeared with Kieran in tow, 'We were wondering if you would take our Kieran out to do a little shopping, for us and for him.' Bill said as they arrived at the office. 'We need a few bits from town, I was going to get them myself later, and Kieran here needs to get a few items of clothing.'

'Absolutely!' I said, feeling a positive surge.

Bill gave me a list and some money, the list was for foodstuffs and an added note that from the money I had been given Kieran had £50 to buy some clothes, particularly socks and pants, a couple of tee-shirts, a jumper and a pair of jeans.

'Tall order, all that from fifty quid I know' Bill whispered to me as we walked out to my car, 'but I'm sure you'll do your best,' he sighed. 'The youngsters don't seem to understand hand-me-downs like the old'uns. Despite being here they expect everything new and given, like a birthright.'

Kieran folded himself into the passenger seat of my Mini and I headed straight out towards Truro.

'So how's it going?' I asked

'Okay.'

'Do you have any real objection to shopping at Matalan?'

I caught the merest shrug from beside me.

'It's just that we'll get the best chance of finding all you need for the money we've got to spend there.'

'Sure.'

'Okay.'

We drove a while in silence, while I tried to think of a topic of conversation I could engage Kieran in.

'Why d'you do this?' Kieran suddenly asked.

'Do what?'

'Do this stuff, at the hostel, Bill says you just do it for free like.'

'Yes,' I said slowly, trying to think through where he was coming from, why he was asking, 'I guess it's to give something back.'

'Give something back?' he echoed.

'Um, yes sort of.'

'So, were you in there sometime?'

'No,' I said suppressing the small disparaging laugh that would normally go with such a denial. 'No, but I realise that any one of us could be there at some time in our lives, when things just go badly wrong.'

'Like the old soaks that were roaring it up last night?'

'Simon and Micky, yes, have you talked to them at all?' Knowing the answer from the way he talked about them and the sneer I felt him form as I said the words.

'No, why would I?'

'Well, Simon used to be a solicitor, before everything went wrong for him.' I could sense the disbelief. 'I'm sure he wouldn't mind me telling you that, and that it was his wife leaving him that made him turn to drinking and that which led to him losing his home and everything he had, leaving him to wander the streets until he found St Piran's as a refuge.'

He was silent for a while as the countryside unreeled beside us.

'And the other one, he was never a solicitor!'

'No, but he was a bookkeeper, not quite an accountant but a responsible line of work.'

'And?'

'And he was very good with numbers, thought he could beat the odds, developed a gambling habit – addiction even, and for him that was his downfall, fiddled the books he was dealing with to skim off money to gamble and then got done for fraud. Nothing left for him when he came out – he only knew bookkeeping and no one is going to take you on in that role with a sentence for fraud behind you, are they?'

'Guess not.'

He was silent again.

'Well, I'm not like them,' he muttered. 'Never got the break in the first place, never had a bloody chance anyhow.'

I remained silent, not saying that he had every chance education offered as I still knew so little about him, other than he'd washed up at St.Piran's because the police had found him sleeping rough so many times and, as he was over eighteen, social services had washed their hands of him.

''n if I had, if I'd been a bloody solicitor I'd not have chucked it away, that's for effing sure!'

'So, Kieran, what do you want to be?'

He looked at me as if I'd asked him a rude question; I glanced quickly at him and returned my eyes to the road.

'Shit knows,' he muttered.

'Well, what are you good at? What do you like doing?' letting the silence hang, letting him think through the answer. He still hadn't answered when we pulled into a car park and decanted ourselves into Matalan.

Luck was with us, seven pairs of socks for a fiver, three pairs of boxers; a fiver with a buy-one-get-one-free offer making it six pairs, two tee-shirts; a fiver; leaving a healthy thirty five pounds for a 'jumper' and jeans. The jumper became a sweatshirt with a logo across the front – with me dissuading him from a hoodie as such – the jeans, just a nondescript pair that he said were okay, so I threw in three pounds to the remaining two quid for another pair of tee-shirts. The bags felt reassuringly full.

We'd bought all the items on Bill's list and a Snickers bar for each of us and were on our way home when Kieran began talking. 'You knows, I grew up in Camborne?' Rhetorical question, it was one of the few things I did know about him. 'Cornwall, innit, but not nice Cornwall like the 'oliday places, bloody great estate we were on. D' y' know? Well, my brothers an' me we used to get up to all sorts, all the time. Got Mum in hell of trouble. Got us asbo's – fat lot of good that did. Anyways, one time we were given this holiday, Mum, me and my brothers, in like a 'oliday cottage on a farm. They 'ated it. What the hell do you do on a farm? Jus' roam around, nothing to do, nothing to see. Well, we all said it were shit.'

He was silent again.

' 'cept it weren't. This farmer was okay, if he seed you about he'd say 'want something to do?' and we'd usually say fack off and mooch back to the 'ouse. One day I was on me own so I says 'what like?' and he says, well you could come with me to see to the hens.'

Kieran shifted in his seat. 'So we went along to this bloody big shed and in it were loads of chickens, all running around when they saw us, some dashing out the little holes all along the sides, others squawking and fussing over in the boxes. We went along and he says we got to check all the drinkers were clear and clean, fresh water getting into all of them, then the feeders were the same, then we could collect the eggs.' I could feel him smile. 'I was shit scared that one of those chickens was going to peck me! Imagine, scared. And the farmer shows me how to slide my hand under a sitting chicken and gently pull out those warm eggs. One nest had four eggs in it, all beautiful and clean and neat. For the rest of our fortnight there I'd slip away from the others and go and help with the hens, never did tell them mind.'

He was silent for a moment. 'So, I never told anyone before coz they'd all laugh anyhow, but I wouldn't mind doing that, being a chicken farmer,' he said softly.

'Told no one? Not even at school, careers teacher perhaps?'

'Never saw him, weren't there often enough. Skived off – couldn't stand being indoors all the effing time.'

'Well, not too late, there must be apprenticeships or training for farming, at least starting off working on farms,' I said, wondering how this was done, was it only farming lads and lasses that were taken on? I promised myself that I'd find out as soon as I could. He shrugged and we turned down the lane leading back to St. Piran's.

Bill seemed pleased to see us back and with a good haul for the money, 'Have to send you out again Mrs Johnston,' he beamed as Kieran took his new clothes away to his area.

'And it was good to be able to chat really informally with Kieran,' I said. 'I think he found it easier with me driving and almost just listening in, you know?'

'Now that's interesting.'

'And he does have a grain of ambition that might help us, he's had a bit of experience at a chicken farm, egg production one that is, and he really liked it – would like to do something in that line, something towards running one of his own some day perhaps.'

'Really?'

'So, do you know of anywhere that takes on youngsters for work experience on farms, or training?'

'I might do at that, leave it with me and I shall see what we can come up with. You're sure?'

'Pretty well, came quite unexpectedly from him.'

'Good, good, now would you like a cup of tea?'

'Gasping!' I grinned at him, feeling so much happier than I had before I'd turned up on his doorstep.

Micky and Simon had still not woken when I left. We both looked at them, both spoke to them, gave them light shakes, but nothing seemed to wake them. Bill stood there pulling at one earlobe and puffing a tuneless rhythm through his lips.

'No, I'll risk leaving it until tomorrow,' he said with finality about it. 'They just seem asleep to me, deeply asleep. I'll call the quack tomorrow if they aren't up and about by breakfast.'

I drove home sedately, thinking about Kieran and perfectly clean warm eggs filling nests, filling egg boxes. I was really hungry and so ready for a quiet night. What I really needed was a good film that I could get involved with, a large glass of red and a quick filling meal. What I found when I got in destroyed all that carefully planned scenario.

The Angel Bug 20

Luke 27th October

The small round table overlooked the sea and we sat slightly turned in that direction yet opposite each other, looking for all the world like a couple out to lunch or on an assignation.

Sapphira sat tall and haughty and picked just about the most expensive items on the menu, not that it bothered me, I wanted to be in her good books.

'So, why the lunch then, Dr Adamson?'

'Luke, please, Luke,' I smiled. 'Lunch because I feel we got off to a bad start, I had no idea that you were new to the post, that you were not being supported as well as you might have been,' she inclined her head, 'and that you were so worried about what I might say or do to harm Eden or your reputation. And because it is a pleasure to share lunch with you.' I half expected the stench to fill my nostrils, it was just such a line as I would use as an opener to the bedroom scene, but none came and perhaps this was because, now, I had no wish to nail this woman, desirable as she appeared.

'Come now, can we get to some kind of agreement? I get to work on the Moringa nodules and the tree and Eden gets second billing for any research work that comes out of it? A deal?'

'Actually, Luke, didn't you say that both Eden and myself would feature?'

'Yes, of course, both.'

'And perhaps that should be 'in association with Dr Luke Adamson',' she smiled sweetly, pushing the posts back further.

What the hell? 'Yes - that's okay, it really doesn't matter to me, Eden and yourself – in association with, yeah okay.'

'That sounds better. Now what assistance can we give you? Our lab facilities …'

'Are crap,' I finished for her. 'I have my own, no, I just want the access to the tree.'

'I really feel I have to insist that a member of the Eden staff accompany you throughout all your experiments and especially when you are accessing the tree.'

'Why for heaven's sake?'

'Why, to ensure that you do not take any … liberties with Eden's good name or make any untrue claims for your findings?'

'What are you talking about, what reason would I have to make untrue claims?'

'I have no idea Dr Adamson, only that you told me yourself that you thought it might be the nodules that caused your coma.'

'And what if it did? I am not pursuing any legal redress, I've said I'll sign anything to prove I won't.'

'I am very intrigued as to why you would do that? Why would you sign away all your rights to compensation? Why would you happily allow other people's names on to your research at your own cost? This doesn't sound like the man that I have heard about in academic circles.'

I looked at this woman, unable to see the hand she was playing. 'To start with it was made quite clear by Mrs Johnston that it was through my own fault that I became contaminated, despite her reminding me to wear protective gloves, so I feel I have no loss there, and, as I see it, there was no real harm done, coma for three days and now fit as a fiddle,' I drew breath. 'As for the other thing, perhaps this is just a fancy of mine – I can afford to have fancies and follow them up – the movie has done that for me.'

She just sat there looking at me over her sole bonne femme á la maison.

'Look, I don't know what game you are playing, or what you want of me, but if I have to have someone tagging along then okay, sure,' I gave in.

The gleam in her eye told me I had acquiesced too easily.

'Not that I'm happy about it,' I added. 'Do I get to choose which member of your staff I work with?'

She flashed her eyes at me. 'No, Dr Adamson, I choose,' she said. 'When he can be spared I will send along Mr Peters.' She must have seen that I didn't recognise the name and added, 'Our plant pathologist.'

Then I did – the bear. 'Really, he has time?' I said, thinking there could not be a man more antagonistic to me in Eden.

'I will make time for him, and when I can't, it will be Jim Borlase.'

'Who is?'

'Our chief horticulturalist.'

'Huh! And a fat lot he'd know about my research.'

She smiled. 'That's not the point, as you well know, Luke.'

   The food that looked and smelt so good seemed tasteless as I swallowed this information. She was going to interfere as much as she could, cause as many problems as she could, yet wanted all the glory, should there be any, for herself. It really didn't make a lot of sense and I felt myself growing angry.

'I don't understand you? You want your name on the research but don't want me to succeed in any research.'

'No. You have that wrong, I don't want you to waltz off with the real results, the ones that matter, while putting a set of simplistic results under our name.'

'Why would you think I would do that?'

'Therese Manilaut,' she said, her black eyes fastened on mine.

I sat frozen. Therese was an excellent young, beautiful, sexy ecologist. Yes we had met, yes we had fucked, and yes we had put our joint names to a paper on 'lichens and man'. She did accuse me of taking one of her ideas and turning that into a new piece of research, nothing proved of course as I had actually done all that research alone.

'You know Therese?'

'Extremely well,' she settled back as the waiter brought our desserts. 'I am god-mother to her daughter.'

'She has a daughter now?'

'Oh yes, about four years old.'

'Four?' When was it I last saw Therese? Far more than four years ago I was sure. 'That figures, haven't seen her for at least that long'

'No,' Sapphira said, leaning forward to slice her spoon through the crisp surface of the crème caramel.

'No, wait a minute, she didn't suggest this daughter was mine?'

'She didn't.'

'She didn't. So what the hell are you dragging this up for.'

'You asked how I knew Therese. And Therese warned me that if there was anything good to come out of the research I was to watch you like a hawk.'

'This is ridiculous, you would jeopardise the research just on the say so of a girl.'

'An excellent scientist, who has had dealings with you before. Yes.'

I stared at her.

'Coffee sir, madam?' the waiter said suddenly at my elbow.

'Please, black,' Sapphira said and as I gave my order she excused herself from the table.

Therese Maniluat! I remembered something else about Therese, she had a vindictive streak. I couldn't have anyone looking over my shoulder all the time it was impossible for what I had in mind. What I had in mind would never be published, if it worked it would be far too dangerous for that. I needed Sapphira to leave me alone with my research, or even better, to be on my side. The coffee came, and the answer was before me, no time to think things through, no time for anything except to stir the contents of one of the folded papers into Sapphira's coffee. She returned to the dining room as I set the spoon down and arrived back at the table while the coffee was still turning slightly in the cup.

I almost stopped her drinking it, having now taken a moment to think what might happen next, but it was too late as she brought the cup to her lips. The old guys were snoring their heads off at St. Piran's, they didn't seem to have come to permanent harm, but they'd been crazy before they fell asleep, what would I do with a crazy Sapphira. I thought quickly, if the effect followed the usual pattern, if two exposures could be called usual, then she would probably be fine for a few hours, then after a few more manic hours would fall asleep. How could I manage her behaviour, make sure she was safe but out of the way, where no one would wonder at her sudden malaise, especially anyone who could put two and two together with my previous condition and my presence.

If the old guys were anything to judge then I had about four or five hours before she went crazy. There was no way she wouldn't be going back to Eden, so I had to arrange to meet her after she finished, perhaps even a little earlier so that I could be sure she was with me and safe before the manic stage set in.

Sapphira put down her cup of coffee, and consulted her watch. 'Well, really now we must get back to Eden, I have a busy schedule.'

'Of course,' I said calling for the tab, signing it to go on my bill. 'Of course, and it was good of you to find the time to talk to me, and I am sure we will do well out of this, you and me.'

'Quite probably,' she smiled, 'now we both know exactly where we stand and I have my contingency plans in place'

'Well, Sapphira,' I said standing, ceremoniously lifting her chair slightly for her to stand, oh so the gentleman. 'Would you like to look at the research I have been doing so far?'

She looked at me, her head tilted a little, eyebrows raised. 'Well, well, you have been busy.'

'Most certainly, I can show you straight after you finish at Eden this evening it you like,' I paused, glanced at my watch. 'Well, perhaps you'd have to take the last half hour or so off otherwise the facility will have closed by the time we get there.'

I tried to look nonchalant, but inside I was tight, this had better work.

'Half an hour?'

'Or so, the labs are about twenty minutes away from Eden, so I guess I'll really need you from about four?'

She looked at her watch again and I could sense that she was going to refuse me. 'Sapphira,' I said, using the tone that I usually reserved for the pre-seduction phase, 'Sapphira?' She looked at me again. Slowly, looking deep into her eyes. 'It will be really good for you to see this research now, you'll be able to say with all honesty that you were in on it from the very beginning, with me.'

She blinked, and I knew I had her.

'From four?' she said. 'All right, I think I can re-schedule things to be available for you from four.'

And I was not sure what she meant either, but I knew then that I would have her away from Eden and in my care by the time she went ape, and that was what really mattered. Now I had to think of what I would do with her after that.

I dropped her back at Eden and drove off back to the hotel, grabbed a quick shower, changed into fresh jeans and shirt and lay down on the bed. What the hell was I going to do with Sapphira, not only while she went mad but afterwards, for the two or three days when she would be out of it. I thought of booking her into the hotel, but soon realised that even if I used a 'do not disturb' sign there was a possibility that she might wake when I was not there and cause a disturbance. And I couldn't sit with her the whole time; I needed to carry on with the research. There had to be someone who was able to help me, someone who could spend time that I could not.

There was only Gabriella, dear sweet Gabriella, suspended from work at Eden, Gabriella. She had the time; she understood the need for research. I reasoned, forgetting that I had not quite confided in her the full extent of the research or what I thought had happened to me, what I thought would be possible if I could find a safe level, an effective level of inoculation that would make people unable to be greedy, whatever form that passion took in them, perhaps an end to so many of the world's most destructive behaviours. I called her number, only to be put straight through to her voicemail. Damn! I tried again, this time her home number and listened to the ringing in her empty house.

By the time I had to leave for Eden I had left three blank messages, two pleading with Gabriella to 'get back to me as soon as she got this message, whatever' and had let the phone ring in her house half a dozen times each until it was cut off by the phone company with a saccharine, 'Please try later'. I had briefly contemplated keeping Sapphira at the Lab, taking her back there using my own keys and codes after I expected everyone else to be gone, the security and the secrecy levels there were tempting, but almost all the lab was visible from the glass panel in the door and besides I was concerned that she might be seen on some security cameras I was unaware of and her non-reappearance be noted and followed-up without me even knowing. Privacy had only been guaranteed for the actual research I was doing, not for myself. So I booked a twin room in Gabriella's name, ready for Sapphira, requesting one next to my own and being lucky enough to get that at least. My plan was that Gabriella would 'baby sit' Sapphira while I got on with the experiments, making sure that even if she awoke unexpectedly Gabriella could call me. All I had to do was get Sapphira into my room at the hotel and I could think of only one way I might to do that.

I waited outside Eden for a few moments, wondering whether to go in and 'collect' her or whether she would rather not draw attention to the fact we were going out together yet again. In my book either option had its advantages and disadvantages, I could see that I could spin a story either way gossip took it. Ten past four, time was pressing I got out and walked into reception when I saw her hurrying down the stairs. She smiled briefly and snapped 'Book?' at Karen who had been looking at me and had not turned the signing-in book round ready for Sapphira. Blushing Karen fumbled the book round and tried to proffer the pen, it flipped from Sapphira's hand as she took it and flew, clattering down somewhere behind the desk. Muttering 'sorry sorry' Karen ducked down to retrieve it and as she did so Sapphira mouthed, 'Go! GO!' at me, so by the time Karen bobbed up the door would have been closing behind me and

Sapphira berating her for her slowness would be taking her mind off my absence.

I held the car door for her to get in then scooted round and settled myself quickly in the driver's seat. There was no way that the potion had taken effect yet, this woman was still in command of all her faculties and her reaction to being seen with me again was promising, creating an illicit feel to our relationship already. I set the car on the road to the labs, I would have to take her there, explain, show her what I was doing and watch and wait. Timing was everything, I didn't want her to become manic at the lab and I had to get her to come quietly to the hotel, either a manic or a comatose woman would cause problems for me.

I introduced Dr Ananias to the receptionist and we were buzzed in. She looked surprised by the range of labs we passed but did not say anything until we entered my lab.

'You got this set up very quickly. Had someone told you that you were going to find something at Eden before you arrived?'

'No, not at all, to be honest there was a moment when I may not have even come. This place, well it exists and my contacts were able to put me in touch.'

I led her to the incubator, indicated a lab stool for her to sit on. 'Here are the samples that I have been incubating, waiting to see if there is any growth into the agar plates.'

'Yes, I can see, but what is your hypothesis, why are you interested at all?'

Not the question I wanted to answer at this point, perhaps not a question I ever wanted to answer when it came from her.

'If I can show that the nodules do continue to grow when not attached to the Moringa then it will give me an indication of the type of growth we are dealing with here, parasitic or symbiotic.'

'Your hypothesis?'

'My hypothesis…' I hesitated, I turned again and slipped out a microscope slide, fiddled with it a bit and placed it under the lens, gave it a twist to focus it and turning to her indicated with a tip of my head and a smile that she should come and look. She roused herself from the stool and came to where I stood, raised her eyebrows at me then bent to look though the microscope.

'What?' she snapped. 'What exactly am I supposed to be looking for?'

I leant one arm on the bench beside her, pressed my body gently against her, spoke through her hair softly to her ear. 'Whatever you want. I'll make it be there for you.'

It was hell of a risk, she went still but did not shrink back nor push me away. Still looking through the lens she spoke. 'I think you'll have to show me clearer than that.'

I slid my hand softly down her spine, resting the heel in the small of her back my fingers caressing the cleft of her buttocks. I heard, perhaps only felt, her intake of breath. She straightened and turned in the circle of my arm, our faces so close we breathed the same air. I did my classic, stolen from old movies it usually worked, brought my other hand up to gently cradle her jawline, caressing, my forefinger touching her earlobe, I felt the gentle pressure of her responding to me, slid my hand round the nape of her neck and brought her in to the kiss.

It was as I imagined it would be, demanding and hard, yet though my body responded I was quite taken up with the realisation that there was no stench filtering its way to me, wondered if my hypothesis was already in tatters. Here I was determined to get this woman away from the lab and quietly into the hotel, by deceit if necessary and I was not being put off in any way.

She began to giggle, not the most rewarding response from a kiss that I have ever had. I held her gently away from me and looked into her eyes. She shook her head and another stream of giggling ensued.

'What is it?' I asked. 'You are denting my ego.' I smiled at her, somehow it was not easy to be angry with this silly sound coming from her.

'Nothing, nothing,' she put a hand to her chest, and the giggling continued. 'Nothing, nothing.'

Then it hit me, I had been expecting some signal that the manic stage was starting, some kind of withdrawal from reality, and then I was expecting dancing or singing, or whirling round, or something else, giggling hadn't been described, but here must be the onset of the manic stage.

'Do you want to go?' I asked.

'Go? Stay, whatever, what … ever,' she tilted her head as if listening to her own words. 'Wha at eeh ver' she said, splitting the word into separate parts, making it a whole phrase. 'Wha attt eeh vv errrr,' and giggles threatening to overrun into something more raucous.

'Right, we will go, back to my hotel I think, do you, would you like to come with me?'

I was escorting her out of the room now, turning to set the alarm, leaving everything as it was, untidy and unpacked.

She grabbed me halfway down the corridor, forced me to look at her. 'With … You?' her face alive with laughter.

'Yes,' I said pulling her along, desperate to get out of the building. I posted her into the car seat and clipped her in, but by the time I had got round to my side she had flung open the door and was trying to get out without releasing her seat belt. I leant across and pulled the door shut. She grabbed my hair and forced my face into her lap.

'Naughty, naughty!' she squealed and set off into peals of laughter, releasing my hair as she did so. I drove quickly away from that place, trying to think through the crackling of laughter now filling the car, emphasising every twist and turn in the road as she swung deliberately from side to side in hysterics.

There was no way that I could take Sapphira in this state into the hotel. There was nothing for it; I headed for Gabriella's.

I pulled up outside her small house. Her car wasn't there. Damn, still out. Thank goodness it was an isolated place, as one look at Sapphira laughing manically in the passenger seat would have brought questions from anyone.

Perhaps I could get in; perhaps she'd left a window ajar or something.

'Stay here!' I said to Sapphira.

She grasped my arm, her fingernails digging in. 'Stay here, without you?'

'For a moment, just,' I tried to wrench my arm away.

She found this hilarious, clamped her other arm right round my arm. 'Never! never!'

'Please, Sapphira, I …' I looked into her eyes. 'I need to get the place ready for you, for you and me.'

'You and me?' she said, she pulled me close kissing me again, I kissed her back and the grip was released and the giggling resumed.

I slipped quickly from the car and only just pressed the lock button on the key quickly enough to stop her trying to open the door. How long before she figured out how to open the door I didn't know, it wasn't hard but she definitely wasn't in her right mind; that was for sure.

A quick scan of the front told me there were no opportunities to get in there; and even the back was done up tight. There was no choice, I picked up a rock from the edge of the garden, took off my jacket and wrapped it round my hand then, rock in wrapped hand, smashed the glass in the back door. Fat lot of good it did me. The door was locked and she had not left a key in the back of it. I looked round, the kitchen window looked easiest, I smashed that too, and this time was in luck as Gabriella hadn't pressed in the little button that locked it tight. I opened it up and heaved myself in. The front door was on a Yale lock and I opened it up quickly, locking it open, and ran out to the car to fetch Sapphira in.

Easier said than done, as by the time I got back to the car Sapphira had not spent the time trying to get out of the car but trying to get undressed, without removing the seat belt, she seemed to be tied in by jacket and blouse half taken off half trapped by the belt. Reaching across to unclip her meant that she had the chance to force me against her again, this time with loads of groaning followed by peals of laughter that sounded like mockery.

I extricated her from the car, pulling her blouse round her, and bundled her to the house and in, dropping the latch to lock the door behind us. Freed from my grasp she now whirled away from me, removing her blouse as she did so, stumbling into the lounge while she tried to unclip her bra. I followed.

'Sapphira, don't do that!' I pleaded. I really didn't want to cope with her half naked.

'Yes,' she said. 'You promised me, yes!' she managed the clip and her full breasts fell loose as she flung the bra away, now wrestling with her skirt clip, she slipped the skirt down and tripped, I leapt to catch her before she fell, last thing I wanted was her injured. I managed to get my arms around her but toppled back myself as the force of her sudden dead weight unbalanced me.

The Angel Bug 21

Gabbi 27th October

There, in front of my house, was a car, the passenger door hanging open, and it looked like the car Luke had hired. I pulled up behind it, clambered out quickly, but went towards it cautiously. As I came up to the open door I noticed something hanging half out of it. It looked like a woman's jacket, dark blue with scarlet lining. I glanced round, then picked it up and notice the distinctive perfume favoured by Sapphira. I looked up and around again, completely puzzled, all was quiet.

I left everything in my car, buzzed it locked and went to my own front door. I was half aware of a sound as I turned the key in the latch, but though quiet as I opened it I knew immediately that there was someone inside the house.

'Luke?' I called experimentally, though baffled as to how he could be in there, hoping I was right and had not come across a burglary in progress, and if I had that they would scarper out the way they had come in.

'I'm home,' I called, hoping to drive them out.

'Gabriella, in here,' Luke's voice; from the lounge. I threw the front door closed behind me and hurried to the lounge. Luke lay on the floor, between the end of the coffee table and the sideboard, his feet hidden behind the end of the sofa and most of the rest of him hidden by Sapphira's semi-naked body. I gawped. I know I did, stood there, mouth open, while questions and rage fought for control. As I did, he struggled to push her off him, but I could see he was trying to do this and still hold her head to stop it hitting the coffee table or the legs of the sideboard.

'What the?' I found myself saying. 'What?'

'Help me, support her head.'

I stepped over and did as he asked, as he wriggled out from beneath her.

179

'Luke? What the fucking hell are you doing Here with Her like This, in My House!' I knew I was shouting. Rage had burst through, bringing with it words I rarely even thought, let alone used. Between us, at our feet, lay Sapphira, wearing only tights and a thong and breathing heavily into the carpet.

'Gabriella! Gabriella!'

'Don't bloody Gabriella me! You are mad! You are so fucking full of yourself!'

'It's really not how it looks – she did this herself – took her clothes off! Look Gabriella, please, please, help me get her comfortable – she's, she's sick. Needs care.'

I looked at her, I hadn't thought about why she just lay there, and now realised I had thought her dead-drunk or something. 'Sick?'

'Please, let's get her in a bed, I'll explain, honest.'

I snorted at his 'honest'. He really had no idea what the word meant.

Her face was terribly pale, I dropped to my knees and took her pulse, slow but steady. Shook her gently, 'Sapphira?' Nothing, her skin felt cold to the touch, but then the house wasn't that warm and she was naked. I looked up at Luke, he looked at me and tipped his hands open in supplication. I nodded, couldn't trust myself to say anything for a moment.

Together we lifted her and staggered up to my spare room, making the mistake of putting her down on the bed before pulling back the duvet. An indecent rolling and tugging took place to get the duvet back and her into the recovery position and covered up cosy. It was then, putting her into the recovery position that I had the creeping feeling that there was something else going on here, a sense of the familiar that was trying to filter itself through to make sense of everything.

Luke stood and looked down at her. 'Seems okay, don't you think?'

'I really don't know what you mean, but if you are talking about her basic health, yes, she seems okay as far as it goes, though you have some big questions to answer.'

'I know,' his voice for once sounding hesitant and not as sure of himself as usual. 'Think we can leave her and go downstairs to talk?'

'Yes, yes let's do that,' I said thinking that if I hadn't needed a glass of red before I arrived home, I certainly did now. I led the way down and headed straight for the dining room cupboard, pulling out a bottle, glasses, ignoring him standing aimlessly behind me. I relented, 'I'm having a drink, you?'

'Yeah, thanks, yes please.' I poured him a glass and as I turned round to hand it to him I suddenly noticed the shattered window and the glass across the sink unit.

'What the hell?'

'Sorry! Sorry, I'll pay to get it fixed, and the door. I had to get in,' Luke said, coming over quickly to my side.

'And the door?' I stepped through to the back hall to find glass all over the mat and a gaping hole in the pane. 'I just don't believe you,' I said coming back into the kitchen.

There were tears trickling down his face.

'Luke?' what the hell was going on now. 'Luke, look, let's sit down.' I said indicating the dining table, there was no way I wanted to revisit my lounge just at the moment. He nodded brushed his sleeve across his eyes as we took up stations opposite each other across my solid oak dining table.

'Now, what the hell is going on?'

He rested his elbows on the table and for a moment hid his face in both his hands, then pushed them back over his head, sweeping his hair back. He looked tired.

'I'm not sure anymore,' he said. 'It's been a hell of a day and when it started I thought I knew what I was doing, now I am confused and concerned my hypothesis was wrong in the first place,' he looked at me, a rueful smile on his lips.

'And?' I said, as he'd not yet told me anything though he looked as if he thought he had.

'And? And? I need to do some tests, to see if the hypothesis was right or the...'

'No Luke, let's try again. What happened here, today?'

'Here, well, I didn't want to come here, but after Sapphira went into the manic stage I couldn't take her back to the room at the hotel.'

I could feel the anger boiling up inside me but before I exploded I think Luke must have seen it, as he shook himself and reached across the table towards me.

'Gabriella, sorry, I'm not making much sense, I will have to explain everything from the beginning, though you know a lot of it.'

So he started at the beginning, by acknowledging that he should have listened and worn the gloves when prepping the original nodules and then he told me about his coma, not from the outside, that I already knew, but from the inside and he told me about the stenches, as he called the effect that he now had whenever he sought to take advantage of someone for some kind of gain.

I was fascinated, found myself leaning forward to catch every word as he softly voiced all that had happened to him The news about the lab he'd hired and the way he'd produced 'inoculating' samples amazed me but when he came to the point where he said he'd been looking for some way to test the hypothesis on other people, I suddenly shot bolt upright. The connection was made, two other people left to rest in the recovery position, waves of fire and ice rushed through me.

'No! You didn't give it to Simon and Micky? Say you didn't do that, something so, so..'

'Inhuman? Unethical?'

'Yes, exactly! You did though, didn't you?'

He nodded , his eyes closing again. He licked his lips. 'In my temporary madness, yes, I did, I figured that they would be better off if it worked and no worse off if it didn't. I didn't die, they wouldn't die, they were in a place where they'd be cared for, it seemed safe and if I could talk to them, test them, I could find out if it was just me or whether the stuff really does work.'

'But they are…' I began, slamming my fists on the table.

'They are sleeping it off!' he grasped my hands. 'No, listen,' his eyes were shining now. 'Imagine a world without greed. No theft of any kind, no material theft, nor emotional, think of all the evils caused by people being greedy, just wanting something that wasn't theirs, wanting to have more than they need.'

'But, you have no idea if this stuff could harm anyone…'

'No!' he barked. 'No,' softer again. 'No, I didn't, but I hope to show it is safe, albeit after a time asleep, but safe and that it revolutionises people's behaviour. Come on Gabriella, can you think of any evil committed by man that is not down, at its very core, to greed of some kind, you can't can you? The more you think about it, the more you'll find that it's true.'

I wrested my hands away. 'And Sapphira?' I saw her in a flash as I had come upon them. I had no love for the woman but the … state she was in brought a whole new flood of suspicions into my mind.

He sighed, in such a way that it was almost a laugh. 'Sapphira, well she forced me into it, into giving her some.'

I gasped. 'She knew? She asked for some?'

Now he did laugh, a single bark, 'If only, no, she boxed me into a corner whereby there would be someone else looking over my shoulder at all times to check on my research – had me over a barrel as they say, I couldn't let that happen, had to either have her out of the way, or on my side, or both. Gabriella, it was a split-second decision, once made unable to be taken back. That's the devil of it, once she started into the manic stage she became,' he stopped, obviously searching for words, looking inside himself, remembering, 'she became over-amorous, I guess you'd say, in between laughing like a hyena – I couldn't take her back to the hotel, as I'd planned to do. I had planned to call you, you see, ask you if you'd look after her while she slept it off, even booked you a twin room.'

I could scarcely believe what he was saying, as if he had taken it for granted that I would do whatever he wanted – even as far as aiding and abetting kidnap. 'You realise this is kidnapping?'

He looked momentarily shocked, he had obviously not thought about it in those terms, but he came back with 'No, it wouldn't be, it would be that she was taken ill when out with us, we were just looking after her.'

I shook my head in disbelief. 'And now?'

'The same, only you can look after her here instead of the hotel, even easier.'

'Until she wakes and then what? I am not exactly the person she would voluntarily have gone to for anything!'

'She'll probably not remember anyway; I didn't.'

Somehow I found myself talking to him as if what had happened was completely normal and alright, just a few wrinkles to be sorted out.

'Look, I am so hungry at the moment I can't even think straight,' I said after a few moments.

He nodded.

'Nothing's going to happen for a while is it? We might as well eat, and look at all this sensibly.'

I rose and went through to the kitchen, pulling open the freezer and dug out two frozen portions of Irish stew I had made the week before, popped them in a casserole and set it to heat up in the microwave. I cut some slices of brown bread and brought them with butter and cutlery to the table where Luke still sat. He took them from me and laid them neatly in mirrored pairs. I directed Luke to sweep up the shards of glass while I found some plastic and tape and then covered the holes in the windows, pressing the lock home tight.

'You really are amazing, so practical,' he said, as we ate. 'Does nothing completely floor you?'

'Well I'm feeling pretty floored right now to tell you the truth,' I said, 'and I've run out of steam for now but we've still got to sort this out you know.' I mopped the last of the stew with a chunk of bread. 'So did you go to see Simon and Micky today – how did you know how they were?'

'I went, took a cheque to your friend Bill, and he told me all about it, didn't sound too worried at the time. I called back later too, but they were still snoring. I didn't think I could ask again without raising suspicions, he already half accused me of slipping them some cash.'

'Instead you slipped them something else entirely!'

He looked up at me to see if I was laughing. I wasn't. 'Were you there today? How were they when you left?'

'Yeah, yeah, I was there today. Actually Bill wanted my opinion on how long he should leave them before calling the doctor in. He's decided to wait until tomorrow.'

'Okay, I was going to ask you to ring him and ask how they are now.'

'Well Bill probably wouldn't be there now, he does have a home to go to, you know. It'll be Agnes or Peter.'

Luke looked alarmed. 'What if they don't leave them?'

'Well that's up to them, I guess, but Bill will have said something when he handed over, I'm sure.'

'So you won't call?'

'Is there a point?'

He took a deep breath. 'Well, since I gave the stuff to Sapphira, now I am really concerned, I just want to know how they are.'

'Want to know if you are busy poisoning people, is that it? You really should have thought of this before.'

'Gabriella?'

'Oh, what the hell,' I got up and went to the phone, pressing in the numbers for St. Piran's.

Agnes' reedy Scots voice answered.

'Hi, Agnes, Gabbi Johnston here. Look I was in this afternoon and Bill told me about the binge that Simon and Micky had been on, I was just wondering if they are awake yet?'

'Well, as a matter of fact they are, I am looking at them right now, tearing through a powerful pile of supper, like as they'd been starved.'

'Oh! Oh that's great, no after effects, I mean no hangover then.'

'Not that it seems, though where the blighters got it from we still don't know. If I had my way they'd be out, at least for a few days, remind them why it's good to be here, rules or no rules.'

'I understand how you feel, Agnes, and thank you for letting me know.'

'It's no bother hen, good night.'

I put the phone down and looked at Luke. 'You got that I guess?'

'Awake and with no after effects,' he nodded, his eyes bright.

'Apart from a dreadful hunger, they seem fine.'

'Tomorrow I must go and talk to them, see if they experienced anything like I did.'

'And that won't raise any suspicions?'

'Well, I hope not, I'll not be blurting it out and I need to test them, see if there is any change in their reactions to…' he stopped.

'Test them? How? Not another unethical experiment?'

'No, forget them a minute, that's not what I was thinking. I was thinking about you,' he said stepping over to me, too close, I involuntarily moved back a bit, my back came up against the kitchen unit where the phone was.

'Gabriella? You know I couldn't quite believe we'd been thrown together again after so many years, there was something else from the Moringa effect I didn't tell you about. Before I went into the manic stage, before the talk even, I had a powerful out-of-body experience and it was all centred on you, I had to get close to you again, it mattered.'

He reached out one hand towards me, 'You know, you are an amazing woman,' he touched my face lightly, just below the jawline, caressing it with one finger. It felt good to be touched, and the years melted away momentarily, I felt my eyes close, his palm cupped my face, a finger touched my ear. I opened my eyes to look deep into his, God he still had that certain something, I thought, and he's going to kiss me, his hand slipped to the nape of my neck as I felt myself lean into him, wanting to feel his lips on mine.

The Angel Bug 22

Luke 27th – 28th October

Her lips were soft and her body moulded itself against mine as I pulled her closer. All of a sudden the switch flipped; I wanted her, all of her. I didn't want to stop kissing her but in an instant it was all I could do not to shove her away from me. My stomach turned, threatening to spew its contents, as the foulest of stenches filled my mouth, my nostrils, my lungs, my guts. I stepped back, suddenly breaking away, gulping in air, I could see confusion on her face.

Another unethical experiment, I thought. Result, however! The hypothesis stands.

'What?' Gabriella said, her eyes wild.

'Sorry!' I gulped, I hadn't wanted to hurt her, 'The, the stuff – it won't let me. Soon as I, soon as I, uh. The stenches, they just came.'

'So, you can't kiss someone without that happening?'

'Not exactly, the kiss was fine, it was what I wanted to do with you after that,' I raised my eyebrows and I think she got my meaning as I saw a blush rush to her cheeks.

'Huh! Okay, saved by the Moringa? Is that what you are saying? Oh my God! It was a test wasn't it, you were so, so worried, something had made you think it had stopped working, and that was a bloody test.'

'No, yes, the kiss wasn't - that was real, Gabriella, I, it's only when it goes to the greed part, when I just wanted to possess you, your body, take it, have it, then the Moringa took over. Look, that's good isn't it? That's like, no more rapes, not by anyone who's had the Moringa, if, if I can prove it.'

She closed her eyes and then flashed them open and stepped away from me.

'I've had enough for one day! Too much! I'm going to bed, I'll find you a duvet, you can use the sofa.' and almost ran away to return after a few minutes with a duvet which she dumped on the back of a dining chair, sighing then starting to clear the table.

'Leave it, I'll do that,' I said. She looked at me, then seemed to make up her mind about something and turned on her heels and left the room.

I quietly removed the bowls and sat them in the sink, running water into them while I wiped the table down. I gave them a wash and left them upturned on the draining board, noticing as I did so a tiny sliver of glass and gingerly picked it up and consigned it to the bin with the rest.

I could hear Gabriella moving around upstairs, it sounded as if she went from the bathroom to the spare bedroom then back, I assumed, to her own room. I wondered if I should check on my patient myself, decided I ought to but waited until there were no more sounds from upstairs before I did. I crept up and pushed open the door. I could hear the steady breathing, noisy, not quite a snore, but reassuring in itself. I closed the door and went to the bathroom, splashed water on my face, rinsed my mouth with some mouthwash I found there and washed my hands, God I looked wrecked. Quietly I left the bathroom and turned to go downstairs. I stood on the landing looking towards what had to be Gabriella's room, seeing again her confusion when I'd pulled away, and worse her hurt as she figured out that I was running a test. I felt unease in my heart, really, right there, an ache within my chest that was totally unfamiliar. I crept downstairs and made my long frame fold itself to some semblance of comfort on her sofa and to my amazement slept right through until Gabriella herself touched me in the morning.

'Coffee,' she said, setting down a huge steaming mug on the table, gathering up Saphirra's cast-off clothes, and leaving me to it. I sat up, finding my muscles cramped and unwilling to stretch, retrieved my shirt from the back of the sofa and shrugged it on before taking a sip then a long draw on the coffee. It felt good, the heat of it radiating out. I stretched, my arms, my back then, pushing the duvet off my legs, stood and put my jeans on. Taking the remains of the coffee I went into the kitchen-diner, only to find it empty, I turned back and saw myself in a mirror and ran the fingers of one hand through my hair to try to tidy it. I drained the cup, took it to the sink and stood looking out of the part of the window that had not been obscured by plastic and tape, and took in the amazing view.

'Wonderful, isn't it?' Gabriella said from behind me, 'Always works its magic on me, especially in the mornings. I think it's why I didn't leave.'

It was as if I couldn't trust myself to speak this morning, I nodded and grunted assent.

'Breakfast?'

I nodded again. Then looked up at the ceiling, thinking I ought to check on Sapphira.

'She's okay, still sleeping,' Gabriella said as if reading my thoughts.

'Thanks,' I managed to say, even that sounding strange.

We munched through some kind of oat-based cereal and sank another cup of coffee in silence.

'I am not saying what you did was right, not even okay,' Gabriella said suddenly. 'But if we don't want a hue and cry about Sapphira she needs to let people know she's, she's .. indisposed.'

I nodded, it was something that had run through in my mind but I hadn't seen a simple answer and had gone on to thinking about other things.

'Just so you know, I don't think what you are doing is right, but I seem to be caught up in it now, should have done something, said something last night, that would have been the right thing to do, it's too late now. So, I think I can send an email to the team as if it came from her, saying she's poorly or something. I checked just now, she doesn't seem to have changed the password yet for the senior botanist's work mail.'

'Great, that would really help,' I said. 'Hey, d'you think you could add a bit to that. Say that she's given permission for me to

examine the Moringa tree at the other site? It'd mean I could get in there before she can add on any more conditions.'
She nodded.

While she went off I thought hard about what she had said. It was obvious that she still didn't see the total good this could lead to, anyone who did couldn't condemn what I was trying to do. I could see such a world, perhaps it would only be those convicted at first who would have the Moringa treatment, the prisons would empty, then the politicians would see that this went further, that crime could be prevented before the perpetrators even thought about committing it. The mission of it filled me until I felt I was glowing. I had to have Gabriella on board with me; something told me she was important.

'Okay, that's done, suspected food-poisoning, she'll be away for at least three days, and permission passed on.'
'You realise the old guys woke up before three days, actually only asleep twenty-four hours, if that.'
'Long enough,'
'Yes, but better than I had thought, if the results are the same. I really have to get over there today, are you going to be okay looking after Sapphira?'
'Do I have a choice? Though to be honest with you I really don't want her here.'
I stepped towards her, resting my hands on her shoulders, 'Gabriella, it will be okay. Promise.'
She shrugged me off, 'Don't you promise things you know nothing about. Just go, see that Simon and Micky are okay, just … oh, and just don't be away long.'

I drove from Gabriella's place to the hotel and freshened up, clean shirt and clean teeth, minibar whiskey slipped in my pocket then headed out to St. Piran's. How to play this? I decided that I wouldn't know how the guys were, after all there was no reason for them to assume that I knew what Gabriella knew.

'Hey, Bill!' I greeted the guy cheerfully. 'Have an hour free this morning, on my way over to see Gabriella, thought I'd look in. How are they today – hungover eh?'

'Good morning, good morning. Pleasantly surprised to find them both awake and none the worse for wear, haven't actually grilled them myself as such to point out the error of their ways, but go on in, have a chat, do, do.'

Simon was there, reading a newspaper, no sign of Micky. That suited me as I preferred to speak with each of them alone.

'Simon!' I said, drawing up a chair to the table where he was.

'Hmm?' he looked over the top of the paper, then folded it down swiftly and stuck out his hand. We shook. 'Good to see you again,' he said his English accent sounding quite plummy.

'Would you like a coffee?' Bill called from over by the kitchen.

'Oh, yes, thanks, Simon you?'

He nodded. Ideal! I thought.

'I'll come and get them, Bill,' I added, standing up again and going to take them from Bill as he poured.

'I um, heard about your little bit of fun the other evening,' I said putting the cups down on the table. 'I know it's not legit, but I brought a hair of the dog in for you, good brand, a nip in your coffee?' palming the whiskey bottle in my hand, showing it to him.

I could see the battle going on behind Simon's eyes, he licked his thin lips.

'Bit mistaken that, I didn't have anything to drink at all the other night.'

'Oh? Sorry, it's only what I was told, the singing and dancing…' I let my voice trail off.

'Humph, well if that's true, what you have been told, then I can understand it, but I can assure you I did not imbibe.'

'Oh! So I'd better put this away, mustn't tempt you, must I?'

'No indeed,' he said his eyes fixed on my top pocket where I had returned the little bottle.

We started to talk about other things, but his eyes kept straying to my top pocket. After a while and half his coffee later he broke. 'I think,' he said, 'if the offer is still open, I little nip wouldn't do any harm. Just as a restorative.'

I grinned, and conspiratorially opened the bottle under the table then tipped about half into his coffee cup. His hand reached across for it then he sat upright, his nose flaring, looking round, then looking straight at me.

'What?' I asked, though I had a good idea.

'Hells bells man, can't you smell it? Enough to turn your stomach.'

'No, there's nothing.' I said, making a play of sniffing.

It must have subsided as he went to pick up the cup again, and as quickly let it drop with a clunk; a splash of laced coffee jumped from the mug and pooled on the table top.

'Oh God!' he said, clamping his hand over his mouth and staggering out towards the gents.

I smiled to myself. Now I wanted to ask him about other things, how did he feel if he thought about stealing, would the same thing happen? This would be trickier, but I had to know.

I cleared away the coffees before he came back and before anyone else could offer to wash them up and discover the extra contents of Simon's mug. As I returned from the kitchen he was back in his place, looking a little green but otherwise fine, I knew exactly how he felt. He eyed me suspiciously as I sat down again.

'I, um, I thought you probably didn't want the coffee after all.' I said.

'Humph,' he snorted.

'Have you ever tried any type of aversion therapy?' I asked.

'No, no time for that sort of stuff,' he said. 'Though I'm not saying it doesn't work, just that I wouldn't want to try it, you never know where it would end.'

'How do you mean?'

'Bit 'Clockwork Orange' I've thought, the aversion might boomerang, not work as they expect.'

'But if it could be guaranteed?'

'Well, if it could, I suppose it might make things simpler for you if you were trying to kick a habit.'

'Like drinking?'

'Like drinking, or smoking, yes, I suppose.'

'Or thieving?'

He regarded me down his long nose for a moment. 'Well, I suppose there are those who are kleptomaniacs, that would be a bit like a habit and perhaps that would, could be affected by aversion therapy, but I think a lot of theft is due to need.'

'Need, not greed?' I asked.

He rested his chin on his chest for a moment while he considered this. 'Fifty, fifty perhaps.'

'So you are saying that those people who steal because they think they need something, they do not have any greed in their action?'

'Not as such, they might be starving you know, or driven by another need.'

'Like for drugs or alcohol?' I added.

He looked at me again; I could see he was thinking of himself. Suddenly his cheeks blew out and he clamped his hand across his mouth. His nostrils were flaring and sweat stood out on his skin. He stumbled away again.

'What's wrong with that old bugger?' came Micky's voice behind my shoulder.

'After effects of your session, I'd guess.'

'Stuff and bloody nonsense. I'm right as rain and I can't remember no dancing and singing, certainly not with that stuck up prick.'

'Sounds like it was even better than you thought, wiped your memory too.'

'Shut up, what the fuck do you know?'

'I'm willing to bet you that Bill will say Simon here was drunk as a skunk the other night and you with him, fifty quid on it,' I said pushing the offer of a bet on him.

'And you know what you can do with your fifty quid, you can go stick it up where the sun don't shine. No ways you going to get me in on a ringer like that!' he grinned, 'Beside, I wouldn't be wanting to waste my money now would I?'

No reaction, no sign of him smelling anything strange, I was a little disappointed after the good result from Simon. Perhaps that was it, he knew I was onto a winner and wasn't even tempted.

'So, you do remember getting drunk?'

'No I don't, but I do remember you playing a mean game of chess wiv me last time you came, so if you'd like to play again, this time with a small consideration on the side,' he winked.

'Well,' I started, but his top lip was curling and he was backing away. 'Yer dirty bastard, dropped a bad one then, stinks like yer shit yer pants!' he waved his hand in front of his face and stepped back again.

'Did I?' suddenly I understood, he thought the stench assaulting his nose came from me. I laughed.

'Bluddy funny eh? Disgusting, I calls it. Don't you yanks have any manners?'

I could hardly keep a straight face. 'I really don't know what you are on about, Micky,' I said, 'I can't smell a thing.'

I left St. Piran's with a spring in my step that hadn't been there when I'd woken up. This stuff was going to work, the thought that it could be worth a fortune slid into my mind, and just as swiftly came the smell. Involuntarily my thoughts reeled back and I agreed with myself that this was something for mankind as a whole, a gift, a new beginning. Perhaps it was that thought that started me thinking about why me, and how it had all happened. I called Gabriella and told her the guys were fine and everything was fine. She told me that Sapphira was still sleeping, wanted to know when I'd be back, but I put her off saying I had to drop into the lab and at Eden.

I headed next for the labs, I wanted to build a supply of the powder, it had been the most useful method so far and I was down to just two papers. I had to plan out what I was going to do and how I could convince people that this was not only safe but a truly viable option for the world at large.

What can I say about how I felt, rushes of amazement kept flowing over me, that this could be an end to evil. Not only evil, to meanness of all kinds, to all selfish behaviours.

I worked fast and hard in the lab, total concentration yet somehow my mind was flying, making connections, lighting up like it hadn't done for years. Here was something truly important, really special and somehow I was the one to bring it to the world, but in such purity, not diminished by self. Through this I had become altruistic by default – me! I cringed at the thought of my previous behaviour, dreading the stenches that might overtake me if I allowed the memory of the pleasure I had derived in carrying them out, to surface.

I left samples drying all over the lab and rushed away to get to the Watering Lane site to look at the tree. I had no idea if the email would have been circulated as far as this outpost, but I hoped that it had.

I pulled in beside the oversized garden shed and went in, announcing that I was here to look at the Moringa, and had they had the message from the senior botanist she'd promised to send. There was a bit of searching around in inboxes but they came up smiles. Yes I could look at it and they would page Jim Borlase to show it to me.

'No need to bother him,' I grinned, 'just point me in the right direction, I only want to look at it at this point.' They looked at each other and, with a shrug, said okay and directed me up through the greenhouses to where it had been installed. They'd send Jim up when he called in, they said, as helpful as you like. I thanked them and walked as fast as possible without drawing attention to myself, up the way they had indicated.

What I really needed to do was to take some cuttings, root and stem. If this was the only tree that produced these nodules then it was imperative that there be more of this tree. If the world supply of the nodules lay back at the lab facilities I had, then the possibilities that I had foreseen would be severely curtailed and instead of being available to all it would have to be reserved for the worst-case candidates. I waved goodbye to the girls in the shed as I left fifteen minutes later, cuttings tucked into plastic bags under my jacket.

I stopped by a garden centre and collected compost, pots and a pack of sandwiches, all of which I took back to the labs. Once there I devoured the food and set to potting up my cuttings and said a makeshift prayer over them for their growth. The samples I had left earlier were almost dry; I rotated the infra-red lamp around them encouraging them to dry out quicker. When I left the labs I had two sets of supply, a sheaf of ten papers that I folded into my wallet and twenty more that I locked in the small safe at the lab.

By the time I had got back to Gabriella's house I had a theory worked out, a crazy theory, I would have called it not a week ago, but a theory that seemed to fit, it felt right. It might be the understanding that I needed to break through the resistance that Gabriella had to the miracle that was the Moringa treatment.

The Angel Bug 23

Gabbi 28th October

I was getting really angry with Luke by four in the afternoon. I was beginning to wonder how much longer I would have before Sapphira woke up, and I had no wish to be alone with her when she did.

I had already endured a tense day, first the difficulty of finding someone to repair the broken windows at all and then being told it was today or the end of next week, that he was away in-between. I opted for today, only to have the man arrive within half an hour, as if he'd been sitting around waiting for a job, and noisily replace the windows, whistling and casually throwing the broken shards into a large bucket he'd brought. I felt he was overly curious about my 'break-in', wanting to know what had been taken. When I said I'd done it myself as I had been locked out late at night he seemed strangely suspicious. And all the while I was terrified that he would wake Sapphira and she would cry kidnap or worse. When I tried calling Luke and his mobile went to answerphone I cursed him for turning it off, but later figured he could've been in the lab as I knew he couldn't get a signal in there.

When his car drew up at nearly five I had checked on Sapphira twice in the past hour, I was sure she was not sleeping as deeply, but I did not dare shake her to see.

I snatched open the door as he came to it, 'Thank goodness you are back, I was getting worried.'

'Why? Has she woken up?'

'No, not yet at least.'

'So, there was nothing to worry about, was there?' Luke said in such dismissive tone that it only served to make me more angry. 'Look, let me in, I could murder a cup of coffee, I haven't stopped today, don't you want to know how the old guys reacted?' he said squeezing past me.

I looked at him; yes I did want to know about Simon and Micky.

I followed him through to the dining room then went and put on the kettle. He leant against the breakfast bar and started talking. 'Gabriella, this is something so big I am only just beginning to comprehend what it means. Let's see, what would you say was the one thing that Simon needs to be free of to start his life again? What has he done anything to get hold of, pissed his life away on?'

'Well, as you obviously know, he's an alcoholic.'

'Exactly, so when I slipped some whisky into his coffee,'

'You what?'

'He knew I was doing it …'

'That's not the point!'

'Listen, damn you, listen! Listen, he knew I had it, I showed him the miniature and offered it. He said no, at first then, yes, then well, as he went to sip he got it – the stenches.'

'How could you be sure, he might just have realised how bad it was to start … '

'No! I'm right! He almost puked at the smell, I know, I saw it!'

'Ok, so perhaps he did. So what?'

'No perhaps about it! And further, when I drew his mind back to a time when he stole to get alcohol, even that caused the same reaction. Like it does for me, when I remember some things I have done that were, let's say 'regrettable' though I thought them fine and dandy at the time.' He shook his head. 'It was the same with Micky, though he's probably got a stronger stomach for smells, he was still affected badly. He hasn't worked out where the stenches come from yet, and I didn't dare ask about the dreams he had while under the Moringa, whether he experienced the memories and the stenches as I did. But, this you will need to know, they both seem fit as a fiddle and quite unharmed mentally by the Moringa.'

'Well that's a relief anyway,' I said thinking of Sapphira upstairs.

'Gabriella,' he said, fixing me with his clear blue eyes, 'I've had a sort of revelation. I think I know what the Moringa is, why it is. Please listen to me.'

I don't think I had ever heard him sound like this, it was unnerving. I looked away out of the window for a second, I could neither keep his gaze nor stray from it for long. When I looked back he was holding out one hand. It seemed natural to take it. He drew me over to the dining area and we sat down, he still held my hand though now rested lightly on the table top.

'What's the common name of the Moringa?' he asked, then answered himself immediately. 'The Miracle tree, I know there are others, but the Miracle tree is the one. Where did this Miracle tree grow, the only one to have these nodules that leak 'blood' with miraculous properties, at Eden, a new Eden, manmade for manmade woes. This really is a new chance for mankind, a start of a new mankind without any manmade evil in it. Human nature changed by the blood of the Miracle tree in a new Eden. This is a gift for the whole of mankind, a second chance.'

I looked at him, his eyes shining brightly, his face lit with a fervour I don't think I had seen in anyone ever before.

'And who are you in this, the new Messiah?' I knew my voice carried the scepticism I felt.

He closed his eyes and shook his head in a small movement of disbelief. 'I know it's hard, you think you know me, anyone who knew what I was like would agree, but this has changed everything. This *will* change everything and Gabriella, I know you need to be with me on this.'

'I don't need to be anywhere with you on this, crazy idea or not, deep down I don't like it, I don't like the way you say it takes away...choice.. free will.'

'Free will? Do you think Simon has free will in the grip of alcoholism or Micky with his gambling? What kind of free will do you want people to have, to be kind and generous? That's still there, to be cruel and mean? That would be gone. Face it, this is something that has come from something bigger than all of us, from God if you like.'

I shook my head again, not meeting his eyes now.

'Please, Gabriella, I need you to believe me.'

'I believe you,' a voice said from the doorway. 'The blood that washes away your old life, the death of your old life, then you awake renewed, in a new life free from the sins of greed.'

I didn't remember standing, but I was, and back from the table, against the wall. There in the doorway, agreeing with Luke, stood Sapphira, dressed but untidy and somehow soft and vulnerable-looking. It took me a moment to realise that she wasn't angry or about to fly at me or Luke for imprisoning her here; for my heart to stop thumping against my chest.

'Sapphira?' Luke said, his voice taking on a questioning tone. Then as quickly, 'Come, here, sit down, how are you?'

'Fine, thank you. I, I have to confess, I have been listening for a while. I don't understand all that was going on here but I do know that some things you have said are right. I have found that out already.'

Luke was beaming.

'And when you talk of dreams do you mean ones where you feel smug and good about getting your own way, making someone pay, and then you are,' she wrinkled her nose, 'assailed by the most vile, vile smells?'

'Amazing!' Luke said, 'That is it exactly! See! See, Gabriella, now you must believe me.'

I remained where I was, watching Sapphira, waiting for the sly glance to arrow its way across to me. It didn't come. Instead she clasped her hands together and bowed her head, 'Thank you, Lord,' she said.

This was too much for me. I don't know where it came from but I laughed. Both Luke and Sapphira looked at me as if I'd become unhinged. 'Sorry,' I said, 'Nervous reaction I suppose. Don't mind me.' I went into the kitchen area and made three cups of coffee took them back to Luke and Sapphira who were deep in a low conversation.

'Thanks, Gabriella,' Luke said. 'Look we think it's a good idea if I get Sapphira back to her place, then we can see what needs doing from there.'

'Fine,' I said, both relieved and a little miffed that I and my house were suddenly not of use anymore.

'Then tomorrow we can start on the whole new Moringa project,' Sapphira said, her eyes shining.

I raised my eyebrows questioningly towards Luke but he was nodding at what she said.

It didn't take long before both Luke and Sapphira had gathered anything of theirs together and put it in his car. Luke came back to me and gave me a big hug. 'Gabriella, please think about this, I know I need you at my side when we take the Moringa public. I don't know why at this moment, but I do know I need you in this thing.' He held me away from him and searched my eyes. I shook my head a little and he hugged me again to him. 'Think it over. Take care!' he said as if he was not going to see me for a long time. He released me, turned and strode to the car where Sapphira waited for him.

The Angel Bug 24

Luke 28th – 29th October

'You'll have to direct me,' I said after Sapphira had given me her address.

'Of course,' she said and without looking I could tell she was smiling at me.

Sapphira's place turned out to be a large apartment in an extremely modern set of buildings, new build by the look of the illuminated sparse perfection of the landscaping around them and near the coast by the sound of the surf that filled the night air. She led me though to the kitchen and put on some real coffee. As it perked and she went to change, I looked round. You could tell she hadn't been there long as the place had that showroom atmosphere, just the bare essentials of décor, a few elegant but innocuous paintings on the wall, no clutter, no personality, except for the photo of the blond guy in the blue robes which seemed to be in pride of place.

'The Reverend Elliot Ashe,' she said as she came in behind me, 'and Luke, this is one man we must talk to. I believe he will have the answers to many of the questions that the Moringa has offered us.' She spoke as if she had been in on the secret of the Moringa from the start.

'And what might those be?'

She pushed a cup of coffee towards me and sat down with her coffee in front of her and, elbows on the table, interlaced her fingers forming an arch over it.

'From my dreams, from the tests I ran on myself while lying half awake before you came back, I decided something very strange had happened to me. I didn't know then what had caused it, I did feel a sense of a dramatic shift in myself, all sorts of petty incidences kept surfacing. Things I had not thought twice about, had put down under 'management of people, decisive action,' which suddenly were shown to me to be manipulative, prejudicial, demonstrating my, huh, *power* over others. Ugh! Even thinking about it now, telling you, has sent a whiff, you'll know what I mean.' She shook her head as if to clear the stenches. I really did know what she meant.

'So then you came back and I listened, and then I knew what it was and everything you told Gabbi was right, I am sure this is the second chance for mankind, this is the new redemption and that's why we need to talk to Elliot Ashe.' She pointed to the photo I was looking at earlier.

'A preacher?'

'Not any preacher, a man who has been preaching the New Redemption for a while now, I know him. He told me, personally, that he had a vision that the new redemption was at hand, that man was to be given a second chance. He had assumed, as the Bible tells us, that Christ will come again, that it would be a new coming of the Messiah, one in an age when His message can reach everyone all at once,' she sighed. 'I think he was right, and wrong, the new redemption isn't in a person but in a substance, a new manna, a way to cure man of his evil ways. As you yourself said, a miracle from the Miracle tree, from a new Eden. The Lord has made so many pointers in this to make sure we did not miss His intention, and I believe that Elliot Ashe is the prophet and the conduit for His means of distribution.'

'Whoa, this is going a bit fast. This is an untested substance,' I started.

'Not true, you've tested it, on yourself, on someone else, I heard you say two men? On me? You wouldn't have given it to me if you thought it was dangerous, because IT wouldn't have let you,' she looked smug.

She was right, it wouldn't have let me. I had used the lack of stenches already to guide me as to whether something was safe, ethical even, under the strange new circumstances of ethical only meaning 'for good not ill'.

'Tell me,' she asked, 'how did you give me the Moringa?'

'Uh, as a powder stirred in your coffee after the meal.'

'What dose?'

'About point two of a milligram – the result of drying five millilitres of Moringa nodule juice. The dose needs to be refined, I was out for three days, you and the guys for twenty-four hours, the results appear to be the same. I really don't know if even that shortened length of time is necessary, whether the results would be the same with an even shorter time. And then there's administration, mine was direct to the bloodstream, yours via the digestive tract, and you know what difference that can make.'

'Exactly, so it's basically safe, though still untested in many ways, yet needs to be refined quickly, no going through the usual agencies, years and years of animal testing before they let you try a single other human, and what use would that be, how can you judge a change in morality in a mouse? This is too important for that, and I am sure there would be many willing volunteers from Elliot's followers.'

'I don't know,' I began but again she cut into my words.

'People swallow all sorts of untried and untested stuff everyday, call it homeopathy, natural remedies, herbal. It's what this is - herbal – from the roots of a tree that has been eaten as food and taken as medicine for hundreds of years. No, there'll be no problems finding volunteers.'

'There might be a problem with supply though,' I said, though thoroughly caught up in the vision Sapphira was painting. The Moringa tested and refined to the minimum dose needed to create the change of heart needed, the worldwide acceptance of the benefits to mankind as a whole. Greed; without greed even the environment would benefit, I thought of my beloved rainforest, being slashed down by greed and felt a new fire burst up though my body. This was good. This was *so* good. 'There are only thirty or so nodules and I haven't been able to culture them alone, off the tree.'

'Then we need to culture them on the tree,' Sapphira said, then looked at me her face horror struck. 'The tree. Oh! I had it removed, didn't I? What if it had to stay where it was?'

'I don't know. I have taken cuttings though, hoping to infect them with the nodules.'

She brightened again, colour flooding back into her face, 'Yes that might do it, I will get Jim Borlase on to it, as I understand it, that man can make anything grow.' Her eyes were shining now and she downed the last of her coffee, leapt up and went to the phone.

'Hi, Sapphira here, can you patch me through to Jim?' she said, 'What? Yes, I'm ok!'

Realising she was talking to Eden I hissed 'We told them you had a bug.'

Her eyes widened, then she said into the phone, 'It was just a bug,' then looking straight at me, her hand over the mouthpiece she added, 'an angel bug.'

'Jim, Hi, look I would like you to take as many cuttings of the Moringa we had moved as possible without damaging the viability of the original tree. …Yes, as soon as possible. I know, I realise it would have been better if I'd asked earlier when you had to shorten it, and I'm sorry, but something has only just come to my attention so we have to make the best of a bad job……Yes, it is my intention to get a sapling from this tree back into the Moringa's original position as soon as is possible……Yes, I know I asked you to plant a new one already …. you have done that .. ok, that's fine, but I'd still like a viable cutting put back in that place too, alongside if necessary. Yes, thank you Jim, I will be back soon, see you then, thank you.' She put the phone back in its holder.

'That's one thing done. I am sure He will make sure they grow if we need them.'

I couldn't tell if she meant Jim Borlase or the Almighty, but while she'd been on the line I had run through the idea of contacting the Rev Ashe, it seemed a good way to get the testing done, sure, but was it the way to spread this miracle to all mankind? It really didn't seem the route to take, after all if it came from a Christian preacher how many of other faiths, or none, would be willing to take it up? I looked at Sapphira's shining eyes and kept this observation to myself.

'And, is this not His planning or what?' she continued, 'Reverend Elliot Ashe is in the UK right now,' she paused, 'and the closest he comes to us is Exeter, and I'm booked to go up to see him there in just three days time.' She paused and looked puzzled for a moment. 'What day is it today?'

'Friday, why?'

'Hang on,' she disappeared into another room and returned with a diary. 'I seem to be out of sync with the days. It's on the thirtieth, so, only two days away.'

'So we could talk to him then, I guess.'

'Never mind talk, I don't see why we couldn't start the process of testing, Elliot always travels with a Church of believers, to give him strength in the work of the Lord and to minister to all those who hear the word and become believers at the rallies, these would be the best people to approach through Elliot.'

'We need to talk to him first though, get him on board if possible.'

'It is possible, I am sure. Leave it to me, I shall talk to him, I can contact him wherever he is.'

I looked at her, she was shining with a fervour that was almost frightening, yet she was right, this might hold the key to successfully testing the dose needed, the smaller the amount the better, especially as we were so limited in supply. I had hitched my hopes to two wagons, one that I could inoculate the roots of other Moringa trees with the nodules, as you would if they were essential for plant growth, and the other that the active agent in the process was alive, a bacterium that infected the new host and grew in the host to create the same effect as a larger initial dose. If the latter were the case then a delayed reaction could be expected but the result should be the same, and perhaps the deep-sleep part would be reduced, perhaps short enough not to cause concern. So many variables to test for, I needed to write this down and set up the possible testing regimes to find out the answers that I needed.

I asked for some paper and started sketching out a testing regime while Sapphira got us something to eat. I took very little notice of her but was aware of her humming and singing snatches of hymns that tugged at my childhood memories in a not unpleasant way.

After we ate we reviewed and amended the testing plan I had sketched out. She offered me the spare room and I was glad not to spend another night on a sofa, slipping into a dreamless sleep quickly and easily.

The pale light of a cold, crisp dawn woke me, the curtains being tidily hooked back as I'd left them, and tucked up warm in bed I had little inclination to get up. I lay there thinking of the enormity of what we were about to do, to change the lives of a whole group of volunteers forever. Sure, if they were truly of the Christian persuasion then their lives should not change too much, but I really didn't believe that there is anyone without some hint of greed in their psyche. I thought of Gabriella, wondering why it was I had this feeling she should be involved with all of this. I tried to dismiss it as my old self, where to fancy a woman equals to have her, but it didn't seem to be that simple. After all I had really fancied their ethnobotanist, Mikaela, but didn't have any inclination for her to be involved in this adventure.

I stirred myself to get up when I heard Sapphira on the phone. I could not make out the words but the passion in her voice carried. I heard her sing out 'Hallelujah' and she came running towards my door. I opened it to find her about to knock.
'He's with us, he really believes, I knew he would.'
'That's, that's amazing.'
'He's travelling with forty-eight members of the Church, is that enough?'
I did some mental calculations based on the amount of dried nodule I already had and what there was left of the original nodules. Plenty for testing especially if I cut the dose down a

little, but I was concerned about using any more of the fresh ones until I was sure of infecting other Moringa trees or the cuttings, or somehow growing more in vitro. In vitro! The idea came in a flash, I knew that Gabriella had run tests on the chemical make-up of the nodules, and they were extremely interesting, but I felt sure a DNA test would reveal that the nodules were more, much more, than a simple collection of sleep inducing and hallucinogenic chemicals

'Sapphira? What are the chances of getting a DNA scan of the nodules in this country?'

'DNA? Well, there's the TGAC up in Norwich, they have the best gene sequencing machines but that's run by the biotech and biological sciences research council and there'd be a long waiting list to get anything sequenced. There are companies doing sequencing for people, DNA health scans, you might be able to buy an early slot in one of those.'

'No, I'm not after human sequencing, this stuff might be a lot harder so I'd prefer an academic outfit, besides if, just if, it is a bacterium, only those working in that area could offer me a short cut, so, who would be the top people to go to, because I'll need to try them first?'

'I have a contact in the micro-biotech world,' she said, adding 'I'll see what I can find out,' as she turned away from me and headed off to what must have been her study.

DNA. What we needed was a self-replicating organism, something that would produce as much of the inoculate as we would ever need. Much of the work in this area had already been done, and even somewhat prematurely released to the public under the pseudo title of 'Man Creates New Life' in the newspapers. No, man had not made life, he had merely joined-up a new combination of DNA strands and inserted them into the nucleus of a bacterium cell minus its own genetic material and waited while the bacterium triggered and completed the binary fission of itself. Yes, truly amazing, but not 'Life'. However, that might be exactly what I needed to happen, nothing more or less, if my hypothesis about the nature of the 'blood' of the nodule was correct I might have to get in touch with Craig Venter at the Venter Institute labs in Rockville, where they had performed this feat.

Sapphira came back with the news that as far as her contact knew there were only a few universities working on DNA scanning of anything other than the human genome, and that Queen Mary's, London was the closest and the best. I was torn between wanting to get the doses worked out and set up for the Exeter visit of the Reverend's contingent and wanting the scans run and to be there when the results came through. I decided I would have to see if I could get the scanning going, then wait for the results while pressing ahead with the other testing.

First up, I had to set up a DNA scan, so spent some time researching the internet from my phone to come up with the name of the Queen Mary's head of department that dealt with gene sequencing. Then I put a call through to a guy I knew who could wring just about any information you liked out of the internet which got me a personal mobile number that, he said, should get me through to the head of the right department, even on a Saturday. With promises of returned favours and thanks, I rang off and prepared my pitch, then hit the keypad to call Dr William Vaughan-Hallam.

'Hello, Vaughan-Hallam' a cultured voice answered.
'Good morning Professor, my name is Dr Luke Adamson, I'm an ethnobotanist currently in the UK.'
'Good morning. Luke Adamson? Have we met?'
'Not yet, though I hope we will soon. You may have come across my lecture tour and film on the Rainforest, Jungala?'
'Ah! Yes, thought I'd recognised the name, you don't mind me asking, how the devil did you get this number?'
'A friend of a mutual friend I'm afraid, I had urgent need to contact you, I am sorry to disturb your weekend.'

'Hurmph, well, what is so very urgent?'

'I have a pressing need to have a nodule of vegetative origin with contents probably of bacterial constituents sequenced. This is something new and unscanned, however if bacterial I am assured that your facility is the foremost in this country on bacterial DNA sequencing and therefore you may be able to save me a lot of de-novo time in mapping a DNA sequence for this.'

'Really! Well just put this research project in writing and have it submitted, we could then allocate a time, resources and personnel to complete it for you. This information is available on the university website, it really did not need you to call me on a Saturday!'

I could tell the man was not delighted. 'Unfortunately... sir,' a little sweet talk never hurt with some of these old-school professors, 'I have a very tight schedule and that also means I have some substantial funding to get this work done in the minimum time. I am talking this week, starting this weekend if possible, I can have samples to you by first thing tomorrow morning.'

There was a pause on the line, I waited, listening to an open silence, then began to get concerned that he'd cut the call, I was just about to speak when he said, 'And what would you call substantial?'

Here was the rub, what would it be worth? How much could I afford and what would be the tipping point?

'I was thinking twenty thousand.'

'Pounds not dollars?'

'Sterling, yes.' Another silence followed.

'And this is a sequencing of the bacterial matter only, not the vegetative part?'

'Yes.'

'Give me a number I can get back to you on.'

'This number is fine,' I suddenly realised he might not be able to get through to me if I was in the labs, 'Um, the reception can be really bad where I am, if you can't get through please email me at

adamson at Jungala dot org and I'll call you right away. Thank you, sir.'
'Hmm, we'll see,' he said.

We set off for the labs as soon as we'd had a bite of breakfast and we set to work as soon as we arrived. I logged my phone into the lab wi-fi and put it on the bench-top ready to pick up any emails from Vaughan-Hallam. It was about two hours later when the email alert sang out for the sixth time, but this time it was him. I clicked on open to find a brief message. 'Adamson, looks like you are in luck, call me' and his number. I showed Sapphira and took my phone out of the building to get a signal to make the call.

'Vaughan-Hallam,'
'Dr Adamson here, thank you, what can you do for me?'
'Tomorrow morning you said? Right, when you arrive I'll have a contract to the effect that we are sequencing bacterial DNA only, and the total fee to be paid before any results are released,' Vaughan-Hallam said slowly.
'Absolutely fine, any idea how long the sequencing will take?'
'I couldn't give you anything definite – if you are lucky it could be as little as sixteen hours, if not, anything up to two months. Call me, on this number, anytime after seven am tomorrow and I'll give you directions on how to find us.'
'Thank you, I look forward to it.'
'I'll see you tomorrow, Dr. Adamson.'

Two months sounded a lifetime, but sixteen hours would be amazing, I thought as I headed back into the lab. We still had so much work to do to set up the testing regime I had worked out last night so that we would be ready for Exeter. Now I had a definite 'yes' on the sequencing I also had to prepare a suitable sample ready to be taken to Queen Mary's.

The end of a concentrated day saw Sapphira driving up to Exeter, the lab packed up, the doses in differing amounts and in differing conditions safe in a chill bag, and me flying to London ready to deliver the sample to Queen Mary's the next morning. Sitting on board the tiny craft, unable to rush around and do things for a short while my thoughts bounced around what had to be done, what was set up, and how, even though I had promised, I had failed to speak to Gabriella.

The Angel Bug 25

Gabbi 29th October

I could still feel the shape of his hug in the morning, sounds daft and romance-novelish but as I woke I swear I could feel his presence and that warm pressure to join in this mad scheme he was swept up in. Not for the first time I considered whether the Moringa infection could have damaged his mental faculties. Yesterday, talking to Sapphira, he just didn't sound like himself at all, and come to that she didn't seem like the old Sapphira either, in fact that was the more unnerving change, the acid and the edge had gone completely. She had not shown any dismay at finding herself in my house, in her condition, in anything other than the possibilities that the 'Moringa project' offered.

I roused myself from bed and with no work to go to planned for myself a leisurely breakfast, a walk, if the weather was good enough, and then a trip to St Piran's not least to check up on Simon and Micky and to see how things were going with Kieran. I popped the last piece of toast into my mouth and the phone rang, chewing madly to be able to speak clearly I picked it up and pressed the button. 'Hello?' I mumbled.

'Muumm?' Emma's voice wailed all the way from Australia. 'Oh Mummm!!'

'What is it Emma?' my body tingling with the adrenaline that surged round it from the pain in Emma's voice.

'Oh Mum,' her voice breaking, 'Oh Mumm!'

'Emma? What has happened? Tell me, please!'

'I was, I was....attacked.'

My heart thumped, like someone hitting me, I felt winded, went hot and cold.

'How are you, what happened?'

'Nothing broken,' she started boldly. 'I'll live,' she broke into a sob.

Gently, softly, 'Emma, what kind of attack?'

'He, he knocked me down, ripped my bag from my arm and he, he,' she choked up, 'dragged me.. it was...' another sob, 'Oh Mum, I just want to come home.'

'Of course, book the first plane you can, I'll pay,' This had to be bad, I thought, Emma would never abandon her PhD on a whim. 'It is ok for you to go? Have the police taken your statement and everything?'

'Yes, yes, Mum, they haven't got him though and I can't bear to stay knowing he's here somewhere.'

'Emma? Do you know who did it?'

'Yes and no, I have seen the guy around but I don't know him, his name, nothing like that - just seen him hanging around.'

'Right, love, get straight onto Quantas, or whichever can get you back fastest and I'll put the money straight into your account, don't worry about cost, go for the first. Let me know when your flight is.'

'Oh No! I can't! He's got all my cards, now they're blocked. Mum, I'll email you the flight, please can you book it for me?'

'Of course! Of course, I'll be online waiting.'

'Ok Mum, bye.'

'Bye love.'

I sat back on my chair, my heart pounding and my imagination filling in the blanks. The bastard, how could anyone hurt Emma, she was the gentlest soul around. Ok, so I am her Mum, but she is, she's always been the one to care for others. I went to the computer and got it up and running, my email open and waiting. Within minutes an email popped through and I set to and booked the flight. She would arrive at Heathrow on Monday evening at five-thirty, I couldn't wait to see her and wrap her safely in my arms.

I sent the confirmation back to Emma and sat there just staring at the computer screen for a while, sightless, viewing instead horrible possibilities in my mind's eye. I shuddered and shook myself to shut down the computer and get on. The thought of a quiet walk was out of the question, quiet would only give my imagination free rein and I had just been there. I had to get busy and as Eden, my familiar salvation, was closed to me I decided on St. Piran's.

Even the drive was therapeutic, the beauty of the austere landscape seeping into my consciousness and easing the ache that Emma's news had put there. I pulled in to the familiar entrance and parked. The morning was crisp and bright, not quite a frost but it must have been a close thing and the sun had yet to warm the air, I took a deep breath, composed myself and went in.

The place seemed empty at first, it was so quiet. I noticed Bill's door was ajar and headed in that direction. I saw through his window that he was there but totally absorbed in reading something on his computer, I tapped gently on the open door and he looked up. His face looked blank for a second then cleared and broke into his usual smile.

'Gabbi! I hadn't expected you today?'

'No, I know, Bill... you know I said I'd have a bit more time for a while… well, and..' thoughts of Emma broke through and must have shown on my face.

'Why? Whatever's the matter, Gabbi … Gabbi sit down, what's wrong?'

I shook my head still trying to control the sob that was threatening to break my voice. I swallowed. 'It's Emma, you know, my daughter Emma?'

'In Australia, isn't she?'

'Yes, yes, she called this morning… It's just I feel powerless, so far away, she's been attacked, mugged by the sound of it.' I took a deep breath, blew it out. 'I, I'm sorry, I thought I had it under control.' I sat, brought my fist to my mouth as if pressing it there would somehow dam the cries that were trying to burst out, all it did was to force the tears into my eyes. 'Sorry,' I muttered against my hand, 'I'd better go.'

'Don't you dare!' He tugged a tissue from a box on the windowsill, 'Here, I'll get us a fresh cup of coffee, don't you move, I'll be back in a tick.'

I mopped my eyes and blew my nose, taking deep breaths to clear my mind again. Bill appeared balancing the two cups of coffee and a plate of biscuits, I was honoured.

'Thank you Bill,' I said hugging the coffee mug like a lifebelt, 'I'm really sorry, I don't know what came over me. You'll be fed up with me crying on your shoulder so much.'

'No need to be sorry, we all have times when it gets too much.'

'I suppose after losing my place at Eden and,' I stopped myself, and all the other weird stuff surrounding Luke that I couldn't mention, I thought, 'and I think Emma's news was just the last straw,' I sighed, and took a sip of coffee.

'Any news of that? Eden, I mean, it was only a suspension, there must be some kind of tribunal?'

'No, no news at the moment,' I thought of Sapphira, would her change of personality mean that there would be a reversal on her decision to cut me out of Eden? A sneaky little frisson of hope ran through my mind, if for nothing else perhaps the Moringa effect would be good for me. 'And here, Bill, how are our reprobates now, fully recovered?' I asked, thinking I knew the answer from Luke already and relaxed in the reply I expected, but Bill's face clouded a little.

'Well, I'm not sure..' he began, my heart raced, 'perhaps you better go and see for yourself. Since the binge they have both been a bit strange. In fact you could help, you could perhaps persuade Simon that he ought to stay here for a while longer.'

'Why is he going to leave? Is it because he broke the rules or something?'

'No, not that, and he still denies it by the way, no, he is determined to get himself a job, get himself sorted out, as he puts it, and has the theory that he'd be discriminated against if he put our address on an application form of any description.'

'But, surely that's a positive, it looks like he's turned a corner, though I can see why you'd want him to stay a while longer, until he was settled.'

Bill nodded, looked down at his hands, 'It seems to show little faith,' he said, then smiled up at me, 'but the change is so sudden

I can't quite believe it, anyway, do me a favour and talk to him, will you, Micky too if he's back, he has taken to going for a walk in the mornings, and that's something new too.'

I found Simon poring over the local newspaper, as I arrived I could see that it was turned to the job ads.

'Hello Simon, what have you got there that's so interesting?'

He looked up at me and there was a definite sparkle in his eye, he sat up straight and it was as if he had grown imperceptibly, somehow taller, his shoulders back more than was usual. 'Gabbi, how very nice to see you.'

'Bill tells me you want to leave.'

'Not want to, I believe it might enhance my job prospects. Good as St. Piran's is, everyone knows the type of clientele, not exactly the best start to an application.'

'But you don't actually have to leave do you, you could use a box number for your replies,' I suggested having had time to think this one through.

He looked at me, his head turned a little. 'What a good idea. Why didn't I think of that? It would solve my catch 22.'

'Catch 22?' he'd lost me.

'Can't apply for a job without a suitable address, can't get an address without a job to pay for the renting of the address.'

'Ah!'

'Thank you, dear girl, thank you.'

'And what jobs are you looking for?'

'To be honest with you, anything that this frail body and reasonable mind can do.'

'Anything there?' I said indicating the newspaper.

'Solicitor's clerk, though not sure my computer skills are up to that. Or there's an invoice clerk, whatever that is, same problem I suspect.'

'Then it seems to me, Simon, that what you really need first off is a computer course to get you up-to-date and ready to go.'

He leaned back and looked at me, 'Again, right to the point, thank you, Gabbi.'

217

'And I happen to know they run courses at the local college, free, gratis and for nothing. Shall I ask Bill to get the information for you?'

'No, thank you, Gabbi, I shall ask him myself, an excellent idea.'

'Sure?'

'Yes, it's about time I was more…'

'Proactive?'

'Is that the term? I was going to say self-motivated, used a bit more get-up-and-go.'

'If you want more of that you should get up off your backside and get some exercise,' Micky cut in as he passed us, cup in hand, towards a different table.

'No need to be rude, Micky,' I said, 'there's nothing like the newly converted for evangelising is there?'

'Huh, what you on about?'

'You, I hear you are into early morning walks now.'

'What of it? I just don't want to crumble away.'

'And Simon, here, just wants to try to get a job, start again.'

'Huh! He's not the only one.'

'But he's doing something about it, like you are doing something about your health.'

'An' who's you to say I ain't?'

'I didn't say that, just he's looking for jobs..'

'Well,' he muttered, 'so am I, fed up with dossing round 'ere. Not much going at the moment though is there. I don't think I'll apply for the bar job down the local, somehow.'

'Perhaps you could go on the computer course with Simon. Up-to-date computer skills would help.'

'What's that then?' he asked, his wizened face tilted like a bird.

'At the local college,' Simon said, 'and, apparently, it is free. I'm going to speak to Bill about it later, do you want me to say you are interested too?'

'Won't do no harm, I s'pose.' Micky said giving Simon an unaccustomed half smile and a nod.

I asked after Kieran as I saw Bill on the way out, telling him only that I'd had a useful chat with both Simon and Micky and so allowing Simon to follow up the initiative himself. If I heard nothing more about it I might mention it to Bill later, otherwise, I was happy. More than happy, Bill had got Kieran onto an introductory course at an agricultural college and the reason I'd not seen him round was because the minibus picked him up at some unearthly hour in the morning and it seemed he was getting himself up and out under his own steam. I set off for home in a much more positive mood than I had left it.

It wasn't until quite late that I realised I hadn't heard from Luke. Part of me was glad that I hadn't had to think about what havoc he might be causing, and this lapse in memory meant I didn't quiz myself over the ethics of keeping quiet about what he had done. And what had he done exactly? There were Simon and Micky, both as well as they had been before Luke used them as guinea pigs, perhaps even better than they were. Mentally they seemed more positive, as if they'd had a blockage to progress removed in some way. Could that have been any part of the Moringa effect? Impossible to know but another aspect to think about, watch and note. Yet, the fact he had used human beings, without their knowledge or consent, against all the rules of ethical testing still worried me and I had no idea exactly what I ought to do about it. To report him at this stage somehow seemed to implicate me in the event, after all it had been me who'd introduced him to St. Piran's. To compound that, I had not reported what I'd discovered straight away, I'd even made calls on Adamson's behalf. It was an uneasy sleep that I drifted into later that night.

It's certainly not every Sunday that I go to Church, but this Sunday as I awoke I felt the need, to touch base, as it were. I dressed a bit smarter than I usually do and set off for, not my local parish Church, but the one closest to St. Piran's, preferring the down-to-earth sermons that the vicar there delivered.

I was a frequent enough visitor to feel part of the congregation, to be welcomed as such, but not so much that I'd been roped into any of the regular jobs in the Church, no one had asked if I'd join the flower arranging or the cleaning rota. After taking communion, I lost myself in my personal version of prayer, calling to mind each person I was concerned for, an exercise very much like prayer but without petitioning God to do something, only dragging myself back to the present as the final benediction was said and the congregation rose for the exit of the vicar. I sat for a few moments after that, drawing in the peace of the place, considering what I had heard there that day. The vicar had taken Luke 12 from verse 15 as his text for the sermon, 'Beware! Be on your guard against greed of every kind, for even when a man has more than enough, his wealth does not give him life'. There was something in it that was nudging my memory, something that Luke Adamson had been saying about greed being the root of all evil.

I was still thinking about this as I returned home and logged on to check my emails in case Emma had sent me any other messages. There was nothing from Emma but there was one from Luke. I opened it, Luke started with an apology for not calling me yesterday, at which I shrugged, I hadn't expected him to, then it told me he was in London and would be for at least a couple of days, perhaps more, so not to expect to see him around and that he would contact me as soon as he got back to Cornwall, he had so much to tell. I set the computer to shut down and put the kettle on, just as I was pouring the boiling water into a cup of instant coffee my phone rang, it was Luke.

The Angel Bug 26

Luke 30th October

Less than five minutes after seven in the morning I put the call through to Dr Vaughan-Hallam. He answered quickly enough.

'Good morning Dr Adamson, where are you now?'

'I'm staying at the Hotel Indigo, Tower Hill,' I said naming the moderately priced smart hotel I'd found as close as I could to Queen Mary's in the East End.

'Ah! Good, not too far away then. Make your way to Queen Mary's university. When you arrive come in through the entrance for the School of Biological and Chemical Sciences. Once inside follow the signs for the CCG – that's the Centre for Comparative Genomics. Have you got that?'

'CCG, yes, thanks,' I said, jotting down the relevant names. 'I shall get to you as soon as possible.'

I took the chill-pouch containing the sample nodule out of my small suitcase and put it in my laptop bag, checked I had everything I needed for the day and left the room. At the front desk I asked them to call me a taxi and within five minutes I was on my way.

I was dropped outside the university and soon found the signs to the CCG as directed. It didn't take long to find the professor; I could hear him talking to someone in the department as soon as I reached it.

'Ah! There you are. I was just talking through today's procedure with Gordon here, he'll be running your scan, very able PhD student, been doing this sort of work for his doctorate the past two years and knows what he's at.'

'Dr Luke Adamson, pleased to meet you, Gordon,' I said, shaking his hand, not sure if I had been offered his first or his last name.

'Right, so if we can get on, do you have your sample?'

'Yes, here,' I said, holding up the laptop bag.

I handed it over and they both looked at it carefully without touching it.

'What actually is it?' Vaughan-Hallam asked.

'A nodule from the root of a tree, though I don't believe it is usual, not nitrogen-fixing, I believe it is the cause of some unusual effects,' I said. 'And I need to warn you that it may have toxic effects if absorbed by the human body in any way,' I added looking at the student, 'You must take precautions when analysing it.'

He nodded, 'No probs. I'll get started, shall I?' he looked to his professor who nodded.

Gordon snapped on some gloves, mask and goggles then picked out the nodule with tongs and moved it over to a prep area. He was obviously taking my warning seriously. Professor Vaughan-Hallam and I stood and watched him working methodically for a few minutes.

'Well, Adamson, not much point you and me standing round watching, I have the contract in my office for you to sign then I suggest you go off and wait for Gordon to report back, I have given him your contact details and told him of the urgency involved.'

'What?' I said coming out of a reverie where I was fast-forwarding what I could do once I had the results, the options that were open to me depending upon the results, 'Oh, sure, after I sign, will it matter if I stay here a bit longer?'

'No, not at all,' he said in a tone that suggested it was not the expected or acceptable thing to do.

I chose to take it at face value and said, 'Thanks, I won't get in Gordon's way. Just interested in the procedures.'

We stepped out of the lab facility and down the corridor to his office, where he printed off the contract. The first three pages were full of legalese but the core content stated that the sequencing of a bacterial sample would be done with payment before results were released, but I noticed it also said that the sequencing would be added to their data bank of bacterial sequences to enhance the facility's information and delivery.

I hadn't thought of this, though it was obvious; after all I was going to them because they'd have the jump on a bacterial sequencing merely because they had done so many already that the core constituents would be recognised and sequenced far quicker and this could only happen because everything was kept on record.

I hesitated. Could the DNA sequencing of this nodule be allowed to be kept on a semi-public database? What about industrial implications of someone else getting hold of the DNA sequence; somehow using it to manufacture this in the future. I sniffed, there was a funny smell, no, there was an awful smell! I realised that my mind was working along the lines of industry secrets and the subsequent profit advantages of keeping it secret. Ridiculous, I thought, I wasn't thinking of making money out of this in any way, yet, even the hint of that sort of thinking, albeit subconsciously, had brought the warning.

'No problem,' I said half to myself, and signed the agreement.

'As for the payment,' the Prof added, 'here are the university's bank details, I suggest an instant bank transfer as the fastest way to get your results released to you.'

'Absolutely,' I said, 'the faster the better.'

I went back to the lab to watch the lad working. By the time I got there he was operating the centrifuge, leaning back on the edge of the bench just waiting for it to do its thing. He smiled as I came in.

'Going ok?' I asked.

'No probs,' he smiled briefly.

'So what're you working on for your PhD?'

'Pombo bacteria,' he answered with another small smile.

'As in?' it was like drawing blood from a stone.

'As in, they have an anomalous behaviour and we are trying to find the DNA basis for that.'

'What do they do?'

'Make a kind of methane, but much more that should be possible, can't really say anymore,' this time he grinned.

'Ok, so, hypothetically, if these bacteria do what you hope, how would you get to make truckloads of the stuff?'

'Oh, that's simple, get a big tank of medium and let it go, right conditions and bingo – a big tank of bacteria.'

'This would work for any bacteria?'

He tilted his head a little as if contemplating the answer. 'Well, depends, the right medium and the right conditions are vital, but basically, yes.'

'Ok, so how would I go about finding the right medium for my bacteria, if that's what I have here?'

'This lot? Well they are in their medium aren't they? The vegetable part, though to be honest they are probably only there for what they can get. The right conditions? Where you found them I guess.' He was obviously less sure of himself on this but I realised that I already had the knowledge that I needed, I just hadn't been thinking along the right lines. There wasn't much I didn't know about root associations and symbiotic relationships between plants, it had, after all, been the basis of my life's study. 'Cheers! I owe you one,' I said. He looked momentarily puzzled, but then turned away from me as the centrifuge slowed to a halt and he returned to his concentrated scientist mode.

I leant back against the bench top and watched distractedly as he worked on the sample. Perhaps I didn't need to extract the DNA and put it into another bacterium after all. Perhaps I already knew how to make this bacterium multiply. I thought of the basic constituents of the photosynthates carried in the phloem, the food that a plant manufactures from the nutrients in the soil, carbon-dioxide and sunlight, and decided a vat of that was well within the capabilities of man to devise. The temperatures would then have to be that of the Humid Biome, around thirty-six degrees and then it was only a matter of time. At optimum conditions an average bacterium will divide every ten minutes or so, the exponential results of this over a mere twenty-four hours can be an awesome figure, taken that a millilitre of bacteria could have over a million of the beasts in it. I was so entranced by my thoughts that I didn't realise at first that Gordon was all packed up and was shrugging on his overcoat.

'What's going on? You can't have finished yet?'

'Yeah, I'm done here, I have to take the extract over to the Galton labs where the Analyser is, I'm not sure you'll be allowed in there, bit fussy on access and a Sunday would be a real pain.' He walked with me out of the building.

More relieved than anything I sighed, 'Ok, I'll be seeing you. You have my contacts?' He nodded. 'Hey, do you know where I can get a cab?'

'Um, yeah – outside the tube station – just past that bridge there,' he said pointing down the road.

'Great, thanks, I'll be seeing you,' I repeated.

'Bye,' he said, gave me a brief wave and headed off. I stood in the chill wondering where to go while I waited for the call, I glanced at the time, eleven already, and thought of Gabriella. I found her name and pressed call, in seconds her phone was ringing. And ringing, there was no answer.

What was my real aim? Not for gain, that was certain, nor for glory, I had a sneaking suspicion that the stenches wouldn't even allow that. It had to be for a better world, there wasn't anything I could reasonably see that would militate against this. It would have to be everyone though, because everyone was subject to some temptation. What was it Sapphira had called it? An angel bug? That was it, something that could make angels out of everyone.

At the taxi rank I asked for the Natural History Museum, though I wasn't sure if it was open on a Sunday, however, the cabbie assured me it was. As I walked the short distance from my drop off point to the entrance, I paused for a moment and tried Gabriella's phone again, listening to it ring all the way down in Cornwall.

'Hello?'

'Hi Gabriella, did you get my email?'

'Hello Luke, yes I did, what are you doing up there?'

'Hey, I'm getting the nodule's DNA sequenced.'

'What? Why, what will that do?'

'I'm beginning to wonder myself, had a bit of a brainwave about that, something I want to talk over with you later. How are things with you? Did you go to St Piran's at all? How are the old guys?'

'The old guys are fine, both thinking of looking for jobs they tell me.'

'Okay!'

'No, not just okay, it's strange, not like them at all.'

'Perhaps once they are off the hard stuff, you know whatever their poison is, perhaps they can think about other things.'

'You'll still not persuade me it was ethical Luke, just because I'm not saying anything.'

'You know it's right really though, don't you? Something like this that could change people for the better.'

'Change is one thing, force is something else,' she persisted. 'Anyway, I'm heading up to London tomorrow.'

'Why? What for?' I said feeling just a little suspicious of her motives as she was definitely not on board with my experiments, then realising she knew nothing about the plans.

'Nothing to do with you, Emma, my daughter Emma, she's flying in on Monday evening. She's coming home for a while.' Suddenly there was a catch in her voice, 'Oh Luke!'

'Whatever is the matter Gabriella, aren't you happy she's coming?'

'I am, to see her, but not, because she's only coming back because some … bastard attacked her out there and they haven't got him yet … it's driving her mad so she's coming home until they get him.'

'No shit? That's bad.' And it's just that sort of behaviour that I'm talking about curing, I thought. 'Wait, how are you getting here?' I added, suddenly feeling I needed her near me.

'Driving.'

'So you just have to hop in your car and drive? Why not come today? Come and stay with me at the Indigo Hotel.' I offered, adding swiftly, 'I'll book you a room. We could go out, have a meal, talk about this more, then tomorrow, well, I'm only waiting, we could go around a bit, see London, until her flight comes in.'

'I don't know Luke.'

'It would be better than you driving up and then back down in the one day,' I added persuasively. She was silent for a few minutes as if working something out.

'Okay,' she said at last, 'what was the name of the hotel again, better still, do you have a postcode for it? The sat-nav should get me there then.'

'Brilliant,' I said, having fished out their card and given her the precise details. 'Can't wait, how long before you should be here?' I felt alive.

'You'd better give me six hours at least. I'll call you when I'm there. See you later Luke.'

'Can't wait,' I said, and meant it.

The Angel Bug 27

Gabbi 30th – 31st October

I sat there by the phone for a few minutes after he rang off, composing myself, analysing why I had agreed to go. He was so right about it being better to drive up one day and return the next, but the thought of being with him was definitely a pull and I really wasn't sure if it was a good thing at all.

I took one of my home-made meals out of the freezer and put it in the microwave. Setting it to defrost then heat, a total of twelve minutes, I went up to my room, pulled out a small suitcase and started to fill it quickly, jeans, jumper, and favourite blouse. Dress, suitable for an expensive restaurant, another, less dressy, in case, a pair of high heels, another top and jumper, all went in the case, wash-kit, night clothes, and I was done. I chose to wear casual trousers, tee-shirt and jumper with a pair of flat shoes to drive in that would also be good for walking round London.

The microware had signalled it had finished its job a minute or two before I brought the case down. I tipped the meal out onto a plate and grabbing a knife and fork devoured it quickly. I washed the plate and left it draining. I put the house phone on answerphone and locked up. Out at the car I shoved almost everything on the back seat, set the sat-nav up with my destination but left it in my handbag in the front with me. I knew I wouldn't need it until I came off the M4, but also knew I'd be stopping before then.

I played upbeat music as I headed out of Cornwall and up past Exeter. After a quick break at Gordano services and a longer break near Reading, I set the sat-nav to guide me to the hotel. It worked better than I could have hoped, leading me safely there.

It was nearly seven and I was exhausted. I asked for the booking in my name, but was told, apologetically, that there was no room booked for me. I then wondered if it was in the name of Dr Adamson? This resulted in the receptionist smiling and saying, but of course, and that Dr. Adamson had the adjoining room and giving me the key card. I went up and found the right number, unlocked my door then paused, turning back to tap on Luke's door.

A moment later he opened the door. He looked great, or it felt great to see him, I didn't know which, but his arms came round me in welcome and I leant into him.

'Gabriella, I'm so sorry to hear about Emma, it must have been a shock.'

'Mmm,' I mumbled into his chest, loving the secure feeling it gave me. 'I'm worn out,' I sighed, pushing myself away slightly, but not breaking his hold.

'It's a long drive,'

'Yeah. I'll feel better once I've freshened up.'

'I've booked a table for eight o'clock downstairs.'

'Don't worry, I won't be long,' I smiled and stepped away into my own room.

Downstairs, at least I wouldn't have to go far, I thought, but the less dressy option was probably best. The shower refreshed me, and I stood letting the warmth seep through to my bones, suddenly aching from sitting tensed at the wheel for so long.

The room was very modern but pleasant and well equipped and I was soon drying my hair, lifting the hanks and flicking the powerful hairdryer back and forth under them to get it dry without causing a frizz. I dressed, then with my hair still not quite dry I twisted it up into a pile on top of my head and fixed it with a clip. I teased out a few tendrils to soften the effect, looked at myself in the full-length mirror and, quite liking the effect, smiled.

'Hi,' Luke said softly as I opened the door to his knock, 'You look great,' he smiled.

'Thanks, you're not too bad yourself,' I said and, to hide my embarrassment, turned and grabbed my handbag and key card.

'So,' he said, the ordering of the meal over, 'tell me about what happened to Emma?'

'To tell you the truth I hardly know much, but I do know that she would never leave her doctorate studies without a good reason.'

'But you said she'd been attacked?'

'Yes, those were her words, seems she was mugged for her bag, but somehow I feel there's more, worse. She said attacked first, the she said she'd been dragged, least I think she had been dragged, it might have been her bag, she wasn't very coherent. Whatever, the guy who did it is still free and she is plain scared I think.'

'Asshole!' he said, 'It's greed, and in this case aggravated by hurting someone to get something.'

'And I suppose you are going to say that your Moringa potion would be the solution to all these problems?'

He leaned back, looked at me, raised his eyebrows a little and turned out one hand, palm up; a silent suggestion that I think it over. I thought, but I still came up with an uneasy feeling that people ought to be free to choose between right or wrong, at least until they proved they couldn't handle the choice properly.

'So, perhaps,' I looked him right in the eye, 'Perhaps you have something, where, say, convicted criminals are concerned, perhaps.'

He smiled, and we were interrupted by the arrival of our first course.

'Explain about the DNA scan,' I said as we sat back over coffee, for him, tea for me.

'I felt the need to know what it was inside those nodules, it's my bet that it is a type of bacteria.'

'So are you having the whole nodule scanned?'

'Unless someone has already run a scan on Moringa then that would take months, six at least, no, I'm betting on the bacteria and hoping that the scan will give me an idea of where to go next.'

'Why? What do you want to do with it?'

He looked at me for a second then something shifted in his eyes and he smiled. 'I just want to know what it is that affected me so, so much that it has changed me, made me see what a shit I used to be. I got away with it, all of it and people thought I was a good guy, and that only makes it worse 'cos the more you get away with it the more you take it for granted.'

'But weren't you a good guy? Your work for the environment is good, the way you…'

He cut me short, 'Oh sure, the environment, but what of the man, how I treated anyone else in my way? How I treated any woman that came my way?' he raised his eyebrows and his nostrils flared a little. 'I can't even think about the way I used to be without being reminded that it was not good, not acceptable, that I was taking advantage of other people. Worse, I did damage to people and their careers to make sure I came out on top.'

I reached out my hand and touched his where it lay on the table, 'We're not all perfect, it's part of being human.' He turned his hand and held mine.

'You're a good person Gabriella, and probably too protected, or too naïve to have any idea what I am capable of, what I was capable of, and am not now because that stuff in the nodule changed me, totally. This is something really big, really important and I need to understand it. So, yes I'm having its DNA scanned, but that is just one aspect of what we are doing. Tomorrow we are running a proper test of the Moringa juice.'

'We? What kind of test?'

'Sapphira has forty-eight volunteers willing to try out the Moringa in a double blind test, so we can see if it works on larger numbers, what the effects are and how they manifest themselves.'

'You have got to be joking!' I said, pulling my hand back, 'That has to be off the scale in taking advantage of people and unethical in the extreme?'

'Tell me, is or is not the Moringa oleifera edible and harmless in root, branch and fruit?'

'Yes, but..'

'And have there ever been any cases of harm from ingesting it?'

I shook my head 'But..'

'So these volunteers have been told that. Just that, they will have an herbal remedy that is from the Moringa.'

'But it's not is it? Is it?' I could hear my voice rising. 'It's like saying you can eat mistletoe berries because they grow on apple trees and you can eat apples!'

'No! It's not like that, if there were any difference, if we were taking advantage of these people we would know, I would know, IT would tell me.'

I looked down trying to think straight. 'I can't handle this,' I said, 'it just doesn't seem right.'

'Perhaps you'll understand when you see the results, this is okay, it really is, there's no harm I can see to anyone, it can only help even the most righteous of us.'

'I'm too tired to get into an argument with you tonight, Luke. Let's call it quits for now.'

He smiled, whether he just thought he was right, or whether he thought he'd won I didn't know nor care, for it was true an enormous weariness had come over me. We parted, agreeing to meet at breakfast, and I headed off to my room. It really didn't take me long to get to sleep, easily glossing over my qualms over the ethics of what Luke was doing, in essence he had it covered, it was a plant that had been used extensively and widely in many forms and for many uses, all beneficial, with no harmful effects whatsoever.

We breakfasted late, a full continental, and talked over what we were going to do for the day while he waited to hear from the university and I waited for the time to collect Emma. I was feeling quite excited about seeing her again after so many months away, despite the unfortunate circumstances that meant she was coming home. We decided to split the day between the National Gallery and the Natural History Museum and left the dining room to get ready.

The day was bright and looked a lot warmer than it was, so I was shivering by the time we reached the Natural History Museum and I realised that it had to be almost twenty years since I had been there last, when Emma was quite young. I remembered her being mostly interested in the dinosaurs, being in that dinosaur-loving stage that children seem to go through, whereas I was fascinated by the human evolution displayed alongside so many other species. It was a keen reminder that we were part of nature, just another one of the species of animals on the earth, and that not every version of man had survived.

Looking at a vastly re-vamped display of the same basic material I remembered the effect it had on me back then. Brought up an Anglican and believing, in a comfortable way, I had a revelation, here, in this very building.

We were not saints who sometimes made mistakes but animals that mostly tried very hard not to behave true to our animal nature, and often failed. That there was no such thing as a soul, no God, just a set of social rules that meant we could survive, and as a group thrive, on this planet. That we had made God in our own image, rather than God making us in his, suddenly seemed obvious and that it was this 'god' that gave us the social rules that were our key to survival in a world where the human animal was neither strong, nor fast, had neither sharp teeth and claws nor huge bulk to protect itself. This human animal had only a growing intelligence and ability to use its social group for protection or aggression, for hunting and for caring. It was here I became what I am, not totally casting aside my cultural church-going inheritance, just keeping only those bits that seemed right, love your neighbour as yourself, that became my creed from then on, and it had all happened here in this building.

'What's wrong, you look like you've seen a ghost.' Luke said coming up beside me as I stood unseeing before one of the exhibits of early man.

'I have, it was me,' I said, and smiled up at him. 'It's okay, I was just remembering something.'

'Are you ready for some lunch?' he asked, I nodded and we headed out to the sunlight.

'Luke, you don't believe in God do you?' I asked as we strolled in the sunshine towards the restaurant he'd found recommended on his mobile five minutes before and booked immediately.

'Well,' he began, 'had you asked me that a month ago I would have said 'no, ma'am', but to be honest, now I am not sure. I really don't think you appreciate what happened to me when I was out, in that coma, or how I think and feel now. What the hell else do I put it down to? There has to be something behind it.'

'Altered states of mind don't have to have God behind them. Someone on drugs doesn't say that the effect must be caused by God!'

'It's not the effect while I was out, it's the lasting effects and, yes, the effects of the dreams that seem to explain everything, and that in the terms of good if not explicitly God. But you, you believe in God don't you, isn't this why you find this experimenting sort of wrong?'

I smiled, 'No, Luke, I don't quite believe in God, as in the God of any of the religions. I believe 'God' is in our social make up, it's part of what makes society work and that is important. I also believe that it gives us time to reflect and guidelines to live by. That's where I have my objections, free will is important, it's part of what makes the human being the wonderful animal it is.'

Luke stopped. I stopped. He looked at me, 'You know,' he said taking my hand as if it were the most natural thing in the world to do, 'you amaze me, I really thought you were a believer, Church on Sunday the lot.'

'Well, I do go to Church on Sunday, sometimes, it's … comforting, and gives me a time to focus on people I care about. Doesn't actually mean much else, you know. I reckon there's a lot who go because it was expected of them, then go about their daily lives doing others down. The building doesn't mean anything, no more than feelings mean there is a god out there somewhere.'

'Whew! Did I get you wrong!'

I shrugged. We walked on and suddenly there was the sound of cheering and clapping and Luke dived into his pocket and retrieved his phone.

'Adamson.'

The sound of another male voice burbled from the phone.

'Great, and thanks Gordon, can I come over right away?.......Sure.....As soon a I can buddy!' Luke said, putting the phone back in his pocket. 'Do you mind if we skip lunch and get over to Queen Mary's, the scan results are in?' His eyes were alight and I could almost sense him bouncing up and down like a small boy.

'No problem, if I can come along too. You'd better cancel that reservation, hadn't you.'

He looked unimpressed, 'I will?'

'Otherwise you'll have them keep a space open for a non-existent customer, that's not fair to them.'

He pulled his phone out again, looked at me, as he re-dialled their number. 'You're right – odd, but you're right. Hi, yeah, hi, sorry, I just made a booking, like ten minutes ago, name of Adamson, sorry but I have to cancel, yes, sorry, called as soon as I knew, and thank you too, yes, yes, I'll have nice day,' he shook his head. 'What is it coming to when a nice class of restaurant tells you to have a nice day like a MacDonalds? We yanks have a lot to answer for!'

Luke led me through an entrance that said School of Biological and Chemical Sciences and down a number of corridors following the CCG signs. Eventually we opened a door into a lab area.

'Hi, Dr Vaughan-Hallam, Gordon,' Luke called as soon as he saw them, full of bonhomie and thrusting out his hand to shake. 'And this is Gabriella Johnston, botanist.'

'Well, Dr Adamson, shall we just complete the financial details and then once confirmed we can look at your results,' the professor said.

'Will you be okay here for a while?' Luke asked.

I shrugged, 'Sure,' and gave Gordon a small smile, 'looks like we both have to wait.'

'Do you know what was being scanned?' he asked, darting his eyes to the door that the others had just gone through.

'Yes….why?'

'Well…what was it from?'

'I'm not sure I can give you that information unless Dr Adamson says it's okay,' I said cautiously. 'Why do you want to know?'

'Well, it was bacteria, as he suggested.'

I nodded.

'And it was related to a strain of Frankia, that's not usual as he brought me a nodule-like piece, and that's a nodule forming bacteria, nitrogen-fixing, you know?'

'Okay… but you seem .. concerned?'

'Er, perhaps I'd better not say anymore until we tell Dr Adamson.'

'I'm with Dr Adamson on this … don't tell me the results, just what you are concerned about.'

'Well it's not so much concerned as, well, a bit confused. The DNA read out identified a lot of chromosomes that flagged up the Frankia, but more, a lot that flagged up Agrobacterium tumefaciens.'

I shook my head, I was none the wiser.

'It's the favourite vector for GM,' he explained. 'And they weren't in two separate bacteria.'

Just then Luke and the professor reappeared in the room, both looking pleased.

'Well, here's the man who can give you the full interpretation,' Dr Vaughan-Hallam said as they approached, 'I've told Dr Adamson that he was right about it being bacteria, do use the office there,' he said, then turning to Luke held out his hand. 'Good bye, Dr Adamson, I do hope that your work progresses well, thank you, I'll leave you with this young gentleman, I'm sure he can explain anything you need to know now.' And having shaken hands all round, he left.

'Well,' said Gordon, and indicated with a tip of the head the office. We all went in and sat down.

'Okay, the results showed that your sample did contain bacteria, and the scan was fairly swift because many of the genetic combinations on the chromosome strands were coming out as matches for bacteria that we have already sequenced.' He stopped and took a deep breath. Luke nodded. 'So,' Gordon continued, 'initially they were matching with Frankia, do you know it?'

Luke nodded, 'Nitrogen-fixing, nodule-creating on non-leguminous plants.'

'Yeah, that's him. So, okay, as expected, but the scan didn't stop there, strands of another recognised bacterium were flagged, this one was Agrobacterium, do you know that one?'

Luke pulled a face, 'Something somewhere tells me I've heard of it, but, no... you tell me.'

'Agrobacterium tumefaciens is the most favoured vector in plant GM. It carries the required genes into the plant cells to create, for example, disease resistant plants.'

'Okay. So, is the Agrobacteria genetically modified to do this?'

'No, it's a natural bacterium of plants. It just already had the mechanisms for transferring genes into plant material and that's why it's used to get selected genes into plants and possibly animal cells, but that's not the point, there was something else,' he was obviously intrigued by what he'd found, 'not only were these two sets of recognisable genetic material in one bacterium, together in one bacterium, but another whole pair of chromosomes that have not been sequenced before by us, or any of the labs we collaborate with, they were in there too. This pair of chromosomes could do anything!'

'What sort of anything? Could it make analgesics, or sedatives?'

'I guess, I really don't know exactly, but many of those have plant origins, why not? As I said it could be anything.... Anyway, here's the whole read out, my conclusions from the recognised parts and the full sequence of the un-recognised chromosomes. You know, I'd love to know what the sample was, sir, to have a hybrid of those two bacteria in it?'

'Thank you so much, Gordon, hell, I'd love to tell you but the research is at a very delicate stage. I really can't, but I promise you that you'll get a mention when the paper is published for your work on this. I have your details here?' he said indicating the sheets Gordon had handed him.

'Yes, sir, thank you.'

'And for a job done well and fast,' Luke fished out his wallet, 'with my thanks, especially giving up your weekend, buy yourself a drink,' and passed the young man a wad of twenties. He took them, saying, no, really, thank you and looking a bit embarrassed. I smiled at him and we all shook hands and left.

Luke had a real spring in his step as we left the university. 'A late lunch,' he said cheerfully, 'with champagne!'

We were both ravenous and enjoyed lunch and he did order champagne to go with it, incongruous as it seemed at three in the afternoon and he had to drink most of it as I knew I'd be driving shortly afterwards.

'So,' he said, leaning back and twirling the stem of his glass between his fingers, 'don't you find this amazing, a natural pairing of two plant bacteria that can change human behaviour.'

'Yes, but, like the lad said, analgesics and sedatives, not to mention hallucinogenics have all come from plant sources, long before men found out how to combine chemicals to make them,'

'True, but here is something revolutionary, something that is a gift to the world. It is not a temporary high or short-term pain relief, this is behaviour changing, permanent, bad-behaviour changing and that is big, so big I think I need to talk to someone in my government about its possibilities.' He sounded tipsy.

I looked at him in surprise. 'Look, Luke, aren't you forgetting something, this is untested, and where it has been tested, to admit to it would be tantamount to destroying your reputation and besides you only have a handful of nodules left, if that.'

'Ah, my lovely Gabriella. Forget the old guys,' he held his hand up as he could see I was fired up to argue, 'for now, forget the old guys, they are none the worse for the experiment, maybe a whole lot better, but forget them, perhaps that was unethical but no harm was done and they don't even know they were dosed.'

'And Sapphira?'

'No need to worry about Sapphira, she is so much on-board that she is helping run these next trials, set them up in fact, and these can be talked about, are ethical in that the facts have been given and permissions obtained and these results can be used.'

'Yeah and you know what I think about that,'

'Yeah and I would ask you, most respectfully, to keep your thoughts to yourself, for this is for the greater good, and eventually you will see that. It has been tested on the two people running the experiment, what better guarantee can they have that we believe it to be safe?'

'Even if you had good results, what would be the point in taking it any further with such a limited supply?'

'Ah! Pretty one, that's where you are wrong, as long as we have some, we can grow more.' Definitely tipsy.

'But we tried culturing the nodules in the lab, nothing happened.'

'No, not culturing the nodules, culturing the bacteria, the lad suggested it and I checked it out last night. The bacteria can be grown in vats of the right medium and will multiply exponentially. Sourcing shouldn't be a problem.'

'I think perhaps you are crazy. I suppose you see a killing to be made in this stuff?'

He actually looked surprised. 'Oh, no, Gabriella, I couldn't do that, this is a gift for mankind, hand on my heart, I can't profit by it. *It* wouldn't let me.'

It was my turn to look surprised.

We headed back to the hotel, checked out and retrieved my car. I had agreed with Luke to pick up Emma and drop him off at a hotel and conference centre near Exeter on the way down.

I was jumping up and down when I saw Emma coming though the terminal, I wanted to make sure she saw me and I knew I had the biggest grin on my face. She rushed over, hugging me tightly. 'Oh Mum, It's so good to be home,' she said. We were both in tears. Luke stood a little way back watching, I felt his eyes keenly on us both.

'Emma, this is Luke Adamson,' I started.

'Oh Wow, so it is! I saw your film!' she said, sticking out her hand to shake his and looking at me again, 'Wow, mum?'

'Luke is …. an old friend,' I decided to say. 'We, your father and I, knew Luke at University.' Stretching a point but it felt the safe way to introduce him. 'We're giving him a lift down to Exeter tonight. Come on, let's go.'

After the usual questions about how the journey was and what we had been doing in London there was a lull in the conversation as we drove down the motorway towards Exeter. I suppose being a Monday the road wasn't too busy and we were making good time. Regardless there came the need to take a break and we did so with Luke making much of unwinding himself from my back seat and stretching. Emma, dear girl that she is, offered to swap places for the next leg of the journey, which, with one eye on me, Luke gladly accepted.

As we set off again, Emma, leaned forward from her new position on the back seat and addressed Luke.

'So,' she said, 'apart for being an old friend of Mum's what are you doing in the UK?'

'Well,' he said, 'I have just finished a lecture tour, last talk was at Eden, and believe it or not I recognised your Mum, not changed all that much in all those years.'

I could feel Emma smiling at that. 'And up in London? With Mum?'

I had the distinct sense of one and one being added together to make three.

'Luke was up there visiting a university,' I said, 'and then I came up to collect you.' Hoping to put an end to filial speculation.

'I was having some plant material DNA scanned,' Luke added.

'So what are you working on?'

Luke looked across at me but didn't wait for me to react, 'A substance that if taken makes sure that you can't do anything to someone else just to get something for yourself out of it.'

'Sorry, what?'

'Once someone has taken this it is very hard, I'd say just about impossible, to steal, hurt, wield power over someone, just for your own gain.'

'There can't be anything like that, surely? Did you find it in the rainforest?'

'Sortta,' he said. 'I guess you could say that, a rainforest.' There was a small silence then Luke asked. 'If they caught the guy who jumped you, would you think it was right to give him some of this stuff, so he'd never do it again?'

'What, like just inject him with it?'

'Well, similar, make him take it like a pill say, or give him the choice, take the tablet or take the prison sentence.'

'Stuff choice!' Emma said. 'He didn't give me any choice. Yeah, make him take it, make all of them.'

Luke tipped his head in acknowledgement and looked across at me, I focused on driving.

The Angel Bug 28

Luke 1st – 2nd November

I had hardly slept for thinking of what this day could bring. The Reverend Ashe was a very charismatic guy, though not the sort I'd usually cotton-on to, but it was obvious that what he said, how he said it, won over a lot of people. He was conviction itself and what blew me away was the way he'd seen the good in the Moringa treatment. He was sure, positive, God-given, certain sure, that this gift was from God and that it was for mankind as a whole. I'd even drawn Sapphira away for a few moments and checked she'd not delivered him a surreptitious dose of Moringa as she had the same sort of conviction. She hadn't, she had only explained, using herself as a truth-laid-bare-example of what it had done to her.

Today was the day. We were going to give forty–eight people the Moringa treatment, and they were ready to be part of this amazing experiment. On the Monday, Sapphira had gathered them together and explained that we had a remedy made from the entirely edible plant, Moringa oleifera – they could check it out on the internet if they liked - so it was an herbal treatment that we wanted to test. She told them we needed them to take a quiz both before and after they took this treatment, as we knew it had beneficial effects, we'd both taken it ourselves and knew, but didn't know quite how it worked, and that was where they came in. They were told that the whole experiment was to be anonymous, no one would know who had answered which questions, their identification being only a number allocated blind. We would ask no questions that might identify the actual person in any way, not even gender, and pointed this out to the volunteers to gain their honest and open responses. They were told that the remedy was made totally from the Moringa, nothing else added except orange squash, and that it may make them excitable and later drowsy, so if they felt like sleeping, they should. We also asked them not to discuss any sensations or feelings that they had during the two days with anyone but us, and especially not with any of the other participants. To my amazement every one of them agreed, and signed a form to say they would participate in this trial with full understanding and permission.

We had decided to do a double blind experiment, telling them all that they were taking the treatment, while secretly giving it to only half of them. They were asked to take one of the tumblers when they were brought out, drink the contents then turn it over to see which number was written on the base. This, they were asked to memorise as they were required to write this number on the top of their question sheets.

We had labelled the cups with the numbers and dosed all the odd ones, then muddled the groups up a bit before asking a few of the volunteers to come in, put cups on their trays and take them out to the other members of the group. Both the waiters and the recipients were to be oblivious to any order they were in, and all could select whichever they wanted from the tray as they came to them. This way we couldn't know who had taken the treatment and who hadn't, we would have to wait to see the results.

The quiz was designed to seek out their weaknesses with regards to greed of any type, but surrounded by other questions that muddied the waters so our objective was not obvious. We'd put together the questionnaire back in Cornwall, brainstorming the types of behaviour that would demonstrate greed and mixed in those that might merely be thought of as having health benefits. The final layout and production of the questionnaires had been one of Sapphira's jobs to do once she had gotten to Exeter.

When I'd looked over the finished questionnaire last night I'd read: Put the number from the base of your cup here. There is no way we can link any one person with their answers so please give your honest and open responses, thank you for helping to help mankind. Please tick all responses that apply to you. 1, Have you ever given into the temptation of eating/taking/doing, (even though you thought you shouldn't) any of the following: cookies, made a false insurance claim, candies, cheating in an exam, cigarettes, taking home stuff from work, flirting, cannabis, sex outside a firm relationship, adding to your expenses bill, putting other people down to gain an advantage over them, bet to get yourself out of money troubles, lying to get some kind of advancement or power, exaggerating your expenses on your tax form, alcohol, hurting someone because you could, chocolate, downloading pirated films or music, 'insider dealing'- using information to gain a unfair financial advantage over others, a Big Mac or similar, and so on for a total of thirty questions of which two-thirds were the ones we were really interested in. These were followed by a similar range of questions for a more serious level of participation in, or addiction to, these behaviours or substances. Finally there were two questions: Do you still do any of the behaviours listed in question one, with 'yes', 'sometimes' and 'no' options and the same for section two. Every substance or behaviour had a tick-box beside it. I looked it over; I felt it would give us a good baseline.

I picked up the second questionnaire; unlike the first two-page quiz, this was on six sheets. I skimmed through it, from the start with the same request for the number, this would be the link between the two papers, and the same reassurance that we'd not know who had filled in what, there the simplicity ended, and I could see this would take a long time to fill in.

For each of the listed behaviours, as in the first questionnaire, it said: If you ticked this box on the first questionnaire briefly describe one real example where you did this, and it offered four blank lines to fill in. Each of these was followed by the request to 'State any feelings or sensations that you experienced while recalling this event' and two blank lines. I knew what I'd be writing down and hoped these people would be as honest, but was a little concerned that they wouldn't know what they were experiencing and would be shy to write down that they were having olfactory hallucinations, 'smelling shit' where there was no real stuff around. I slipped the questionnaires back into the folder; it wouldn't do for anyone to see these too early.

The group straggled into the conference centre, some chatting excitedly, others looking a little less keen this morning. When ten o'clock came, we called them to order and eventually even the last few sat down. They were all there. The Reverend Ashe led us all in prayer and we reiterated some of the most important points from Sapphira's talk the previous day. They were given a last chance to skip the whole event, but everyone stayed put. The volunteers to collect the cups went into the side room and filled their trays and brought them back, handing them out at random, finally taking the cups that were left for themselves. We encouraged everyone to check their numbers in secret and then the trays went round and the cups were gathered up at random.

'Okay!' Sapphira called, 'Please pick up a clipboard from the back table and go and complete it. Please do not leave the conference area but there are tables you can use at the back, a comfortable seating area in the side room, or you can stay as you are, just answer honestly and without anyone else seeing your responses or your number and when you are done slip the sheets into the box here,' she finished, indicating something like a ballot box beside her. 'Any questions?'

The volunteers looked thoughtful, some glanced at each other, but no one had a question, I breathed a sigh of relief and watched as they got up and collected the clipboards. Some people's faces were fascinating to watch, so revealing as they went from a smile to a deep frown, to something that raised a blush just by ticking it, other faces remained passive or thoughtful throughout. I could feel the excitement building in me and was on the look out for the first signs that the treatment was working, the excitable stage as Sapphira had called it. It was going to be interesting to see the reactions when some people became excited and others didn't.

This is why scientific testing has to be done so carefully, I thought, as I watched the scene before me. At least three quarters of the volunteers were behaving in a hyper-active, inebriated way, yet we knew it ought to be only half. We'd laid on a film to watch in the main room and music to listen to in the side room. The volunteers had been encouraged to bring games or books to occupy themselves but most didn't bother with anything they had brought with them. The music was a general mix of easy listening and current pop but some of these guys were jumping around and dancing to it as if it were the most exciting music out, even where people were watching the family-rated film, there were those flinging their arms around and hooting with laughter or calling out to the screen like demented children. There were a few very puzzled faces, some looking at their friends and compatriots with thinly veiled disgust. One of these came up to me.

'Sir, are you certain sure this stuff isn't just a type of amphetamine?'

I smiled reassuringly, 'Certainly, and yes it may look weird but this is normal and wears off soon.'

'So, I suppose it's not working on me then?' he sounded a little disappointed.

'It can affect different people in different ways,' I said, not wanting him to know he probably hadn't had a dose at all.

We had a buffet brought in and some people ate, mainly those who were calm, some of the others too, but all seemed thirsty and the range of soft drinks that we'd ordered soon disappeared and we had to send out for more. Slowly they all calmed down, tiredness overcoming them, some more than others. We took it in turns to escort these people back to their rooms and held on to a key card for each twin-room so we could check on everyone on a regular basis. It seemed a hell of a long day, but by eleven o'clock even the ones who probably hadn't had a dose of Moringa at all had decided to go off to bed. I was so wired I wasn't sure if I was tired or not. We decided to split the night into four-hour shifts, each of us taking a turn at checking that everyone was okay and waiting up in case there was a problem. Mine was the middle shift, though I didn't feel much like sleeping when I returned to my bed, worrying about how long it would take for each one of them to wake up, remembering the over-long sleep that the old guys had taken.

Next morning Sapphira was knocking on my door. Somehow I had slept right on through the alarm I had set. My first concern was how everyone was, whether we'd had any problems in the last section of the night. I needn't have worried. Apparently over half of the people were up, dressed and breakfasting, just over a third were still snoring away to one extent or another.

By lunchtime there were only three people who were still sleeping. We kept a close eye on them, checking them more and more often. Eventually, by two-thirty, everyone was awake and the late-risers were eating a hearty lunch.

By four we had everyone gathered again and, after prayers led by the Reverend Ashe, we asked them to take the new six page questionnaire and complete it, as before putting their unique number on the top and not allowing others to see what they were doing. I had to smile when I saw the first person curl her lip and put her hand to her nose, disgust written all over her face. I saw her look round for the source of the stench, but she was very much in an area alone. I made a mental note to ask Sapphira what her dreams were like. Mine had been explanatory, but then I had been out of it for much longer. Perhaps with the shortened time you only had the smells without understanding what they were or why they came. I could tell now, I thought, which candidates had taken the odd-numbered cups with the Moringa treatment in, they were the ones with nostrils flaring, or occasionally hands over their mouths, or looking round suspiciously. The ones who kept eyes down and just wrote were those who hadn't, though the occasional blush could be seen colouring a face if you studied these people close enough. They were also the ones who managed, on the whole, to finish earlier, I guessed because they had not been distracted by the effects of the treatment.

Just after six we thanked all of them and said that they were free to leave. Sapphira and I stood looking at the 'ballot' box full of responses.

'After we've eaten, I think,' I said, with great restraint.

Over the meal I asked Sapphira what she remembered of the time she was asleep, after I'd give her the Moringa.

'Why, Luke?' she said. 'What's bothering you?'

'The way some people obviously treated the stink that they were smelling as coming from somewhere else, not from inside their heads.'

'Ah, I see. Okay, so I don't remember a lot to be honest, I don't remember going to Gabbi's house for instance, I think the last thing I remember is getting into the car. Then the next was waking up but not opening my eyes, lying there feeling something had changed but I didn't know what. Then I remembered snatches of these strange dreams, like very short clips from my life, each one where I was feeling smug because I got what I wanted because I could, and you know, the stenches.'

'And did it make sense to you?'

'Not right then, no, I ran a few experiments on myself as I lay there, I think I told you, and it happened, not just in the dream, but right then. Besides, it wasn't long before I heard you talking to Gabbi, heard what you said, and then it made so much sense.'

'So, today, these people who were looking round for the smell, perhaps they just hadn't put two and two together?'

'Perhaps, though I think that if you watched they soon stopped looking round for the smell….'

She was right, I had thought I'd just stopped noticing that particular behaviour, whereas, people had gradually stopped.

'Interesting… are you finished? Personally, now, I can't wait to get to those response sheets.'

We'd divided the papers into odds and evens, paired up the first paper with the second, then each took half of the number. First of all we just skimmed through the answer sheets, we weren't too worried about what they had actually said, what each person's memories of bad behaviour actually was, it was the responses we were looking for, and there they were, time after time on the odd numbered sheets. A typical example started with, 'Revolting' then added, 'and I can smell something funny', after he or she'd described taking home a pack of computer paper, the same person by the time they'd got to near the end of their questionnaire simply wrote '!! That Stink again!!' when asked for any feeling or sensations on describing how they'd added to their expenses claims.

Hours later I put down my last sheet. We'd gone from skimming to enumerating the results. There wasn't one case of true greed, described by an odd-number respondent, that wasn't accompanied by signs of revulsion and the evidence of stenches. Whereas some of the confessions on the other sheets, even accompanied by regret, made us wonder if we shouldn't give the even-numbered volunteers a dose just to be on the safe side.

I knew I was right, that I had in my grasp a wonderful discovery to help all mankind, a new beginning, and I was afraid, me, afraid to go to the big wide world alone with this thing. And that's when I told Sapphira of my bigger plan.

'Sapphira, I am hoping to take this home to the US, make something really good come out of it, something big, not for me, I'll not be taking anything out of it, but for everyone. Do you want to come with me?'

'Luke?'

'A business partnership, I mean, offering just enough to live on, maybe. Do you have the same objectives as I do for this, the Moringa treatment for the good of mankind?'

'Oh, a business deal, with no profit, just a small salary? Yeah, that smells right!' she smiled. 'That's it isn't it? We can't make money out of this.'

'You got it.'

'I'm on board. I'll send my resignation to Eden at once. How long before you go back?'

'I'll be off as soon as I can, but you'll need to apply for a visa I guess.'

'No, no, it's not a problem, I have dual nationality, I'll come with you.'

The Angel Bug 29

Gabbi   November - December

I didn't quiz Emma on the journey home about her trouble in Australia because, not far out of Exeter, she fell asleep, so I listened to the radio and pushed the car as fast as she would go to get us home as quickly as possible.

The next morning Emma looked so much better and we went for a walk along the coast, the wind whipping up spray and the waves crashing on the rocks.

'He didn't just snatch my bag you know, mum,'

'No, I thought not.'

'But it wasn't, he didn't rape me or anything, well…' she closed her eyes, 'He didn't, but I think he might have, if, if, you see some joggers came by and,' she stopped and took a deep breath. 'You see he'd tripped me up, then he was all over me, lying on me, I was fighting him off, but not screaming, when I think back I might even have been holding my breath with the effort. Stupid or what? But then I heard them, felt feet pounding, and I screamed and screamed, he must have seen them 'cos he looked towards the hedge, let go of my arms, snatched my bag up and ran. Suddenly this guy bursts through the hedge. A jogger, I mean. He took one look at me then took off after the other guy, and others come through the hedge, some women in the group and they helped me out. The jogger came back, he'd lost him, but you see, Mum, I'd seen this guy hanging round, sitting on a wall near the halls,' she shuddered. 'I really couldn't hack being there, knowing he might just turn up.' She stopped walking, turned to me, close to tears

'Be a real idiot if he did though,' I said, pulling her in for a hug.

'Probably a smack-head, you just don't know with some of them,' she shook her head against my shoulder and stood away again. 'It's good to be back in Cornwall anyway, if a mite chilly,' she tugged her coat closer and snuggled her nose down into her scarf as we turned for home.

By a week or so after we had got back from London I was getting used to having Emma around. We'd just been out to Truro on a little shopping spree and had been delighted to find plenty of nice things to look at and buy. We'd stopped and watched a mad group of border Morris dancers, their black and gold tattered jackets flying as they crashed their huge sticks and twirled round in their dances, the musicians pounding out toe-tapping music from concertinas, accordions, drums and flutes. As we came in the door, still humming the rhythmic tunes, I heard the phone ringing.

'Hello?'

'Hi, Gabbi?'

'Yes, Tim?' I asked to be sure.

'Yes. I was wondering, could you come in on Monday, or whenever suits next week, I've wanted to talk to you since I got back and now I can, as I have a proposition for you.'

'Oh! Well, yes, of course, Monday is fine. Is it about the suspension?'

'Well, sort of, but you don't have to worry about that now, um, how about nine o'clock, in the Foundation building?'

'Fine,' I said, 'I'll see you then,'

'Thank you, Gabbi, thanks,' Tim said and rang off.

I stood there with the phone in my hand, listening to its hum for a moment before putting it gently down.

'What was that?' Emma asked, staring at me.

I shook myself. 'It was Tim, from Eden, he wants to see me. He said I wasn't to worry about the suspension now… or did he mean don't worry about it *just now*? I'm not sure.'

'And you're going to see him, soon?'

'Oh yes, Monday morning.'

'Then there's no need to worry about it at all, you'll know soon enough,' she said with confidence. It doesn't work like that for me, I worried at it the rest of the weekend, making sure I had my defence ready if this was about the suspension after all. I really wanted to have my place at Eden back.

Monday morning I was up, showered, smartly dressed and as nervous as if for a first date. I called to Emma, who hadn't even stirred from her bed, that I would be back by lunchtime and left. There was ice on my windscreen, so I had to run back in to get a jug of warm water to defrost it, then back in to drop it off again. Emma called down, 'Everything all right?'
I shouted back 'Fine,' and left again. Typical, all hot and bothered before I'd even left home, I thought, as I met another car on a narrow stretch of road and had to whiz the Mini back to a passing place.

I parked in my usual space outside the Foundation building and it felt so right. Karen was all smiles and would have kept me talking if Tim hadn't come along.
'Gabbi, great, shall we go through here?' he said, leading the way through to office space on the ground floor.

'Do take a seat,' Tim said indicating the comfy chairs. This obviously wasn't going to be formal, but then formal wasn't Tim's style. When we were comfortable he leant forward, his hands clasped before him.
'Gabbi, will you come back?'
'Oh Tim, I'd love to.'
'The post of senior botanist is going to be advertised soon.'
'Oh! What happened to Sapphira?' I asked, but as I spoke I had an inkling I might know, she and Luke had seemed close when I'd last seen them in Exeter.
'She resigned, and left immediately. Her post will be advertised this week and I would really like it if you'd consider applying.'

It took a second or two to assimilate that, and then the objections came rolling in.

'But, well, Sapphira made pretty clear that my level of qualification wasn't high enough, even though I'd not applied.'

'But not me, and anyway this new post is being pitched as more managerial, after all we can call upon the best specialists to work out any science needed, having everyone as a team, as a *happy* team, is far more important here.' He looked at me, raising his eyebrows a little. Ungratefully I was thinking that I didn't want to work full time and give up on St Pirans and juggling that with the thought of being back with the gang again, and the fact that it had worked well while I was covering the job before. 'It would be on the same terms as when you stepped in before, but with the enhanced salary, you managed everything perfectly well while you were holding the fort back then,' he added as if reading my thoughts.

I smiled, 'Thank you Tim, yes I'll apply.'

He beamed at me, 'Great!' he stood and picked up a sheaf of papers from the table behind him and handed them to me. 'Here it is, I look forward to seeing it.'

I looked at the application forms in my hand and smiled.

I was just about to leave when Naomi came down the stairs. She hurried over and threw her arms around me. 'Oh Gabbi, so good to see you, has, have…' she began. Tim, from somewhere behind me, said 'Yes, I have asked her.'

Naomi straightened, 'When Tim asked us what we felt about him offering you the job, well, it made us all very happy, you will take it?'

'Well, I will apply,' I said looking from her to Tim. He grinned and turned away, she beamed at me.

'Oh!' she seemed to suddenly remember where she was going, 'I have to go, so great to see you Gabbi, I can't wait to tell the others,' and she hurried out of the building. I turned to follow and caught Karen's eye.

'It will be nice to have you back here,' she said smiling at me

'It would be nice to come back,' I said with feeling.

I read the application forms and filled them in. It was as if someone had studied exactly what I had done for those few months and put them onto paper, including the hours I had wanted. The job description fitted me like a glove. However, the proper procedure still had to be gone through. The post was advertised, at least internally, and then the board met to discuss applicants. With no other applicants I was told that they had made the unanimous decision to take me on as the Botanical Manager as from the fifth of December, and I couldn't have felt happier.

That Monday came at last and I drove happily into work, parking my Mini in its place and heading into the Foundation building. I was early, hoping for a quiet half hour to sort a few things out and, as no other cars were in the car park, I thought I was on a winner. I heard a scraping noise just as the door eased its way closed behind me, but thought nothing of it as I climbed the stairs. I stepped out onto the floor and nearly fell back down in shock as happy shouts of 'welcome back' came from behind me where the team had been hiding out of my line of sight. They came rushing round to greet me and I had tears in my eyes before I knew what I was doing, hugging and being hugged by Karen, Naomi, Mikaela, and even Andy.

We took the drawers out of the senior botanist's desk and together carried it ceremoniously back to where it belonged, shuffling the other desks into their old familiar pattern. The filing cabinets followed and within half an hour the place truly felt like home.

'So,' I said when we were comfortably ensconced in our old format, 'update me on where we are with things.'

'We've had a bit of a problem with sparrows in the Warm Temperate biome. Breeding at this time of the year! Not quite sure what the house policy is going to be on this, it was one thing them coming and going, and even the first nest last spring wasn't a bother but we've located two nests, with eggs, just last week,' Naomi started.

'Hmm, interesting. Are they degrading any of the plants?'

'Not that we've noticed,' Andy said.

'Okay, watch and wait for now, any other worries?'

'The Moringa, still,' Mikaela sighed.

'But it was taken out? Didn't Sapphira just leave the Neem?'

'No, it was all panic stations, she had a replacement put in then, just before she upped and left, she ordered Jim to take as many cuttings as possible from the original and get one back into the same place as the old one as soon as it had struck.'

'Oh right. Has he been able to do this?'

'Well, he has put the replacement in, but what with her not returning he didn't quite know what to do about the cuttings, he has a row of cuttings that he says have taken and wants to know whether he's to put one of these back in as asked.'

'Why not?' I said, knowing what the aim must be even if I was still not sure about the outcome. 'Let him know it's okay to go ahead and do it when he thinks it is right.' I looked around at the crew, they seemed happy, 'If there's nothing else I'll let you get on and after I've checked anything pending,' I waved my hand at the computer, 'then I'll take a walk around. It's good to be back – thank you,' I added, knowing I had the biggest smile on my face as I said it, and seeing it reflected in the faces of those around me.

Like seeing your child after they've been away at camp for a week, coming back to Eden made me notice all sorts of small changes that I would normally just absorb and probably ignore on a day-to-day basis. I noticed where some plants were encroaching on others, to their detriment, where a sign was looking tired, and later, in the afternoon, a new face in the greenhouses at Watering Lane.

He might have felt me looking at him, as he suddenly looked up from what he was doing; caught out I smiled, said 'good afternoon' but then turned away and hurried out because I was feeling so hot all of a sudden, which I didn't like. Even once back outside and I'd put it down to being inside the warm greenhouse after being chilled outside before, I was still uneasy. I asked at the Reception building who the new guy was on the horticulture staff, and when I'd described him, tall, dark-hair, lean-looking, they told me he wasn't with Eden at all; he was Dr John Keyes, a scientist from the Royal Horticultural Society at Wisley, doing some kind of research at Eden.

At home that evening I found myself looking up the RHS website, finding him listed there. Googling his name and finding out more than ought to be possible about someone you don't know, from multiple entries ranging from papers he'd had published to his Facebook page. He'd been circumspect on that, apart from the very basic information it was all 'friends-only', but his photo was there, that's how I knew I'd found the right John Keyes out of at least twenty offered. From this and the rest I discovered he was a highly educated man in his early fifties, specialising in plant pathology and genetics, single and living in Berkshire. After a few minutes flicking around extracts from papers he'd published I wondered what I was doing and embarrassed with myself turned off the computer.

I didn't see him around at all Tuesday or Wednesday and was beginning to think he'd finished his stuff and was off back to the RHS when he walked up the stairs and hesitated at the top, looking round. The others were all out and about and I was working through paperwork and sorting out schedules for the Christmas period.

'Can I help?' I said, slightly rising from my seat. He turned on an amazing smile; it went right to his eyes.

'I was told to come and see Gabbi?'

'Well, that's me,' I said, standing properly as he strode across, hand held out. We shook, his hand firm and dry in mine.

'John Keyes. From the RHS,' he said.

'Take a seat, John,' I said, swivelling my chair and indicating one of the other computer chairs nearby, thinking of how I'd been looking him up already. He sat in Andy's chair. Damn, I was feeling all flustered again.

'How can I help?'

'Well, we were sent some samples from nodules on the Moringa, back in late October.'

'Pardon?'

'The RHS were sent some sections of a root nodule from Eden …' he started.

'Who the hell sent them?'

He looked a little confused, 'Well, I understood that *you* had, well, to be accurate, you had sent them to the University of Reading for SEM and they sent us a section as a follow-up.' I must have looked a little surprised as he continued, 'It's standard procedure if they come across something that they have not seen before, they double check with us.'

'I see,' I said, waiting for the revelation, after all I knew the bacterial make-up of the nodules now.

'And it wasn't anything we'd seen before either. I suspect that we have a new nodule forming bacteria here and as it also seems to be a nitrogen fixer that is associated with a non-leguminous plant. We, at the RHS, were interested and contacted Eden,' he looked at me, 'You haven't been told any of this have you?'

I shook my head. 'I've been away and our last senior botanist left after, after a short illness, rather abruptly, there's been no handover.'

'Ah! I understand now. So you won't know that Tim gave me the go-ahead to study the tree the nodules came from, the soil, everything.'

'No, but that's fine. Did you know Dr Adamson is interested in the nodules as well?'

He tilted his head. 'Well, there was more left unsaid than said, but I did hear,' he smiled. 'I have to admit that though people have been very friendly they've not been exactly chatty with me over the past week.'

'I would guess that is because the people you needed to talk to weren't aware of your study. It's been a little chaotic with the sudden change-over, so I'm sorry, usually we are very helpful.'

'Ah! No! I didn't mean to criticise.'

'Don't worry, it's not a problem. Look, shall we go back to the start and you can tell me what you'd found out and I can fill you in with what we know here,' I said, feeling cooler and in control again.

'I've a better idea,' he looked at me and smiled, 'how about we get some lunch and I can tell you about it while we eat?'

I found I was delighted with this idea, but tried not to show it as I could feel the heat travelling up my body again. 'Great idea,' I said standing and turning round to unhook my fleece from the back of the chair, hiding the blush that was hitting my face at that moment. 'Shall we go down to the Link or up to the Visitors Centre?'

'You choose,' he said, standing, 'it's your place.'

The Angel Bug 30

Luke   November - December

I ought to have felt exhilarated coming back to the States, but as we touched down I felt a strange regret at leaving England, and certainly at not having seen Gabriella to say goodbye. I'd sent her an email, but that wasn't the same.

I'd already been talking to people I knew back home. Reminding myself of the people I actually knew who were now in positions of power within the Justice system. I had the theory that if I could get this idea taken up, we would be able to empty our prisons. Okay, not right in one go, and there were always those people who clamoured for people to be locked away to teach them a lesson and act as a deterrent for others. It didn't work, that much even I knew, recidivism was rife, three quarters of those in jail had been in before, many came from families who had other members who were, or had been, in jail, it wasn't much of a put-off. The best it did was keep the criminals off the streets for a while. Good as that was, it also had the unintended consequence of putting them in a place where they learned, not how to be a model citizen when they came out, but how to get away with it longer before they were caught.

Gerry had been with me at Johns Hopkins University and he was now head honcho of the penitentiary system within the Department of Justice, only two steps away from the President when it came to matters concerning convicted criminals. A few hours after we landed I had a meeting with him all set up, informal of course, old friends catching up, but I had signalled that I was on to something really big that could help his position in the department. He was curious as hell, but I made him wait.

The first call I took, once back on American soil, was from the laboratories I had worked with before, and that I had asked to price up and be ready to order all the equipment I'd need for large scale bacteria culture. They had said it was no big deal as long as we were operating with non-virulent bacteria, and I was pleasantly surprised at the price they quoted and gave the final okay. They assured me we would be ready for work by the end of the following week.

I knew I had the staff at the labs that I could call on to oversee the actual operation of making the bacteria cultures, and I had asked the lab to find me a specialist who could make sure everything went according to plan and without contamination. Over all this I put Sapphira, to run the day-to-day operation and tasked her with keeping me up-to-date on everything. That someone might leak information about our trials, or worse still, about what the Moringa treatment actually did, before we were ready, worried me. We could be blown out of the water before anyone had the chance to evaluate the wonderful opportunity it provided to the world, and I was determined to prevent that happening. Ashe had readily agreed to save the announcement for the opportune time, as we'd persuaded him that premature revelation would only harm the cause, the volunteers were asked by him to wait until he was ready to reveal the message, and it appeared they were happy to follow him.

It was an expensive restaurant, and Gerry looked as if he was used to dining well and perhaps a little too often. He grinned, half stood and held out his hand, 'Well, what do you know, Luke Adamson.'

'Gerry, great to see you after all this time,' I said giving a firm handshake and sitting down opposite him.

'So, I saw your movie. Was it all real? Nothing faked? Come on, you can tell me,' he said winking.

'All real, just cut out the boring bits, of which there was about eighteen months, but hey, I think despite the distractions it did bring the rainforest's problems into focus.'

'Sure, sure. But I'm fired up to know why it is that you dug up this old acquaintance, sure as hell I don't have any rainforests in my pocket,' he smiled and tilted his head indicating that the question was the real point.

'Well, no you don't, but I have something from the rainforest in mine and that something might be an answer to one of your problems.'

'It might? And which of my many problems were you thinking about?'

'Probably, recidivism.'

'Recidivism? Whoa, what do you know about recidivism? I'll have you know we try both carrot and stick, all the time. And every so long a guy comes up with some new psychological notion on how to persuade these sons of bitches to go straight when they get out, and it works, maybe, for a week or two and then boo! It all disappears and the assholes are back in.'

'What is the re-offending rate would you say?'

'Last year it came in at sixty-seven percent after three years.'

As I had researched, give or take. 'What if I could give you a treatment that meant the recidivism reduced to zero to five percent?'

'There's no course on earth could do that,'

'I didn't say course, I said treatment, a simple drink with a remedy in it after which that person would find it hard, very hard to re-offend.'

Gerry sat back and looked straight at me. 'Let's order,' he said, 'then you can tell me more.'

We made our choices and while we waited for our first course to arrive Gerry shook his head. 'If you weren't Dr 'Saviour of the Rainforest' Adamson I think I would have walked away by now, you do realise you sound like a kook?'

I smiled to myself, when put like that I guess he was right. Perhaps I needed to go back to the beginning and explain it in more scientific terms. 'Okay, when we've finished here would you accompany me back to my hotel, I have statistics set up on my computer that will probably help me appear a little less kooky?'

'Agreed, I don't want to spoil this meal with too much talk anyway, the food here is just too good.'

'It'll only take a minute or two to call them up,' I said as I set up the laptop. 'A nightcap?' I asked, indicating the minibar.

'No thanks,' he said, seating himself comfortably on an armchair opposite the screen.

'Okay,' I turned the projector on and my desktop appeared on the screen. I flicked up the charts that I had created out of the results of the trials. There was a little bamboozlement in the headings, nothing that wasn't true, or that caused me to suffer any stenches though. I had grouped the responses under headings that you would usually see in indictments. So the results from the questions about 'exaggerating expenses claims' and over-estimating outgoings on tax forms' and 'claiming against insurance' were under the heading 'Fraud' other headings were 'Theft' 'Assault' 'Sexual harm' 'Addiction' – none of the titles covered the health benefit questions, though I'd had a chuckle to myself over the thought of putting them in under a title of 'Indulgence' while I was completing the charts.

'Hmm,' Gerry started, 'I don't see any murder or extortion?'

'No, you won't, my sample just didn't include those.'

'Your sample? Who was it? Where did you do this testing?' he was going fast. I had to remind myself that Gerry, amiable and full of smiles as he appeared, was one of the best brains in our year, and hadn't got to where he was through being a fool.

'I did the testing in the UK, it was where I was at the time,' I galloped on, hoping he'd be happy with that and not ask what prison gave me the opportunity. 'Here are the results of these behaviours from the sample.'

I pressed a button and up came a simple bar chart showing how many had offended in each way for the whole sample

'How big was this sample?'

Damn! A question I had hoped to avoid. 'Not large, I agree, mainly because we were carrying out a double-blind experiment, we had forty-eight in total and only gave half of the number the treatment.'

'And this was okay under their government, I mean, I usually hear they are far more squeamish than us about these things.'

'Each and every participant was a volunteer and gave their full informed consent,' I said. True. 'So, half were given the treatment, double-blind, we didn't know who had received the treatment and they weren't aware that only half of them would receive it. They were later asked to recall the events they had enumerated before the treatment had taken effect. Now I've split the groups for you to see. Here's the group without the treatment and their responses to being asked to write down what they had actually done. See, mostly neutral, some justifying their actions, some ashamed but nothing much.' I took a deep breath, 'Now, here's the group who took the treatment, here's what they did,' I clicked on their bar chart folder, 'and here are their responses. Mostly revulsion at the thought of what they did with ninety-seven percent writing the words, stench, stink or vile smell.'

'Weird, but what does it mean?'

'It means that if you even think about doing something bad, something based on your greed, you get an overwhelming stench that seems to fill your nostrils, and if you don't stop, it will make you gag, even vomit.'

'You sound convinced of that.'

'I am, I, I took a treatment myself, in the early stages.'

'You mad or something? Scientists doing tests on themselves went out with the ark!'

'Not so, but then, what I was testing was what you might call an herbal remedy, and from a plant that man has used and consumed, for years.'

'An herbal *remedy*? You *are* having me on?'

'Yes. No, it's from a safe herbal background, let's say, but this treatment, this version, is different, it is new and it works. What I need, is to try it out here, in the States, but this is so big it can't hang about waiting for the FDA. Look, over a time it could nearly empty our penitentiaries and jails, isn't that worth looking at?'

'You really have taken this stuff? Any side effects?'

'Only that I am a better man than I've ever been. And I know I couldn't go back to how I was even if I wanted to.'

'So, you want to run a trial?'

I nodded.

He took a long indrawn breath between his teeth, 'I might be able to help, I don't know if you remember Jock Mackay?'

I shook my head, 'What discipline?'

'Politics, same as me but he didn't do our sports, so you might not remember him, basically, he owns a private medium level penitentiary in Louisiana, and he might be interested. We have a scheme whereby these private places take on our worst recidivists and get a bonus, first for each month, then after a year, for each year the jailbird stays out of the system after they have left. He might be interested, and I wouldn't know anything about it,' and he winked.

Jock, or James as he was christened, Mackay was a hefty ex-football player and filled the room when I welcomed him into my hotel suite in Louisiana.

'Hey, great to meet you. Know all about you from that movie and Gerry tells me you were at Hopkins with us?'

'Sure,' I said pumping his meaty hand, 'Biological Sciences, but rowing and baseball with Gerry.'

'Sure,' he said as we sat, him leaning back, confident and at ease. 'So, what have you got for me, Gerry was telling nothing definite except this might be real interesting for me.'

'Well, he was telling the truth there. As I understand this you get a bonus for every month, then each year that a guy does not end up back in the justice system, is that right?'

'Just about, meant to encourage us to build into our system as many deterrents and facilitators to go straight when they leave, as is cost effective in the long run. You take it, if our clients would keep their noses clean we'd be making money by the shed load.' He grinned and shook his head, 'They just don't seem to get the idea though,' and laughed.

'Okay, as you say, but what if I could supply a drink, an herbal drink, that once taken would really help deter these guys from committing another crime?'

'Huh? An herbal drink, is this some kind of scam?'

'No, you know who I am. I am not a scam merchant. This is from a rainforest tree that has been consumed and used by man for hundreds of years, however, this preparation is new, and it works.'

He narrowed his eyes at me, 'Side effects?'

'Well, apart from finding it hard to commit most crimes, barely any to speak of, a short few hours of hyperactivity followed by a deep sleep for twelve hours or so and that's it.'

He showed his hand, 'Gerry said that you're a mad skunk and had tried it yourself.'

I grinned, 'Yes, I did.'

'So, we only have a wee problem of ethics then, of this potion of yours not having been trialled here in the US,' he leant forward resting his hands on his legs.

'Well, to tell you the truth, I can see no way to test the efficacy of this on rats or mice or even primates. They are not going to tell you how they feel towards the thought of committing a crime. And, as you say, I believe it is safe, it's an herbal remedy from a plant consumed for hundreds of years.'

'And you want me to dose up my felons with your herbal remedy and let them out.'

'Only as they are due to leave, what difference does it make, except I am sure that you'll not be seeing most of those faces back at your door, which would make you plenty.'

He threw himself back and looked up at the ceiling. I could tell it was time to keep quiet and let him work it out.

'It can be taken as a drink?'

'Best way.'

'And this will cost us nothing? Gerry hinted this was by way of a trial.'

I smiled to myself, perhaps Jock needed a dose too; he was obviously counting up his bonuses already. 'That's right.'

'So all I need to sort out is a way to get their consent to taking this stuff and we have a deal.'

'You probably already have it, you have to use medication on these guys at times, am I right? And their induction documents will have included a treatment waiver?'

'Yeah, sure, for medical problems.'

'And mental problems?'

'Sure, some of these guys are psychotic without their meds.'

'There you go then, for this treats a mental condition that causes recidivism.'

He looked thoughtful then said, 'I'll run it by my lawyers, but it looks like you have a deal, when would you want to start?'

'I have to get the production running here in the US first, say in a month? You'd need to give it to the prisoner say a week before release. The guy would need twenty-four hours care while the effects work through, then he'll be fine to release.'

Sapphira had certainly been busy. The 'New Life' Laboratory, as she had dubbed it, was up and running and the first batch of medium was ready to inoculate. The constituents of the synthesized food substances carried in the phloem of plants were well known, what we had to engineer was the delicate balance required as different elements were consumed by the bacteria in their own multiplication. We'd started with ten smallish containers and inoculated each with a differing amount of the unusual red bacteria from the nodule. The temperatures were set and we waited and watched. By the next evening one container was showing a pink tinge. By the following evening all of them were and the first was a definite red.

We decided that when the container was thoroughly red we'd try to harvest some for the drying process and already we were wondering how we could check that this man-made batch of Moringa bacteria was as effective as the naturally occurring. This was going to be a problem, I thought, until I recalled my first experiments and wondered about where I'd find some local refuge like St Piran's. Did the idea stink? No. So I searched the internet and found one such place not two blocks from the apartment I had in Washington DC.

Hostels for the down-and-out are always cash poor, so donations were a good way in and I played both benefactor and friend to the inmates. It was a re-run of the Cornish set-up. I got to know a few of the guys, chatted to them and found out from them, or those that ran the show, what their particular devils were. I selected just two and gave them a measure in their coffee and waited for the results. I made sure I visited later the same day and was around to help when they got boisterous, and to reassure when they settled into raucous sleep. Next day I was back, concerned and conciliatory. Later, when they were recovered, and after they'd eaten well, I ran the tests. The new batch appeared to be working as well as the natural. I donated an extra five-hundred bucks to the outfit, went home elated and called Sapphira to tell her that full production could go ahead.

The fifteenth of December saw me heading out to Jock's facility in Louisiana. I flew into the nearest airport and hired a car. I had very little with me except a medical chill box in which were enough doses for a thousand people. Jock's institution held over fourteen-hundred inmates, most of whom were on one to five year's detention. This meant that in an average year they might be releasing about 750 inmates at a rate of thirteen or fourteen a week. The first batch would be those due for release a week from now, I thought of it as the best Christmas present they would ever receive.

After a two hour drive, I hit the small community that bore the same name as the jail, drove past the red-brick elementary school and library, through the streets lined with white painted clapboard homes and out the other side to the junction where Prison road joined the highway through town. I turned down that road, the fields stretched out bare and flat on either side between stumpy hedges that led off left and right in long straight lines, the ploughed soil red, the grass spare. About a mile along the road was a dark clump of fir trees but after that nothing to give shelter or a hiding place for miles, only the gate to the prison was visible way up ahead of me, blocking the road like a toll-booth, and as I neared, the miles of fencing stretching away on either side.

I was expected, but was still treated as if I were trying to smuggle in weapons or drugs to the inmates. Patted down, pockets turned out, contents of the case prodded. It was only with firm brandishing of my authority from Jock himself that I managed to stop them opening one of the sachets to check for drugs. I was allowed to proceed through the gate and down to the facility. A good clear half mile on and I had to go through the same procedure at another gate. Then I was in. The jail before me had a large concrete frontage, though only four stories high. The administration block I was directed to was right in front of me, and I parked up outside the low redbrick building and went to the door. Identity checked I was admitted and at last met by someone who really was expecting me. An overweight African-American woman with a pockmarked face came round from behind a table to greet me, introducing herself as Dr Sally Bernhard, facility medic and she thought she knew all about me.

Dr Bernhard led me through to her own office and after making sure I had coffee and cookies before me, she started.
'Well now Dr Adamson, I hear you have some kind of untried herbal remedy that you'd like us to test on our clients in this here place?'
'Well, I wouldn't put it that way,' I began.

'And I am supposed to be happy to administer this stuff - do you realise what trouble I could get in?'

'Bur, Jock … Mr Mackay, has sanctioned this.'

'What does he know, *Doctor* Adamson? And I guess you aren't a real doctor, not a caring-for-the-people type doctor? No, I thought not, you just see them as some kind of lab rat?'

'Dr Bernhard, Sally,' I said trying to be placatory. 'That is not the case. I have already done the tests. The tests were run in the UK and I can vouch that it is safe for the… for your clients, to take, why I even took it myself.' I found myself unconsciously imitating her cadences and style of speech.

She tipped her head at an angle, 'You did?'

'I sure did.'

'So', she said later after I had explained everything as clearly and in as much detail as was possible without outright lying. 'If I took a dose of this herbal treatment it wouldn't harm me?'

'No, you'd would be fine, but, like anyone, you'd need to be watched for twenty-four hours after you'd taken it. Like I explained, there is this euphoric state when you don't know what you are doing and there is a deep sleep state when you just need keeping an eye on.'

She made a small noise in the back of her throat. 'Okay, you can leave it here and I will contact you when the first batch has been administered.'

'I was hoping I'd be around to make sure….'

'Oh. No, Dr Adamson, I don't want anyone suspecting anything, you will *not* be here, nor anywhere near. Give me an email address where I can get hold of you.'

'But, surely, for the first…'

'Do you want me to do this or not?'

We stared at each other for a moment, I shrugged. 'Here's my card,' I said, sliding one out of my wallet, 'it has my email and my cell number on it…do not hesitate to call me if…'

'What? If something goes wrong? You've just taken half an hour persuading me nothing will.'

'No, not goes wrong, if you have any questions. And I'll need to know who and when. We need somehow to put markers in the system so we are alerted if they are picked up anywhere for any crime.'

'Sure, we can do that. Goodbye Dr Adamson,' she held out her hand.

I left the prison with an uneasy feeling. I hadn't seen inside the jail, I hadn't met the prisoners who would be taking the first set of treatments, hadn't been able to talk to them, I wasn't even sure that Dr Bernhard would administer the doses. This was not how I had expected things to go.

The Angel Bug 31

Gabbi   December – March

It was the most pleasant lunch I'd had for a long time. John proved to be not only interested in plants and their problems but also in art and literature, chiming with my own interests easily. The meal over and the table cleared except for coffee, eventually John got round to the Moringa.

'So, can you tell me the history of this Moringa problem?'

'Well,' I said, 'back in October, one of our workers noticed the leaves were changing colour.'

'To red? I noticed some leaves on the trimmed down tree had red undersides.'

'Exactly, to red, however we couldn't find any particular reason for it, no parasites, no damage, the leaves were not falling off nor were they flaccid. They seemed just to have partly changed colour.'

'Did you have the leaves tested?'

'We tried cultivation of the cells, looked for fungal invasion, we tested for nutrients, water content ...'

'Did you cultivate for bacteria?'

'Not as such, no, maybe we would have got there, but then Dr Adamson arrived on his lecture tour and, sort of, took control of the matter. Almost like it was a personal affront that the Moringa was doing something he didn't understand.'

John was smiling, 'I can understand that,' he said, 'if you are the world expert on something and you can't answer the questions you might be a bit put out.'

'Anyway, he found the nodules, we'd not even thought to look at the roots, we were still focussed on the leaves. The nodules were a challenge – well you've seen them, quite unusual.'

'Actually, Gabbi,' he said. Somehow I liked hearing him say my name. 'I haven't. All I have seen is a section. I had hoped there would be more to see but I understand that they have disappeared.'

I know I went red, an instant flash as I remembered obtaining a single nodule for Luke and then his appropriation of the remaining ones from the tree. 'Well, I'm not sure about that….' I started. There would, should have been two nodules left untouched. I had no idea what might have happened to them while I was gone, but I could look. He was looking at me expectantly. 'Oh! Well, we did have at least one more, I haven't yet had an opportunity to check what happened between when I left and Dr Ananias left. Can I get back to you on that?'

He smiled, 'I'd really like to see one, handle it, before I go back. I was shown some pictures that your plant pathologist took of it but I have to say they were not very informative.'

I smiled, 'I'll have to speak to the team and find out what has happened. Have you asked to see them?'

'Yes, I asked Jim and he gave me the photo.'

'Okay, let me get back to you on that after I've spoken to my team.'

'That would be great, but you know I'm catching the train back to Reading this evening?'

'Ah, no, I didn't. What were your plans for this afternoon, will you still be around?'

'Nothing much, and yes, why?'

'Give me your mobile number and I will call you as soon as I can find out what we have for you.' I said. He seemed happy with that and handed over his card.

Back in the Foundation building I ran into Naomi and remembered that Sapphira had told me that it was Naomi who had alerted her to the missing nodule, the one I had taken for Luke.

'Hey, Naomi, I was wondering if the remaining nodules from the Moringa are still down at Watering Lane, would you know?'

'Well,' she said slowly, 'last time I saw them they were, in fact Sapphira took them from me and put them under lock and key herself.'

'Really, where would she have found to do that?'

'She took them into the back of the Reception building and locked them in Jim's 'dangerous chemicals' safe.'

'Oh!' I said feeling a bit lost. 'I suppose Jim has the keys for that then.'

'I suppose so,' Naomi added. This left me wondering why Jim had only offered our research colleague a photograph when he had access to the real material.

I called Jim up on his mobile.

'Hi, welcome back, Gabbi,' he said.

'Hi Jim, good to be back. Look Jim I've a query about the Moringa nodules.'

'Those damn things,' he muttered.

'Yes, those, I understand Sapphira locked them away in your chemical safe.'

'She did.'

'And Dr Keyes of the RHS asked to see them but you just gave him a photo? Was there a reason for that?'

'To be honest, Gabbi, I didn't know what to do. Sapphira has told me not to let anyone, no matter who they were, to have access to them. Failing other orders and with no one in the job to ask I just stuck with it. Why, is it a problem?'

'No, not at all.' I sighed, relieved, 'I'll come down and collect them now Jim, I think.'

'Sure enough, I'll be around.'

I called John Keyes' mobile and asked him to meet me at Watering Lane at half past three and headed out there myself. I found Jim and collected the remaining two nodules. They looked smaller than when I'd seen them last and I wasn't sure if it was my imagination or whether they'd suffered some dehydration effects.

I was in the lab when there was a knock on the door and John came in. Stupid, I know, but I felt it was lovely to see him again, when it had only been a couple of hours since we'd finished lunch.

'John, here are the remaining nodules,' I said, indicating the Petri dish they were sitting in.

He came over and stood beside me, leaning down to get a better look. 'Hmm, may I touch them?'

'Sure, here're the gloves,' I said pulling a pair from the box. He tugged them on, then tentatively prodded one nodule, picked it up and looked at it carefully. 'I think that they have lost a little turgidity since they were dug up,' I said.

'Mmm, that's probable.' He turned his dark eyes on me, 'I don't suppose I could actually cut one open, could I?'

There we were, that was the big question. I knew that Luke had taken all the rest, that he'd had them analysed, that he'd turned some into a potion that did strange things to people. Would it be safe to let this man cut one open, investigate it further. And if I did let him, how much should I tell him about Luke and what he was doing.

'How much of one were you sent from Reading?' I asked.

He smiled and shook his head. 'Not much, a single slice, strangely pink.'

'Ah! Well, if you think the pink was strange,' I made my mind up. 'Let me,' I took the nodule from him and set up a board. 'Will you want to take this part away with you?'

'That would be marvellous.'

He was leaning close to me as I sliced through the slightly rubbery skin of the nodule, the blood blooming viscous and deep red from it as the blade sliced through.

'That's, hmm, extraordinary.'

'Yep,' I said, 'That's what we all thought when we first saw it. Not only that but it may be dangerous as we believe contamination from this onto broken skin caused Dr Adamson to be hospitalised.'

John suddenly stood up straight. 'Really? I'd heard about that! You think it was this?'

'Pretty certain, he'd not been careful and he got this red liquid on his hand and his hands were abraded. The tests we have run on the nodules showed levels of an hallucinogen, an analgesic and a sedative-hypnotic amongst other things.'

John looked round, found a chair and sat down; I pulled out a lab stool and perched on the edge of it.

'And is that why I wasn't given the chance to see these earlier?'

'No that was because our senior botanist at the time had given very specific instructions that no one was to have access. I suspect to stop Dr Adamson taking them.' I said before I had thought it out properly. John raised his eyebrows a little. 'I mean,' I added, 'he already has all the rest of them.'

'Why's that?'

'Because, because, he wanted to find out what it was that had happened to him, he wanted to find out because if it was the Moringa, like you said, he needed as many as he could get to run all his experiments. Look you really ought to contact him, save replicating anything. I believe he's already had them DNA sequenced for instance.'

'Interesting, that is something I was thinking of doing, do you know what he found?'

'Not really,' I lied, 'well, not in any detail, I know you are right to think the nodule is bacterial. Look,' I tried to distract him from his questions, 'I can let you have his contact details before you leave.'

'Thank you, and a sample?'

'Yes,' I said, moving towards a drawer for a sample tube, 'I'll put it in here for you now.'

'Thanks.'

'We had been keeping them chilled, but since Dr Ananias had them locked away they've not been chilled so I guess it won't hurt as it is for the journey,' I said as I busied myself with placing half of the nodule in the pot, sealing it and then wrapping the other part and putting it with the remaining whole nodule into the fridge.

I fished out Luke's contact details and wrote them down. 'Here's Dr Adamson's contact details and mine,' I said, 'I'd like to be kept informed.'

He took them from me, glanced at them, then looking back at me he smiled right into my eyes. 'I'll do that, Gabbi. I'll keep in contact,' he said, and I found myself hoping that it wasn't just words.

*

Emma and I had a family Christmas together, which would have been wonderful if we hadn't been missing James' presence, it is always these set-piece family times that upset the carefully maintained front, but we made the best of it. At New Year we drove up to Derby to James' sister and really did have a wonderful time surrounded by her children and grandchildren, all of whom had remained nearby. The New Year also brought news for Emma, her attacker had been apprehended. He had done something similar again and this time had been caught; she was asked to return to identify him and be available for the trial. I didn't know how I felt. It had been good to have Emma home but it was obvious that she wanted to be doing something positive rather than hanging around in Cornwall waiting. Now she had the chance to put it behind her and to get back to her PhD studies, so it was with a mixture of happiness and sadness that we booked her return ticket.

*

Life at Eden settled into a pleasant and controlled existence. We had no major upsets with the plant life or the personnel. Everything seemed to be working well, with Naomi booked on her management course, Andy working towards a new paper on plant relationships and everyone forgetting about the Moringa problem.

At St. Piran's, Simon and Micky were both enrolled on computer courses and, by their own accounts, were enjoying it. Kieran had gone from the introductory course into a full-time animal management course that was part-time in the college and part-time on a farm. They had found him a place at a free-range egg producing farm and he was a different lad when I met him, happy and looking forward to the future. There were new faces at the refuge too, others with stories of a life wrecked by drink, drugs or gambling – nearly always the same three culprits. It really made me wonder about Luke's Moringa treatment when I saw the difference it had made in Simon and Micky, could it be the answer as he had said?

*

The daffodils were making a terrific show already with huge clumps of them in the borders of my garden, in patches round the road signs on the way into work, and at Eden, with the glorious show of tulips that we have each year waiting in the wings ready to take over in a heady, fiery show. I was just picking a few daffodils from the back garden when I heard the phone ring, I nipped indoors and with one hand still clasping the bunch, I picked the phone up. It was Emma.

'Oh Mum! The trial's over.' She didn't sound as happy as she ought to.

'What's up?' I set the daffodils down gently.

'They only gave him six months, six months! And he'll only serve four if he behaves himself. I can't bear it, what if he comes after me again?'

'He'd have more sense than to do that,' I said, but feeling panicky myself at the thought.

'You don't know, it was as just I'd guessed, he *is* a smack-head, shit for brains.'

'Emma!'

'Sorry Mum, it's just. I'm just shaken; I really thought this would be an end.'

'Does he have to do a drug rehabilitation programme?'

'Yeah, yeah, there was something about that, but he'll be out, just have to attend.'

'I don't know what to say Emma, how long now before you finish,' knowing she still had a year and a bit to go, but playing for time to think and subtly pointing out it wouldn't be forever.

'Too long, Mum?'

'Yes?'

'You remember Dr Adamson asked me, what if I could give the guy something to make sure he never did it again?'

'Yes,' I said, hesitantly, trying to remember how much had been said, how much she knew.

'Did he really have a substance like he said? That could do that?'

'Well, maybe. It's pretty untried, why Emma?'

'No matter, just a thought.'

'Emma?'

'Seriously, just curious. How's Eden, how's everyone there?'

'Fine, everyone seems happy. No crises to report,' I said, and knew I sounded relieved.

'Great, well, I better go Mum, don't worry about me, I, well it was just the first shock! I just had to tell you. Bye then, love you.'

'I understand, take care, love,' I said, hugging the phone, 'love you, bye.'

I put down the phone and picked up the daffodils staring past them out of the window at a place half a world away, I made a silent prayer for her safety.

The more I thought about it the more I wondered if it was possible that I could make a little of the potion up like Luke had done. I wondered if it was the right thing to do. I had access to the remaining one and a half nodules, what if I just took a little bit of the cut one, no one would know. I'd have to ask Luke how he'd done it, how much to give, I thought, then dismissed the idea again as unethical and wrong.

I slept on it. That night and the following, or should I say I barely slept on it, as the thought of it, the possibility of it, set my conscience and my maternal instinct into a war, and a battle raged whenever my mind was not fully occupied with work.

The Angel Bug 32

Luke   December – March

Just before New Year I had an email from Dr Bernhard asking me to make an appointment to see her. So it was that on the tenth of January I took the flight and the long drive out to the prison facility in Louisiana again. This time the clapboard houses looked dingier than ever against the recent fall of pristine snow in their front yards. Travelling down Prison Road with all the features wiped out was an eerie feeling as if man should not be out and about on such a day, as if all the human population had vanished with the snowfall.

The welcome at the gate however was just as thorough and I was quite chilled by the time I reached her office. It was just as well her name was still on the door as the woman who greeted me appeared different, her face was slimmer, more shapely and, as she stood to welcome me with an outstretched hand to shake, I thought she had to have lost at least twenty pounds.

'Do sit yourself down Dr Adamson, please do,' she said, wreathed in smiles.

'Thank you, you are looking very well,' I said, trying to keep the wonder out of my voice.

She smiled, 'Ah, well, fancy you noticing. I have lost twenty-eight pounds in about twenty days, and do you want to know how?'

I wasn't really here for an evangelical weight-loss programme, but I did want to keep this lady sweet so I nodded and said yes I did.

'Dr Adamson, I took a leaf out of your book. I felt I really couldn't try this herbal potion out on my clients without being sure, so I took a dose of it myself, just the way you did.' She must have seen the shock on my face as she held up a hand to stop me saying anything and ploughed on. 'Oh don't you worry, I made sure that I would be well cared for, and that there would be no questions asked, I did it that very first weekend.'

'I don't understand, I mean, I understand what you did but not the link to the weight loss.'

'Well, you told me yourself, you said it would stop the clients wanting things as they shouldn't have, that it took the greed out of them. I know you didn't explain just how it worked, and I can tell you that the stink is enough to put a person off their food on its own.'

'Oh? It has put you off eating? That's not happened before. Oh no! Have any of the pri .. clients reported anything similar,' I said getting concerned.

'Whoa, you've got the wrong end of the stick. It's only when I lets myself get greedy I smell them, and let me tell you that was far too often for my health but it did me no good telling myself that before. Sure enough, before I would say, Sally you must stop eating this stuff between meals and before I knew it the cookie jar was empty. This herbal remedy is a godsend, let me tell you, and it comes not a minute too soon for this here nation of ours. I am not the only obese person in the USA.'

'Hold on, are you telling me that it stops you eating only when you've eaten enough?'

'Sure thing, I'm not starving, I had a lot of weight to lose and it has fallen off me.'

'Oh my!'

'Tell me Dr Adamson, are you able to make money out of this herbal remedy?'

I looked at her, did she already know the answer? 'No, it seems I can cover expenses all right but no I won't be making money out of it.'

'I thought so. One day last week I was thinking to myself that this herbal remedy would be a gold mine in the slimming market and if I could get myself a slice of that action I could start over as a dietary clinician. It took me a few minutes to work out why the stinks were coming, I wasn't thinking of eating you see, then I worked it out, that would be greedy wouldn't it?'

'Apparently so.'

'Then I have something I must say to you. I believe this is the biggest thing that has hit America, and it works. Let me tell you our figures right now, I have dosed up one hundred and twenty two clients before their leaving this facility. I have made sure to follow-up on each and every one. Dr Adamson we have had none, not one, turn up under any justice department. Now I know some of them have only been gone a day or two but we cleared a lot just before Christmas, so over half have been gone two weeks. Re-offending rates usually show that forty percent will have transgressed within a month, and of those, eighteen percent in the first week. Zero? That is a miracle.'

'That's very interesting,' I said, feeling like laughing.

'So with that and with the weight-loss programme, you Doctor, have a winner that you cannot cash in on. But, beware, anyone who hasn't taken your potion could cash in on it and it is too big and too special for that.'

The laughter in my mind was doused with cold water; she was not only right but I had missed this point altogether, too focussed on the fact that I could not profit from it I had not thought of the danger of someone else profiting from it. She must have read my face because she continued, 'And you hadn't thought of that had you? No, you had not! The fact is, this is such a blessing for this nation I think you should get it into the hands of the government, where it can do the best for the people without cost to the nation.'

There it was, Dr Bernhard had thought this through further than I had, too busy concentrating on proving it rather than on looking long-term.

'You are so right,' I said, 'And thanks, and when I do just that, would you come and testify for me that it works,'

She beamed at me, 'Better than that, I'll bring along my husband and a couple of my girlfriends too,' she said. 'We were all a little hefty and I've put them all on your herbal programme this last week.'

I was really shocked then, it seemed wrong and right at the same time.

As soon as I was back in Washington I put a call through to Gerry's department and booked an appointment, then tried to call up Jock Mackay.

He was out for the day but I left a message for him to get back to me. I was so fired up, Dr Bernhard was right and I needed to make sure this was used in the right way.

Jock called me later that evening.

'Adamson, just the man, I have had a report from Dr Bernhard, and I think we need to talk.

'Yes, I spoke with her today, she is very positive...'

'Positive – that's an understatement! This stuff is going to revolutionise things for us. I want you to expand this to another prison set up I have an interest in where we are on the same recidivism deal, it's in Colorado.'

'I really don't think so at the moment.'

'Why the hell not?'

'I need to talk with Gerry first before we expand the experiment.'

'Experiment be damned, you said it was all tested and safe.'

'I meant in dosing prisoners.'

'Now you look here Adamson, I want this rolled out to my Colorado interest, now, before the world and his wife want in on it.'

I held my temper. 'I'll see what I can do, you must realise,' I extemporised, 'that at this early stage the supply of the drug is very limited.'

He was silent. I thought he'd bought it.

'Okay, but your word that we get the next batch for our places, exclusive.'

'I think I can say that.' I said, the whole conversation had not only gone the wrong way but was flagging up just the problem that Sally Bernhard had spotted.

I was better prepared when I went to see Gerry. He was sitting behind an impressive carved mahogany desk made in an era before we realised we ought not to be cutting down these trees.

'Luke,' he said in greeting, 'take a seat.'

'Hi Gerry, thanks for seeing me at short notice. I want to talk to you about the Moringa drug and the recidivism problem.'

'Sure thing, but you mean the Moringa herbal remedy, don't you?' he winked.

I looked blank then shrugged. 'Yeah, the herbal remedy.'

'Well, I hear that it is showing some very positive signs, in fact, I have never known anything like it. If it continues it would not only be marvellous but it will also break the bank on our anti-recidivism programme,' he held his hands up, 'not that I would mind – after all we'd be able to ditch it altogether if this is as good as it looks, but don't tell our friend Jock that.'

I smiled, he had his eye on the financial aspect already so what I was going to say would be easier.

'Gerry, there's more. Have you ever met Dr Sally Bernhard, the facility medic at Jock's place?'

'No, why the hell should I?'

'No problem,' I thought, wishing I had 'before and after' photographs of her, 'What is the biggest health problem in the US?'

'Full marks for dodging the question – cardiac arrest? Diabetes?'

'Linked; obesity.'

'Yeah, yeah, sure obesity – a time bomb, they say.'

'What if I told you that this herbal remedy may also help obese people lose weight?'

'You have got to be kidding me?'

'That's why I asked if you'd met the good Dr Bernhard, she is what you might call, on the large size. To check out that the remedy was safe she done took a dose herself, though on her it worked so that when she went to overeat it stopped her. The weight is just dropping off her.'

He was silent for a moment or two; I wondered what he was thinking but carried on 'Gerry, I want to put this herbal remedy exclusively into the hands of the government to be used for treatment of obesity sufferers and for felons, at no extra cost.'

He now looked at me full-on, his eyes wide. 'But you could make millions out of this.'

'I know, but I don't want that, what I want in return is the backing of the United States government to stop the exploitation and degradation of the Rainforests, forever – that's my price,' I said, and the thought smelled sweet.

When I got back, with Gerry's promise to talk it over with those who mattered in my pocket, I rang Sapphira. I told her what I had found out from the prison and what I had asked for, and was surprised when she wasn't pleased. Well, when I say not pleased, what she intimated was that I was selling the Moringa short, that it ought to be aimed at every single person in the whole world. I had forgotten her fanaticism, forgotten that she saw the Moringa treatment as the New Redemption. I warned myself to be more careful next time, that I ought to have called Gabriella to share the news with, she would have understood.

*

Gerry came back to me after a couple of weeks. I was to go before a Senate committee and present all the evidence I had for the Moringa treatment, and that committee reported directly and only to the President. I was not to worry, he said, as it had been obvious to the people he dealt with that this whole discussion should be held under the highest degree of secrecy, in the government's interest. I wasn't even to know who would be on the committee but was assured that it would be peopled by those who would understand and appreciate the potential as well as those policy makers and scientists who could evaluate its scope and risks. I was given three weeks to prepare my proposition; I was going to be beyond busy!

*

It was just as I was getting my final figures and other data into some easily understood form that I got a longer-than-usual email from Gabriella. We'd been exchanging quick emails every so often, me telling her how I missed England, asking about Simon and Micky, letting her know how well the Moringa therapy was working in the prison trial. She answering with news about the old guys and telling me about her job at Eden. The last one I'd sent after my run-in with Sapphira, telling her I thought I had a plan to save the Rainforest that would work and how I was going to be too busy for words over the next few weeks, so not to worry if she didn't hear from me for a while.

So I was surprised when this one arrived, as this one was different. She told me in great detail about Emma, how she'd gone back for the trial, how she was distraught that the guy who'd attacked her, and others, was going to be out on the streets in four months and how Emma had asked her if the treatment I'd spoken about was real. Gabriella said she didn't know what to do, that she just kept thinking of the Moringa treatment and whether I was right when I had said it would stop the guy ever doing it again, did I believe that, know it even, by now? How hard was it to make the powder out of the nodule, how much was in a dose? Reading between the lines I knew Gabriella wanted me to step in, but if I didn't she was preparing herself to make some up. Gabriella, and Emma, needed my help, no matter how busy I was. I replied asking for Emma's contact details, so I could talk it over with her and explain things, I said. If I could help them both I would, it was just a matter of whether Emma would be able to administer the dose.

The Angel Bug 33

Gabbi   March - April

John returned to Eden frequently to look at the progress the cuttings were making and to look at the roots of the replacement Moringa that had been planted first – a careful and painstaking job to look at the roots without disturbing even the finest root hairs. There was no sign of any nodule development.

The more I saw of John, the more I liked him, and we had gone out to eat on a few occasions when he visited. Like me he'd lost his partner. Elaine had died of cancer of the liver, a devastatingly swift and untreatable end, leaving him with two teenage boys of thirteen and fifteen. Liam was now doing his A levels and Sean was in his first year at university.

This time we set out on a cliff walk together, ostensibly talking about the Moringa.
He did in fact start by talking about the Moringa, or rather how he'd contacted Luke but heard nothing, even sending a repeat email in case the first had ended up lost, and still had no reply. I was a little confused as I knew Luke had found the time to reply to me and to help out Emma, but didn't say this to John. John had booked in the nodule at TAGC, the national DNA analysis centre, for sequencing, but he knew from something I said that Luke had already had it done. It occurred to him that if he took it to the same place then the matter could be dealt with much quicker. In view of Luke's rudeness I decided to give John the information he needed and told him to contact Dr Vaughan-Hallam at Queen Mary's. He laughed, no problem, he said, my PhD alma mater and I even know William.

*

I began to suspect that John was not only coming down to Cornwall to see the Moringa when I returned to the Foundation building one afternoon to find him perched on the edge of my desk chatting to the others.

'Here she is now,' Andy called as I topped the stairs and walked into the sort of silence you get when everyone was talking about you and hasn't had time to think of a new subject. John was the first to break it by pushing himself off from the desk and stepping forward to greet me with his fantastic smile and a handshake, held a fraction longer than necessary, his dark eyes looking into mine. I knew I had a huge smile on my face reflecting his. Within seconds the others began to melt away with mutterings of work they had to get to, leaving the two of us alone. 'I'm afraid I have to admit we were talking about you,' he said, 'all good, I might add,' and he smiled. 'I was wondering if you'd like to come to see a play with me this evening?' I was surprised, but also delighted.

The play was on for three days that week in the town hall, and Mikaela had recommended it to John having seen it the night before, even phoning the town hall for him to reserve two seats. Surfing Tommies was put on by Bish Bash Bosh, a very small touring company, and told of the Cornish miners who went into the First World War digging the tunnels that undermined the enemy positions, and about shell shock, or post-traumatic stress disorder, as we would call it now, or cowardice as it was seen then, to be dealt with by a firing squad. I had a lump in my throat and tears in my eyes before the end and clapped so hard my hands stung and it was obvious how much John had enjoyed the play too.

The next day we got down to the official reason John had turned up that week.

'I have the sequencing results,' he said, looking keenly at me.

'Yes?'

'Did you know it showed a new, possibly symbiotic, relationship between two bacteria, one of which was Agrobacterium tumefaciens?'

The name rang a bell, the student had said something like that, it came back to me. 'Is that the one used in GM?' I asked.

'Yes, so you knew, and you weren't concerned about that?'

'Not really, it was just something the student doing the work mentioned, that this bacteria was used in genetic modification work. Should I have been? Remember John, this was Dr Adamson's results, I just happened to be there.'

'But the nodule came from here, from Eden, under your jurisdiction surely?'

'No, not then, just then I wasn't even part of Eden,' the memory of the suspension still had a sting.

'Never mind, this is irrelevant. Agrobacterium tumefaciens has been shown in a small study, under certain conditions, to invade human cells. Research is very new and so far limited, but enough to warn workers using the stuff to take precautions. It's carcinogenic, it's what the bacterium does in its wild state to plants, causes rapid growth.'

I felt my heart thump, carcinogenic! Luke, Simon, Micky, Sapphira and how many others? 'Does Luke, Dr Adamson know?'

'I haven't told him yet, but I intend to, I hope he pays more attention to it than he did my last email, especially if he's handling this stuff himself.'

'Oh John, he's into something really big out there to do with saving the Rainforest, I don't think he'd ignore you otherwise. However, you are right, this is very important, very important that he should know. I know he gets my emails, I'll send him the information too.' Thinking that it was really so important that Luke knew and not only for himself, Simon and Micky, he'd talked about testing the stuff on others, volunteers he'd said, and goodness knows how many other people were now involved too with the prison trial up and running. And then there was the guy who'd attacked Emma, I thought with a flood of heat through my body, he may have deserved to be 'made good' but he didn't deserve to be given a death sentence by cancer.

I moved the conversation onto other things as I thought through what I was contemplating doing, in the end it seemed the right thing to do. I told John about the nodule's effect on people who took it. Everything, from the start with Luke's accidental infection to the milder manic sessions and the deep sleep that Simon and Micky and Sapphira went through and I said that wasn't all, as I understood there were trials going on in the US right now, involving prisoners. He nodded.

'Interesting. Fascinating,' he said. 'And now something else makes sense too, there's been rumours coming from the States about a treatment that has been getting amazing results in preventing recidivism, but no one has had any idea what it is, speculation is that it's some pharmacological intervention, but not this.' He shook his head and gave a little grimace, 'It sounds such a perfect solution, it'd be a shame if the stuff is carcinogenic, because cancer is a terrible thing, Gabbi, and no one should be condemned to that sort of death.'

The Angel Bug 34

Luke   March – December

I was too busy really, certainly far too busy to answer some complicated requests from a Dr J Keyes about the Moringa nodule, and disinclined to do so anyway as discussions were at a delicate point, but this was Gabbi and this was Emma her daughter. I phoned Emma and asked her if there was any way she could give this guy a cup of tea or coffee, where she had control of the drink at sometime, failing that if there was any way she could get someone else to slip it into his drink. I emphasised that it should be done while he was still in the prison so that he'd be cared for in the tricky times after administration.

Gabriella had already talked to her about the possibility of my providing some of the Moringa, she said, and there were two chances she could see. There was the victim apology interview, where he was supposed to apologise to her face for his actions. Doing this earned him brownie points that got him out quicker if she agreed to meet him. Apparently, and not surprisingly, a lot of victims didn't want to do this but it was encouraged by psychologists as they said it helped the perpetrator go straight if he recognised his victim as a real person with feelings, and apologised. Otherwise it was possible to actually be a visitor, to actually ask to see the guy, but she felt that would look weird. Seems, that with either process there is always a guard present, but from what she'd found out it was possible for them to have a drink together, a coke or fruit juice but not a hot drink after one victim threw the scalding liquid in the face of her assailant.

I said it would do, and agreed to send her a dose of the Moringa therapy; it would be so thin that I didn't think customs would bother opening it, but to be sure I slipped it inside a birthday card and sent it off. I sent an email back to Gabriella too, letting her know I'd sent it, then put this to the back of my mind as I had to meet the committee in three days.

*

I went before the Senate committee with all the information I had so far. I had the latest from Dr Bernhard. Most importantly, still not one felon had returned to the system, secondly, I had her weight-loss details, including weight loss charts for herself, her husband and friends and in the 'before and after' photos the weight-loss was noticeable – and as it was only over a couple of months, at the longest, this was amazing in itself. I had the production costs figures too. The government would be offered the therapy at cost price, and it wasn't a lot, I estimated it at forty cents a pop, less than the cup of coffee it would be served in.

I recognised two of the committee, one an eminent scientist, the other the senator who headed up the health and welfare of the nation committee. Gerry was there, but as he explained, he was only there to introduce me to the committee and laid it on the line that he had given the go-ahead for the trials I had been running in Louisiana.

I greeted the committee and launched into my spiel. I had learned a lot from my lecture tour. I had the talk almost off pat. I painted a picture of life as it is now. The degree of recidivism, the causes of the crime in the first place, which led me nicely on to addiction both to alcohol and to drugs. It was enough to start with; I offered a therapy that works. I put up impressive charts. They now covered more than just the misdemeanours that my original sample admitted to, they included some worse cases according to the previous crimes of the participants. The statistics of the numbers usually expected to be already back in the judicial system after this short time versus the numbers from those who had been given the therapy was stark. Forty percent against zero. Who could argue with that?

There were a few questions at this stage. In fact I think most of them had thought I'd finished so looked a bit surprised when I said I also wanted to introduce them to a different aspect of the treatment, one that Dr Bernhard had noted and that I had been unaware of as I had not been looking for it. I started as she had done, I asked them to tell me the biggest health concern for the nation. Obesity was soon hit upon, and it was recognised that almost all the other biggies in health terms were consequent on obesity. I told her tale, how she'd decided to make sure the therapy was safe for her clients, painting her in glowing terms, and how she found her own addiction, to food, quelled. I brought up on the screen her before and after photos, and then those of her husband and friends with their weight charts beside them.

'Hells teeth, man,' said the portly senator from Illinois, 'give me some of that stuff!'

And the others laughed a little, but their faces told a different story, they were hooked.

'I understand you are willing to give this to the nation at cost price? Is that so?'

'It is, I do have a price though,' I said glancing at Gerry wondering if he'd filled them in on it. He nodded. 'The Rainforest protection scheme?'

'I've had some number crunching done on this already,' Gerry intervened. 'The costs of the penal system, alone, are fifteen times greater than the cost we envisage in complying with the Rainforest protection scheme as Dr Adamson set it out, the key strategy is to use satellite monitoring and fast response teams. With a little more input, we believe we can get universal agreement from all countries involved.'

'Ah, okay, but I still can't see why you are giving it away, this could make you the richest man in the world and then you could set up this scheme yourself.'

I smiled, 'That brings me to the only other stipulation I have with this before it is handed over. Everyone who has any leading role in its manufacture, distribution, or the decision-making about these, must, as a condition of their employment, take a dose of the therapy themselves.'

'And why the hell would they want to do that?'

'If they want the job then they would, it is a show of confidence I guess sir, and I would hope you'd all do the same before you recommended it to the President. Look at Dr Bernhard, she is an inspiration.'

'And what about you?'

'I, sir, was the first person to try it,' I said, quite honestly.

'What about smoking? Dr Adamson? I've been trying to quit for years,' asked another.

'I don't know sir, it is not one of the things we have been looking for,' I said and wondered why I'd not thought of it.

'Well you just have a look, and if it's a yes then send me some of your stuff right along!' There was another smattering of laughter.

'Dr Adamson,' the scientist put in. 'Up to now we have been kept in the dark as to what this therapy is based on, understandably, but I, for one, expected *this* committee to be told.'

'I'm sorry, sir,' I said. 'All I can tell you at this point is that it came from the Moringa oleifera and that it is an extract of one part.'

'What's a Moringa oli, oli whats-it?' asked the senator from Illinois.

The scientist snorted and gave an answer before I could. 'Asian rainforest tree with leaves, beans, flowers and roots, all edible and, coincidentally, this gentleman's speciality.' He turned back to me and raised his eyebrows.

'Thank you, succinctly put,' I said.

The chairman of the committee shuffled some papers then looked around the group. 'If there are no more questions?' he paused. 'Then, thank you Dr Adamson, we will let you know our decision in a week,' and he smiled.

It was both a fast week and a long one. I went up to the production plant to see how things were getting on, how easy it would be to upscale and to talk to Sapphira, to see if she could ask the Reverend Ashe to find out how many of his travelling church, our guinea pigs, had been smokers before the treatment, and how many were now. She was remarkably quiet and I asked her if anything was wrong. At this she burst out crying.

When I got her to calm down enough to tell me, it seemed that Elliot Ashe had pressured her to siphon off some of the production to give to him to use in his ministry. He had convinced her that it was for the Lord's work. He then gave it to converts in a healing cup, to drive out the spirits that held them captive; addictions of all kinds, to drink, drugs, cigarettes, sex and gluttony. He was fast becoming a miracle worker. She had believed it was right, but then had found he was encouraging these people to donate all they had, or much of what they had, to his Foundation, and Sapphira was not happy; it smelled wrong.

I knew immediately what I had to do, what *we* had to do. Ashe had to be given a dose of the Moringa therapy himself, and Sapphira was happy to do it, her penance, as she called it. In the meantime I already had part of my answer, if Ashe was releasing people from the evil spirit that bound them to cigarette smoking then it obviously worked. I wondered about the power of the tobacco and alcohol lobby and decided the benefits were going to outweigh whatever pressure even they could bring to bear on our government.

The following Monday I was on edge, waiting for the call. It came at half past two, Gerry on the other end of the line sounded really upbeat from the off. 'Luke, we've done it!' he said. 'All penitentiaries, all rehab clinics, all hospital obesity clinics as from when you can supply.'
I knew he was referring to all government controlled facilities, 'What about the private ones, like Jocks?'
'Yeah, we'll bring them in as soon as your production meets our requirements,' he said.

'At no extra cost,' I added, remembering that Gerry had not yet had a dose, nor had the accountants who were pulling his strings, thinking that accountants needed to be included in those obliged to take the Moringa therapy.

'Sure, sure, at no extra cost,' he assured me. 'How much have you got made now, how much can you get in say a month?'

'I've enough made in stock now for thirty thousand doses, with the go-ahead I can step up production and make that much each week.'

'Got to it!' Gerry said/ 'And put this date in your diary, you are going to meet the President!' and he reeled off a date and time for me.

*

By the morning of April tenth, the date of my appointment to meet with the President, the programme was up and running in every state-run prison in the land, with a few private ones, notably those in which Jock had an interest, also on board. By sharing out the doses on a week by week basis, with only as many as were required for those in charge in the first wave, and then for all those leaving the institutions from then on, there was enough with the stockpile and the rolling production to cover every place, plus the first of the rehab centres to start using the therapy.

I was just wasting a little time, all togged up and ready to go when I got an email from Gabriella. I scanned it through and came up short. She'd been seeing this guy, John Keyes, and that name rang a bell, she said he was looking into the nodule and had had it sequenced, he was concerned and that made her concerned. He was concerned that one of the two bacteria in the nodule may cause cancer in humans. Had I realised Agrobacterium tumefaciens had been cited as being able to carry its genetic facility for multiplication of cells into the human? He said it was a new, and at the time unsubstantiated, theory but probable, given its proclivity for doing just that in plants. I was stunned. I sat there looking at the screen. Had anyone suffered from cancer that had taken the Moringa treatment long enough ago to tell? Was there, right now, something eating away at me, growing within me? Or Simon or Micky or Sapphira? It was the last thing I wanted to think about just before I went to meet the President, but I would have to think about it. I emailed back my thanks to Gabriella, and asked after Simon and Micky, I was sure she'd see through my request but left it at that. I checked the time, I just had time to book myself in for a full health screening, money no problem, and I soon had one set up for two day's time.

*

I rolled out of the MRI scanner and waited until I was told to sit up. It was the last and most expensive part of my full body and brain check-over. I had not said what I was concerned about, I didn't want anyone even suspecting I was concerned about cancer, but I knew which results I would be looking at the hardest. While I had been lying there immobile I had decided two things, to run some trials, away from the US, and to get Simon and Micky a full health check too, after all, if it was good enough for me then I ought to accord them the same treatment. They still had no idea that they'd taken anything and I might find it hard to convince them, but I felt I owed it them to try. And it would be good to see Gabriella again, I had missed her.

I was on the plane the following Monday, with an onward flight booked to Newquay and a rental car set up at the other end. I'd emailed Gabriella and she'd insisted I came and stayed with her. I had no objections; it would be good, I thought.

Cornwall in April was absolutely stunning, the hedgerows full of early wildflowers in blues, pinks and white with the occasional burst of narcissi and I felt so at home when Gabriella's small cottage came in to view. I pulled up outside and before I could get out she was coming out of her front door, looking wonderful. What I hadn't expected was her to be followed by some tall guy. Gabriella and I hugged and gave each other a peck on the cheek, then Gabriella introduced me to John Keyes. He had a good firm handshake and though he smiled I felt he was summing me up. 'John's going back to London this evening,' Gabriella said, 'he stayed on just to meet you.'

'I think I may owe you an apology,' I said. 'You asked for information at a rather difficult time and I am afraid I never did get round to helping you out.'

'Not at all,' he said, his voice cultured, 'I went to Queen Mary's anyway and the sequencing was more of a matter of matching.'

Ouch, I thought.

Gabriella ushered us inside before we could get stuck into any further argument, but he was not to be deterred, over a welcome drink he asked if I had considered the carcinogenic properties of the Agrobacterium tumefaciens since they'd sent the information on. I admitted I had and had just had myself checked out for any insipient signs, I could see Gabriella's beautiful eyes shining, knew she was worried for me. I reached out and touched her hand. 'It was all clear,' I said 'and that's why I'm here now, I want the same for my first two subjects, I'm going to provide a full medical check-up, just in case.' She was smiling now, the sort of smile that made me feel good.

'Forgive me,' John said in that unassuming but still patronising way that the Brits have of talking when they are in the right, 'but don't you think that this therapy should have been fully trialled before it was administered to anyone?'

I looked from Gabriella to John, she must have trusted him if she told him what I was doing in the States, but what to say? The man was right but he couldn't know the half of it, not even Gabriella knew everything that happened to me in my coma. I smiled ruefully.

'Well, it jumped the gun in the first place,' I said. 'I was inoculated by it before we had any idea of its amazing effects. It seemed to me the first priority was to see if it was a one off, or whether it worked on others too, and you sure can't check subtle personality changes in mice.' I stopped, listened to myself using my scientist ears and heard someone talking like an evangelist. 'You are right, of course,' I continued. 'I should have done the trials for side effects, but I was feeling fine and the Moringa has a long record of being used as a food and medicine source for humans, without problems. As for now, well now I'm here to set up screening for Micky and Simon and put into place the trials that are needed. To that end, would you be available to oversee them? I don't see the point in involving more people than we have to.'

'And you'd stop it being used until you have the results?'

I thought for a moment. Could I? Was it the right thing to do?

'How firm is the evidence to show transference of the A. tumefaciens genes to humans?

'Hmm, not firm at all, to be honest. Reports suggest contact of cell matter with broken skin a possible cause of reported cancer. It's under investigation, but has been of enough concern for a warning to be issued to all personnel handling A. tumefaciens in their work to take precautions.'

'Okay, well do bear that in mind for your investigation, but, no, John, I can't stop the therapy program on that basis. This thing is bigger than me now and the potential good outweighs the potential harm at this point. I promise you I'll close it down if there is a proven link, hell, you can close it down. But until then I'd insist on the security clause being in force. As I see it, the trials should include the worst case scenario, direct inoculation intravenously, and the method we use, administered orally. Let's test both to be sure,' I said knowing I was the only one who had ever had direct contact.

He shifted in his seat a little, I could guess that the security clause was bothering him, but it was standard practice for research funding and would also serve to exonerate him if he thought about it.

'You said yourself that the link was tenuous,' I continued. 'One murder not committed, one rape, one life not messed up by drugs or alcohol is worth it against a tenuous link, and here we are talking hundreds of crimes that will not be committed over the time your experiments will take. Even if the program is running in the whole of the US by the time your trials finish, if they show a causal link, I'll pull the plug. It doesn't hurt me, I am not making any money from this. It won't let me. Until then, nada, not a word. Do we have an agreement?'

He looked at me for long moment; then nodded his agreement.

John Keyes, once this problem was out of the way and rather to my annoyance, turned out to be a really pleasant guy, the type I can get along with fine, and as the afternoon turned into evening and he prepared to leave I could see that he and Gabriella had something special between them, even if they didn't realise how special it was yet.

I had expected to roll up to the hostel the next morning and talk to Micky and Simon and whisk them off for a medical the next day. It was only as I was explaining to Gabriella my plan that she pointed out that they had straightened themselves out so much they were both working and with luck wouldn't even be in the St Piran's for much longer as they had been offered a place in a half way house. I could tell she was really proud of both of them, Simon at a call centre where his clear modulated tones were of benefit and Micky in a basic data inputting job, both of which had been gained with help from St.Piran's. Both on a short trial period to start with, but they were doing well and expected to be taken on permanently. They wouldn't want to take a day off, I was told. This was going to be harder than I expected, I needed to get an out-of-hours check-up organised, and that would cost me, but to be sure they were in the clear it would be worth it.

Suffice to say that I managed to get the screening set up, and with a lot of persuasion, including from Gabriella, I got the old guys to go along. Their read outs were interesting, to say the least. They had problems, all caused by the type of life they had led, but none that was going to kill them in the short term, and none of them cancer.

I returned to the States, to find that we were now at peak production and expanding the production facilities again. The 'Rehab Therapy' as it had been officially renamed was now being rolled out to all addiction clinics of all types, from the hardest drugs to 'giving up smoking' classes, and hospitals treating obese patients. On the streets it was being called 'the angel therapy' or the 'the stink therapy' but everywhere people were asking for it, so much so that the government decided to open up access to private businesses on the condition that the owners, managers and accountants were all dosed up first as per the agreement.

*

You can't keep something like this a secret. By late December I heard from Gerry that Britain was knocking on the door, they had a serious prison overcrowding problem and they'd heard whispers of this new therapy that worked. The President wanted to share this miracle.

As the only supplier I was able to take a stand, make sure that profit was not going to be taken, even when it was not my own country, after all I figured it belonged to them as much as to the US. The argument didn't hold so well when it extended to the rest of Europe, or when most of the countries in South America entreated us to supply their need, but we did it anyway, to everyone at cost.

At home the evangelical far right, led by Reverend Elliot Ashe, was pushing Congress for inoculation at birth with the Rehab therapy. It won support in a few fundamental Christian states but was fought off by all other religious groups and the majority of the rest of the government.

The Angel Bug 35

Gabbi   April – January

Luke set the trials up in the labs he'd hired before – they were already licensed with an equipped suite of labs and trained, licensed assistants to care for and monitor the mice. The trials would be done under the auspices of Dr. Brandon who ran the labs with John as consultant advisor - seems that got round yet another license - and somehow Luke got the permission for the trials through the red tape in record time. This meant that, from the middle of May, John had reason to visit Cornwall frequently, and when he did, he made time to see me.

*

I won't go into that here, but suffice to say that as Christmas approached he asked if I'd like to spend it with him and his boys, and I was glad to accept and had a wonderful time.

It was a few weeks after I'd returned to Cornwall, a crisp January morning when I answered the door to unexpectedly find John standing there.

'John? Come in,' I stepped forward to kiss him, he took a second longer to respond than usual, 'What's wrong?' I asked as we went through to the kitchen and I reached for the kettle.

'I've just come from the labs,' he said. 'They called me down because some of the mice are showing signs of cancer.'

'Oh no! Which ones?' I stood frozen with the kettle mid-air.

'Well, it's the intravenously inoculated ones, but ...'

'How many?'

'All of them,' his voice flat.

'All of them? Hell! And the others, are they alright?' I put the kettle down, clicked it on and turned back towards him.

'So far,' he looked down, then back at me. 'Do you know anything about the Moringa therapy being used in the UK?'

'No, no, I don't. Do you think it is?'

'I'm not sure – I just heard a whisper that would mean nothing to anyone else – just talk of trialling the American system in our prisons.'

I thought about that comment. Could be the Moringa therapy – could be any other system from the US – they were always trying something, but I was as suspicious as John.

'And this new result – have you told Luke?'

'No, not yet. I wanted to tell you first.'

Maybe I looked surprised, after all the research was for Luke, paid for by Luke.

'It's the moral question. If this is carcinogenic and they are thinking of trialling it here should I breach the contract and tell our government?'

'Did you say the orally administered mice were fine?'

'Yes, and I've brought forward their next scanning to double-check. It's the others though …'

'But the others were inoculated intravenously, no human has had that form of inoculation.'

'Except Luke, and that's the other reason I wanted to talk to you. Luke needs to know that it's in all the mice in that batch.'

He left the unasked question hanging in the air. As the kettle came to a rattling boil and clicked off I absorbed the meaning behind John's words.

'Do you, would you like me to tell him?'

'No, well, to be on hand. I know - it's a hard thing to do.'

'And where has the cancer shown itself?'

John stepped forward and took me in his arms, holding me.

'We noticed some behavioural changes first,' he must have felt me tense, I didn't want a preamble. 'It's in the brain, in the brain,' he whispered.

We stood there holding each other, I have no idea of what was going through John's mind, marked as he was by his wife's cancer, but I was experiencing nausea at the thought of cancer affecting Luke's brain.

'I'll tell him,' I said.

The Angel Bug 36

Luke (2023) *(Ten years after last entry – EM)*

I am sixty-six today and won't see another year. It's cancer, as predicted by the trials Keyes ran; I guess there has to be one sacrifice. Brain surgery hasn't moved on enough to excise the piriform cortex, ironically an area to do with the sense of smell, and leave me a going concern. In the meantime palliative drugs do what is needed. The effect of the Moringa therapy, however, remains as strong as ever, which means it must operate from the most primitive parts of the brain where the memory of smell can lurk and not in the piriform. So even in dying I have learned something new about the Moringa.

It's amazing what has happened since I let go of the reins on the Moringa therapy…or rather since Mother Nature took charge. I'll try to summarize it here though it took us a while to find out what and how it had happened. Firstly, as we now know, Agrobacterium moringarhodofaciens, as it has been officially classified, replicates in the body once ingested, creating enough of the chemical stimulus to alter the brain, and also creating more bacteria which are then excreted.

The first batch of doses that went to the prison resulted in some bacteria leaving the prison via the sewerage system before Christmas. As we all know sewage is actually cleaned up by bacteria at the treatment plant. Our bacteria joined them and also went out with the treated sewage. What do you call treated sewage? Organic fertilizer - and this stuff is just sprayed out on the land. That's what happened, and that first year's crop on all the fields that got a share as top-dressing after February, were amazing; bigger, stronger, more bountiful but with red tinged leaves. Just happened it was only on one farm. Did the farmer kick up? Hell, no, he had no idea what it was, but to cut his losses he put it about that he was trying out new varieties, and it seems that carried him through. Vast cabbages coloured like lollo rosso lettuce and corn with huge orange cobs. Seems the buyer was a mite funny about the slight pink tinge to the wheat and wouldn't pay top dollar, but, as there was so much extra, the farmer was happy anyway.

Where did that first batch of wheat go? It went as food aid to Africa. The next year there were many more fields growing red-leaved crops round the prison, the first farmer explained it was no problem and the others happily went along. Besides, by now the program was running countrywide and the scenario was being played out everywhere.

I remember the press speculation about the red-leaved plants in the second year, how it was thought to be a spontaneous genetic mutation to counteract the changes in climatic conditions, or a response to increased ultraviolet or even escapees from a GM facility. The latter got closer than we would have liked, but no one linked it to the Rehab therapy being used and, as soon as we ourselves suspected, a lock-down on all research information concerning the Moringa nodules and the Rehab therapy made sure they never did. Initially there was grave concern that if anything went wrong and the link was discovered, the US would be blamed, so all records were wiped and the few who knew the facts were warned to keep them secret.

That first batch of wheat wasn't the only one to get sent abroad, a lot of the early pink-tinged seed was deemed less than first class and was sent food aid, especially to the war-torn and drought-ridden countries of Africa.

Gradually wars ceased, especially in the poverty-stricken areas of Africa where the damage the people did to themselves was at least as bad as that which the droughts and the floods did. Of those first seeds from red-leaved plants some were eaten by the warring factions, stealing their cut from the food aid before it even reached the people. Other seeds were sown and once placed in the ground took hold swiftly, outgrowing anything else, and providing more food for the people. As the warring ceased, the monetary aid also seemed to get through to the right people and for the first time in living memory, Africa was on its way to being able to feed itself. Even Israel and the Arab states are looking at an amicable compromise after a few years of relatively peaceful negotiations. At the time of writing I cannot think of any part of the world where there is a war going on, or even local conflicts.

Anyway, by the time we realised what was happening, how the Agrobacterium moringarhodofaciens was spreading itself, it was too late to turn back, and within a few years almost all crops came from reddish leaved plants as they grew stronger, were more bountiful and grew even where nothing else would. And Mother Nature got the balance right, no longer did people fall into a deep sleep or have three hour manic sessions, it was far more gradual, one day they woke up and they were transformed. Like a miracle.

We still have to lock some people away, though there aren't many and they are really facilities for the mentally unstable; as some crimes are not driven by greed, but erupt from a disturbed mind.

The US government didn't even have to spend too many years protecting the Rainforests; as people stopped wanting to exploit it, it became safe on its own. I guess I claim that as my legacy.

My only regret? Leaving Gabriella, I still feel she was intended to be with me on the Moringa project. I should have gone back to her earlier, but the project kept me here and when I was free of it I was not about to break up what seemed a happy relationship for her; I couldn't. But now, at the end, I'm sending this to the only person who knows what it really means, I'm sending it to her, to Gabriella.

The Angel Bug 37

Gabbi   2017 – 2043 *(Extract of relevant entries – EM)*

John and I went to Emma's wedding in Australia in 2017 and fell in love with the lifestyle there. We really only returned to resign, sort out our lives and arrange to move out. John's boys were all through with university and Liam was talking about doing the round-the-world trip and cheerfully hoped he could drop in on us.

The only thing I hated leaving was Eden and everyone in it. They really had been my family and my support, even though I was starting a new life in Australia with John, leaving Eden was going to leave big space in my heart.

I told Luke of our plans in one of my monthly emails to him, not that it made much difference to him, an email from Australia is very much like one from the UK. The five years between the Moringa therapy being used and when we moved to Australia had seen such changes already. I knew that the UK prison population was already halved, in less than four years. Each year there were fewer entering than leaving, and none going back. It was an incredibly exciting time, especially as the government brought out the treatment for all sorts of other problems through the NHS. Even I, who had known about the Moringa therapy from early on, had difficulty accepting that it could do so much for so many.

The reports of reddish leaved plants spreading across the world and providing bountiful crops didn't surprise us; Luke had kept us up to date with the, otherwise secret, findings from his researches   on   the   method   that   Agrobacterium moringarhodofaciens used to spread itself. 'And the productivity of the infected plants makes sense,' John had said. 'The Frankia in it is a nitrogen-fixing bacteria, so would give the plant a huge advantage.' What he didn't know, nor did any of us then, was that the advantage was even greater than that, it meant the new red-tinged varieties, like the symbiotic lichen found all over the world and in all extremes, would grow almost anywhere, and farmers and nature made sure that it did.

The wild form of Agrobacterium moringarhodofaciens came to Australia a little later than to most countries as it has always had very strict food import regulations. But, as the Rehab treatment started being used in our prisons, it was not long before the Australian food chain included a significant amount of red-leaved plant derivatives too. As a result, the crime rate dropped by fifty percent within a year and our natural world has a different shade now, with much more red amongst the green.

Luke sent me his notes and diaries just before he died and his request for his ashes to be scattered under a Moringa oelifera; there being no one else, we performed this last rite for him – laid him to rest beneath his favourite tree.

The world is such a peaceful place now that I wonder how I could have ever thought that the work of the Moringa therapy could be wrong in some way. It just shows you how these vague feelings we have can be just so much nonsense in the long run.

John died a couple of years ago, and at eighty-four I now live in an apartment near Emma and her husband, another John. Their family are scattered all over the continent doing useful jobs, nothing exciting, nothing cutting edge, but useful jobs.

The Angel Bug 38

Emma October 2084

EM's Long View
New Blog Post: Save the Human race

The world is changing and I fear for the future.

As I see it, through my old anthropologist's eyes, our race is at a turning point and we must adapt or die.

And that's the problem.

I'm ninety-six this year, and for the last sixty years or so we have enjoyed a time of peace and simple living. You don't see pictures of starving children anymore, or fat people, you don't hear about wars, addiction of any kind, rape or barely any other crime. All the old fears have gone. We have been living in a golden age.

I still remember the global businesses, long gone now, of course. Who needs to build that sort of empire once you have all you need? We are all used to our local markets now, though we still have the net and our fantastic cheap postal system that all governments worldwide fund so that small producers can make and send to anyone. I can also remember the time when you would buy the latest, newest mobile phone and within six weeks it would be old hat, there would be something out there with newer and better features that you just had to have. It was just too much, and it was not just phones, every day there was some step-up in some kind of consumer technology.

When this stopped happening is hard to pinpoint even with hindsight, the change was so gradual. To start with you have to know that back then the US and Britain were amongst the most innovative countries in the world. Sure, there were advances in technology, especially in miniaturisation, in some of the Far East countries, but the breakthrough innovation was often led from the US and the UK. They were also the first to embrace the Moringa Therapy. Its proper name was Rehab Therapy, I've heard it called other names, 'be good-be good' being a favourite amongst the Aboriginals, Angel therapy, Stinks therapy, and eventually, nothing at all. There are only a few of us who can recall a time when we didn't have this inbuilt revulsion to feeling greed in any of its guises, two or three generations have known nothing else.

There are some social historians and commentators, even other anthropologists, who have said we are in a parallel with the Neolithic peoples, the only other time in history when we believe there was enough for all to eat, no reason to war and great public works were pursued just to give people something to do. I disagreed even before this, for back then the Neolithics were still developing, *they* moved on. Historically humans, more specifically, our branch of the human species, has only survived because we have either adapted to a changing environment or have changed the environment to suit our form of life.

Mum had this thing about unintended consequences; she'd rail against politicians as it seemed they were the worst at not thinking things through and landing up with unintended consequences. My teenage years seemed to be peppered with times when she'd say, 'there they go again, not thinking things through, and look at the mess!' I'm sure she'd be upset by the unintended consequences if she could see the problem that the Rehab Therapy has left us.

Forty years ago, sorting out Mum's things I came across these two sets of e-diaries or memoirs. One was Mum's - Gabbi's, the other, strangely, was Dr Luke Adamson's. I was too busy to deal with such things just then. I skimmed a few entries and put them away, but the thought of them had remained with me.

The way things are going now, we need to understand how we got into this situation. I think, perhaps, that it might help with a solution, and I, at least, had an idea of what I was looking for. I have been thorough in my research, however, it seems that anything else on the Rehab Therapy was purged, destroyed or never recorded. I guess I'm not surprised; I remember being told it was highly sensitive when it began, and that we would be wise not to mention what we knew, especially as we could be implicated in its unauthorised use.

These memoirs may be the only evidence left of what really happened, where it came from and how it spread. So I've gone through the two memoirs, Luke's and Gabbi's, and put the pieces that relate to the Rehab therapy, or Moringa Therapy as Mum called it, in chronological order so that they make some kind of sense.

It took a long time for this side-effect of the Rehab therapy to show itself, but we must find a way to reverse it. As it stands the human race seems to have stopped innovating at all, stopped dead. It is as if mankind has totally lost the drive to better its environment or to adapt to change.

This wouldn't be a problem, if everything stayed exactly the same, but as we know; the world is changing.

If you are reading this then you will have found it on the net where I posted it for everyone in the world to access, to understand what happened and how the Rehab therapy changed us all. My hope is that, with this information, someone out there can devise a solution before it is too late.

I hope that person is you, if not, share this blog post with all your contacts, tell everyone you know that this information is here; somewhere we must find a saviour.

[click here to read memoirs]

Notes on Moringa oelifera:

This plant may not be a miracle tree as described in this fiction but it does have wonderful properties.

The Moringa oelifera is the most widely cultivated species of the genus Moringa, which is the only genus in the family Moringaceae. It grows in semi-arid, tropical and sub-tropical zones and, while it grows best in dry sandy soil, it tolerates poor soil including coastal areas. It is fast growing, drought-resistant and a native of the foothills of the Himalayas in north-western India

English common names include Horseradish tree, from the taste of the roots, Drumstick tree, from the appearance of the edible long, slender, triangular seed pods, Ben-oil tree from the oil derived from the seeds or **Miracle tree** as it provides not only food from leaves, flowers, seed-pods and roots, but also medicine, oil, green fertiliser, a water purifier, wind-breaks, shade and forage crops.

***

Note on American English use of indefinite article with the word 'herb / herbal'

Where I have Americans *speaking* or Luke reporting I have used the indefinite article 'an' as in 'an herbal treatment' as that is what they would *say* – so I have rendered it as *an herbal*. I know this will look wrong to British readers – but in American English they do not sound the H in herb – saying it as 'erb' so American English requires an 'an' before 'herb' it as it has a silent 'h' for them. Elsewhere, where US spelling varies from English but pronunciation remains the same, I have used the English spelling

Acknowledgements:

To The Eden project for allowing me 'behind the scenes' and to Dr Alistair Griffiths (Horticultural Science Curator) for answering so many of my science and botanical questions about the Eden Project

Thanks also to Sir Tim Smit for reading through the manuscript and agreeing that I could use him as the only true-life character in the novel

Grateful thanks to my proof reader, Christine Haywood, my excellent beta-readers Nicky Hatherell, Steph Dickenson, Kathy Gilmore, Denyse Keslake, Joan Tall and from the USA Ann Quinn, and Cover designer, Nathan Murphy

**Thank you for reading The Angel Bug by Ann Foweraker
You may review this book and the others written by the
author on Amazon, or Annmade.co.uk
where they are also available to purchase in all e-formats**

Other novels by ANN FOWERAKER

Divining the Line – Ann Foweraker

The first time it happened it felt like stumbling across another avenue to an ancient monument, but this one pulled at more than just his head, there was a tightness in his chest, the lights twinkled and flashed inside his mind, the intensity giving Perran a firework of a headache. Following the line - years later in the early nineties - leads him into Liz Hawkey's ordered life, and together they discover the source of the line.

A story of family, love and loss, Divining the Line brings the ordinary and the extraordinary together into everyday life.

Nothing Ever Happens Here - Ann Foweraker

Living in London suddenly becomes too uncomfortable for the attractive Jo Smart and her sixteen year-old son, Alex, after he is beaten up. so when they are offered the chance to take an immediate holiday in a peaceful Cornish town they jump at it. But not all is as peaceful as it seems as they become involved in a murder enquiry, drug raid and abduction.

DI Rick Whittington has also escaped from London and the reminders of the death of his wife and child, and through his investigations finds himself meeting Jo and being drawn into the events surrounding her.

This is a love story set in the early 1990s which combines the historic Cornish love of the sea and smuggling with hard faced twentieth century crime and detection. The perfect blend for a woman's crime novel.

Some Kind of Synchrony - Ann Foweraker

Faith Warren, married mother of two, is a secretary in a newspaper office. It wasn't what she'd hoped for, but her dreams of university and becoming an author were lost long ago. Telling stories to entertain her lifelong friend on their journey to work and back is all that is left, until she tells The Story.

The real trouble began with the minor characters, just unfortunate co-incidences, but when do you stop calling them co-incidences and begin to wonder what the hell is going on – and how it can be stopped

About the Author

Though a writer of poetry and short stories since my teens I also love passing on knowledge so I became a teacher, gaining my BEd degree in the seventies. Teaching is still in my blood - give me half a chance and I'll teach you everything I know.

Marriage took me from Berkshire, where I was born, to live in Cornwall and the novel writing began while taking an extended break from teaching to bring up our four boys.

My books are all available from PendownPublishing.co.uk in various e-formats and are also available at Amazon for Kindle.

Please follow my blog on annfoweraker.com where you'll get an insight into the things I'm in to, from belly dancing to sand-sculpture and, of course, writing.

Follow me on twitter at @AnnFoweraker for tweets on life, Cornwall and writing, and Like my page on Facebook 'Ann Foweraker' for more info and thoughts.

‶tning Source UK Ltd.
Keynes UK
‵5f0255221113